THE UNDERTAKING OF HART AND MERCY

Praise for

The Undertaking of Hart and Mercy

"A uniquely charming mixture of whimsy and the macabre that completely won me over. If you ever wished for an adult romance that felt like *Howl's Moving Castle*, THIS IS THAT BOOK."

—Helen Hoang, author of *The Kiss Quotient*

"With its wonderfully unique setting, lovable characters, and engaging mix of humor and spice, *The Undertaking of Hart and Mercy* is a truly outstanding romantic fantasy. I loved both its kookiness and its deep authenticity. An instant favorite!"

—India Holton, author of *The Wisteria Society of Lady Scoundrels*

"If Lewis Carroll and Nora Ephron teamed up to write a magical Western, this would be the result. An unabashedly offbeat adventure full of dead gods and mostly dead zombies, family drama, swoon-worthy love letters, and a Very Good Dog, *The Undertaking of Hart and Mercy* oozes romantic fun like a corpse oozes dubious fluids."

—Freya Marske, author of *A Marvellous Light*

"Perfect for readers who love enemies-to-lovers mashed up with a touch of secret pen pal romance. I showed up for the fantastic, fun fantasy setting but it was Hart and Mercy that kept me reading."

—Ruby Dixon, author of *Ice Planet Barbarians*

"This book is a gooey (and hot!) romance immersed in a tasty layer of quirky fantasy, like some decadent chocolate treat. A little sweet, a little spicy, a little sharp, and entirely moreish!"

—Davinia Evans, author of *Notorious Sorcerer*

"A lovely, macabre fantasy romance about life, death, and Actually Living. I cried twice and smiled plenty."

—Olivia Atwater, author of *Half a Soul*

THE UNDERTAKING OF HART AND MERCY

MEGAN BANNEN

This book is a work of fiction. Names, characters, places, and incidents are the product of the author's imagination or are used fictitiously. Any resemblance to actual events, locales, or persons, living or dead, is coincidental.

Cover design by Lisa Marie Pompilio
Cover illustrations by Shutterstock

Orbit
Hachette Book Group
1290 Avenue of the Americas
New York, NY 10104
orbitbooks.net

First Edition: August 2022
Simultaneously published in Great Britain by Orbit

Orbit is an imprint of Hachette Book Group.
The Orbit name and logo are trademarks of Little, Brown Book Group Limited.

Library of Congress Cataloging-in-Publication Data
Names: Bannen, Megan, author.
Title: The undertaking of Hart and Mercy / Megan Bannen.
Description: First edition. | New York, NY : Orbit, 2022.
Identifiers: LCCN 2021058953 | ISBN 9780316394215 (trade paperback) |
ISBN 9780316394314 (ebook) | ISBN 9780316425308 (ebook other)
Subjects: LCGFT: Romance fiction. | Novels.
Classification: LCC PS3602.A6664 U53 2022 | DDC 813/.6—dc23
LC record available at https://lccn.loc.gov/2021058953

ISBNs: 9780316394215 (trade paperback), 9780316394314 (ebook)

Printed in the United States of America

LSC-C

Printing 6, 2024

To Mike—
We've got a good life, honey.

LYONA

MEDORA

REDWING ISLANDS

VINLAND

PAXICO

GALATIA

ARVONIA

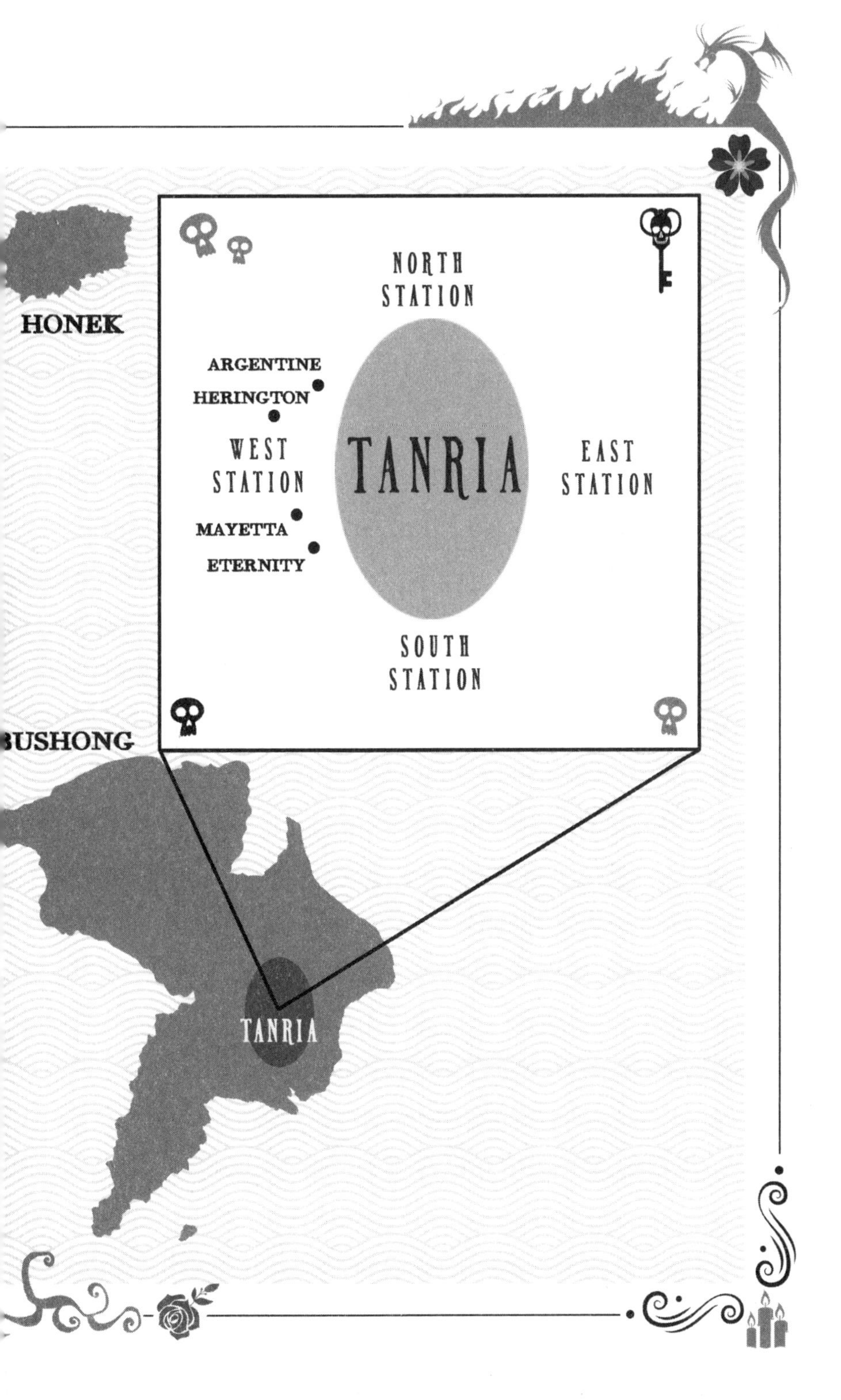
HONEK
NORTH STATION
ARGENTINE
HERINGTON
WEST STATION
MAYETTA
ETERNITY
TANRIA
EAST STATION
SOUTH STATION
BUSHONG
TANRIA

Chapter One

It was always a gamble, dropping off a body at Birdsall & Son, Undertakers, but this morning, the Bride of Fortune favored Hart Ralston.

Out of habit, he ducked his head as he stepped into the lobby so that he wouldn't smack his forehead on the doorframe. Bold-colored paintings of the death gods—the Salt Sea, the Warden, and Grandfather Bones—decorated the walls in gold frames. Two green velvet armchairs sat in front of a walnut coffee table, their whimsical lines imbuing the room with an upbeat charm. Vintage coffee bean tins served as homes for pens and candy on a counter that was polished to a sheen. This was not the somber, staid lobby of a respectable place like Cunningham's Funeral Services. This was the appalling warmth of an undertaker who welcomed other people's deaths with open arms.

It was also blessedly empty, save for the dog draped over one of the chairs. The mutt was scratching so furiously at his ribs he didn't notice that his favorite Tanrian Marshal had walked through the front door. Hart watched in delight as the mongrel's back paw sent a cyclone of dog hair whirling through a shaft of sunlight before the bristly fur settled on the velvet upholstery.

"Good boy, Leonard," said Hart, knowing full well that Mercy Birdsall did not want her dog wallowing on the furniture.

At the sound of his name, Leonard perked up and wagged his

nubbin tail. He leaped off the chair and hurled himself at Hart, who petted him with equal enthusiasm.

Leonard was an ugly beast—half boxer, half the gods knew what, brindle coated, eyes bugging and veined, jowls hanging loose. In any other case, this would be a face only his owner could love, but there was a reason Hart continued to patronize his least favorite undertaker in all the border towns that clung to the hem of the Tanrian Marshals' West Station like beggar children. After a thorough round of petting and a game of fetch with the tennis ball Leonard unearthed from underneath his chair, Hart pulled his watch out of his vest pocket and, seeing that it was already late in the afternoon, resigned himself to getting on with his job.

He took a moment to doff his hat and brush back his overgrown blond hair with his fingers. Not that he cared how he looked. Not at Birdsall & Son, at any rate. As a matter of fact, if he had been a praying man, he would have begged the Mother of Sorrows to have mercy on him, no pun intended. But he was not entirely a man—not by half—much less one of the praying variety, so he left religion to the dog.

"Pray for me, Leonard," he said before he pinged the counter bell.

"Pop, can you get that?" Mercy's voice called from somewhere in the bowels of Birdsall & Son, loudly enough so that her father should be able to hear her but softly enough that she wouldn't sound like a hoyden shouting across the building.

Hart waited.

And waited.

"I swear," he muttered as he rang the bell again.

This time, Mercy threw caution to the wind and hollered, "Pop! The bell!" But silence met this request, and Hart remained standing at the counter, his impatience expanding by the second. He shook his head at the dog. "Salt fucking Sea, how does your owner manage to stay in business?"

Leonard's nubbin started up again, and Hart bent down to pet the ever-loving snot out of the boxer mix.

"I'm so sorry," Mercy said, winded, as she rushed from the back to take her place behind the counter. "Welcome to Birdsall & Son. How can I help you?"

Hart stood up—and up and up—towering over Mercy as her stomach (hopefully) sank down and down.

"Oh. It's you," she said, the words and the unenthusiastic tone that went with them dropping off her tongue like a lead weight. Hart resisted the urge to grind his molars into a fine powder.

"Most people start with *hello*."

"Hello, Hart-ache," she sighed.

"Hello, Merciless." He gave her a thin, venomous smile as he took in her oddly disheveled appearance. Whatever else he might say about her, she was usually neat as a pin, her bright-colored dresses flattering her tall, buxom frame, and her equally bright lipstick meticulously applied to her full lips. Today, however, she wore overalls, and her olive skin was dewy with sweat, making her red horn-rimmed glasses slide down her nose. A couple of dark curls had come loose from the floral scarf that bound up her hair, as if she'd stuck her head out the window while driving full speed across a waterway.

"I guess you're still alive, then," she said flatly.

"I am. Try to contain your joy."

Leonard, who could not contain his joy, jumped up to paw Hart's stomach, and Hart couldn't help but squeeze those sweet jowls in his hands. What a shame that such a great dog belonged to the worst of all undertaking office managers.

"Are you here to pet my dog, or do you actually have a body to drop off?"

A shot of cold humiliation zinged through Hart's veins, but he'd never let her see it. He held up his hands as if Mercy were leveling a pistol crossbow at his head, and declared with mock innocence, "I stopped by for a cup of tea. Is this a bad time?"

Bereft of adoration, Leonard leaped up higher, mauling Hart's ribs.

"Leonard, get down." Mercy nabbed her dog by the collar to drag him upstairs to her apartment. Hart could hear him scratching at the door and whining piteously behind the wood. It was monstrous of Mercy to deprive both Hart and her dog of each other's company. Typical.

"Now then, where were we?" she said when she returned, propping her fists on her hips, which made the bib of her overalls stretch over the swell of her breasts. The square of denim seemed to scream, *Hey, look at these! Aren't they fucking magnificent?* It was so unfair of Mercy to have magnificent breasts.

"You're dropping off a body, I assume?" she asked.

"Yep. No key."

"Another one? This is our third indigent this week."

"More bodies mean more money for you. I'd think you'd be jumping for joy."

"I'm not going to dignify that with a response. I'll meet you at the dock. You do know there's a bell back there, right?"

"I prefer the formality of checking in at the front desk."

"Sure you do." She rolled her eyes, and Hart wished they'd roll right out of her unforgivably pretty face.

"Does no one else work here? Why can't your father do it?"

Like a gift from the Bride of Fortune, one of Roy Birdsall's legendary snores galloped through the lobby from behind the thin wall separating it from the office. Hart smirked at Mercy, whose face darkened in embarrassment.

"I'll meet you at the dock," she repeated through gritted teeth.

Hart's smirk came with him as he put on his hat, sauntered out to his autoduck, and backed it up to the dock.

"Are you sure you're up for this?" he asked Mercy as he swung open the door of his duck's cargo hold, knowing full well that she would find the question unbearably condescending.

As if to prove that she didn't need anyone's help, least of all his, she snatched the dolly from its pegs on the wall, strode past him into the hold, and strapped the sailcloth-wrapped body to the rods with the practiced moves of an expert. Unfortunately, this particular corpse was extremely leaky, even through the thick canvas. Despite the fact that he had kept it on ice, the liquid rot wasn't completely frozen over, and Mercy wound up smearing it all over her hands and arms and the front of her overalls. Relishing her horror as it registered on her face, Hart sidled up to her, his tongue poking into the corner of his cheek. "I don't want to say I told you so, but—"

She wheeled the corpse past him, forcing him to step out of the autoduck to make room for her. "Hart-ache, if you don't want my help, maybe you should finally find yourself a partner."

The insinuation lit his Mercy Fuse, which was admittedly short. As if he would have any trouble finding a partner if he wanted one. Which he didn't.

"I didn't ask for your help," he shot back. "And look who's talking, by the way."

She halted the dolly and pulled out the kickstand with the toe of her sneaker. "What's that supposed to mean?"

"It means I don't see anyone helping you either." He fished inside his black vest for the paperwork she would need to complete in order to receive her government stipend for processing the body, and he held it out to her. He had long since learned to have his end all filled out ahead of time so that he didn't have to spend a second longer in her presence than was necessary.

She wiped one hand on the clean fabric over her ass before snatching the papers out of his hand. Without the consent of his reason, Hart's own hands itched with curiosity, wondering exactly how the round curves of her backside would feel in his grasp. His brain was trying to shove aside the unwanted lust when Mercy stepped into him and stood on her tiptoes. Most women couldn't get anywhere near Hart's head without the assistance of a ladder, but Mercy was tall enough to put her into kissing range when she stood on the tips of her red canvas shoes. Her big brown eyes blazed behind the lenses of her glasses, and the unexpected proximity of her whole body felt bizarrely intimate as she fired the next words into his face.

"Do you know what I think, Hart-ache?"

He swallowed his unease and kept his voice cool. "Do tell, Merciless."

"You must be a pathetically friendless loser to be this much of a jerk." On the word *jerk*, she poked him in the chest with the emphatic pointer finger of her filthy hand, dotting his vest with brown rot and making him stumble onto the edge of the dock. Then she pulled down the gate before he could utter another word, letting it slam shut between them with a resounding *clang*.

Hart stood teetering on the lip of the dock in stunned silence. Slowly, insidiously, as he regained his balance, her words seeped beneath his skin and slithered into his veins.

I will never come here again unless I absolutely have to, he promised himself for the hundredth time. Birdsall & Son was not the only official drop-off site for bodies recovered in Tanria without ID tags. From now on, he would take his keyless cadavers to Cunningham's. But as he thought the words, he knew they constituted a lie. Every time he slayed an indigent drudge in Tanria, he brought the corpse to Birdsall & Son, Undertakers.

For a dog.

Because he was a pathetically friendless loser.

He already knew this about himself, but the fact that Mercy

knew it, too, made his spine bunch up. He got into his autoduck and drove to the station, his hands white-knuckling the wheel as he berated himself for letting Mercy get to him.

Mercy, with her snotty *Oh. It's you.* As if a dumpster rat had waltzed into her lobby instead of Hart.

Mercy, whose every word was a thumbtack spat in his face, pointy end first.

The first time he'd met her, four years ago, she had walked into the lobby, wearing a bright yellow dress, like a jolt of sunlight bursting through glowering clouds on a gloomy day. The large brown eyes behind her glasses had met his and widened, and he could see the word form in her mind as she took in the color of his irises, as pale and colorlessly gray as the morning sky on a cloudy day.

Demigod.

Now he found himself wondering which was worse: a pretty young woman seeing him as nothing more than the offspring of a divine parent, or Merciless Mercy loathing him for the man he was.

Any hope he'd cherished of skulking back to his post in Sector W-38 unremarked vanished when he heard Chief Maguire's voice call to him from the front door of the West Station, as if she had been standing at the blinds in her office, waiting to pounce.

"Marshal Ralston."

His whole body wanted to sag at the sound of Alma's voice, but he forced himself to keep his shoulders straight as he took his pack out of the passenger seat and shut the door with a metallic *clunk*. "Hey, Chief."

"Where you been?"

"Eternity. I took out a drudge in Sector W-38, but it didn't have a key. Decomp was so bad, I decided to bring him in early. Poor pitiful bastard."

Alma scrutinized him over the steaming rim of her ever-present coffee mug, her aquamarine demigod eyes glinting in her wide brown face.

Hart's lips thinned. "Are you implying that *I'm* a poor pitiful bastard?"

"It's not so much an implication as a stone-cold statement of fact."

"Hardly."

"You have no social life. You work all the time. You don't even have a place to hang your hat. You might put up in a hotel for a few nights, but then you come right back here." She jerked her thumb toward the Mist, the cocoon of churning fog that formed the border of Tanria beyond the West Station. "This shithole is your home. How sad is that?"

Hart shrugged. "It's not so bad."

"Says you. I assume you took the body to Cunningham's?"

"No."

She raised an *I take no bullshit from you* eyebrow at him before leaning on the hood of his duck, and Hart frowned when she spilled a few drops of coffee onto the chipped blue paint. It was rusty enough as it was; she didn't need to go making it worse.

"Look, Ralston, we rely on the undertakers. We need them to do their jobs so that we can do ours."

Great. A lecture from his boss. Who used to be his partner and his friend. Who called him Ralston now.

"I know."

"You are aware of the fact that Roy Birdsall almost died a few months ago, right?"

Hart shifted his weight, the soles of his boots grinding into the gravel of the parking lot. "No."

"Well, he did. Heart attack or something. In theory, he's

running the office, but Mercy's the one taking care of everything at Birdsall & Son—boatmaking, body prep, all of it."

"So?" His tone was petulant, but the memory of a disheveled Mercy with corpse rot smeared over her front made a frond of guilt unfurl in his gut.

"So if you're going to patronize Birdsall's, cut Mercy some slack and play nice. If you can't do that, go to Cunningham's. All right?"

"Yep, fine. Can I go now?" He adjusted his hat on his head, a clear signal that he was preparing to exit the conversation and get on with his job, but Alma held up her free hand.

"Hold on. I've been meaning to talk to you about something."

Hart grunted. He knew what was coming.

"Don't give me that. You've gone through three partners in four years, and you've been working solo for months. It's too dangerous to keep going it alone. For any of us." She added that last bit as if this conversation were about marshals in general rather than him specifically, but Hart knew better.

"I don't need a partner."

She gave him a look of pure exasperation, and for a fraction of a second, Hart could see the old Alma, the friend who'd been there for him when his mentor, Bill, died. She dismissed him with a jerk of her head. "Go on. But this conversation isn't finished."

He'd walked a few paces toward the stables when Alma called after him, "Come over for dinner one of these days, will you? Diane misses you."

This peace offering was almost certainly Diane's doing, and he could tell that it was as hard for Alma to deliver her wife's invitation as it was for Hart to hear it.

"Yep," he answered and continued on his way to the stables, but they both knew he wouldn't be standing on Alma and Diane's doorstep anytime soon. Although he and Alma had long since made peace on the surface of things, the old grudge hung in the air, as if Bill's ghost had taken up permanent residence in the space between them. Hart had no idea how to get past it, or if he wanted to, but it was painfully awkward to miss a friend when she was standing right behind him. It was worse to miss Diane. He almost never saw her anymore.

The stables were dark compared to the brutal sunlight of Bushong, and blessedly cooler, too. He went to the stalls to see which mounts were available. He knew it would be slim pickings at this time of day, but he was unprepared for how bad the pickings were: a gelding so young, Hart didn't trust it not to bolt at the first whiff of a drudge; an older mare he'd taken in a few times and found too slow and plodding for his liking; and Saltlicker.

Saltlicker was one of those equimares that bolted for water every chance he got and maintained a constant, embittered opposition to anyone who dared to ride him. Some marshals liked him for his high-spiritedness; Hart loathed the beast, but of the three options, Saltlicker was, sadly, the best choice.

"Wonderful," Hart griped at him.

Saltlicker snorted, shook out his kelp-like mane, and dipped lower in his trough, blowing sulky bubbles in the water, as if to say, *The feeling's mutual, dickhead.*

All at once, an oppressive sadness overtook Hart. It was one thing to dislike an equimaris; it was another to have the equimaris hate him back. And honestly, who did genuinely like Hart these days? Mercy's barbed insult, which had followed him all the way from Eternity, surfaced in his mind once more.

You must be a pathetically friendless loser to be this much of a jerk.

She had a point. Only a pathetically friendless loser would face his nemesis time and again to pet her dog for five minutes.

Maybe I should suck it up and get another dog, he thought, but the second he entertained the idea, he knew he could never replace

Gracie. And that left him with nothing but the occasional visit to Leonard.

Hart knew that he needed to get to his post, but he wound up sitting against the stable wall, shrouded in shadows. As if it had a mind of its own—call it ancient muscle memory—his hand snaked into his pack and pulled out his old notebook and a pen.

When he had first joined the Tanrian Marshals after his mother died, he used to write letters to her and slide them into nimkilim boxes whenever he and his mentor, Bill, made their way to the station or to a town. Then, after Bill was killed, Hart wrote to him, too, mostly letters full of remorse. But he hadn't written to either of them in years, because at the end of the day, it wasn't like they could write back. And that was what he wanted, wasn't it? For someone—anyone—to answer?

Poor pitiful bastard, the blank page splayed across his thighs seemed to say to him now. He clicked open the pen and wrote *Dear*, hesitated, and then added the word *friend*.

He had no idea how much time passed before he tore out the page, folded it into fourths, and got to his feet, relieving his aching knees. There was a similar relief in his aching chest, as if he'd managed to pour some of that loneliness from his heart onto the paper. Glancing about him to make sure he was unobserved as he crossed the stable yard, he walked to the station's nimkilim box and slid the note inside, even though he was certain that a letter addressed to no one would never be delivered to anyone.

Chapter Two

Mercy cranked up berth number five and watched as the unfortunate man whom Hart Ralston had brought in the day before surfaced from the well, which had kept his body chilled at a steady fifty-five degrees overnight. He wasn't overly large, but he wasn't tiny either, and moving him onto the dolly would go easier with two.

"Zeddie? You there?" Mercy called hopefully up the basement stairs, but it was Pop who answered her, his voice too eager for her liking.

"He's not in yet. Need help with something, muffin?"

"No. Nope. I'm good. I wanted to show Zeddie how to work that tricky kink in berth number five's rope." It wasn't a lie, per se, but she didn't want Pop doing anything that required physical exertion, such as helping her move a corpse. He wasn't so great on stairs these days either. His knees popped alarmingly with each step. After his heart attack six months ago, the doctor had said that he needed to retire, at least from the heavy-duty work of undertaking, which was why he was upstairs running the office in Mercy's stead, and she was down here, working as the interim undertaker until Zeddie was ready to take over, which, in theory, was happening this morning. If he ever showed up.

Annoyed with her brother for being late on his first day as the official undertaker of Birdsall & Son, Mercy maneuvered the indigent's remains onto the dolly by herself, rolled the body into the lift by herself, added several more pounds to the counter-balance by herself, and pulled down on the lift rope by herself, hand over hand, until she felt it hit the end of the line. She liked the way her muscles worked, hefting and hauling, pushing and pulling, as if this job were the reason why the Three Mothers had made her bigger than nearly every other woman on the island of Bushong, and taller than most men, too.

Of course, there was one man who towered over her, or rather, one demigod. Too bad Hart Ralston's divine parentage came with a heaping spoonful of arrogance, so evident in the way he cocked his head and put his hands on his hips, drawing attention to their slimness, the way his rapier belt hung off them in the most irritatingly sexy way possible. It annoyed Mercy to no end that after years of putting up with that insufferable marshal, some primal inner instinct continued to think he looked good enough to eat.

She locked the rope in place and whistled as she headed upstairs, the rubber soles of her red canvas shoes making a satisfying *thud, thud, thud* on the treads. Since Zeddie had yet to arrive, she decided that now would be a good time to broach the subject of her father's languishing to-do list. She popped her head into the office where Roy Birdsall sat at her old desk, his reading glasses propped inexplicably atop his bushy eyebrows.

"I don't know if you remember my mentioning this last week, but we're out of cedar and larch, and now we're running low on salt, too. And urns."

"I'll write up the orders this morning as soon as I'm done balancing the books. I promise."

"Very, very, extremely low. And it wouldn't hurt to order more keys. We've had a run on unidentified bodies lately. Should I write this down?"

"I'm old, but I'm not that old. I'll remember."

"Because I can write this down if you want."

He shook his head with a grin. "Sometimes, you are just like your mother."

Mercy knew this was the highest of compliments coming from the mouth of Roy Birdsall. She kissed his more-salt-than-pepper curls and counted off the to-do list on her fingers. "Cedar. Larch. Salt. Urns. And remember to order more keys."

Pop saluted her, but the gesture was somehow less than reassuring.

With that, Mercy left his office. She was about to head to the boatworks when she heard Horatio's familiar rapping at the front door, his talons clacking against the wood. "I've got it," she called to her father on her way to the lobby to let in the nimkilim. The owl stood on the welcome mat as he did every morning, six days a week, his white feathers garbed in a particularly dapper emerald waistcoat and silk trousers, an ensemble that seemed remarkably out of place in a dusty border town like Eternity.

"Ah, good morning, Miss Birdsall," Horatio hooted in a way that also said, *I was once a messenger to the Old Gods, and yet you made me wait on this kitschy doormat.* But Mercy found the owl's old-school hauteur charming, so she gave him her usual bright smile as he stepped his standard three paces into the lobby on his bare bird feet. He fished out a slim packet of letters from the tasteful, soft leather mailbag slung across his back and handed it to Mercy. "I rather like this modern style you are trying on these days. I've never seen anyone make overalls work, yet here you are, the very picture."

Mercy dimpled. A compliment from Horatio, even one sniffed with patronizing admiration, was cause for celebration. Her beloved dress collection had been gathering dust in her bedroom closet upstairs for six months now, but she found that her new coveralls and dungarees offered fashionable opportunities alongside their practicality.

"Thank you," she said, patting the floral scarf that bound up her hair as she took the daily death notices from the countertop and handed them over. Then she fished a coin from the bowl she kept behind the counter and gave it to the nimkilim as well. Horatio sniffed at the silver glinting on the white feathers of his wing and was about to bid her good day when Mercy held up a folded piece of paper she found on top of the stack in her hand.

"There's been some kind of mistake, Horatio. This letter isn't addressed to Birdsall & Son."

"A mistake? I think not." The owl tugged up on a chain around his neck, and a pair of reading glasses popped out from beneath his waistcoat. He plunked them onto the end of his beak with the feathery tips of one wing as he took the paper from Mercy with the other. He studied the blank outer fold as if there were something to read there. Then he thrust the letter at her once more. "As I said, it is for you."

Mercy took the note, frowning at it in confusion. "But... there's no address."

"Yes, there is."

"Where?"

Horatio flapped a wing vaguely toward the paper in her hand.

"Still don't see it," said Mercy.

"Just because human beings can't see it doesn't mean it's not there, my dear. I should add that this missive is not addressed to Birdsall & Son. It is addressed to you, personally."

"To me?" A thrill shivered up her spine. The only person who sent her non-business-related mail was her sister, Lilian, who sometimes found hilariously tacky postcards on the road. "Who's it from?"

"Goodness, how would I know?"

"The same way you know it's for me?"

Horatio gave a tittering hoot. "Darling, reading the direction is the sum total of my powers in that regard. Pesky privacy laws and all that. Which is a shame, I can tell you, for there are so many letters I would love to read prior to delivery. Are we quite finished here?"

"I—"

"Excellent. Ta-ta."

"Bye," Mercy replied absently. She stared down at the folded paper in her hand, bewildered, as she flipped the front door sign to "Open." Behind her, she heard the door to the kitchenette squawk on hinges in need of oiling and turned around in time to see Pop trying to sneak into his office with a steaming cup of coffee.

"No! Nope!" Mercy said, pointing an accusatory finger at him.

Pop sulked like a giant toddler. "Aw, muffin."

"You know what Dr. Galdamez said."

Defeated, he went into the kitchenette to dump out his coffee as Mercy unfolded the note and read.

Dear Friend,

I suspect that I'm writing to someone who doesn't exist. But if you do exist, and you're out there somewhere, I guess this letter is for you.

I have recently been informed that I'm a dickhead, by an equimaris no less, and before you go defending me, please know that it's true. I am a dickhead. I'm not sure when or how it happened, and I don't think I've always been a dickhead, yet here we are. I have to confess that there is one person in particular who brings out the complete and utter dickhead in me, and I wish I knew what to do about that.

Do you have someone like this in your life, a person who rubs you the wrong way, and no matter how often you promise yourself that you will rise above it all, you let them goad you every single time? I hope you don't, for your sake, but if you do, my condolences.

I've been trying to figure out why this person brings out the worst in me, and I have come to the following conclusion: Most days are just days, you know? Just me plodding through the hours between when I get up and when I go to bed. But whenever I'm around this one person, this individual who gets under my skin like no other, I feel more strongly the presence of an undeniable truth that is always there, lurking, hovering, waiting for me around every bend in the road.

Loneliness.

There. I said it. Technically, I <u>wrote</u> it, but committing it to ink makes it truer.

I'm lonely. So this woman who very clearly does not like me reminds me that there are very few people left in this world who do. And my circumstances are such that I don't know how to solve that problem.

Maybe that's why I keep putting myself in her crosshairs. Maybe there's a strange comfort in knowing that at least one person feels something for me, even if that feeling could best be described as hate.

Well, this is a dismal letter. Sorry about that. For what it's worth, I feel better for having written it, to have applied the weight of my loneliness to a piece of paper rather than to my own heart for a change. Thanks for that, my friend. I hope my words haven't weighed you down.

Or are you lonely, too?

Sincerely,
A Friend

Mercy gaped at the inexplicable pouring out of a heart that she held in her hand, from a person as real and substantial as the paper on which it had been written, but as fragile and easily torn, too. Who had sent it? And why had Horatio insisted that this letter was addressed to Mercy when the writer clearly didn't know who she was?

The front door opened, and Mercy folded up the letter and shoved it into the pocket of her dungarees in time to see her brother, Zeddie, saunter into the lobby, brazenly hip in his green shirt and slim-cut pink pants, his golden curls perfectly disheveled, the picture of twenty-year-old callowness. He carried a greasy bag with one hand while stuffing half a glazed doughnut into his mouth with the other. Like Mercy, he was tall, but unlike Mercy, he had inherited their mother's narrow frame and the ability to shovel food therein with little effect.

"Why are you late?" Mercy asked him.

"Because doughnuts." He handed her the bag, which she opened so that she could inhale the fried perfection inside. It was hard to stay mad at anyone who brought her doughnuts.

"Fair point, but we need to make sure Pop doesn't see these."

As if on cue, their father stepped out of the kitchenette sans coffee and beamed when he saw his son in the lobby. "There's the graduate!"

"That's me." Zeddie smiled gamely as Mercy hid the bag of doughnuts behind her back, but there was a tightness to his mouth, a gritting of the teeth that planted a small seed of concern in Mercy's gut. She refused to let it take root, however, certain she must be imagining things.

"So, what are we up to on your first day as undertaker?" Pop asked, clapping his big hands and rubbing them together in giddy anticipation.

"*Zeddie* is going to bathe, salt, and wrap the gentleman Marshal Ralston brought in yesterday, while *you* sit quietly at your desk and balance the books, per the doctor's orders."

"Oh. I thought maybe we'd start with boatmaking," said Zeddie.

"This one's keyless, so it'll be easy-peasy."

"Right." Zeddie laughed nervously. Mercy chalked it up to first-day jitters.

"I'll let you get to it." Pop chucked his daughter affectionately on the chin and went back into the office. With her father safely out of the way, Mercy decided it would be acceptable to stop in the kitchenette to snarf down a doughnut before heading to the boatworks.

"How can the body be keyless?" Zeddie asked her a few minutes later, through a mouthful of half-masticated fried dough. "Don't you have to have an ID key to enter Tanria?"

"Legally, yes, but plenty of people sneak in to poach birds, dig up exotic plants, that kind of thing. There's a whole black market for Tanrian stuff."

By now, Mercy had finished her cruller and was ready to get to work, but Zeddie grabbed another doughnut from the bag and took a bite. "So how do you know what to do with the body or where to send it?"

"We don't. All we can do is salt the remains, perform the incantations, and take them to the burial pits."

"Gods, no wonder we're broke," Zeddie muttered before taking another bite.

Mercy bristled. "These people deserve dignity at the end of life as much as anyone else. That's how we do things at Birdsall & Son."

"But how can you stay in business if you're taking on unpaid work?"

"*We*, not *me*," she corrected him as he shoved the remaining chunk of doughnut into his mouth. "And it's not unpaid. I applied for the Indigent Processing Grant when the new Tanrian ID laws went into effect four years ago. Aside from Cunningham's, we're the only drop-off site for keyless bodies near the West Station, and we get paid a stipend every time a marshal delivers unidentified remains to us. At first, it didn't add up to much, but with the sheer number of people entering Tanria these days, indigent intake has become a steady revenue stream."

"Good to know," Zeddie said with a distinct lack of enthusiasm, which was disappointing. Mercy was proud of herself for having the foresight to apply for the grant four years ago.

"Well, there'll be plenty of time for you to learn the ins and outs of the finances, and that part of the business is mostly my job anyway." She patted his arm, brushing aside her wounded pride at the same time. "Ready to do some bathing and salting and wrapping?"

Zeddie frowned at the greasy doughnut bag. "Maybe I should digest first?"

Mercy laughed at his joke—surely he was joking—and led him to the boatworks, but by the time they had donned their goggles and gloves and rubber aprons, her brother's tawny skin had taken on a ghostly pallor. She almost offered to get the body out of the lift on her own, but she stopped herself. The business was called Birdsall & *Son*, and the son had finally come home to take over what their father had begun. It was time for her to stop babying him and let him get his hands dirty.

"Go ahead and get him on the prep table."

"Right."

She watched as Zeddie rolled the dolly out of the lift and

clumsily hoisted the body in its stained shroud onto the table over the drain in the floor. He was clearly holding his breath, and by the time he'd finished, he had turned positively green. She could make neither head nor tail of his squeamishness. Maybe they used dummies instead of corpses in his training program?

"Are you up for salting and wrapping the body?" she asked him.

A bead of sweat trickled down his temple. "No, I think I should watch you do it first to make sure I learn how to do things the way Pop wants them done."

"All right."

She studied his pinched face. Zeddie had always been timid around the dead, but surely three years of working toward his degree in Funerary Rites and Services would have solved that problem. Shoving aside her misgivings, she went about unwrapping the body.

"The decay is extensive, but you can see that this man was strangled, which is a blessing. Drudges often bite into their victims' throats to kill them before taking over their bodies, as I'm sure you know."

Zeddie swallowed and nodded.

Mercy cut away what remained of the man's clothes, revealing the bloodless skin of his abdomen. "See here? There's a wound where Marshal Ralston ran the corpse through the appendix, which, as you know, is the seat of the human soul and the point of drudge infection, but I always double-check to be on the safe side."

She picked up the scalpel she kept on hand for this purpose, made a precise cut to open the lower abdomen, and fished through the intestines until she found the appendix, punctured as it ought to be. She sliced into it again for good measure... in time for Zeddie to bend over the sink basin behind him and lose the contents of his stomach therein. He fled from the boatworks, the soles of his canvas high-tops squeaking on the clean linoleum floor in his haste, and Mercy was left to loom over the corpse, bewildered, holding the scalpel in midair. She set it down on the tray, washed her hands in the sink—rinsing Zeddie's mess down the drain at the same time—and followed his trail until she found him sitting at the small table in the kitchenette with his head buried in his arms. The now empty doughnut bag was crumpled up next to his elbow.

"Zeddie?"

He sat up, furiously wiping his eyes with the backs of his hands, and Mercy's whole chest ached in sympathy.

"What's wrong?" she asked.

"I need to tell you something."

"Okay." She sat down in the chair opposite him and patted his arm. "I'm listening."

He squeezed his hands between his knees, as miserable and pathetic as a puppy stuck outside the screen door in the pouring rain. "So... when I was at school... I didn't exactly follow the coursework for Funerary Rites and Services."

That seed of concern in her gut sprouted, grew, and bloomed.

"What?" she asked, not certain she wanted the answer.

"I flunked Intro to Death Rituals my first semester, and I had to drop Intro to Boatmaking because, as it turns out, I'm allergic to mahogany. That would explain all those rashes I used to get as a kid. Remember?"

"Mother of Sorrows," Mercy breathed at him in disbelief. "Then what in the Salt Sea have you been studying for the past three years?"

Zeddie shrank into the chair, caving in on himself. "Ancient Medoran philosophy."

"Are you kidding me?"

"I wasn't married to it, but I didn't know what else to do."

"And you're just now telling me this?" Over the course of those seven words, Mercy's voice shot up several octaves.

"Shh!" Zeddie sprang to his feet and closed the door to the kitchenette. "I'm telling you now."

"Does Pop know?"

"No! Gods, no! Please, don't tell him, Merc."

"How am I supposed to keep this from him? I think I'm going to pass out." She put her head between her knees and took deep breaths, gulping down air and steaming up her glasses until she got a grip on herself and could sit up again. "It's okay. We can fix this. You don't have to use mahogany. Oak's better anyway."

She looked hopefully at her brother, but that hope quickly dwindled as she watched him lean against the door with an air of tragedy.

"The job's not that bad once you get used to it," she assured him. Begged him, more like.

"I will never get used to it. And you're right. It's not bad; it's terrible."

"No, it isn't!"

Zeddie clutched the sides of his head, his curls splaying out between his fingers. "I know I should have said something before now, but every time I tried to tell Pop, I chickened out. I mean, how could I do that to him after all he's done for me? So I thought, 'Okay, Zeddie, how bad can it be? Give it a shot.' But that shot lasted all of five seconds. Gods' tits, this is a fucking disaster."

"It's not like this job was a giant surprise. You've always known that undertaking gets passed down from father to son. It's been that way since the days of the Old Gods, and Pop's had this all laid out for you since you were born. You'd take over as undertaker, and I'd stay on as your office manager. Things are a mess, Zeddie. If you don't step up, that's it. Birdsall & Son is done. Finished. Over."

"I know, but I'm telling you, I can't do it. I *won't*."

"Well, what else are you going to do with your life?"

"Not spend it with *dead* people!"

The words were a slap to Mercy's face. Her eyes welled up with hot tears of frustration, but she could see that there was no cajoling him into the undertaking business, not as he melted against the door in mute misery, anyway. Defeated, she rubbed her forehead with both hands. "What are we going to do?"

"I don't know. Please don't tell Pop. Or Lil either. I don't trust her to keep her mouth shut."

"They're going to figure it out."

"I know. I'll tell Pop. I'll tell both of them, I swear. But I'd like to have a plan for my future in place before I do. Can you cover for me until then?"

Mercy wondered if her brother understood that he had pulled the rug out from underneath her. She'd worked her tail off for thirteen years to help Pop keep Birdsall & Son up and running for Zeddie's benefit, and now he was about to smash it to smithereens. She wanted to say, *What about me?* But what right did she have to guilt Zeddie into a job—a vocation, really—that made him miserable? She couldn't do that to this brat she'd adored since the day he was born.

He came to kneel in front of her. "Please? Pretty please?" he begged her.

And she cracked like an egg.

"Ugh. Fine. I'll keep your secret. For now. But at least give boatmaking a shot if you can't handle the bodies. You owe Pop that much. As for telling him about the philosophy degree, make it soon. And until then, you have to help me do all the things that don't involve dead bodies. And you have to help me keep Pop in line, too, because he keeps trying to do stuff the doctor says he can't do anymore. Deal?"

"Yes. Absolutely. Deal. You are the literal best sister ever."

"Be sure to mention that to Lil the next time she's in town," Mercy joked weakly as Zeddie hugged her hard, chair and all.

She had already forgotten about the strange letter, so she paid no attention to the crinkling of paper in her pocket as her brother squeezed the breath out of her.

Chapter Three

Hart had been back in the field for all of twenty-six hours when the nimkilim showed up with his obnoxious "Knock, knock! Mail delivery!" outside the barracks, more than enough time for Hart to reconsider and regret his decision to write and send that letter. What if the nimkilim who collected it out of the box read it or, worse, had a way of returning it to the sender? What if the letter was actually delivered to somebody? What if someone—anyone—figured out that he was the one who had written it?

And yet as he stepped out into the Tanrian gloaming to find Bassareus standing by the deck chairs, Hart couldn't help but hope that the letter in the rabbit's paw was a response to the one he'd sent out into the world like a message in a bottle.

"How you doin'?" the nimkilim said in his incongruously deep voice. His red vest was ratty, but the gold hoop in his long ear gleamed like new.

"Banneker and Ellis are on rounds," Hart told him, since he knew the delivery probably wasn't for him, and he didn't want to be disappointed.

"Good to see you, too, sunshine. It's for you, from the chief."

Hart took the proffered letter and frowned at it, more disappointed than he had thought he'd be. When he realized that the rabbit was still standing there, he said, "Thanks?"

"You're welcome."

Bassareus didn't move, so Hart did, going inside the barracks to read the note, but he didn't fail to hear the nimkilim's muttered "Asshole" behind him as he shut the door. Alma hadn't bothered stuffing the letter into an envelope, so Hart unfolded it and took in the message, delivered succinctly in Alma's neat, unfussy script.

Marshal Ralston,
Your presence is required in my office tomorrow afternoon, one o'clock sharp. See you then.

—A

It was unsettling, the odd balance of former partners and friends turned boss and underling and sort-of friends but sort-of not friends. Hart scanned the terse message again, trying to read between the lines. There was the arm's-length distance of calling him Marshal Ralston and the friendly overture of signing off with her initial. This was why he didn't go over to her house anymore; he never could figure out exactly where he stood with her.

Their conversation the day before about Hart's working solo was no small cause for concern. And yet as he lay in the too-small bunk that night, it wasn't his impending meeting with Alma that kept him up. It was the letter he'd sent to no one. He continued to fret over the wisdom of pouring out his heart onto a piece of paper, so much so that by the time he returned to the station the following day, he felt sick to his stomach.

He arrived a half hour early to resupply so that he could escape as soon as Alma was finished with him, but the chief's voice cut across the commissary at a quarter to one.

"Marshal Ralston."

He looked up from the shelf lined with canned fruit and found her standing by the door. She jerked her head toward the hallway behind her.

Hart pulled his watch from his pocket. "The meeting's not till one."

"May as well get it over with. Come on. And don't say I didn't warn you this was coming."

His stomach soured more as he met her at the door and fell into step beside her. "So you're foisting another partner on me?"

"In a manner of speaking."

"Meaning?"

Alma stopped outside the closed door of her office and studied Hart. One corner of her mouth twisted into a grin.

"What?" he asked, disconcerted.

"You're fantastic at what you do."

A compliment. He was not expecting that, and he didn't know what to do with it. Warmth spread across his chest.

"Which is why I have decided that you owe it to the profession to pass along your wealth of knowledge," she continued, and all at once, Alma's grin struck him as menacing.

"An apprentice?"

She might as well ask him to learn glassblowing or change a baby's diaper. He couldn't imagine how she came to think this was a good idea, but there she was, demigod eyes shining with amusement as she nodded in response.

"No. Hard no," he said.

"It's time for you to pay it forward."

Before he could sputter another protest, she opened her office door. A painfully young man was waiting for them, sitting in the chair across from Alma's desk, his knees bobbing up and down with nervous energy. Actually, the term *young man* was stretching it. The kid probably didn't need to shave the black fuzz off his upper lip on a regular basis yet, and there was something about the close crop of his tightly coiled hair that made him seem younger than he was, as if his mother was the one calling the shots on his hairstyle and buying him socks and underwear. He had a stoppered bottle tattooed on his forearm, which meant that his appendix had burst at some point and a temple votary had had to preserve his soul in the spirit vessel inked on his skin so that it wouldn't go sailing off on the Salt Sea before his body died. Marshals without their appendixes tended to be risk-taking, show-boating nightmares in Hart's experience.

The kid leaped to his feet, clutching a recruitment brochure that said *So you want to be a Tanrian Marshal!* as he gaped up at Hart. "Dang, you're tall."

This is not happening, Hart thought. *I refuse to do this.* He gave the applicant a cool squint, the one that froze the blood of most miscreants, but the kid was so guileless it had no discernible effect on him.

"All right," Alma told the young man. "Have at it. And godsspeed to you."

The kid looked up at Hart with eager eyes the warm brown of a well-worn leather book cover. "I know you're a busy man, Marshal Ralston, so I'll get right to the point. I hear you've been working solo for a while."

"Yep."

"Marshaling is hard work. It goes easier with two, am I right?"

"This is what you call getting to the point?"

The kid licked his lips. "I need a job, and you need a partner."

"You are at least fifty percent incorrect."

"It's a win-win."

"And that is one hundred percent incorrect."

The kid's eyes went from eager to pleading. "Hear me out. My dad died in an autoduck wreck last year, and it's been hard on us, especially my mom. She had to pick up an extra job to keep us afloat. She wanted me to go to school for dentistry, but when my appendix burst a couple of months ago and I managed not to die, I thought, 'Here's my chance. I could join the Tanrian Marshals and make serious bank and help my mom send my sisters and my brother to college.' I mean, do you *know* what a marshal makes?"

Hart didn't answer the question. He was too busy remembering his own mother, used and left by an uncaring god to raise Hart on her own. At least this kid's dad had been a decent father.

"I'm strong, and I work hard," the recruit wheedled, as if he could sense the way Hart was caving. "And hey, since I don't have an appendix, I can't become a drudge, right?"

"But you can be *killed* by one," Hart pointed out, reminding himself that he neither needed nor wanted an apprentice. "This isn't a game. The more people pour into Tanria, the more bodies there are for drudges to take over, and it gets worse year after year. Marshals make 'serious bank' because every time we step onto Tanrian soil, we put our lives on the line. It's dangerous work, and you're only a kid."

The kid in question stood up straighter and puffed out his chest. "I'm nineteen. How old were you when you started marshaling? Who mentored you?"

Hart clamped his lips as he recalled his sixteen-year-old self—gawky, skinny, sullen.

Scared.

Alone.

This guy was hitting every sore spot he owned.

"Hold on a sec," Alma told the would-be marshal before she hauled Hart into the hallway and pointed a stern finger at his face. "I want you to remember who you were when you were nineteen years old. I want you to remember what Bill meant to you then. You could be to this young man what Bill was to you."

All the air whooshed out of Hart's lungs. Alma hadn't uttered Bill's name in his presence since their argument four years ago, and now here she was, playing it like a trump card. What rankled him was that it was working. He should be tearing into her; instead, he glanced into the office at the kid, whose raw hopefulness twisted Hart's conscience into a pretzel.

You could be to this young man what Bill was to you. For a moment—for one heartbeat of his life—he wanted it to be true, wanted it enough to let out a gusty breath of defeat and lean against the doorjamb to give the kid a long, appraising look. It was like staring into a mirror, the reflection of his younger self challenging him to be a better man than he had become.

"What'd you say your name was?"

"Penrose Duckers, but my friends call me Pen." Both answers sounded more like questions than statements of fact, a hint of uncertainty that tightened the pretzel in Hart's gut and strengthened his bewildering resolve to make what was likely to be a very bad decision.

"Well, I'm not your friend, Duckers. Come on. We need to get you outfitted."

Duckers's whole body lit up with puppylike excitement. "Wait, what? Am I hired?"

Hart marveled at the dingy ceiling of Alma's office, as if the reason behind his agreement to take on an apprentice was sticking to the strip of flypaper that dangled near the window. "Looks like it."

"Yes! I won't let you down, Mr. . . . Har—what should I call you?"

"Sir," Hart answered dryly.

"Right." Duckers grabbed Hart's hand and pumped it with enthusiasm. "Yes, sir."

Alma beamed at him, and for some strange reason, his stomach didn't hurt anymore.

Hart and Duckers sat atop their equimares, inches away from the Mist at the western checkpoint, where an archway made of metal and a bewildering array of pistons and cogs stood against the churning fog of the Tanrian border. The portals that punched a doorway into the Mist at each of the four cardinal points of Tanria never ceased to impress Hart. He'd gone in and out of them for nineteen years, but he had no idea how they worked. The engineers had a great enough command of the machinery to make repairs from time to time, and pirated knockoffs were becoming more and more abundant, but the only person who truly understood the ins and outs of the portals was the man who had created them twenty-five years ago, a reclusive scholar at the University of Quindaro named Dr. Adam Lee. Hart had met him once when he came to examine the portal at the West Station. He was a petit, fine-boned man, but although the top of Dr. Lee's head didn't reach Hart's shoulder, he was the most intimidating person Hart had ever met. No one could match that kind of brilliance, which would explain why the pirated portals used to illegally enter Tanria frequently collapsed or exploded.

The engineer on duty at the West Station's portal pushed a couple of buttons, spun a dial, and pulled on the crank. Duckers gawked at the Mist within the archway as it swirled and thinned into nothing more than a gauzy opaque curtain with the shadowy silhouette of the Tanrian landscape barely visible on the other side.

"So I ride through this?"

"Yep."

"Just ride on through? Easy as pie?"

"Yep."

Hart waited for the kid to get moving as the marshals assigned to the checkpoint snickered, but Duckers continued to sit on his docile mare and frown at the dense fog without going anywhere. "Are there any drudges in this stuff?" he asked Hart.

"Nope. They can't get into the Mist, and there are marshals stationed on the other side, so you usually don't see them close to the portals either."

"Usually?"

Hart had no intention of sitting here all day—he had already lost most of the afternoon as it was—so he grabbed the reins from Duckers and dragged rider and equimaris through the Mist with him. The thick silence of the fog seeped into the marrow of his bones as they crossed, a sensation to which he was accustomed by now but had never learned to love.

Duckers was far from loving it either. His dark complexion had taken on a sickly cast by the time they made it through. "Holy shit," he sputtered.

"There," Hart said, tossing the reins back. "Easy as pie."

Duckers looked like he was going to be sick all over the scaly purple hide of his mount, but when he finally noticed his surroundings, his lips slackened with awe. "Whoa."

It had been a long time since Hart had viewed the landscape of Tanria with anything resembling wonder. Now, he gazed at the bizarrely symmetrical triangles of mountains in the distance and the sweeping pink hills rolling before them. He listened to the lavalike burbling of an ambrosial brook and the jarring trill of birds and the comical burps of animals that lived and died only in this strange land—an off-kilter world created by imprisoned gods with nothing better to do. Hart tried to appreciate it once more as he watched Duckers take it all in with new eyes. It didn't work. Tanria was simply a place to him now, no different from any other place. He thought of what Alma had said about this shithole being his home. It wasn't a shithole, but it wasn't his home either.

Duckers, on the other hand, took it all in with enthusiasm, and his smile grew bigger and bigger. He looked back at the portal and laughed. "Holy shit!"

"Yep," Hart agreed.

The portal was still there, with a bored Tanrian Marshal stationed on either side of it, but the archway appeared to be a freestanding door in the middle of nowhere, as if the Mist weren't there at all. The scrubby desert landscape of Bushong was clearly visible from inside Tanria but completely unattainable without the portals. Duckers pressed a hand against the solid yet invisible border and watched a tumbleweed blow past on the other side. "So people couldn't see in, but the Old Gods could see out?"

"Yep."

"Dang."

"Guess the New Gods wanted the Old Gods to see what they were missing." This had always struck Hart as being cruel, but then, it wasn't like he had a high opinion of the gods, Old or New, anyway. He shoved aside the moribundity and nodded at his apprentice. "You ready?"

"Yes, sir." Duckers grinned at him, game for anything, and Hart realized, to his amazement, that he kind of liked this kid and didn't mind his company as much as he'd thought he would.

"Not going to fall off your equimaris, are you?"

"I don't think so, but I'm a city man. I'm not used to equimares."

"Well, get used to them, because autoducks don't work here. Neither do transistors, gas stoves, firearms, you name it. Anything that didn't exist before the Old Gods were imprisoned is useless on this side of the Mist. This place is old school, so if you want to cook something, you do it with fire, and if you want to kill something, you do it with a pointy object, and if you want to get around, you do it on foot or on an equimaris. If you want music, in theory, you make it yourself, but be aware that I will tie you up and gag you if you do."

"Okay," Duckers said, drawing out the last syllable like a long musical note of uncertainty tinged with a healthy questioning of his career choice. "You know this is all Tanria 101, right?"

"Yep. Tanria 101 is now in session."

Hart urged the equimares forward and began his apprentice's first tour of Tanria, keeping to the outer edge near the Mist. Drudges could be found anywhere inside Tanria, but the border was the least likely place to come across criminals illegally mining gems or poaching exotic birds, unless they happened to catch them as they were breaking in. Today's ride would be purely educational. In short, Hart was teaching Duckers about Tanria the same way Bill had taught him all those years ago: by beginning with the basics.

"We're starting with history," he said. "What is Tanria, and how did it come into existence?"

"Oh my gods." Duckers rubbed his forehead in frustration.

"Answer the question."

"The Old Gods were all about war and vengeance and stuff, so the New Gods overthrew them and put them in prison on Earth. That was, like, a couple thousand years ago. The Old Gods lived here until two hundred and something years ago, when they finally cried uncle and the Warden let them out and the Unknown God made them stars on the altar of the sky. Then some guy made the portals twenty-five years ago, and yadda yadda yadda."

"And people could get into Tanria for the first time since its creation," Hart finished for him. "I get that you're annoyed, but I want to make sure you are absolutely clear on how shit works here, because 'yadda yadda yadda' covers a lot of territory. Like how many of the locals weren't too happy with the fact that a bunch of people started pouring into Bushong either to loot a sacred place or to profit off the adventurers and business tycoons making money in Tanria. 'Yadda yadda yadda' also elides the fact that once people could get through the Mist and die in Tanria, they could be turned into drudges, which is why the Tanrian Marshals were formed."

"'Elides'? Who talks like that?"

Hart pinched the bridge of his nose. "The point is, there are a lot of stupid rumors out there about Tanria, and I want you to know your facts from your fiction. Half the population of the Federated Islands believes that dragons are flying all over here and hoarding treasure."

"So, like... they're not?"

"No."

"Oh. I knew that."

"No, you didn't." It was a smug answer from a man who had thought there were dragons in Tanria when he was a kid and had been as disappointed as Duckers was now to discover that they were nothing more than fairy tales. "Why did the New Gods place Tanria in south central Bushong?"

"Uh... I mean..." Duckers surveyed his surroundings as if the answer might be helpfully written on a nearby tree trunk.

"Because it's arid and rocky and shitty and about as far away from water as you can get, so very few people were living here at the time. I'm sorry, what were you saying about this being Tanria 101 and everyone knowing all about it?"

"I guess they didn't teach us that part in school," Duckers muttered.

"I guess they didn't. Now tell me what you know about drudges."

Duckers perked up, ready to hold forth on this subject. He'd probably played Drudges and Marshals a million times when he was a kid, like every other child in the Federated Islands. "No one knows what they are or where they came from. All we know is that if someone dies on Tanrian soil, they can be infected by some sort of spirit and reanimated. Most people think they're lost souls since they infect the appendix, but since souls are invisible, there's no way to know for sure."

At that exact moment, a soul floated past Duckers, the eerie rod of amber light drifting over the pink hillocks of Tanria like a wind-blown dandelion seed. Not that anyone but Hart could see it, and not that anyone knew that Hart *could*—no one who was alive, at any rate. In the days when he and Alma were partners, he had been tempted to tell her that he could see the souls of the departed—his demigod gift—but then he'd remembered what happened to Bill and he'd kept his mouth shut. Since Hart couldn't do anything about a soul when it was disembodied, he kept up his lesson.

"How do you kill a drudge?"

"Can you kill them? Aren't they already dead?"

Hart opened his mouth, then closed it. "Good point."

"Aha! In your face! Who's educating who here?" Duckers pumped both fists into the air in triumph, a gesture he undercut a second later when he nearly fell off the equimaris and had to grapple for the pommel to stay on.

"Who's educating *whom*," Hart corrected him, tamping down the unfamiliar urge to laugh. "How do you take out a drudge?"

"You poke them in the appendix so the lost soul can't stay in the body. It's like an off switch."

"Is that an easy thing to do, to 'poke them in the appendix'?" Hart put air quotes around the ridiculous wording.

"Um, no?"

"No, it is not. The appendix is very small."

"Well, let me tell you, it felt fucking huge when it blew up inside me."

Hart turned his head and pretended to cough when, in actuality, he was barking with laughter. "I imagine that it did. When is a drudge most likely to kill a living person?"

"When the dead body they possessed is all rotting and nasty, and they need a fresh body."

"Good. What happens if a drudge gets outside of Tanria?"

"Seriously? Does that happen?"

"Rarely, but it's not unheard of. Sometimes, a marshal will deliver a body to an undertaker, thinking they've hit the appendix when they haven't, and if they wrap the drudge up in sailcloth so that it can't move, no one's the wiser until the undertaker unwraps it, and the drudge is free to wreak havoc in some border town. Also, a drudge sometimes manages to get through a pirated portal if the criminals using it don't seal it up properly or if it malfunctions. It's been happening more and more lately. So what do you do if a drudge gets out?"

"Pokey-pokey?" answered Duckers, illustrating his meaning with his pointer finger.

"That's right, because a drudge will continue to decay, which means it might try to kill someone on the other side of the Mist. It doesn't understand that it can't infect a body outside of Tanria. That's why you have to be certain that you've hit the appendix before you take the remains out of here for shipment home. Is that clear?" Hart wanted to scare this point into his apprentice.

"Yes, sir. Do drudges infect animals? Are there squirrels and shit that are drudges, too?"

"A drudge can infect anything with an appendix."

"What all has an appendix?"

"In Tanria? Humans, rabbits, opossums, porcupines, and graps."

"And what?"

"Graps. Rabbits, opossums, and porcupines were already here

when Tanria was created, and some of them got stuck inside. But graps were created by the Old Gods. They're like frogs, but they're furry. You'll only find them in Tanria."

"Huh. What about cats and dogs? Do they have appendixes?"

"No and no."

"So they don't have souls?"

Hart brought his equimaris to a halt, and Duckers's mare, sensing authority, stopped in her tracks as well. "Do you honestly believe that dogs don't have souls? Have you ever met a dog who wasn't a hundred times nicer than your average human being?"

"Um, no?"

"Exactly. Don't insult dogs like that."

He gave his equimaris a light tap and got them both moving once more, feeling a bit guilty. The kid didn't know about Gracie, after all, and Hart didn't need to go chastising him on day one.

"Guess you like dogs," said Duckers.

"Guess I do."

"Let me ask you something. If you had to choose between saving my life or saving a dog, which would you choose?"

"The dog."

"That's funny. You're hilarious."

"I'm not laughing, am I?" Hart nudged his mount forward, leaving Duckers to catch up.

"Dang. That's cold, sir."

Hart glanced behind him and saw his apprentice clinging for dear life to an equimaris that had begun to trot. He faced forward again so Duckers wouldn't see him grin.

Chapter Four

Zeddie's confession and its ramifications continued to worry Mercy the morning after her brother's disastrous first (and possibly last) day as undertaker, but since she had no ready solution and a backlog of boats to build, plus a well full of corpses to deal with, she donned her apron and rubber gloves and goggles and got to work. The body on the prep table had belonged to a licensed grap trapper whom a marshal had brought in the day before, a woman killed and reanimated by a drudge while gathering graps for the lucrative Tanrian pet market. Unlike the leaky, keyless man Hart Ralston had brought in two days before, this one came with a prepaid funeral package from Birdsall & Son.

Once Mercy had cut off the soiled clothing with a sharp pair of scissors, she bathed the body with the sink's hose attachment. Then she sang the incantations of the Three Fathers and the Unknown God as she rubbed salt into the dead woman's already sloughing skin.

From water you came, and to water you shall return.
You shall sail into the arms of the Salt Sea,
and Grandfather Bones shall relieve your body of your spirit.
The Warden shall open the door unto you,
and the Unknown God shall welcome you into their home,
where you shall know peace.

Mercy lost herself in the verse, her alto voice filling the room. While it lacked the resonant heft of her father's baritone register, she threaded the words with her own respect and gravitas.

Once the grap trapper was wrapped in fresh sailcloth, placed in her boat—a nice oak cutter—and stowed on the dock to go out for delivery, Mercy fetched the last of Birdsall's keyless indigents for the week and performed the same ritual again. As the salt did its work, she placed a generic key on a cheap chain around the unfortunate man's neck. Then she reached into the bin on the work counter and pulled out a small wooden boat the size of her palm.

Pop whittled them in his spare time, tiny catboats and sloops and cutters. He had always believed that everyone should get a boat to sail the Salt Sea to the House of the Unknown God, no matter who they were or how poor they might have been. It was this small act of kindness and decency that made Birdsall & Son a million times better than a bloodless, soulless, profit-is-everything operation like Cunningham's. She placed the wooden boat over the man's heart, straightened his key, and wrapped him tightly in clean sailcloth.

She was grabbing a quick cup of coffee in the kitchenette when she heard Zeddie say, "Be right back, Pop." He emerged from the office across the hall, closed the door, and rammed his fingers into his disheveled curls.

Mercy leaned against the counter as Zeddie walked past her to pour himself a cup. He added a staggering amount of sugar and stirred it in with a vigorous clanking of the spoon against the porcelain.

"That bad, huh?"

"Gods' tits and testicles, Mercy, I had no idea what you've been putting up with all these years. The books are a mess, and it's not like I'm great with numbers."

Mercy gave an unintentionally maniacal giggle over her mug. "Well, you're better at it than Pop."

"You need to sic the math teacher on him."

"I know, but Lilian's hardly ever in town, and it's unfair to make her deal with the books on her time off."

Their sister had once been a math teacher in Argentine, but when she fell in love with Birdsall & Son's delivery driver, Danny, she was more than happy to abandon her "little shits" to travel the Federated Islands of Cadmus with her husband.

"Sure you wouldn't rather salt and wrap a couple more bodies with me?" Mercy offered.

"Math it is," Zeddie sighed, and he returned to the office, but Mercy was far from giving up hope. Once her brother saw firsthand the importance of the work she and Pop did at Birdsall & Son, he'd come around.

Mercy loaded up the old autoduck with four salted and wrapped indigents and drove south on Main Street, following it as it turned into a two-lane highway. Once the paved road met gravel, she slowed down to navigate the bumps without jostling the bodies in the hold, and she took care as she made the sharp turn onto Shipyard Road. Obviously, the corpses didn't appreciate the effort, but it seemed like the decent thing to do.

She parked at the pits, well away from the small but growing shipyard, where the dead of Eternity, Argentine, Mayetta, and Herington were buried, their headstones spaced in neat rows. She wheeled each body over the uneven earth and deposited them into the open hole where the unidentified and unwanted ended up, the people who entered Tanria by any means possible to get rich or start over, only to be killed by drudges and become drudges themselves.

Mercy batted away a fly as she gazed down at the unclaimed corpses that had accumulated over the course of the week. As per usual, Cunningham's unidentified remains outnumbered Birdsall & Son's by a hefty margin. The Other Undertaker didn't bother to shroud the indigents, which seemed offensively undignified to her. It wasn't so much that she shrank away from the decay and the maggots, from the milky eyes and open mouths, from the muscles taut with rigor mortis—far from it. It was simply that she believed everyone deserved a ritual to usher them into the next life, and if that left no one but her to say a few words over an unmarked grave, she was more than willing to do what was good and right. She clasped her hands in front of her and gave her speech. The words varied each time, but the sentiment remained the same.

"I know this pit is probably not what you would've wanted for yourself, but to be honest, it's the living who care, not you, not anymore. All those folks in their fancy boats getting interred here or shipped home? They're going to the same place as you. Some of them have been preserved in Tanrian heartnut sap. Some of them will be buried in shipyards, in airtight boats that aren't supposed to leak. Some will be burned to ash in their boats and scattered on the ocean by loved ones. But in the end, they'll all sail the Salt Sea, like you. The Warden will welcome them into the House of the Unknown God, and there will be nothing left but what Grandfather Bones leaves behind. It's the way we all go. So safe travels and a happy homecoming to you. It's been a pleasure and an honor to serve you here at the end."

She gave the bodies one last look, as if to say *I see you*, before heading home. By the time she returned to Birdsall & Son, the delivery duck was parked by the dock, which meant that Lilian and Danny had arrived while she was out. Mercy's spirits lifted. She took a quick bath in her apartment above the boatworks, threw on one of her favorite dresses—robin's-egg blue, covered in pairs of cherries—and picked up a bottle of wine before heading to Pop's house with Leonard at her heels and a renewed optimism that everything was going to work out.

Her springy gait was made springier by the raucous laughter of her family, which she could hear from two doors down. She skipped up the front steps, threw open the door, and let the explosion of sound that was her family wash over her.

"Is that the literal best sister ever?" Zeddie called from somewhere out of sight as Mercy dipped fingers into the dish of salt water on the family altar and touched her mother's key.

"I'm right here, you rat," Lilian fired at him, hugging Mercy hard, then dragging her by the hand to the dining room table, where they could sit and watch Danny—the one family member who could cook—make dinner in the kitchen. To Mercy's shock, Zeddie appeared to be helping him.

"I am very alarmed. What is happening?" Mercy asked her sister.

"Do we trust Zeddie with a knife, honey?" Lilian called to her husband.

Danny grinned adorably. Everything about Danny was adorable, from his dark red curls to the tips of his brogues. "He's learning to cook."

"Do we trust Zeddie with *food*?" Mercy asked.

Zeddie gave her a theatrical glower and gestured with the knife, flinging onion bits all over the floor. "Har har. Weren't you the one complaining the other night how terrible our dinners are without Danny?"

"No, that was you complaining. And also not cooking."

"Well, now I'm learning to cook, so shut up."

"Gods help us." Mercy made a show of tiptoeing into the kitchen to grab a cracker off the cheese plate and offer it on the

Hearth's altar to the right of the kitchen sink. "Please, make sure he doesn't poison us," she mock-prayed to the kitchen god.

"You're a riot." Zeddie toed her in the butt to nudge her toward the dining room as Pop came in through the screen door in a cloud of cigar smoke. When he saw Mercy, he grimaced and tried to wave away the evidence.

"Pop! Dr. Galdamez said no smoking!"

He put up his hands in surrender and went into the kitchen to help himself to the cheese plate, which probably wasn't the best thing for his health either. "What are we having?" he asked.

"Roasted chicken, balsamic-glazed carrots, and a nice green salad." Danny uncorked a bottle of wine and started pouring it into the glasses on the table, leaving Zeddie to his own devices.

"Gods bless you, but isn't Zeddie going to burn down the kitchen without you?" Mercy stage-whispered to her brother-in-law as he poured her a very generous glass of pinot grigio.

"Hey!" Zeddie protested.

"He's not too shabby," Danny answered with a laugh. But as he started pouring a glass for Lilian, he pulled up short, sloshing wine onto the tablecloth. "Oh jeez, babe, can you drink this stuff?"

Mercy froze, her body understanding what Danny was implying before her brain could catch up.

"Of course she drinks wine. Who doesn't like wine?" an utterly clueless Zeddie commented as he peeled garlic cloves.

"I like wine," Roy added, also clueless.

Lilian gave Danny a wide-eyed, exasperated look, and her husband's freckled cheeks turned pink.

"Shit! Sorry!" he whispered to her.

"Wait! Are you—?" Mercy began, but Lil pinched her leg under the table.

"We'll talk later," she said out of the corner of her mouth, releasing Mercy's poor thigh.

In her mind, Mercy was dancing on the table, squealing, *Lil's having a baby!* It was all she could do to keep herself from bawling over her sister as she passed her the carrots during dinner. But her joy came with a bittersweet barb after dessert, when Pop raised his glass, directed a meaningful look at Zeddie and a more pointed one at Mercy, and made the same toast he had made at Lilian's wedding. "Cheers to this wonderful family. May it continue to grow."

"Oh my gods, this again?" said Zeddie.

"You? You're still a baby," Pop told him. "But Mercy is thirty years old."

"Oh boy." Mercy put her napkin on the table in case she needed to wave it like a white flag.

"I'm not going to be around forever, and I want to make sure you're taken care of when I'm dead and gone."

Lilian snorted. "Who's taking care of who here, Pop?"

"All I'm saying is that I would like to see Mercy settled."

"That is such an Old Gods thing to say. Are you hiding an alter to the God of Patriarchal Order around here?"

"Old Gods. New Gods. I don't care so long as I know someone is watching out for Mercy, preferably a nice man who makes a shitload of money."

"Can I get one of those, too?" Zeddie interjected.

"If he makes a shitload of money, you can marry a whale for all I care."

"Pop. I'm fine," Mercy assured him. "All in favor of moving on to a new topic of conversation, say 'aye.' "

"Aye," answered Lilian, Zeddie, and Danny. Even Leonard grunted from the couch in the parlor.

"Did you hear the Arvonian polo team is getting a new head

coach?" Danny said to divert Pop's attention, because if there was one thing Roy Birdsall loved nearly as much as his family, it was professional sea polo.

Lilian nudged Mercy. "Let's escape while we can. Want to get another slice of cake?"

"Does the Mother of Sorrows want a vacation? What kind of question is that?"

The sisters sneaked into the kitchen as Pop declared, "I don't care how many times Redwing has won against Vinland. They're no match for Bushong's equimarine front line."

Mercy cut an extra-large piece for Lilian, and not because her sister was pregnant. Lil could always pack it away while maintaining the petite figure she had inherited from their mother. Mercy, on the other hand, was built like Pop, tall and big boned. She liked her curves, but sometimes, she envied Lil's size; it would be nice to find a dance partner who managed to clear the top of her head by at least an inch every now and again. Her ex-boyfriend Nathan had claimed that he was six feet tall on the nose, but when they danced, she highly doubted it.

The thought of Nathan jabbed her in the heart.

"Sorry about Danny," Lil said, taking an enormous bite of cake and talking through the crumbs. "I stopped by Dr. Galdamez's first thing after we got to town to make sure it was true. I was going to tell you after dinner, but my beloved messed up the big reveal."

"I'm so happy for you," Mercy told her, but while she was thrilled for Lilian and Danny, there was a part of her that was envious. She had always imagined herself settling down with someone nice and starting a family of her own, but that notion seemed to be drifting farther and farther from her grasp these days.

The thought of Nathan jabbed her in the heart again.

"I'm trying to wrap my brain around it," Lilian said. "Me, having a kid?"

"You'll be fantastic."

"Well, I had a good role model."

"Mom was pretty great," Mercy agreed with a fond pang of grief.

"Yeah, she was, but I wasn't talking about her."

Mercy gaped at Lil, momentarily speechless. She sniffed, then sniffed harder. "But you don't want to tell Pop yet?" she asked, not quite hiding the sentimental quaver of her voice.

"No. It's early days yet, and I don't want him to get his hopes up in case... well, in case. So please don't tell him. Or Zeddie. I don't trust that brat to keep his mouth shut. But I want to make sure you know, because me being preggo is about to upend how things work at the family business, and it only seems fair to give you as much warning as I can."

By now, Lil had polished off her cake and was pressing her thumb against the crumbs on her plate. Mercy set down her fork and eyed her sister. "Meaning what?"

Lilian sucked the crumbs off her thumb and wiped her hand on her skirt. "I can't travel all over the islands with a baby. And I don't want Danny leaving me on my own for days or weeks at a time to deliver bodies. What's the point of being married if we're not together?"

"No one expects either one of you to stay on indefinitely. We can hire someone else to do the deliveries."

"That's not what I'm getting at. Look, Mercy, Zeddie is the undertaker now, so let him worry about hiring a new delivery driver, and let him hire a new office manager while he's at it, so you can finally get on with your life."

Zeddie's secret roiled in Mercy's stomach alongside the chicken and the carrots and the salad and the second slice of cake. "But if I leave now, the whole business will collapse."

"I'm not suggesting that you abandon Zeddie. You can help him get on his feet, but once you do, the time has come to move on."

"I can't."

"Yes, you can. Sweetie, you're so smart and talented and organized. Stop wasting yourself at Birdsall & Son."

It wasn't that Mercy didn't think she was smart or talented or organized, and it wasn't that she was in love with running the office either. It was more that she couldn't imagine a career outside of Birdsall & Son and everything it stood for. Besides, how on earth was she supposed to make a fresh start at age thirty with no degree and no experience outside of managing the clerical needs of an undertaking business?

"What happens if Zeddie can't make a go of it?" she asked, knowing that it was more than a mere possibility.

"Then he doesn't make a go of it, and he does something else. If worse comes to worst, Cunningham's can handle the dead of the western border towns."

Mercy gaped at her sister.

"Don't give me that. *You're* the one who got stuck with the business after Mom died, and you practically raised me and Zeddie, too. Well, Zeddie and I can take care of ourselves now. You deserve to live your own life for a change."

Mercy took up her fork and speared another bite of cake. "But it would crush Pop if the business went under. And Cunningham's is such a soulless, inauthentic end-of-life experience. People deserve a choice."

"Dead people don't care! Never once has someone piped up from the hold of the delivery duck and said, 'There's too much salt in here,' or 'I told Enid I wanted *teak*.'" Lilian took Mercy by the arms, and Mercy couldn't help but recall that Lil had sucked the crumbs off her thumb and was now touching her with it. "Think about it. For me?"

Mercy nodded, but there wasn't much conviction behind the gesture. She couldn't leave until she had convinced Zeddie to take over, and that might be a long time coming.

Lilian kissed Mercy's cheek. "Good talk, but I gotta go barf."

Not one, but two secrets weighed Mercy down as she walked home with Leonard, and both of them seemed to be herding her toward an uncertain future, one without Birdsall & Son. Normally, when she had a problem, she would talk it through with Lilian, but she had promised Zeddie she wouldn't say anything about his degree in ancient Medoran philosophy, and replacing Lil and Danny was now one of the many plates Mercy had to keep spinning.

"Ugh," she told Leonard as she plopped onto her settee in the apartment above Birdsall & Son, Undertakers. Determined to be a lapdog, he sprawled across her legs and crushed her beneath his weight. How sad that Leonard was Mercy's sole confidant. She couldn't talk to her family about the things that worried her most, and Nathan was out of the picture, and any friends she'd had in her youth had long since left Eternity for greener pastures elsewhere. How on earth had she let herself get this isolated?

It was then that she remembered the strange letter she had received the day before, forgotten in her dungarees pocket in the laundry hamper. She shoved Leonard off her lap and fished it out.

Are you lonely, too? the stranger asked her in precise letters that had more corners than curves. Mercy's heart pounded in reply. She felt a jolt of understanding, a connection to the writer, like magnets set too far apart to snap together but quivering with proximity.

At least she didn't think of herself as "plodding through the hours" as this person did, but she most certainly knew someone who goaded her like no other. The name Hart Ralston displayed itself in her mind like a garish advertisement on an oversized billboard.

She stared at the signature line.

A friend.

Mercy loved her family more than anything in the world, but it would be nice to have someone in her life who wasn't so completely and utterly up in her business, a person who wasn't foisting secrets on her that she didn't wish to keep. In short, *a friend* was exactly what she needed.

She knew it was absurd to write back. This person was a complete stranger, after all, and how on earth could she send a response with any confidence that the nimkilim could get it to the right person? She sat at her desk anyway, pulled out a sheet of stationery from the drawer, and wrote the words *Dear friend* at the top of the page.

Chapter Five

Mentors and apprentices were never assigned to sectors until after the first two weeks of training, and since they were sticking to the least populated areas of Tanria—hence, the least likely places to encounter a drudge—Hart decided to make camp that night rather than stay in a barrack with other marshals. Alma had already foisted Duckers's company on him; he didn't feel a need to foist anyone else's company on himself. Duckers was dozing off on his sleepsack, and Hart was reading his interlibrary loan—*Crossroads: The Intersection of Modern Grammar and Compositional Theory*—in the flickering light of the campfire, when Bassareus's booming voice shouted, "Knock, knock! Mail delivery!"

Duckers shot to his feet and grappled for his unloaded pistol crossbow as the oversized bipedal rabbit sauntered into the campsite on two enormous feet.

"A drudge! Kill it! Kill it!" shouted Duckers.

"How you doin'?" the rabbit greeted him, as if the kid weren't waving a weapon in his direction.

Duckers halted his frantic panic dance. "Nimkilim?"

"No, I'm your grandma. Yes, I'm a nimkilim. Put that thing down before you blow the asshole's balls off by accident."

"It's not loaded," Hart said blandly from his battered old folding stool, where he calmly sipped a cup of chamomile tea.

"It's a nimkilim," Duckers breathed in relief, inexplicably

blocking his own crotch with both hands. "I thought I was a goner."

"A possessed rabbit is not going to be the means of your end, Duckers. I promise."

"What? The rube's never seen a nimkilim before?" the rabbit asked.

"Our nimkilim back home was a lizard," answered Duckers.

"Bassareus, Duckers. Duckers, Bassareus. Whatever he's got, I'm sure it's for you, kid."

The nimkilim took a letter from his pack and squinted at it. "Nah, it's for you, sunshine."

"What?" Hart asked, incredulous. "From the chief?"

"No."

"From whom, then?"

The rabbit looked at Duckers, jerked his head toward Hart, and snorted. "Get a load of Mr. Grammar here. 'From *whom.*' How the fuck should I know who sent it?"

Hart took the proffered letter, studying one side of the envelope and then the other, but it was completely blank. "This has no address on it, smartass."

"It was addressed by heart, *dumb*ass."

"I *am* Hart."

"No, *heart*, with an *e*. Like, thump-thump, thump-thump." The nimkilim shook his head in exasperation for Duckers's benefit, as if to say, *Do you believe this guy?*

"I feel you, man," Duckers agreed.

With the weight of Duckers's and the nimkilim's eyes on him, Hart slid his finger under the envelope flap and pried it loose. He took out the letter, unfolded it, and saw the words *Dear friend* at the top. His eyes bulged, and his breath came in short bursts.

"What? Did somebody die?" Duckers wondered aloud.

Ignoring the question, Hart skimmed down the page and saw

that it was signed *Your friend*. He refolded it and clutched it in his hand. The rabbit was staring at him with an air of expectation, as if Hart were supposed to read the letter aloud.

"What?" Hart demanded.

"He's waiting for his tip," Duckers whispered.

"What? Why? No one tips me when I deliver dead bodies."

Bassareus gave Duckers another one of those *What the fuck?* expressions.

"Don't look at me. He hasn't paid me yet either."

"Fine," Bassareus grunted. He strode to Hart's pack, which was slung over the picketed equimaris, and began rifling through it.

"Hey!" Hart protested, but before he could reach him, the nimkilim had unearthed a bottle of whiskey and blown a layer of dust off it.

"This man needs help," he told Duckers.

"Don't have to tell me twice."

"Put that back," said Hart, but it wasn't very forceful. All he wanted was to read the letter that was practically scorching his fingertips.

"Or what? You'll kill me? I'm immortal. Grab me a glass, kid."

Duckers handed Bassareus a tin cup, and the nimkilim shook his head in disgust. "Guess this'll have to do."

"I keep whiskey around for medicinal purposes, so don't drink it all," groused Hart.

"That's your problem, not mine." Bassareus poured out three fingers' worth of whiskey, handed the cup to Duckers, then clinked the bottleneck against the tin before knocking back a few gulps straight from the bottle.

"Down the hatch, kid," the rabbit said with a belch, toasting the young marshal in training with the bottle raised high in the air.

"He's a minor," Hart told Bassareus. To Duckers, he said, "Put that down." Duckers sulked, but he did as he was told.

"Cheers," said Bassareus, and he sauntered away from the campsite, taking Hart's dusty bottle of medicinal whiskey with him.

The second he was out of sight, Hart rummaged through the pack for a second lantern, trying to hide his shaking hands from his apprentice as he lit it.

"What are you doing?" Duckers asked.

"I need to take a piss, and I'm nice enough to leave a light here with you while I'm out."

With that, Hart made his way to the nearest plausible pissing tree. He unfolded the letter and read it by the dancing light of the lantern as a soul floated between tree trunks in the distance.

Dear friend,

Apparently, I exist, because your letter has found me, although I don't know how or why. Did you really mean to chance upon me, or are you simply sending thoughts out into the universe, hoping they find a home? In either case, please know that I am happy to be the recipient.

I do indeed have "that person" in my life! But I can never seem to muster the meanness I require to put my nemesis in his place. How annoying. I wish I could be cutting, but I may as well try to crack a nut with a pillow.

I've been thinking on your situation, vague as it is to me, and I can't help but wonder if more people are lonelier than either of us will ever know. Maybe lots of people are walking through their days, lonely as can be and believing no one understands what it's like. That's not a very cheering thought, is it?

In general, I wouldn't describe myself as lonely, but lately

I've been feeling... Isolated? Stuck? And yet, I like the things I do and the people I meet between sunrise and sunset, whereas you appear to be alone as well as lonely. They're not entirely the same thing, are they? While I am not alone, per se, there are times when I feel like I'm at a party, standing against the wall when I'd rather be dancing. Everyone else is cutting a rug, completely unaware that I'm there. Or worse, they don't want to dance with me. And I'm a pretty good dancer, let me tell you.

If this letter finds its way to you, I hope it makes you feel less lonely, and maybe less alone, too. In the meantime, I remain,

Your friend

Hart read the words again. And again.

Dear friend.

He had written a letter to no one, but *someone* had written back. And he liked this someone.

He raced to the campsite and barely remembered to slap his usual insouciance in place before stepping into the dying light of the campfire. He didn't want Duckers to know that his whole world had been changed in the course of ten minutes.

"That was a long piss," the apprentice commented. He was sprawled on his sleeping bag, reading, of all things, a Gracie Goodfist comic. Hart decided not to say anything about the now empty tin cup beside him. Because Hart had a letter to write and a person to whom he could write it.

He tore a page from the notebook in his pack and got out a pen. *Dear friend*, he began. *I wish I could tell you what your letter means to—*

"Who was that letter from?" Duckers cut into his thoughts.

Hart grunted with annoyance. "*Whom.* And none of your business."

"Who are you writing *to*?"

"Still *whom*. And still none of your business. Do you mind?"

"Is she pretty?"

Hart didn't answer the question, but now he wanted to know: Was she? Because he got the distinct sense that she was, in fact, a she. Something about the wording, the lovely slant of the letters themselves.

Duckers shrugged and went back to reading his comic, leaving Hart in peace to read what he had already written.

I wish I could tell you what your letter means to

It was too raw, too honest. He crossed it out, then crumpled the page and started over with a new sheet. But he didn't know what to say. He read the letter from his friend again.

I feel like I'm at a party, standing against the wall when I'd rather be dancing.

It reminded him of his mom, of all the times she had forced him to dance with her in the parlor with embarrassingly old-fashioned songs blaring on their gramophone. He touched her key, feeling its familiar outline beneath his shirt where it rested against his heart on a silver chain next to his ID tag from Cunningham's.

No son of mine is going to grow into one of those grumpy men who don't dance, she had told him. He realized with chagrin that he *had* become one of those grumpy men who didn't dance. And it wasn't because he didn't like to dance. He did, actually. But he no longer had anyone to dance with, hadn't for ages.

Dear friend, he wrote, warming to his topic. *It would surprise many people to learn that I am, in fact, an excellent dancer. If I ever find you holding up a wall at a party, I promise to dance with you.*

He paused. Was that... flirtatious? Was he flirting? But neither of them was speaking of dancing here. This was a metaphor, and

Hart was hardly likely to be found at a party anyway. Besides, this was a letter to a person he never intended to meet. That was the beauty of it. He could be completely honest with someone who would never see him, never know him in reality.

There and then, he decided that he would never again cross something out or start over. He wouldn't censor himself. He would be exactly who he was.

He wrote the letter and folded it into fourths, making a mental note to buy envelopes the next time he resupplied. Because there would be more letters. He was certain of it.

Once the lanterns were put out, Hart lay on his back, staring at the night sky, at the stars that had once been gods. He couldn't sleep, and he didn't want to. He listened to Duckers's baby-soft snores, and in his mind, he read the words of his friend's letter over and over again.

For the first time in a long, long while, he wasn't alone.

Chapter Six

It was Sorrowsday morning, six days since Mercy had sent off the letter to her mysterious correspondent, but she'd had nothing in reply, and each day of her new friend's silence tied up her insides more tightly, another string that tangled itself into the knot of Birdsall & Son's impending doom.

Don't be ridiculous, she chastised herself. *You knew all along that letter would probably come to nothing.*

The more depressing thought was the fact that the family business seemed to be coming to nothing as well. Mercy lay in bed every night, her wheels spinning, trying to concoct ways to convince Zeddie that he could fall in love with the work. This morning, for example, she had sent him to Afton Lumber to pick up their order, hoping he would take the opportunity to walk through the lumberyard, admire the raw grain of each plank, smell the unique scent of pine and oak (and not mahogany). It's what she always did when she went.

If nothing else, at least Zeddie's fetching the lumber order freed up her morning. She grabbed the broom from inside the hall closet, shook out the welcome mat, and swept off the front walkway as she did every Sorrowsday morning, but she soon lost focus and gazed up and down Main Street in search of Horatio. There was no sign of the nimkilim, so she gave up and went inside.

In the boatworks, the ribs of her sloop in progress hung off the strong back jig, where she had left them yesterday. The boat was for Mr. Gauer, who had been a Tanrian ornithologist before a heart attack set him sailing across the Salt Sea. Better that than a drudge, Mercy supposed, but it was sad all the same. She remembered when he had come to Birdsall & Son about a year ago to set up transportation home to his wife should he meet his end in Tanria. A middle-aged man with a balding pate and a thick ruddy mustache, he had pulled his pocket watch from his vest and opened it so that Mercy could see the watery portrait of his wife that he kept inside.

"She's lovely," Mercy had said. "Such a nice smile."

His own smile had made the ends of his excellent mustache bend upward as he stared fondly at the photograph. "I'm going to send for her as soon as I get settled."

But from what Mercy could tell, he had not felt settled enough in the year that followed to send for his wife, and now Birdsall & Son would have to mail a death notice to his widow, followed by his body. She hoped this woman loved her husband as much as he seemed to have loved her. Then again, she wondered which was sadder: losing someone you truly loved, or never loving someone to begin with.

It was the wife she thought of as she cut the keelson, settling into the rhythm of the saw, moving it back and forth through the wood, taking pleasure and pride in the steady cut. She would make a fine boat for Mr. Gauer, and her craftsmanship would, in turn, bring comfort to his widow. She was hanging the saw on its peg when she heard Horatio's familiar *clack* against the front door.

"I'll get it!" she hollered as she hurried past the office, scolding herself for her unreasonable eagerness. She threw open the front door, and Horatio fluttered into the lobby, his lemon silk scarf billowing behind him dramatically.

"Oh my, not getting enough sleep?" he inquired. "Your eyes are dreadfully puffy. Tea bags, moppet. They work miracles."

Mercy batted sawdust out of her hair self-consciously. She hadn't been sleeping well lately, but it was dispiriting to know that it showed.

"This feels like money, darling, so I put it on top." The nimkilim winked at her and patted an envelope made of creamy, expensive paper as he presented her with the mail. It was addressed to her father in looping, ostentatious script, and the return address was embossed on the flap: *Mendez, Goldsich & Suellentrop, Attorneys at Law.*

"Thank you," she said distractedly as a deep sense of foreboding churned in her stomach. She was so distracted by the law firm's letter that it took her a moment to realize that Horatio was still standing in the lobby, staring at her with a strained cheeriness.

"Oh! Sorry!" She reached behind the counter to retrieve a tip for him. "I don't know where my head is today."

"I would like to think it's atop your neck, but looks can be deceiving." He touched her arm and declared "Tea bags. I swear by them" before sashaying out the door and on to the mechanic's shop.

Mercy knocked on the office door and opened it in time to see her father wake with a surprised snort.

"What's wrong?" Pop asked her when he saw her drawn face, and she handed him the letter in answer. He took the thick, elegant leaf from the envelope, and his eyebrows lowered as he read.

Mercy lingered in the doorway, chipping polish off her fingernails. "What does it say?"

Roy's lips twisted in distaste before he began reading aloud.

To Mr. Roy Birdsall, proprietor of Birdsall & Son, Undertakers:

On behalf of our client, CUNNINGHAM'S FUNERAL SERVICES, LLC, we would like to extend to you an offer by the aforementioned for the purchase of BIRDSALL & SON, UNDERTAKERS, including property, assets, furniture, supplies, and all goods and services associated therewith—

All the blood drained out of Mercy's face. "A buyout offer?"

"As if I'd sell when I'm sure he knows good and well that Zeddie finished school. Cunningham has some nerve."

Her siblings' secrets felt like a ton of bricks on Mercy's shoulders. She'd promised them both that she wouldn't tell Pop what she knew, but in light of Cunningham's offer, it seemed unfair not to tip him off. And yet if Mercy did spill the beans, would he be tempted to sell? Lil's words hovered over her like a ghost—*You deserve to live your own life for a change*—but selling out to Curtis Cunningham felt like the worst possible outcome. Everything inside her revolted at the thought.

She clamped her lips shut.

Pop folded the letter and stuffed it into the envelope. "I don't want to worry Lilian or Zeddie with this or make them think that I'm about the pull the rug out from underneath them when there's no cause for alarm. Let's keep this between the two of us for now, all right, muffin?"

"Sure, Pop."

And with that, she added one more secret to drag at her heels as she returned to the boatworks. She had every intention of working on Mr. Gauer's boat, its frame like the bare bones of a body, but all she could think about was the doomed future of Birdsall & Son, and the fact that she very much wanted an answer to that letter she sent last week. She could use a friend, preferably one who was not a blood relative with a secret.

She flipped through the remaining letters in her hands, her scant hopes for the future shriveling as each revealed itself to be either an answer to a death notice or a bill. But then the last envelope in the stack had the words *To: A Friend* written on the front in blocky letters, and Mercy was so glad to see it that she thought she might shoot through the roof and rain down sparkles like a fireworks display. Her fingertips tingled as she opened the envelope and pulled the letter free.

Dear Friend,

It would surprise many people to learn that I am, in fact, an excellent dancer. If I ever find you holding up a wall at a party, I promise to dance with you.

Not that the opportunity is likely to present itself. As you astutely pointed out, there is a difference between being lonely and being alone. The good news is that recent developments have lessened the latter (although the jury is out as to whether that's a good thing or a bad thing) while your letter has alleviated the former. Thank you for that.

Actually, "Thank you" is an understatement, but I'm worried that I'll come across as maudlin if I tell you how grateful I am for your words. What can I say? I needed a friend, and a friend wrote back. <u>You</u> wrote back. I'm glad it was you. Is that maudlin? Honestly, I'm not like this on a day-to-day basis. If anything, the word that best describes me is "bristly," so I'll simply say thank you and move on.

I'm intrigued by what you said about many people being lonely. It's a sobering thought. Most people seem so dull to me, balloons full of vacuous wind and empty words. I wonder what I would find if I tried to dig deeper every now and again? After all, there are a few things about me that would surprise most people if they ever bothered to scratch the surface. I'm a voracious reader, for one. I suspect many would find it shocking that a man as taciturn as I am would enjoy words so much when they are written on a page. What else? I have a weakness for pie, especially blueberry. I live for tea and despise coffee. Dogs are my favorite people. (That last one might not come as a shock to anyone.)

What would surprise most people about you, I wonder? I think I might be on tenterhooks until I find out.

Sincerely,
Your Friend

P.S.—Sorry this letter has taken so long to get to you. I live in a remote place and had to wait until I could get to a nimkilim box to post it. You can probably expect similar delays in the future, but I promise I won't stop writing unless you want me to.

Mercy flapped the letter in the air and did a giddy tap dance on the linoleum floor before she read the letter three more times and then a fourth time for good measure. Who was this bristly, dancing, taciturn reader who lived in a remote place? A rancher? A fisherman? A lighthouse operator? She imagined the sort of man who worked hard and had the lean body and rugged weather-beaten face to show for it. As this friend took shape in her mind, he began to bear a striking resemblance to Hart Ralston, an image Mercy batted away as quickly as it formed. She reminded herself that her friend could be anyone and was probably some curmudgeonly hermit with rheumatism who bundled up beside a fire on the warmest of days and played chess against himself. Besides, it didn't matter what he looked like. He was a friend. He was *her* friend. And she was glad of it.

She needed to let Leonard out to do his business, and then she had to finish Mr. Gauer's boat and salt and wrap him and seal him in his sloop. She had a million and one things to do before closing up for the day. Instead, she exhumed some paper and a pen from the supply closet and pulled up a stool to the preparation table.

Dear friend, she wrote at the top of the page in her very best handwriting.

Chapter Seven

Halfway up a wooded slope in northwest Tanria, Hart and Duckers watched from the trees as two teens, giggling with inebriety, sheared a wild Tanrian silksheep on the craggy mountainside. Hart had seen their ilk a hundred times, boys who were old enough to think themselves men and young enough to forget how easy it was to die.

"This is your typical cut-and-run operation," he instructed Duckers in a low voice. "Smugglers cut a hole in the Mist with a pirated portal and pay a few guys to enter the mountains on the border, shear as many sheep as they can pin down, and sell the silkwool on the black market. People are willing to pay an arm and a leg for this stuff, but there's a tariff on the raw material that's legally harvested and processed. Smugglers find guys like this who think it's a lark to bust into Tanria to steal a few bags, usually bored farm kids who know how to handle livestock."

"Okay, so what do we do?" Duckers had a glint in his eye, game for the adventure, and Hard decided that a sink-or-swim method of teaching his apprentice might be in order here.

"*You* are going to go in there and show them your shiny badge. Then you're going to tell them to leave the silkwool and scram or you're taking them into custody. I'll be your backup."

The glint disappeared from Duckers's eyes. "What? Shouldn't you be the one waving around your badge?"

"I already know how to wave around my badge. You're the one learning the ropes."

Duckers regarded the bleating blue silksheep and the drunken teens who were nearly the same age as he was. "Do I have to?"

"Marshaling isn't all fighting drudges and saving the day. You are now law enforcement, and those twerps are breaking the law."

"But I haven't seen a drudge yet."

Hart had already learned not to get drawn into a debate with Duckers. All he had to do was close his mouth and give him a bored look. The kid caved every time.

"Fine," Duckers acquiesced with a sucking of his teeth.

"You can do this. I'll be right beside you. Go get 'em." Hart clapped Duckers on the shoulder, the sort of friendly, supportive gesture for which he was not known, but it seemed to give his apprentice the courage he required. Duckers squared his shoulders and approached the teens, with Hart following close behind.

"Excuse me, gentlemen," he called, his voice ringing with authority. Hart thought it was a good start.

One of the boys giggled uncontrollably while the other froze and blanched in the lantern light.

"I'm Marshal Duckers of the Tanrian Marshals." Here, Duckers floundered. An uncomfortable pause galloped between him and the juvenile offenders. He put a shaking hand on the pistol crossbow at his hip and declared, "Put the silksheep down and I'll let you live."

"Salt fucking Sea," Hart muttered under his breath, bowing his head and rubbing his fingertip across his forehead so the silksheep shearers wouldn't see his exasperation.

The teens glanced at each other and burst out laughing.

"Try again," Hart coughed.

"Go home or we're taking you in," Duckers told them, but they kept laughing.

"And?" Hart prompted.

"And? Oh, the silkwool!" Duckers turned to the boys. "And leave the silkwool."

"Hold on. I've got my license right here," said the more fearless of the pair. He dug around in his dungarees pocket and pulled out his middle finger, to the cackling amusement of his partner.

"Can I shoot them?" Duckers asked his mentor.

Hart was pretty sure he was joking, but to be on the safe side, he said, unequivocally, "No."

Duckers tried again. "This is the last time I'm going to say this. Leave the silkwool and go home, or you're under arrest."

The more obnoxious of the pair tugged a flask out of his pocket and took a gulp. "Ooooh, I'm so scared. Aren't you shaking in your boots, Gerald?" He handed the flask to his buddy, who nodded and guffawed and took a swig.

It was here that Hart noticed a grap moving through the tree branches above the boys—a *possessed* grap. He picked up a rock from the ground and threw it, knocking the small frog-like drudge from its perch. It landed on top of Gerald's pestiferous companion, flailing and crying "Graaaaaaap" in a husky, undead moan.

"Get it off! Get it off!" the young man screamed, but Gerald squealed like a terrified pig and made a run for it, leaving his friend to toss the nasty, furry drudge off his head before he pelted after Gerald in terror.

The reanimated grap rolled on the ground, got to its feet, and hopped toward Duckers. One of its eyeballs dangled out of its socket by a ligament. Duckers froze in terror as Hart drew his rapier and jabbed it three times, hitting the appendix on the third try. The soul billowed out of the wound, and Hart thought, not for the first time, that a human soul would have to be pretty lost and desperate to possess a half-rotted grap. Then again, who was he to judge? He was lost and desperate with increasing frequency himself.

He wiped the blade off on the handkerchief in his pocket and slid it into the sheath before looking at Duckers, whose face was drawn and scared. "Well, there's your first drudge."

Duckers didn't get the chance to respond, because a rustling in the undergrowth and a low groan made both marshals snap to attention.

"And there's your second," Hart said, his eyes fastening on a movement to their left. A drudge emerged from between the trees, a woman wearing a torn and filthy homespun dress. Her throat had red puncture wounds from the drudge that had killed her, livid against her lifeless, waxy skin.

"Oh, fuck. Sir?"

Hart had set aside an hour every day for target practice, and Duckers had proven himself a decent shot. He decided to let the kid handle it.

"This one is fairly fresh, so it's not going to come after you," he said calmly. "Take out your pistol crossbow."

"Fuuuuuuuck," Duckers whimpered, but he did as he was told while Hart came up behind him and began firing off instructions.

"Feet shoulder width apart." Hart put his foot between Duckers's and kicked them to the correct width. "You've got the pistol in your right hand with your finger on the trigger. Your left hand's underneath for support. You know what you're doing." He stood at Duckers's back, slowly unholstering his own weapon. "Hold it about chin high—good. You're aiming for the lower right abdomen."

"Uuungh," the drudge moaned as it shambled closer.

"Fuck!" Sweat poured down the side of Duckers's face.

"You know better than anyone where that appendix is," Hart assured his apprentice. "There. Fire."

Duckers squeezed the trigger. The arrow flew straight and true, and the drudge went down, making an unmoving heap at the base of an aspen.

"Did I get her?" Duckers asked in a tremulous voice, staying put as Hart went to investigate.

"It. Not her," Hart corrected him as he examined the corpse. He watched the soul depart the body, and knowing that Duckers couldn't see the amber light, he said, "You got it. First shot. Took me four tries my first time."

Duckers's face crumpled, and he began to sob. Hart went to him, put a hand on his shoulder, and gave him a squeeze.

"I'm being a big baby," Duckers wailed.

"No, you're not. It's hard. But you need to understand that you didn't kill that woman. She was already gone. What you did—what we do as marshals—is a mercy."

It felt strange to utter the word without reference to a certain undertaker who made him miserable, but there was no other word for what they did when they took down a drudge.

"I know. Sorry." The kid sniffed hard, but the tears wouldn't stop.

"You've got nothing to be sorry about. I bawled my first couple of times."

"You did?"

"Yep, but if you tell anyone that I told you that, I'll rip your nuts off."

"I won't," Duckers said through a wet laugh.

"It gets easier. I promise." Hart gave Duckers another paternal squeeze before he felt like a sentimental ass and let go. "There are some things we need to do before we finish up here: check the body for an identification key, put it into a sailcloth, figure out where it needs to go and when and how. And we should gather up this silk-wool to turn in, too. Are you up for it? It's okay if you're not."

Duckers blew out a breath. "I'm up for it."

"You sure?"

"Yes, sir." He squared his shoulders the way he had done before facing the silkwool thieves, and Hart experienced a kind of parental pride of which he didn't know he was capable. He wondered if Bill had felt the same way about him, and a quiet ache pinched his chest.

Good gods, he thought, *I'm turning into a fucking feelings factory.*

He cleared his throat and got down to business, moving toward the body and motioning for Duckers to follow.

"This one isn't too badly decayed yet. They usually don't become dangerous to humans until the state of decay is so bad that they need to find a new host. But no matter the condition of the body, the first thing I always do is make sure the appendix is punctured. Why is that again?"

"Because if a drudge gets outside the border of Tanria, it might hurt people."

"Exactly." Hart drew his rapier and stabbed the corpse, feeling the tip grate against Duckers's tiny arrow. He pulled it out and wiped it clean before putting it away. "The next thing we do is check for the key. Do you know about keys?"

"Yeah. You're supposed to have a key on you so that if you die here, your soul can unlock the door to the House of the Unknown God."

Hart had no truck with religion, but he wasn't about to foist his bitter opinions on Duckers. He knew that this moment, staring death in the eye, was taking a toll on the kid, but since there was nothing for it, he continued the lesson.

"Right. Also, everyone entering Tanria is required to make funeral arrangements with a licensed undertaker, so the key is going to tell us where to take the remains."

The silver chain resembled a garrote around the woman's neck. Hart fished out the key-shaped ID tag, which had fallen down the back of her dress, and read the directions.

"Fuck," he said, the single syllable cracking off his tongue like a whip.

"What?"

"We have to take this one to Birdsall & Son."

"Are they horrible or something?"

"Yes, very horrible. All undertakers are horrible. Come on. We've got work to do."

Hart showed Duckers how to wrap a body, and he couldn't help but notice how much easier the whole operation was with two sets of hands, especially moving the corpse down the mountain. Duckers didn't shy away from any of it.

"Let's gather up the silkwool and call it a day, huh?" said Hart.

"We're going to camp out with a dead body?"

"Yep."

Duckers blinked at Hart. "Okay then."

After they hauled the silkwool to their campsite, where the equimares were picketed, Duckers dropped onto a fallen log, exhausted. Hart regarded him thoughtfully, then dug around in his pack for a bottle of whiskey. They had stopped at the station two days ago, ostensibly to resupply but really so that Hart could finally put the reply to his friend into the station's nimkilim box. When he'd added two bottles of whiskey to their tins of soup at the commissary, the lady at the checkout had raised her eyebrows, not bothering to cover up her shock. She had never seen Hart purchase a single bottle of whiskey, and now there he was with two. As far as Hart was concerned, she didn't need to know the reason, so he had tipped his hat to her and lugged around two bottles of whiskey for the past forty-eight hours. Now a cup, two tea bags, a small bottle of honey, and the kettle followed the whiskey out of Hart's pack.

He built a fire and went about brewing a pot of tea as Duckers watched him in a slack-lipped daze. When the tea was good and strong, Hart doctored it with plenty of honey and a healthy dollop of whiskey; then he handed the steaming cup to Duckers.

"What's this?" Duckers asked, clutching the cup's warm comfort to himself as if it were a stuffed toy bear.

"Like I told Bassareus, I keep whiskey on hand for medicinal purposes, and you look like you could use some medicine. It's better with lemon, but lemons don't fare well in the pack. Drink up, Marshal Duckers."

Duckers glanced up at him, and Hart knew his apprentice hadn't failed to notice his use of the word *Marshal.* The kid took a sip as instructed, and his eyes went wide. "Whew."

"Definitely better with lemon."

Duckers gave him a crooked grin. "But it's pretty good without it."

They hadn't set up the tent, so Hart saw the nimkilim striding out of the trees before he heard him bellow, "Knock, knock! Mail!"

"Hey, Bassareus," Duckers said.

"Hey, yourself, Master Duckers. You have four letters."

"Four?" Hart asked, incredulous.

"You only get one," Bassareus told him flatly, implying the word *asshole* at the end of the sentence as he shoved an envelope into Hart's hand.

It was addressed *To: A Friend* in a clear, looping, and now familiar cursive, and Hart felt a ridiculous fluttering in his chest.

"Hold on a sec," he told the nimkilim before he rifled through his pack, pulled out the second bottle of whiskey, and handed it over to the rabbit.

"I suddenly like you a whole lot more," said Bassareus as he turned the bottle in his paws, examining the label.

"We're heading into town tomorrow to drop off a body, so we'll be near a nimkilim box, but in the future...you know...if you could pick up our replies the following evening when we get mail in the field?"

Bassareus regarded Hart, studied the bottle in his hand, then turned his attention back to Hart. "She must be a hot piece of ass."

"You look like a rabbit, but you're actually a pig, aren't you?" Hart said, making it clear that this was a statement, not a question.

"You think it. I say it. What's the difference?"

"No, I don't think it. Do you want the whiskey, or do you want to fuck off?"

Bassareus's ears perked up. Then he put his paw over his heart. "Aw, that's sweet."

"What?"

"You're all warm and fuzzy over this girl, you big softy."

"She's a friend." Hart held up the letter, which was clearly addressed *To: A Friend.*

Bassareus grinned, revealing a jagged, broken tooth next to his huge front incisors. "Big gooey softy, that's what you are. You seem all tough on the outside, but you're mushy on the inside for some letter-writing bird. It's cute."

"You can go now."

"Fucking adorable. Isn't he fucking adorable?" Bassareus asked Duckers.

Hart shot eye-daggers at Duckers, daring him to agree. The kid held up his hands in surrender. "I'm not saying a word."

The nimkilim pulled the cork from the whiskey bottle with his teeth, spat it on the ground, and took several hearty gulps. "You've got yourself a deal. I'll pick up your letters for you, Hart-throb. See what I did there?"

Hart-throb was a hop, skip, and a jump from Mercy's *Hart-ache*, and Hart didn't appreciate the reminder. "Go away," he growled.

"Big soooooooftyyyyyyyy!" the rabbit sang over his shoulder as he disappeared into the trees.

"He's right," Duckers said when the nimkilim was gone. "You're one of those hard-on-the-outside, marshmallow-on-the-inside types."

"Remind me again why I hired you?"

"Because I'm delightful."

"Yep, that must be it." Hart rubbed the letter in his hand with his thumb and tried not to smile like a big softy. The envelope pulsed with possibilities on his palm.

"Read it," said Duckers. "Don't let me stop you. Or are you going to go 'take a piss' again?"

"You're fired."

Duckers laughed, but Hart was so glad that the kid was all right after taking out his first drudge, he couldn't bring himself to be annoyed.

"Who sent you all those letters?" he asked, nodding at the papery loot in Duckers's hand.

One by one, Duckers held up the envelopes, identifying each sender. "My mom. My sister Lorraine. My sister Peggy. My sister Nadine."

"Don't you have a brother, too?"

"Yeah, but he's a punk. Anyway, I'm going to bed, so you can read your letter in peace."

"You aren't going to read your letters?"

"Well, I would, but someone got me drunk."

"Medicinally speaking." Hart had to bite his cheek to stop himself from grinning at Duckers, though he couldn't say why he shouldn't.

"Whatever you say." Duckers wormed into his sleeping bag. "Good night, sir."

" 'Night."

"Sir?"

"What?"

There was a pause, and Hart glanced up from his letter to find Duckers gazing at him with artless gratitude.

"Thanks. For everything."

Hart's chest flooded with warmth, as if he were the one guzzling the medicinal tea. "You're all right, Duckers," he said.

With that, Duckers turned on his side, and Hart read his letter by the light of the campfire.

Dear friend,

I definitely do not want you to stop writing. I promise to write to you as long as you write to me.

But we need to discuss more important matters, specifically, your preference for tea over coffee. Are you a monster?? Coffee is a literal gift from the New Gods. How can you prefer to drink boiled weeds instead? This was almost a dealbreaker for me, but since you're a dog lover, I've decided to forgive your ludicrous taste in hot beverages.

What would people find surprising about me? At first, I thought this would be a fun question to answer, but I'm struggling to come up with a single response. I don't think it would shock anyone to know that I like to read novels (bonus points for love stories), that I hate cooking but enjoy eating, or that I sing along to my favorite records at the top of my lungs while soaking in the bathtub.

The one and only thing that might surprise people is the discovery that I take joy in my current occupation. Without going into detail, it's the sort of career that is typically considered disgusting. I must admit, there are occasions when it is. But my job is also a service and a kindness. It allows me to do good things for others and to bring them comfort. How many people can truly say that about their line of work?

Plus, I have the opportunity to meet all sorts of interesting people on their way to or coming from faraway places. Today, for example, I became reacquainted with a gentleman all the way from Timbers Gate in Honek. He had the most wonderful mustache and a miniature portrait of his wife inside his watch case. I always approve of a man who dotes on his wife, don't you? She had a nice smile. I always approve of nice smiles, too.

I worry that you don't see enough doting husbands and smiling wives where you are, although it sounds as if you're no longer alone, or at least, not as much as you were. What has changed? Who is this person or persons? What are they like?

Sincerely,
Your friend

P.S.—I love all desserts, so I won't say no to pie, but my heart will always belong to a well-baked and thoroughly frosted cake, especially chocolate, which tastes particularly good when paired with a cup of coffee (dash of milk, no sugar).

As Hart reread the letter, his eyes kept drifting to the words *I sing along to my favorite records at the top of my lungs while soaking in the bathtub*. He couldn't help himself. He kept imagining a vague woman in a bathtub, the sort who enjoyed eating chocolate cake and had the full breasts to show for it.

She must be a hot piece of ass, Bassareus's voice spoke lewdly in his mind, and yet it didn't prevent him from envisioning a pair of soft legs, bent at the knees, jutting out of the soapy water like two slick, shining mountains of skin hinting at the blessed valley beneath the surface.

You think it. I say it.

Gods, he hated that Bassareus was right. But the more his imagination filled in the picture, the more this vague sense of a woman began to resemble horrid Mercy Birdsall. That put an end to any such fantasies. His friend deserved better. He gave himself a shake and returned his attention to the letter.

Without going into detail, it's the sort of career that is typically considered disgusting.

What kind of job was unsavory but also a kindness? A plumber? A street cleaner? A garbage collector? Diaper delivery service? But would she meet people coming and going in any of those professions?

Then he remembered what he had said to Duckers this afternoon.

What you did—what we do as marshals—is a mercy.

A mercy. A kindness. A service. Could this woman be another marshal? Hart considered the marshals he knew, but he found it hard to believe any of them had written this letter. Then again, maybe some of them were a lot nicer than he was, the sort of people who actually enjoyed meeting all the fortune hunters coming and going across Tanria's border or, at least, the doting husbands and smiling wives she mentioned.

I always approve of nice smiles, too.

Hart knew he didn't smile easily, and when he did, it was rarely in a way that would be described as "nice." Would his friend approve of him? Then again, maybe these letters allowed him to be the sort of person who really did smile, if only on the inside. It was easier to be himself when he was limited to paper and ink, when she wasn't there to stare at him, trying to work out who his immortal parent was rather than trying to figure out who *he* was.

He read her postscript again and was irrationally jealous of cake. He had to remind himself that this woman could be an eighty-year-old granny with a geriatric husband and a houseful of cats.

The image of a naked woman in a bathtub filled his brain again, and why the fuck did that woman insist on looking like Mercy Birdsall? He banished the picture from his mind once more. It was bad enough that he had to deal with Mercy outside of Tanria. He didn't want her messing with the perfection that was this correspondence, this friendship, this one pure and true thing in Hart's life.

Duckers snuffled in his sleep, his face made extra young and soft by the firelight. Hart remembered the way the kid handled himself that day, first with the silkwool smugglers, then with the drudge. He had been scared, but he hadn't hesitated. He had also demonstrated the ability to reflect on his actions, to think about whether or not he had done the right thing. That thoughtfulness was a good trait in a marshal—a good trait in anyone—and it occurred to Hart that these letters weren't the only welcome change in his life recently.

Who is this person or persons? What are they like?

He got out his paper and pen as well as the packet of envelopes he had purchased at the commissary. He gave Duckers the small smile he'd kept hidden up till now before writing *Dear friend* at the top of the page. His smile broadened when he remembered that he and Duckers would be heading into Eternity tomorrow to drop off the body, which meant he'd be able to slip this letter into a nimkilim box sooner rather than later.

Chapter Eight

It had been two days since Mercy slipped her last letter into a nimkilim box, so she knew that she was unlikely to receive a response from her friend this morning. He'd warned her to expect delays, this mysterious wheat farmer / forest ranger / soldier on the freezing military outpost of her imagination. And yet, with her family's secrets weighing on her and the future of Birdsall & Son hanging on by a thread, she offered up a silent prayer to the Bride of Fortune that a letter would arrive nonetheless, a reminder that she had the support of a friend, wherever he might be.

Sadly, it was not to be.

"I am afraid there is no letter from your paramour today," Horatio confided behind his wing when she opened the door.

Mercy's cheeks went hot with mortification. "I don't have a paramour."

The owl didn't have eyebrows, and yet he seemed to be cocking one at her. That scrutinizing gaze made her cheeks go hotter. "If you say so. Here are some bills. I suspect they shall be as depressing as a silent lover. Kiss, kiss."

The nimkilim flapped away, leaving a humiliated Mercy to open the bills, which were, as the owl had predicted, very depressing. One was an overdue notice on the gas bill, and she made a mental note to speak to her father about paying the bills on time, adding it to the ever-increasing list of mental notes that were beginning to leak out of her ears.

She glanced up from the sad stack in her hands and found herself face-to-face with a wall of tall, gangly male. Mercy screamed with fright before she realized it was Zeddie standing in the doorframe.

"What?" he said, as if he hadn't scared the living daylights out of her.

Mercy looked at the clock. Nine seventeen.

"Where have you been?" she demanded.

"I made a batch of cinnamon rolls. Want to try one?" He held up a plate, like an enthusiastic golden retriever offering his owner a stick to throw.

"Your job is not baking. You're supposed to be helping me with—" She glanced at the office door, which was slightly ajar, and whispered, "Stuff."

At least Zeddie had the decency to appear cowed. "I know that."

"Do you? Because you're late. Again. Futzing around with flour and sugar or whatever." Mercy sniffed in righteous indignation, but she caught a whiff of cinnamon and sugar wafting through the air. She did her best to maintain her dignity as she snatched a roll from the plate. "Make sure Pop pays these bills," she told him.

He took the envelopes from her and gave her a side hug. "You got it."

"And once you've done that, come to the boatworks to help me with Mrs. Callaghan's cutter."

Over the past week, she'd salted and wrapped and boated bodies in the evening after Pop went home, while during the day, she'd roped Zeddie into sawing and sanding and gluing and nailing. She had hoped he might perk up at the notion that they were building a new boat today. Instead, Zeddie pouted at her.

"It's a boat, Zeddie. Nary a dead body in sight. If you don't want to help me, feel free to tell Pop all about the tenets of ancient Medoran philosophy."

"You're mean."

Mercy walked past him with her chin up, but she couldn't walk past the fact that Zeddie didn't seem to be taking to boatmaking. How was she supposed to get him on board as the new undertaker if he couldn't get excited about the sharp scent and lovely grain of cedar? Plus, she would have thought he'd be moved to work on the cutter for a woman he'd known his entire life.

Mrs. Callaghan had opened a general store down the street with her husband when Eternity was founded twenty-five years ago. When Mr. Callaghan died, she had handed off the business to their daughter. While Mercy was sad to bid farewell to a neighbor, it was nice to make a boat for someone who had lived well and died peacefully. She placed the keelson into the slots across the ribs, relishing the way the frame came together like a puzzle. Then she began the process of fairing the wood, making sure the surfaces were smooth and flat for the planking.

She had learned all of this from her father in bits and pieces over the course of her life, always there to lend a hand when he needed it. And he had needed it more and more even before the heart attack. Now, as she put her whole body into her work, she could turn off the worries spiraling inside her head and focus on muscle and movement, on the medicinal scent of fresh-cut pine, on the buttery softness of sanded wood beneath her hands, on the comfort that a finely made boat brought a grieving family. She was so engrossed in her work that she forgot about the napkin-wrapped cinnamon roll on the counter behind her and the fact that Zeddie was supposed to get his tail to the boatworks to help her.

She did, however, keep her eye on the clock. It was Bonesday, which was pyre day at the shipyard. That meant Mercy or someone from Birdsall & Son would have to drive out there around three o'clock to collect the ashes of their pyre this week. All at once, a deep sense of dread bashed her from within. She flung open the supply-cabinet doors to find the shelves alarmingly bare.

"Pop?" she yelled, hurrying into the office, where she found him feeding bits of cinnamon roll to Leonard while Zeddie frowned over the bills. "What are you doing?"

"I'm teaching Leonard to shake hands. Watch." He turned to the dog, holding up a wad of soft, buttery dough. "Shake."

Leonard was mesmerized by the promise of food in Roy's fingers, but he was deaf to the command. Pop grabbed Leonard's right paw off the floor and shook it, declaring "Good boy!" as he let the dog mouth the treat from his hand.

Mercy could already imagine the horrific dog poop that would result from this dietary deviation.

"Have you tried Zeddie's cinnamon rolls?" her father asked her as, aghast, she watched him feed another chunk to Leonard. "They're fantastic. Who knew he had it in him?"

"Thanks for the vote of confidence, Pop," Zeddie said without looking up.

Mercy waved away all talk of baked goods. "You remembered to order more urns, right?"

By now, Roy had torn another sticky wad of dough from the giant roll on his desk, but he froze, holding out the treat and sitting as still as the very expectant Leonard before him.

"We're out! Completely out!" cried Mercy.

"I'm so sorry, muffin. I promise to order them today."

"Today? Which is Bonesday?"

Her father's face fell. "How many do we need?"

"One. Only one. Do we have any? Anywhere?"

Roy scooted away from the desk that was formerly Mercy's, her old wooden chair groaning a staccato of protest. "I'll fix this. And I'm going with you to the pyres."

"Pop—"

He held up a trembling hand, and it broke Mercy's heart to see that tremor in a hand that had once wielded saw and hammer like an artist. "I'm going with you. It's my mistake, and I need to see this through myself."

Roy handed Leonard his reward for doing absolutely nothing, then shuffled past Mercy like a schoolboy on his way to the dunce's corner.

"Do you have time? I'm not heading out there until two thirty, and I thought you were leaving early to get groceries for dinner tonight."

Zeddie snapped his head up from the bills piled on the desk. "I'll get groceries and make dinner."

Mercy and Roy gaped at him in stunned silence. Pop recovered first. "There. Problem solved. I'll meet you at the dock at two thirty."

Roy showed up right on time, holding a bundle wrapped in a stained tea towel. At least he had found an urn substitute that was valuable enough to be fragile. They had driven over halfway to the shipyard before Mercy broke the silence.

"Dare I ask what you found to use as an urn?"

Her father squirmed in his seat.

"Pop?" Mercy filled the single syllable with commination.

"Desperate times call for desperate measures," he answered, staring straight ahead through the bug-splattered windshield.

"Oh my gods, what are we using?"

He slid the tea towel from the item in his lap, and Mercy took her eyes off the road long enough to see a pink glass cookie jar—her *mother's* pink glass cookie jar—jouncing in his lap. "It's all I could find."

Mercy teared up. True, the jar had been empty and collecting dust on Pop's kitchen counter for years, but she could recall in vivid detail baking cookies with her mother.

"I'm sorry, muffin." He hung his head, and Mercy didn't have it in her to stay mad at him. She would have reached out to touch him, but the old autoduck required both hands on the wheel.

"It's all right, Pop. It's not like we ever bake cookies."

"Who knows? Zeddie's cinnamon rolls were fantastic this morning." Pop rewrapped the cookie jar and cleared his throat. "How's he doing?"

"Fine." Mercy kept her eyes on the road. She was a terrible liar and didn't think she could get away with it if she so much as glanced at her father.

"Think he'll be ready to take over soon?"

"Working on it." Guilt sat in her stomach like the pound of butter Zeddie had used to make his cinnamon rolls that morning.

"It isn't right. I should be the one overseeing his transition. It's unfair to you, Mercy."

"I'm fine, Pop. Don't worry about me."

"I'm your father. Of course I worry about you."

This time, she did glance at him, and the sad smile he gave her made her tear up all over again. But as she parked the autoduck by the pyre site, her father frowned through the windshield.

"Mother of Sorrows," he said with heat in his voice.

Curtis Cunningham, the founder of the most lucrative chain of boatworks and funeral services on the Tanrian border, was standing with several of his employees as if he, himself, had come to oversee the raking out of the pyres that afternoon. Dressed in a fine three-piece suit, he seemed godlike compared to the rest of them in their dungarees and plaid shirts, Mercy included, although Mercy's shirt was tied at her waist and coordinated with the red kerchief that wrapped up her hair.

"Well, look what the cat dragged in," Cunningham said with what appeared to be an authentic smile as Pop got out of the duck. "Didn't expect to see you here, Roy."

Pop shook Cunningham's hand. "Curtis. How are you?"

"Business is booming, so I can't complain."

Mercy didn't think she could stand any more insincerity on either side, so she asked, "What brings you to the pyres, Mr. Cunningham?"

"You do."

"Me?"

Cunningham offered her his arm. "Care to take a jaunt?"

Mercy's eyebrows came together in consternation. "A lovely stroll by the pyres?"

"Perhaps along one of the shipyard paths." He gave her a charming wink and continued to hold out his arm.

Whatever this was, it couldn't be good, but Mercy thought it best to get it out of the way. "Do *not* rake out that pyre by yourself," she warned Pop before taking the arm of her family's rival.

Once they were out of earshot, Cunningham nodded toward her father and feigned concern. "How's he holding up these days?"

"He's fine."

"And your brother and sister?"

"Also fine."

"And how are you?"

Her already tight smile tightened. "Very well. Thank you."

He gave her an appraising look as they reached the nearest shipyard trail that meandered through the grave markers. "I know you think I'm a big, bad, heartless businessman, Mercy, but I hope you know that I sincerely wish you and all your family the best."

Mercy brought them to a halt. "What do you want, Mr. Cunningham?"

"I'm sure you know by now that I want to buy Birdsall & Son."

When Mercy remained silent, Cunningham continued, his tone appallingly paternal. "I know your father, and I know you, and I believe I can guess how things have played out at Birdsall & Son since Roy's... misfortune. You're young. You have your whole life ahead of you. Why should you let a dying business weigh down your best years?"

Mercy regarded Cunningham's smug, self-satisfied face, with his calculating green eyes and perfect aquiline nose and teeth that were too straight and white to be real, and a bluff of which she did not know she was capable came flying out of her mouth.

"I don't think you'd offer to buy us out if Birdsall & Son were dying. I think you're offering to buy us out because you're scared of us."

Curtis Cunningham was shorter than Mercy, but he somehow managed to talk down to her as he spoke. "My dear, Cunningham's has locations in six border towns. We can process up to a hundred bodies a day. Our newest heartnut-based embalming patch to cover unsightly wounds and make the departed appear more natural and at peace is pending patent, and our embalming practices are quickly outpacing the salted method. Our wholesale buying power allows us to offer valuable products to our consumers at affordable prices, and we can ship a body anywhere within the Federated Islands of Cadmus within two days." He nodded toward the direction of the pyres. "Look over there. That's eight Cunningham pyres to your one, and none of our remains will be ending their days in a cookie jar."

Mercy refused to be rattled. "You gouge your customers by upselling mass-produced boats at a criminal markup, and you convince people that they need to be preserved in Tanrian heartnut sap because it's 'sanitary.' And then you gouge them for that, too. Well, Birdsall & Son is catching up to you in the local market, plus we've made substantial inroads in prepaid packages this year. We take in roughly twenty-five percent of the keyless bodies coming out of the West Station, and we do it out of kindness and decency, while you use your Indigent Processing Grant status as self-promotion. So please don't pretend you have good intentions toward us, when you want to squash us like a bug. We're not selling out to you."

Cunningham pulled a handkerchief from his pocket and dabbed his shining forehead. "And how are you going to keep your doors open when Roy retires? My newest recruit was a classmate of your brother's and has informed me that Zeddie flunked out of Funerary Rites and Services his first year. That leaves no one but you holding the reins, Mercy, and competent as you are, you're one woman. How long do you think you can hold out against the full force of Cunningham's if I decide to force you out of business?"

Gods, he knows about Zeddie, she thought in a panic. Mercy felt as though he had poured ice water over her head, but she kept the sharp smile fixed on her face. "I guess there's only one way to find out," she challenged him, adding "Curtis" before releasing his arm and walking back to the pyres without him.

"I assume he asked you to convince me to sell?" Pop asked, clutching the makeshift urn as the autoduck bounced over the gravel road. He had raked out the ashes in the afternoon sun by himself, against Mercy's strict instructions, while she and Cunningham had had their "jaunt," and now he was troublingly pale. Tempted as she was to spill the beans about Zeddie, she decided not to upset him further with an accurate report of her conversation with Cunningham, but the truth behind the well-timed buyout offer gnawed at her insides.

Before Mercy could answer her father, the autoduck sputtered and slowed, and Mercy was barely able to pull it off the road before it died completely. That was when she realized that the gas gauge read *Empty*. She leaned against the headrest and asked her father, not for the first time and probably not for the last, "Forgot to fill the tank?"

He bowed his head, a sight that was all too familiar these days. She missed him as he was, confident and quick to laugh, the way his capable hands built boats and his big-barreled voice sang the incantations for the dead. Ordering urns and paying the bills and filling the gas tank were the day-to-day details that would never be in his wheelhouse.

Mercy patted his shoulder. "You stay here, out of the sun, and keep the windows down. I'll grab the jug and walk to town for gas."

"I'll come with you."

"No. Nope. I'll be back in forty minutes, tops." She kissed his cheek and hopped out of the cab before he could object. It was a mile or so to Eternity, but the blazing heat and treeless, shadeless road made it feel much longer. By the time she arrived at the gas station to fill the jug, her perspiration-soaked shirt clung to her back, and her boob sweat made the underwires of her bra chafe her skin. She was heading for the road out of town again, carrying a jug heavy with gasoline, when the city hall bell began to ring. Mercy froze out of instinct, a frisson of fear shooting through her spine, until she remembered that it was four o'clock on the first Bonesday of the month.

A drudge drill, not a drudge warning.

"Oh, for gods' sakes," she muttered, freezing in place while sweating buckets under her armpits. She thought of Pop in all this heat, and here she was, stuck in a drudge drill when never, in the twenty-five-year history of Eternity, had a drudge gotten loose in town. Argentine and Herington had each had a few incidents lately, sure, but not Eternity. What could it possibly hurt if she sneaked out of town this one time?

She was a block west of Main Street, but there wasn't anyone out and about this close to the south edge of town. Glancing around, she began to tiptoe toward the road leading to the burial pits... in time for a sheriff's deputy to turn the corner around a clapboard house and witness her clear violation of the law. And it wasn't just any sheriff's deputy. It was Nathan McDevitt. Her ex-boyfriend. Who had broken her heart and stomped on the pieces.

"Hello, Mercy," he sang, swaggering his way over to her.

"Hi." She attempted to smile.

"Were you aware that there is currently a drudge drill underway?"

"Yes, but—"

"And were you aware that during a drudge drill, one is required to remain perfectly still and silent so that one is prepared to respond appropriately in the event that a drudge gets loose in the great city of Eternity?"

Mercy thought that calling Eternity a "city" was stretching it and then some, but she had no desire to quibble. She wanted to get back to Pop as soon as she could. "Please, Nathan—"

"Because if a drudge were to get loose, the quickest way for the sheriff's deputies to find it and get rid of it is by tracking down the only thing that's moving, and a drudge whose eyes have been picked clean by vultures can't see the living and is less likely to sense their presence if they're standing perfectly still."

"I know. We ran out of gas on our way home from the pyres, and I had to leave Pop in the autoduck." She hoisted up the jug, which sloshed with gasoline, but she knew there was no way she would squeeze a drop of sympathy out of a man who'd made it clear to her that he should have come first in her affections, not her father.

"So," he said, drawing his ticket pad from his pocket along with a stubby pencil. "Disobedience of City Code 47-R-9A, wherein all citizens are required to follow drudge-drill protocols."

The sound of the pencil lead scribbling over the paper reached into Mercy's ears and poked a headache into her tired brain.

"Come on, Nathan. Give me a break? Please?"

His demeanor softened, and his face—which tended toward weaselly—became more handsome as a result. The memory of what they'd had together and all the hopes Mercy had once cherished for her future tugged at her heart.

"Have dinner with me tonight, and I'll pretend none of this happened."

Nathan's offer was the last thing Mercy had expected. For months, she had hoped he would come groveling to her and beg her forgiveness. Now here he was, offering an olive branch, and she was tempted. Sorely tempted. But then she thought of Pop in that hot autoduck a mile away, and she remembered what little regard Nathan had had for him in the aftermath of his heart attack.

"Why don't you stuff that ticket in your mouth and eat it instead?" she proposed, sounding braver than she felt.

"Pretty sure this ticket is going to wind up on *your* plate, sugar." Nathan scribbled as he continued to speak his bitterness. "Sheriff Connolly is retiring soon, and guess who's a shoo-in for that promotion? I sure hope you don't have any code violations over there at Birdsall & Son that I'll have to investigate. It would be a crying shame to shut you down." He tore the ticket free of the pad with a flourish and offered it to Mercy as if it were a rose. "For the lovely lady."

Mercy crushed the paper in her hand and made her slow march to Pop and the autoduck. By the time she'd driven her father home, she was a bedraggled mess. Zeddie was putting away groceries in the kitchen, but he did a double take when he saw the miserable pair trudge through the screen door.

"What happened to you?"

"Don't ask. Can you fill Pop with ice water, please?"

She didn't wait for his answer. She shuffled out the door and dragged herself to Birdsall & Son on aching feet to finish up for the day. The second she stepped into the boatworks, she burst into tears. She tore off pieces of the cinnamon roll she had abandoned that morning, and stuffed them into her mouth. It had gone stale, but it was very tasty. The clock read 4:56, which meant in four minutes, she could flip the sign to "Closed" and call it a (wretched, horrible, awful) day.

But it was not to be. She heard the front door open, and the bell on the counter rang. Mercy didn't need a mirror to know how she looked—sweaty, tearstained, and disheveled—but there was no one else around to answer the summons. She wiped her fingers on her dungarees and made a feeble attempt to smooth her kerchief with sticky hands before heading to the counter, where she found a young marshal she had never seen before waiting in the lobby.

And standing next to him was Hart Ralston.

Kill me, she begged the unfeeling gods. *Kill me now.*

Chapter Nine

Hart was taken aback by Mercy's appearance as she stepped behind the counter. Her clothes were in disarray, her hair mussed, her face gleaming with perspiration, as if he'd interrupted her in the middle of a passionate embrace with some Lothario.

That thought brought him up short. Had he? Was there a half-dressed man waiting for her in the boatworks? The mere idea of such unprofessionalism filled Hart with indignation, even though he knew he was responding to suspicion rather than fact, which illogically made him even more indignant.

"Oh gods," Mercy groaned. "I'm having a day here, Hart-ache, so I'd appreciate it if you would make the barest effort at civility, just this once. Okay?"

He hadn't even spoken yet, and she was already laying into him, when *she* was the one being uncivil. Unbelievable. Well, he wasn't about to make an effort now, especially if she planned to pawn him off so she could return to some smarmy asshole in the boatworks.

"Thanks for rolling out the red carpet, Merciless. It's an honor to be here."

"Is this what you call civility?"

"Best I can manage under the current circumstances."

Hart scanned her up and down, noting the sugar crystals stuck to her hair and the smear of icing on her pant leg. He hadn't caught her in flagrante delicto with some lover in the boatworks; she had been making love to baked goods. But given her nasty greeting, the evidence did nothing to cool his temper. He made a show of scanning the lobby as Duckers watched in confusion. "Out of curiosity, does anyone but you actually work here?"

"Are you capable of piecing together two nice words in a row for anyone, Hart-ache, or is that too much to ask?"

"That's rich," he fired back.

She waved him away and leaned over the counter in Duckers's direction. Her shirt was unbuttoned to her sternum, and Hart had to will his eyes away from the resulting cleavage. *That is* enemy *cleavage*, he reminded himself.

"Hello. Welcome to Birdsall & Son. I'm Mercy."

"Thank you, ma'am. I'm Penrose Duckers, but you can call me Pen."

Mercy smiled at him, showing Duckers the dimples Hart himself had not seen since their fateful first meeting four years ago. He tapped the countertop with impatience and was trying to come up with a cutting remark when Mercy's brother burst through the front door with a large book open in his hands.

"Merc, do you have any capers? They didn't have any at the store," he bellowed before he realized she was standing at the counter. When he saw Duckers, his expression went from distraction to very focused and very obvious attraction. "Well, hello."

"Hi," an oblivious Duckers said with a wave of his hat.

"I'm Zeddie. And you are?"

"Pen."

Zeddie Birdsall leaned on the counter next to him, a mirror image of his sister. "Charmed," he said with a brash grin.

This time, Pen did notice, and he gave a bashful, nervous laugh. Good fucking gods, all Hart wanted to do was drop off a body and be on his way. He cleared his throat and announced, "Marshal Duckers is my new apprentice."

Mercy's smile melted into a sympathetic frown. "Oh, you poor thing. Chocolate?" She picked up a candy dish from the counter and offered it to Duckers.

"Don't mind if I do. Thank you."

She glared at Hart and set the dish out of his reach without offering him any. The juxtaposition of her lovely manners toward Duckers—a complete stranger to her—and her surly and unmerited dislike of himself stuck in Hart's craw.

"We've got a body for you, prepaid and tagged. That is, if we're not putting you out. I can see you're incredibly busy."

He gestured around the lobby, which was empty save for himself, the two young men making eyes at each other, and the absolute shrew behind the counter. The latter tilted her chin up. "We've been swamped today, I will have you know."

"You've got a little..." Hart gestured to his own chin and watched Mercy's cheeks darken with embarrassment as she swiped away the icing on her skin with a floral hankie. If he were a cat, he'd purr with satisfaction.

"Zeddie will meet you at the dock," said Mercy as she stuffed the hankie back into her pocket.

Zeddie, who was busy flirting with Duckers, said "You bet" before Mercy's words hit their mark. He whipped his head around so fast it was a wonder that it didn't fly free of his body and roll across the lobby.

"Won't you, Zeddie?" Mercy made it clear that this was not a question, and there was a tiny piece of Hart that thought, *Good for her*. (The rest of Hart wanted to throttle that tiny, traitorous piece.)

Zeddie glanced at Duckers, who cluelessly grinned at him, and he visibly and audibly gulped before setting his book down on the counter. "Sure thing," he said and turned to make his way toward the dock, his long, lanky form moving slowly and stiffly. Duckers ogled Zeddie's backside, and if that was the way the wind was blowing, Hart thought his apprentice could do a lot better than a Birdsall, or any other undertaker, for that matter.

"Come on," he told his apprentice with a nudge, but as Hart reached the door with Duckers at his heels, he lingered, glancing at the green velvet chairs over which Leonard frequently draped himself, and he felt a twinge of sadness to find them empty.

Mercy smirked at him from across the counter, her arms folded over her chest. "Sorry to disappoint you, Hart-ache. My dog is upstairs in my apartment. But I'll be sure to send him your love."

Without taking his eyes from Mercy, Hart handed his keys to his apprentice. "Get in the duck."

"Can I drive, sir?"

"No."

Hart stepped up to the counter to loom over his adversary, but she hardened her glare, refusing to be intimidated.

"Fine," said Hart. "You caught me. I like your dog. Your dog is nice. You, on the other hand, and all your undertaking ilk, are a bunch of grubby opportunists on the Tanrian border, trying to make a buck off other people's tragedies. But I'm trying to be a professional here, so I'm going to do my job and drop off this poor woman's dead body at your dock. I'm going to hand your brother the paperwork I filled out so that *you* can get paid. And tomorrow, I'll return to Tanria, where I keep people safe from drudges while also trying to educate and protect that nice kid who is now in my care."

Hart jerked his thumb toward the door, but to his surprise, Duckers's voice came from right behind him. "Oh, I'm still here, sir. Sorry."

Again, Hart's gaze did not waver from Mercy's fierce brown eyes. "Get in the duck, Duckers."

"So I can drive?"

"No." He leaned in. "This is your last chance to abuse me before I head out, Merciless. Going once. Going twice."

To Hart's shock, Mercy's eyes welled up, and a single tear dripped down her soft, round cheek. Without a word, she marched out of the lobby, her spine ramrod straight, her arms stiff at her sides like a soldier's. The abrupt change in her demeanor knocked the air out of Hart's lungs, as if she had punched him in the stomach.

"Dang, sir," Duckers murmured, not having moved an inch.

Hart glimpsed the book Zeddie had set down on the counter. *The God of the Hearth's Guide to Cooking.* It was open to a recipe for chicken piccata. The thought of that carefree, curly-headed boy cooking dinner threw Hart for loop. He'd always thought of the Birdsalls as seedy undertakers, but it occurred to him now that they were also a family—a daughter who filled in for her dad when he could no longer do his work and a son who got dinner on the table. Between this and Mercy Birdsall's crying, Hart's understanding of the universe tilted, and he didn't like it one bit.

"Get. In the fucking. Autoduck," he ordered Duckers as he strode past him to the door.

"Yes, sir," his irritatingly unfazed apprentice answered with a salute.

"Can I ask you something, sir?" Duckers asked as they drove the short distance up Main Street to the Sunny Hill Hotel.

"No."

"Why were you so mean to Mercy?"

"Me? *I'm* the mean one?"

"Kind of?"

Hart shook his head, but the specter of Mercy's teary eyes haunted him. He pushed it away, refusing to feel guilty for making her cry, when she was the one who had started it.

They drove past Cunningham's, the most respectable building in town, larger and classier than the temple. "Why couldn't that lady have purchased a package from Cunningham's instead of Birdsall & Son?" Hart grumbled.

Probably because she couldn't afford it, he answered himself in the private recesses of his mind. He might loathe Mercy, but he knew by now that Birdsall & Son offered some of the most affordable packages on the border. That didn't make them less opportunistic than any other undertakers, though.

"Know what I think?" Duckers asked as Hart parked the autoduck in front of the hotel and got out of the cab.

"Do I care?"

Duckers caught up to him as he wrenched open the door of the cargo hold. "You've got a thing for Mercy, and you've got it bad."

For a moment, Hart was rendered speechless, before he told his apprentice in no uncertain terms, "I would rather have dinner with a rotting corpse than with Mercy Birdsall. A more infuriating woman I have never met."

"Are her boobs infuriating? Because you definitely got an eyeful of those."

Caught. Fuck.

"I notice all boobs, regardless of their owners."

"All I'm saying is that from what I can tell, it wouldn't kill you to go out with a nice lady like Mercy. You know, live a little, sir."

Telling a demigod to "live a little" was a particular choice of words, one that made Hart stop and consider his apprentice. Duckers had never asked him about his parentage, and as Hart studied his open, earnest face, he wondered if Duckers was so naive that he didn't know there were demigods who didn't live a little, but who lived a lot—lived on and on and on.

"I'm fine," he said as he yanked his bag out of the hold and stepped aside so that Duckers could get his own things.

"Are you, though? Because I think you hang out with drudges too much. You need some quality time among the living."

"I'm spending quality time with you. Are you trying to tell me you're dead now?"

"See, that's just it. You're all gruff, but you're actually a decent human being once a person gets to know you."

"You don't know the first thing about me." Hart walked to the hotel and opened the front door with Duckers dogging his heels like a terrier.

"I know you took me on when you didn't want to because you felt sorry for me. I know you're teaching me what I need to know to do my job. I know you were nice to me after I took out that drudge."

Hart ignored him and stepped up to the key counter. "Two rooms, please," he told the concierge.

"I get my own room? Sweet!"

The concierge raised an eyebrow.

"My new apprentice," Hart explained curtly.

"Really?" The eyebrow shot higher.

"Really. So two rooms." By now, Hart was practically growling.

"Know what else I think?" Duckers asked at his elbow.

"No, and I don't want to."

"I think you're afraid to be nice to Mercy, because you wouldn't be able to handle it if she didn't like you back."

The concierge, overhearing this, turned around with a key in each hand and a mirthful smile spreading across her face. "Two rooms," she declared, but her tone made it sound as if she were singing, *You like Mercy Birdsall! You like Mercy Birdsall!*

Hart took the keys, then ushered his apprentice away from the front counter.

"Duckers, if I want your advice, I'll ask for it."

"You should definitely ask for it, but I don't have time for that right now." Ducker snatched one of the keys from Hart's hand. "Unlike you, I've got a date tonight."

Hart gaped at him in stunned silence for the second time in as many minutes before he said, "You're a pain in the ass."

"But you love me anyway." Duckers shot him a bright, toothy grin before opening the door with his butt and exiting with a flourish.

Salt Sea and all gods of death, Hart did kind of love that brat.

He went to his room and dumped his pack onto the bed. He had been looking forward to this respite from his apprentice's constant and very vocal company, but now, standing over yet another bed that did not belong to him, he felt the weight of his loneliness sink in again. Duckers had arrived in town a half hour ago, and he already had a date. Hart hadn't so much as held a woman's hand in months.

He'd always told himself that marshaling didn't lend itself to love or romance. It was a dangerous line of work and one that kept him in the field for long stretches at a time, which, until recently, had been fine as far as Hart was concerned. There had been many lust-filled one-offs during his early days with the marshals. Then, when he was twenty-one, he had fallen hard for a married woman in one of the northern border towns. When she ended it to return to her husband, he put a hard stop to any notions of love in his future.

After that, Hart's romantic life—if it could be called romantic—consisted of loveless but companionable relationships that stretched on for months at a time. For a while in his early twenties, he slept with a middle-aged widow, who finally taught him his way around a woman's body. Then there was the waitress from Galatia. Eventually, he wound up dating a fellow marshal in a truly mechanical and passionless liaison that ended, to the relief of both, when she returned home to Paxico to take care of her ailing mother.

Clearly, love was an impractical and unlikely thing for a man like Hart, so how had Duckers come to the conclusion that Hart liked anyone, much less Mercy Birdsall? He hated her—*loathed* her—and she gladly reciprocated. But the memory of that single tear sliding down her face prodded his conscience, and he found that he wasn't too proud of himself for what he'd said to her in anger that afternoon.

He sat down at the tiny desk in his hotel room—honestly, was this thing built for children?—thinking he would begin a new letter to his friend, even though he still needed to mail the last one. What would she advise him to do, he wondered?

As soon as he thought the question, he sat up straight, knowing exactly what she'd tell him to do if she knew all the ins and outs of his life. It was the same advice Duckers had offered.

You need some quality time among the living.

There were two living, breathing people Hart sorely missed, and for some reason, the memory of Zeddie setting his cookbook down on the counter at Birdsall & Son made Hart miss the mundanity of a family dinner, so much so that he grabbed his hat and locked up his room. Then he slipped his letter into the nearest nimkilim box and headed for his autoduck.

Chapter Ten

Mercy Birdsall consumed Hart's thoughts for the entire half-hour drive. As he rolled past the cacti and acacias lining the country roads, his wheels kicking up a mini dust storm in his wake, he tried to figure out why he and Mercy had hated each other from the beginning. Their mutual loathing was a fact he had always accepted without examination, but now that he'd made her cry, it was all he could think about.

The first time Hart met Mercy was two months after Alma ditched him for a desk job, two weeks after his dog Gracie died, and two days after the new ID law went into effect in Tanria. Prior to the law, he could take a cadaver to any funeral services provider he chose, which for him meant Cunningham's. The staff were barely tolerable, with their fake sympathy and bogus, hushed respect for the dead, but at least they had intake down to a precise and efficient science. The new law stipulated that everyone entering Tanria had to have a prepaid funeral package from a licensed undertaker and a corresponding ID tag, which meant Hart and every other Tanrian Marshal had to schlep a body to whatever Podunk undertaker in whatever Podunk border town the tag indicated.

That day four years ago, the tag read *009758, Birdsall & Son, Undertakers, Eternity, Bushong.* He had never patronized Birdsall & Son before, primarily because the sign out front had always turned him off. That day, he stood before it, shaking his head at the faded, folksy, hand-painted lettering.

BIRDSALL & SON, UNDERTAKERS
Meeting all your end-of-life needs
We can ship a body
Wherever! Whenever! However you please!

This was exactly the kind of place his mentor had resented, and in his mind, he could hear Bill's voice, clear as a bell.

You see this shit? That tells you everything you need to know about this place. These mom-and-pop shops are the worst, falling all over themselves with cookies and smiles and "customer service," as if that could hide what they really are: grubby opportunists profiting off of someone else's misfortune. They may as well squirt perfume all over a decaying body and pretend it smells like flowers.

It was one of many ways Bill had shaped Hart's understanding of the world, making sure his apprentice saw Tanria for the death trap that it was beneath its odd but bucolic surface, and the way these undertakers had poured into the border towns to take advantage of a terrible situation.

Hart didn't often let himself think about Bill, so he was already a bit unmoored when he stepped into the lobby of Birdsall & Son and hung his hat on the coatrack that afternoon. The first thing he saw was Leonard lounging on one of the green velvet chairs. He reached out and stroked the top of the dog's warm head, the way he had patted the soft space between Gracie's ridiculous ears before her body had given out in a great heave two weeks earlier. Without a warning, a vise in his chest clamped down hard, and he lost control of his self-possession, his eyes welling up fast and leaking fat tears down his thin cheeks.

He heard a door open in the hallway beyond the lobby, and a

very tall, very buxom young woman with dark hair coiled into a neat bun on her head and a pair of horn-rimmed glasses perched on her nose walked into the room, frowning down at a sheaf of papers in her hand. Her sunny yellow dress seemed like the only color in the world. Hart frantically scrubbed his face with his hands before she looked up.

"I'm sorry. I didn't realize someone had come in. Did you ring the bell?"

He shook his head. He wondered if she could tell he'd been crying, and it made him feel defenseless. She was so pretty. Salt fucking Sea, did these places hire attractive women to match the chipper decor now? Was she about to offer him a plate of muffins?

Her smile broadened, dimpling her cheeks, and those dimples in combination with the fact that she may or may not have caught him bawling all over her dog robbed him of speech. With each passing second that he stood there gawking at this ridiculously lovely woman in the lobby, his embarrassment, and the irritation that went with it, deepened.

"Sir?"

"I'm a marshal," he finally choked out.

"I see that. I'm Mercy Birdsall, office manager of Birdsall & Son." She held out a hand for him to shake across the counter. He stepped forward to take it.

"Hart Ralston."

Sweat beaded on his forehead, and his hand pumped a distressing amount of dampness between their joined palms. He tugged his hand back and resisted the urge to wipe it on his pants.

"I usually go to Cunningham's."

Her smile faltered. "Oh. Well, I hope you'll find our services superior. We take good care of our marshals here. Can I get you something to drink? Coffee? Tea?"

Falling all over themselves with cookies and smiles and "customer service," he thought. Aloud, he said, "No. I've got a prepaid body for you."

Mercy's smile remained, but the dimples disappeared. "Of course. The dock is around back."

"Right."

He drove the duck down the alley and backed it up to the dock, berating himself for crying over a dog and acting like an adolescent in the presence of an attractive woman. But he was discombobulated all over again when Mercy was the one who pulled up the dock gate rather than the undertaker or the son that the sign out front purported he had. Now that she was out from behind the counter, Hart could see the way the yellow dress hugged her ample chest and cinched in at the waist and flared out around her generous hips. He was beginning to resent this woman for making him feel perverted.

"I thought you said you were the office manager."

"I am. My father is the undertaker, but he's at the pyres this morning."

"The sign out front says there's a son."

"The son is sixteen years old and probably in biology class right about now, so you get me."

She may have been the office manager, but she didn't flinch at the stench of death that wafted from the hold the second Hart opened it. She continued to soldier on with that smile, which in and of itself was infuriating. Why should she or anyone else for that matter be so sunny, especially at an undertaker's? She had no right to be full of life when she was surrounded by death.

May as well squirt perfume all over a decaying body and pretend it smells like flowers, Bill said in his mind.

"What happened to this poor man?" Mercy asked as she handled the odd, lumpy remains. The drudge had been so vicious that Hart had had to dismember it before lancing its appendix, but Mercy's comment sounded like an accusation, and from a woman who had probably never left the safety and comfort of her father's business, which profited off the dead.

"I did what I had to do."

"Mm-hmm," she answered doubtfully, and Hart cursed the federal government for the new ID tag law that forced him to interact with this judgmental office manager.

The body stowed, he followed her and her yellow dress into the lobby, where the dog still lazed across the green velvet chair.

"Leonard, off!" Mercy commanded, but the dog gave her a confused expression that said, *I'm sorry. I have no earthly idea what you mean.* The boxer mix looked nothing like Hart's own dog, but Leonard's demeanor was all Gracie, and a sharp pang of grief pierced his lungs. He scribbled his way through the paperwork in an attempt to get out of Birdsall & Son all the sooner.

"Is something wrong?" Mercy asked him in a tone so snotty he nearly offered her his handkerchief.

"No," he barked, signing the last document and slapping the pen down on the countertop.

A strained grimace replaced her bright smile, and when she spoke it was through gritted teeth. "Well, feel free to never come back again."

It was as if Hart were an overheated autoduck engine, and Mercy had opened the hood. A hot plume of words heaved out of his mouth. "Lady, I can't tell you how much I don't want to come back here, but the government has other plans. So if you don't want to see me again, feel free to stop fleecing the suckers who come to Tanria to seek their fortunes, only to get turned into reanimated corpses."

She propped her fists on those (admittedly glorious) hips. "Feel free to maybe *not* chop up those corpses into bits and pieces before my father has to send them home to their grieving families."

"Your father is free to join the Tanrian Marshals any time he likes if he thinks he can do a better job, and so are you."

She opened her mouth but seemed to think better of whatever it was she had planned to say. "You know what. I'm not going to waste one more second of my life on you. Don't let the door hit you on the way out, Marshal."

He was a waste of her life. Not her time. Her *life*. Seconds ago, he had merely disliked her. Now he loathed her from the depths of his soul. He glowered at her before snatching his hat off the coatrack and heading for the exit. Behind him, he heard her mutter, "Arrogant demigod."

Hart spun on his heel, trying and failing to come up with an answering sting as she stomped down the hallway to the office. And he was furious with himself for watching her ass until it disappeared out of sight behind the slammed door.

Four years later, as he drove toward an uncertain reception at Alma and Diane's house, Hart tried to imagine how that first meeting could have panned out differently.

He came up empty.

He stood on the front porch, bending and unbending the brim of his hat in his hands. He could hear a record playing inside, something jazzy and soulful, a melody that hit him with a wave of nostalgia for days gone by when he practically lived in this house. It had been so long since his last visit that it seemed almost offensive to show up unannounced like this. But he was here now and didn't see the point in going back to his hotel room, so he combed his shaggy hair with his fingers and rapped on the door.

The door swung inward, and there was Diane, her petite figure drowning in a loose-fitting sundress, her ash-blond hair as short as ever, her cheeks and nose more freckled than Hart remembered. A smile overtook her face, and the crow's feet at the corners of her eyes lashed him with guilt for staying away so long. She let out a happy squeak and hugged him around the middle, her head barely reaching his breastbone. Hart hugged her in return and forced out an awkward laugh. "It's good to see you, too, Diane."

She held him at arm's length to examine him, her blue eyes shining. "You need a haircut."

He laughed again, less awkwardly.

"Who is it?" Alma's voice called from inside, inspiring in Hart the urge to hightail it to his duck and drive off before she got to the door.

"It's Hart!"

"Really?" Alma appeared in the doorframe and squinted up at him, clearly wondering why he had decided to show up. It occurred to Diane to wonder the same thing, her inner mother hen bursting to life.

"Is something wrong?"

"Does something have to be wrong for me to pay a visit?"

"Is that a trick question?" asked Alma, and Hart felt like he should either raise his hackles or be prepared to lick his wounds.

"You invited me."

"So I did. Come in."

Diane hugged him again and took his hat as he stepped into the parlor with its overstuffed chairs and colorful afghans and pillows and stacks of books. A cat he didn't recognize grazed his shin as he followed Alma past the dining room and into the kitchen, where she pulled a bottle of beer and a can of soda from the icebox.

"Thanks," he said when she handed him the soda, surprised

that she and Diane still kept his favorite brand in the house, when he knew neither of them cared for it.

They made their way through the screen door to the deck that overlooked Alma and Diane's acreage with the neat vegetable garden and the chicken coop and the cows grazing on the taprooted grasses that managed to grow in the sandy soil. Hart dusted off the chair that was tacitly his and sat down. His long legs popped up like a pair of mountains in front of him, and he wished Diane hadn't taken his hat, so that he could set it on one knee and fiddle with it. He felt like a child bereft of his security blanket.

Alma reached over and clanked her bottleneck to the rim of his soda can. "I'm glad you came."

"So am I," he said, although he wasn't certain as to the veracity of that statement. An unexpected wistfulness overtook him as he surveyed the familiar surroundings. This place was more home to him than anywhere else he had lived or slept since his mother died, but coming here had lost its homey luster over the past few years. He missed the comfort this place had once provided. He missed the comfort *Alma* had once provided.

"How's your dad?" he asked her, a genuine question that sounded like empty small talk.

"Good. I wish he'd let someone else take over the vineyard, though. He's too old to care for it like he should, but you know how he is."

Hart nodded, feeling guilty about the fact that he couldn't remember the last time he'd inquired after her aging father.

"Seen your mom lately?" he asked.

"A few months ago. She says hello."

Hart nodded again. Unlike him, Alma knew who her immortal parent was—Bendena, whose tiny creek snaked to the north of her father's grapes in central Vinland. She even called her Mom. It blew Hart's mind.

"How's Duckers doing?"

Hart rubbed his chin and took a gulp of soda, letting the too-sweet bubbles fizz and pop almost painfully between his teeth. "He irritates the shit out of me."

"Aw, you like him."

"Yes, I do," Hart agreed in defeat.

"So that means I was . . . ?"

"Right. You were right."

"Mm-hmm."

Alma pursed her lips in smug superiority, which had the ironic effect of putting Hart more at ease rather than less, because it was an expression that belonged to Alma-his-old-partner, not Alma-his-boss. He sipped his soda and set the can on the wrought-iron table beside him. "Thank you. For making me take him on."

"You're welcome. I know you'll look out for him, and he's going to need it, with the drudge situation as bad as it is these days."

"It does seem worse than usual lately."

"It is worse. I've seen the numbers. There's a huge uptick in the keyless."

Diane backed out the kitchen door with a tray of carrots and celery sticks and crackers and cheese, and it occurred to Hart that he was ravenously hungry, something he generally failed to notice until it was hard upon him.

"You'll stay for dinner, won't you?" she asked.

Hart had come here with a family dinner on his mind, but he worried that accepting the invitation would mean committing himself to a lengthier stay than he wanted. Alma skewered him with her fierce blue-green eyes, and he knew she saw right through him.

"I don't want to put you out," he told Diane, but of course, Diane was un-put-out-able.

"There's plenty." She planted a kiss on top of his head, making him go watery on the inside.

Alma cooked chicken on the grill while Diane put together a bowl of mixed greens and pulled some leftover potato salad from the icebox. They ate outside on the east-facing deck, with Diane catching Hart up on all the improvements they had made to the property recently. Hart answered the many questions she threw his way, but mostly he watched and listened, letting Alma and Diane's easy way together wash over him.

After dinner, he and Alma stayed out on the deck, a silence thickening between them, while Diane cleaned up in the kitchen, humming along to the songs spinning off the gramophone. The old quarrel lingered in the air, as dense and swirling as the Mist that shrouded Tanria.

You were a kid when we partnered up, and I always thought you'd grow out of it, come to terms with it, whatever. But you're in your thirties now, and if anything, it's worse.

Can we not talk about this?

We've been friends for over ten years. When are we going to talk about it?

Never.

This is what I'm talking about. Bill's death is as fresh for you as if it happened yesterday. That's not normal. You need to deal with that baggage.

Bill was not "baggage."

You act like he was the father you never had—

He was.

—and I know he did you a lot of good, but you never stop to consider the fact that he was also a sanctimonious pain in the ass.

Are you serious? All this time, all the years you've known me, this is what you thought of him?

Yes. This is what I think of a hypocrite who liked to tell people, especially you, how to think and act and live, when he was the one who abandoned his wife and child in Honek.

It was as if she had taken a sledgehammer to everything he thought he knew about Bill Clark, and in the process, she had smashed their friendship, too. Years of trust pulverized in an instant. He supposed he could apologize for his part in it now, but once again, he couldn't muster the nerve to broach the subject with her.

In the uncomfortable silence, he let his mind drift to his letter-writing friend, to the unfair hopes he had already begun to pin on her for no good reason. But she seemed to get him, and he seemed to get her, and she made him want to...

Live a little.

Which was why he'd come here, wasn't it?

"Thanks for dinner," he told Alma, pulling them both out of their brooding reticence.

"You bet. It's good for you to be social every now and again. You're working too much overtime these days."

"Don't have anything better to do, do I?"

She shook her head. "You are a lonely bastard."

The combination of Alma's endearing bluntness and Hart's soda-spawned sugar high made him laugh.

"It's a choice, you know. It doesn't have to be that way."

"I know," he said, but it didn't feel like a choice. It felt like the hand he'd been dealt.

"Maybe you should get another dog."

"Don't want another dog."

"Maybe you should make some friends who aren't me. Date somebody. Take up Parcheesi."

Hart could feel her eyes on him, but he kept his gaze turned toward the darkening horizon.

"How old are you now? Thirty-five? Almost thirty-six, right?"

"Yep."

"So when are you going to stop being nineteen?"

This time, he did meet her unwavering stare. Nineteen was how old he had been when Bill died, and she knew it. The unsavory truth hung like a ghost over him, but Alma didn't push it.

"At least get another dog," she said. "A puppy. Puppies are cute. You haven't been the same since you lost Gracie."

Hart pictured his dog exactly as she had been the day she came wandering into the campsite, sniffing out the spitted rabbit roasting over the fire, a half-starved mutt, gangly in adolescence, her ribs showing through a ruddy coat threaded with black. Alma had tried to shoo her off, but Hart called to her and held out a fist for her to sniff. She ambled to him on long knobby legs and licked his knuckles, then pressed the side of her face against Hart's chest and gazed up at him with unfettered adoration. The adoration was immediately mutual.

Gracie had been the salve Hart had needed after Bill's death, the light that had brought him back from a place of grief and darkness. For eleven years, she went everywhere with him—his shadow whose worshipful eyes reflected back to him a better version of himself—until she grew thin with age, and Hart had to carry her more often than not. After she spent three days laboring to breathe, sleeping fitfully, her body gave out in one great heave, taking his heart with her.

"A copper for your thoughts?" Alma said to his profile.

Hart was tempted to tell her about the crushing loneliness and the friend he had found by chance, but it felt too fragile to share yet, as if the letters would break apart in his hands and disappear forever if he confessed their existence.

Diane came out, and the three of them stayed on the deck, laughing over old memories, the kitchen window throwing a square of light onto Hart's feet. Around midnight, a bone-weary exhaustion caught up to him when he thought about returning to his empty hotel room, and unable to withstand the force of Diane's hospitality, he found himself curled up on the too small bed in the guest room with roughly fifty homemade afghans piled on top of him. As he dozed off, he sensed Alma and Diane hovering in the doorway like a pair of mothers watching over a sleeping child.

"I worry about him," came Diane's hushed voice in the darkness.

"So do I, love," said Alma, gently stroking her wife's back. "So do I."

Chapter Eleven

Fess up. Did you get takeout to dazzle this guy?" Mercy asked as she and Zeddie set their plates beside the sink at the same time.

"No!"

"You cooked dinner tonight? All of it?"

"I mean, you follow the directions. It's easy." He nodded toward the cookbook from the library, opened to a recipe for chicken piccata. The pages were splattered with lemon juice and olive oil, but the end product had been phenomenal.

"I'm so impressed with you."

"Thank you." Zeddie preened.

Pop's nightly food-induced coma had overtaken him, and one of his wall-shaking snores rattled its way into the kitchen from his recliner in the parlor.

"No higher praise than that," Mercy said, jerking her head toward the door. "Are you going to amaze us with some dessert?"

"No way. Pen and I are ditching you losers to get ice cream."

"You should rescue him from Pop's snoring before he experiences hearing loss."

But Pen saved Zeddie the trouble, entering the kitchen with an armful of dirty dishes. "Need help cleaning up?"

"You didn't want to hang out with the old guy who fell asleep in a puddle of delicious, lemony sauce?" Zeddie asked, relieving Pen of his burden.

"He didn't seem to be enjoying the pleasure of my company, but the dog did. Leonard and I are best friends now."

Mercy turned to her brother and mouthed the words, *I like him*. Aloud, she said, "Zeddie, you finish clearing the table, and I'll wash up so you two can get out of here."

Zeddie mouthed *Best sister ever* before heading through the kitchen door into the dining room.

Pen ferreted through the drawers until he found a clean dish towel to dry the dishes. This guy was getting better by the second.

"So, Mercy," he half said, half sang.

"So, Pen," she sang in reply.

"Guess you and Marshal Ralston aren't best friends?"

Mercy put a sudsy hand to her chest. "Whatever gave you that idea?"

"How did that start?"

"It didn't start. It was, is, and will always be an infinite loop of fated and mutual dislike." She sank her hands into the soapy water to scrub a plate, wondering at the strange juxtaposition of pleasant, thoughtful Penrose Duckers having to learn his trade from dour, scowling Hart Ralston. "I feel for you. I can barely stand the man for five minutes, and you have to be in his presence for days on end. How do you do it?"

Pen shrugged. "I like him."

"No, you don't," she said in disbelief, handing him a slickly clean platter.

"Yes, I do. He's nice once you get to know him. You should give him a chance."

"He's had many chances with me. He has blown them all."

Zeddie returned, holding four wine goblets and two sweating glasses of water in his long fingers. "Did you talk about me while I was gone? Did you have nice things to say?"

Mercy took the breakables from his hands one by one. "No and no."

"Well, fix that." He waggled his eyebrows at Pen and whisked himself into the dining room once again to retrieve more dishes.

Pen tilted his head at Mercy as he finished rubbing the platter dry. "Have you given Marshal Ralston a chance, though? Because you didn't even let him say hello today."

"That's because he's as mean as a back-alley dog. Better to cut him off before he ever begins." Except she hadn't managed to cut him off this afternoon, had she? She had let him cut her down. She had let him see her weakness and her tears. It made her shudder to think on it.

"You've got him all wrong. I'm telling you, he's a marshmallow on the inside."

"Who? Me? Can't argue with that," said Zeddie as he entered with two bowls mostly empty of the potatoes and the haricots verts amandine they once held, plus a couple of smaller bowls containing crudités.

Mercy flicked dishwater at her brother. "We're not talking about you, you narcissistic twit."

Pen took the dishes from Zeddie, and Mercy caught the way his fingers brushed her brother's hand. A twinge of envy jolted through her. Zeddie's usually confident grin turned bashful as he pulled away to finish clearing the table. Mercy frowned at the sink as she spoke the next words.

"He called me a 'grubby opportunist,' as if I'm gleefully rubbing my hands together, waiting for the next dead body to show up. That doesn't seem very marshmallowy to me. I'm so mad that I let him get to me today. I practically handed him his victory on a silver platter."

Pen took a handful of cleaned silverware from her. "Is it a game? 'Cause if it is, it seems to me like you're both losing. Badly."

"Hmph."

"I think he likes you," Pen told her as he went in search of the silverware drawer.

Mercy gaped at him for a full five seconds before sputtering, "He hates me. And I hate him."

"I think he likes you. A lot," Pen said, dropping knives and forks into place with a *plink, plink, plink*. "A *lot* a lot."

Mercy scrubbed at a stubborn chunk of potato stuck to the bottom of a pan, as if by doing so, she could scour Hart's sneering face from her memory. "You must be a hopeless romantic."

"Nothing wrong with romance. It's not always hopeless."

"Agreed. But me and Hart-ache? That's the definition of hopeless."

"All I know is he couldn't take his eyes off you."

"He was probably staring at my boobs."

"Gross," said Zeddie as he came in with the last of the dishes.

"You're right," Pen laughed, directing his comment to Mercy. "You two are hopeless. But I'll hold out hope all the same."

"You're going to be holding out hope for a long, long time." Mercy bumped Pen away from the sink and toward her brother with her hip. "Don't you guys have ice cream on the agenda? Scoot. I'll clean up the rest."

"Best sister ever," Zeddie sang in falsetto as he nabbed Pen by the hand and pulled him toward the door of the kitchen.

"You think on what I said," Pen told her.

She laughed and shook her head. "Good night, Pen."

Mercy heard them giggling like a pair of schoolboys as they tiptoed past Pop and left by the front door, and the bittersweet twinge of envy stung her again.

Once she had the kitchen cleaned up, she kissed her sleeping father on the forehead and let herself out. On the way home, she and Leonard walked underneath a new banner that stretched across Main Street:

Mayor Ginsberg courteously invites you to celebrate
FOUNDERS' DAY: 25 YEARS OF ETERNITY!
Petting zoo! Equimaris rides! Barbecue dinner!
Dancing under the stars! Fireworks display!

Normally, she loved a good party, but the prospect of being dateless and, therefore, danceless at the Founders' Day party dampened her spirits.

When she got home, she poured herself a bubble bath and drank a glass of merlot as she soaked her weary body in the tub, trying not to get the pages of her romance novel wet. It was her favorite way to unwind at the end of a tough day, yet she felt listless now, unable to relax or focus on anything. Giving up on the bath and the wine and the book, she got out, dried herself off, and put on her oldest, raggediest, most comfortable pajamas. Leonard crawled into bed beside her, but his usually comforting presence depressed her tonight. She loved her dog, but he was no substitute for another human being. Not that Nathan had ever spent the night at her place. They'd always had to go to his apartment.

She stared at the night-darkened ceiling with its jagged crack running from the window halfway to the light fixture, her mind busily turning over everything that had happened that day: the bills piling up, running into Cunningham at the cemetery, Nathan McDevitt with his thinly veiled threats of shutting her down once he was sheriff, and Hart Ralston's vicious words cutting her to the quick.

I think he likes you, Pen's voice echoed in her mind.

"He's got a funny way of showing it," she muttered at the ceiling, making Leonard whimper in his sleep.

No, Mercy did not for a minute believe that Hart Ralston liked her, but she found herself thinking about the last letter from her anonymous friend, seeing in her mind the way the blocky letters marched across the page.

There are a few things about me that would surprise most people if they ever bothered to scratch the surface.

What if Pen had a point? What if there was more to Hart than she knew? What if he was the sort of man who, like her friend, was hard to get to know in person? What would surprise her if she made the effort to dig a bit deeper? For the first time in four years, she wondered if she didn't have Hart Ralston entirely figured out.

But she still couldn't stand the guy.

Mercy dragged herself out of bed the following morning, maneuvering around the boneless pile of dog that was Leonard. *Today cannot possibly be worse than yesterday*, she promised herself as she turned on the coffeepot, but when she returned to her bedroom to get dressed, she caught sight of her disheveled appearance in the dresser mirror. "Don't tempt fate, Mercy," she warned her reflection.

A half hour later, garbed in blue coveralls and a matching headscarf, Mercy came downstairs in time to see Zeddie letting himself in, carrying a plate covered with a napkin, and whistling cheerily as he pushed the door closed with his foot.

"Look at you, showing up on time," Mercy marveled.

"Cherry scone? They're homemade."

"How are you so cheerful and well rested when you got up early to make scones?"

"Who said I went to bed last night?"

"If dating Pen means you get to work on time and bring baked goods to boot, I vote for keeping him around awhile."

Mercy nabbed a scone from the plate, took a bite, and savored the buttery sweetness as it dissolved in her mouth, pairing beautifully with the bitter taste of coffee on her tongue. Yes, today was already far superior to yesterday, although as Zeddie set the plate of scones on the counter, he visibly deflated.

"What's wrong?" she asked.

"Pen had to go back to Tanria this morning. That's why I got up so early, to make him breakfast. He's not sure when he'll be in Eternity again."

"Sorry. I like him."

"So do I," Zeddie agreed before taking an enormous bite out of a scone. "What non-corpse-related things do you need me to do today?"

"Do I smell something fresh baked?" Pop hollered from the office before Mercy could answer her brother.

"Yes, but you can't have any. Doctor's orders," she yelled.

"I like Pen, by the way."

"Thanks, Pop. Me, too," Zeddie shouted in reply.

"Pen would want me to eat whatever you baked."

Mercy relented and brought a scone to Pop before putting Zeddie to work cleaning the lobby. It had been too long since she'd done more than run the feather duster over everything, so she had him wash the baseboards and ferret out spiderwebs in addition to all the sweeping and mopping and dusting and polishing that needed to get done. It seemed like a solid plan until, shortly before opening, she heard Horatio's *clack* at the door. A Klaxon of panic blared inside her at the thought of Zeddie getting his mitts on a letter from her friend. She didn't attempt to remove the thick layer of sawdust coating her arms and glasses as she raced for the door in the feeble hope of beating her brother to the punch.

It was not to be. Horatio was in the lobby, studying Zeddie through a pince-nez clipped to his waistcoat. "I don't believe I've had the pleasure of making your acquaintance."

"Horatio, it's me, Zeddie Birdsall. Remember?"

The owl noticed Mercy and hooted, "My dear, I didn't know you had a brother. Why didn't you tell me?"

Zeddie pointed at the sign next to the door. "That says Birdsall *& Son*. Who did you think the son was?"

"Oh, I don't know. I thought it was rather catchy." To Mercy's horror, Horatio handed the mail to Zeddie and helped himself to the tip jar. He gave Mercy a saucy wink and whispered, "I do hope you enjoy *all* your mail this morning, darling. When you write to your inamorato, be sure to tell him that I send my regards. Ta-ta."

"What in the name of the Unknown God was that all about?" Zeddie asked as he watched the owl sashay out the front door.

"Horatio being Horatio. I'll take the mail."

"What's an inamorato?"

"No idea."

She reached for the mail, but he stepped away, flipping through the stack. A brick of despair landed in her stomach as an evil grin spread across her brother's face. He plucked a letter out of the stack and flourished the envelope in front of her like a magician at a magic show. She read the words *To: A friend* before Zeddie oozed, "And what, pray tell, is this?"

Mercy lunged for the letter, but Zeddie darted away, forcing her to chase him around the lobby as he cackled with delight.

"Who's your *friend*, Mercy?"

"None of your business." She snatched her letter away from her brother.

"Mercy has a boyfriend! Mercy has a boyfriend!" Zeddie sang, prancing around the lobby.

"Shh!" she begged him, glancing at the closed office door. "It's not like that."

"Then what's it like?"

"We're, you know, pen pals."

"Right," he said, but his shit-eating grin made it clear that he didn't believe her for a second.

"Can we keep this between us? This friendship is new, and I... Can we keep this between us?"

"So Pop doesn't know about this guy?"

"No! And you're not going to tell him."

"Wait. Does Lil know?"

"No."

"I know something about you that *Lilian* doesn't know?" Zeddie threw both fists into the air. "Right on!"

"Don't tell her. Or Pop. Please?"

Zeddie slung an arm around Mercy's shoulders. "Sis, as long as you keep giving me all the time I need to tell Pop about not studying to be an undertaker at school, mum's the word on this pen pal. Deal?"

Mercy had no idea how much longer she could keep Zeddie's secret from Pop, but she desperately needed some wiggle room to figure out a way to fight off Cunningham's buyout, plus she really didn't want Zeddie blabbing to anyone about her friend. She let loose a deep sigh of resignation. "Deal. Now get to work."

"You're no fun." Zeddie released her and wrung out a rag over a bucket of soapy water, but as Mercy made her way to the boatworks, she heard his teasing voice behind her. "Tell your lover boy hi from me."

She growled under her breath, but by the time she stepped into the boatworks, she couldn't wait to tear into the envelope in her hands.

Chapter Twelve

Dear Friend,

I choose to ignore your accusation that I am a monster, because it is clear to me that you have never known the perfection that is a cup of good black tea. Incidentally, coffee tastes like the sum total of humanity's bitterness brewed into a brackish swill to be slurped with a grimace.

While your hot beverage consumption leaves much to be desired, your occupation cannot be more horrific than my own. At least it is viewed as such by the general public. Personally, I find the interest rates at the bank repugnant, but for some reason, that line of work is considered squeaky clean. I prefer my own career path. It is a kindness, as you said, something that allows me to do good in the world.

As for my not being alone these days, yes, I have a new coworker. He is young and naive and irritating, but I was young and naive and irritating once, so I won't complain. He keeps nudging me out of my grumpy, crotchety, curmudgeonly ways, something I never dreamed possible a few weeks ago. It's annoying, but also kind of nice. I would never admit this to him, but I will admit it to you, since we are always honest with each other: I like him, and I like having him around. Wonders never cease.

So, your heart belongs to cake? To what else does your heart belong? A specific place? A particular memory? Certain people? I hope you don't mind my scratching the surface. It's so much easier to do by letter than face-to-face, and the more I get acquainted with you, the more I want to know.

I wonder, would either of us bother to scratch the surface if we knew each other in person? Or would we pass each other on the street and never bother to look? Knowing myself (grumpy, crotchety, curmudgeonly), I suspect the latter, which is why I'm grateful for your letters. I hope you'll write soon.

Sincerely,
Your Friend

Dear friend,

Why tea? Why??

Now that the most pressing question is out of the way, I must tell you that your letter could not have arrived at a better moment. I needed a friend this morning, and there you were. Thank you so much for that.

I already like this new companion of yours. There's nothing

like youth to snap you out of a funk. Not that I'm old, but I no longer qualify as young either. How old are you, I wonder?

No, don't tell me! I like the fact that we stay away from the banalities of age and appearance and occupation, and I worry that the day-to-day facts of our lives would get in the way of our friendship. Could you be fully open and honest with me if you discovered that I was a hag with stringy hair and objectionable political views? Or I with you if I discovered you were six inches shorter than myself and overly fond of onions? So, don't tell me anything about yourself except the important things. That's all I want to know.

Although a tiny part of me does want to know where you work, what you look like, how old you are—you see, I refuse to lie to you—because those things are a part of who you are, too.

But, seriously, don't tell me.

As to your question, re: To what does my heart belong other than coffee and cake? I love my father and my sister and brother. I cherish the memories I have of my mother, who died when I was seventeen years old. I also love my family's business, which is unfortunate, since it seems destined to fail . . .

Dear Friend,

My mother got up with the sun every morning and worked her fingers to the bone until sundown, but she always made time to sip her tea and read a chapter from a book before facing the day. She raised me to value the very best of hot beverages. Hence, tea. I shall not be moved.

Don't be mad at me, but I laughed when I read your letter. I assure you, there is no earthly way you are six inches taller than I am.

I'm glad to have been there for you, but I'm sorry you were having a bad day when you received my last letter. Does this have something to do with your family's business?

Your family sounds great, by the way. My new coworker comes from a large family, and they all seem to adore each other. Even when he refers to his brother as "a punk," he makes it sound endearing. I'm jealous, to be honest. I don't have a family. Like you, I lost my mother at a young age, and she was all I had. (I'm sorry for your loss, by the way. I know how hard that must have been for you.)

So, you want to know the important things about me? I'm not sure how to answer that. I get up in the morning. I go to work. I go to bed. Lather, rinse, repeat. I suppose that's why my new coworker recently informed me that I need to live a little. How does a person go about living beyond getting up, going to work, and sleeping? The more I think about it, the more I'm certain that my inability to "live a little" is the cause of my loneliness. So it's self-inflicted, whereas your problems seem to be a result of circumstances outside your control, which is a shame. You deserve better.

In other news, you have found me out: I live on a steady diet of garlic and onions and moldy cheese. I fully intend to breathe all over this letter. Now, about this stringy hair of yours...

Dear Onion Breath,

Hmm, I'm not convinced that your loneliness is entirely self-inflicted, although as your friend, who is always honest with you, I can't completely absolve you. Maybe the question we should both be asking ourselves is what do we have the power to change?

For example, there is a circumstance in my life over which I have some control, but I have chosen to do nothing about it. I'm trying to figure out how to confess this without getting into the particulars we have sworn to avoid. Basically, each of my family members has entrusted me with a secret that affects the other two, and I'm keeping my mouth shut because their respective responses are likely to upend my life and my future. But by keeping those secrets, I'm robbing each of them of the information they need to make decisions about their own lives and futures, especially as concerns my father. Does that make me a terrible, selfish person?

Actually, don't answer that. I know the answer. Boo.

Moving on. I think my favorite thing about you so far is your sense of humor...

...Your current situation sounds tough. As your friend, I should advise you to come clean with everyone, especially since it's clear to me that you love and value your family. However, as the King of Avoidance, I don't have a leg to stand on when it comes to this sort of thing, so I'll offer my support, no matter how you decide to play this.

I find it hilarious that you think I have a sense of humor. There aren't many people who would describe me as funny. At all. Whatsoever. Although I do have one friend with whom I let it fly. She and her wife put me more at ease than most, I guess. Then again, we've grown a bit distant over the past few years due to a long-standing argument. See? King of Avoidance, right here...

...Oh my gods, you are one of those terrifying grammar nuts, aren't you? "With whom"? Really? And who is this friend of yours? Maybe you're not as alone as you think you are. Tell me all about her and her wife.

I'm about to head out the door to my family's house for dinner. My brother loves to cook, as it turns out, and he's pretty good at it. Amazing, in fact...

...When I was young, I practically lived at my friend's house, and her wife mothered me, which, truth be told, I needed back then. But then she became my boss, which has made things awkward. We had a falling-out a few years ago, so I don't go over there much anymore. I'm not sure why I can't talk to her about it. I should probably unpack that.

Speaking of dinner, your letter has made me ravenous. Do you have any idea how rare a decent meal is for me? Please don't torment me with words like "pork tenderloin medallions," not when I'm sitting here with a plate full of canned beans. Do you think your brother might be willing to send a care package? My coworker's mother sends cookies on a regular basis, which is nice, but I'd give my eyeballs for a well-cooked meal.

I'm writing to you tonight under a starry sky. When you live in the middle of nowhere, you can see the stars—all of them—without town lights getting in the way. Do you ever look up? I mean really look? I find myself staring at the stars more and more lately, wondering what exactly it is I'm doing here. Here, meaning the universe.

Uh-oh. I guess I'm getting philosophical...

...I stepped outside this evening, but you're right; the lights in town make it hard to see the stars, so I hopped into the duck and drove outside of town for a better look. The night sky is incredible. Why have I never bothered to appreciate it before? It's been right there all along, but I've been so busy thinking of this thing that needs to get done and that thing that needs to get done, that it never occurred to me to look up. I don't know the names of most of the Old Gods, much less which star is who. (Or which star is whom? See what you've done to me, you grammar monster.) If people can't remember gods, think how easily forgotten any of us are.

It made me think about how I want people to remember me when I'm gone, for however briefly I'm remembered. When I'm on my deathbed, will I honestly be thinking, "Good thing I finished that to-do list"? I suspect that I'm more likely to think, "I should have told Pop about that Big Secret sooner," and "I should have figured out a way to save the family business."

I drove straight to my father's house and touched salt water to my mother's key and to the keys of every ancestor on the family altar. You'd think I'd be depressed after all this thinking and wondering, but I felt oddly light. Still do. I suppose it puts things into perspective—or it's more accurate to say that _you_ put things in perspective for me—to gaze up at the night sky and feel a part of something bigger than myself.

I'm guessing that you spend a lot more time outdoors than I do. My job keeps me inside most days, and when I get time to myself, all I want to do is curl up with a good novel, preferably one that ends with "happily ever after." Not that I'm able to sit down long enough to enjoy a cup of coffee most days, much less a good book.

Wait a minute! I can't believe it's taken me this long to ask you what kinds of books you like to read when I've known all this time that you're an avid reader . . .

. . . which star is who. "To be" is a copular verb that takes a subject complement rather than a direct object. Good job, you.

Yes, I love to read, but like you, I often find

myself busy when I'd rather be stretched out with a good book, my ankles crossed, the spine resting on my chest. My tastes lean more toward nonfiction—history and politics mostly. Not many happily ever afters there, I'm sorry to say. To be frank, I have a hard time suspending my disbelief for happy endings, whereas I think you must be a hopeless romantic. Or a <u>hopeful</u> romantic? That seems more accurate. You keep on putting hope into the world; someone needs to, and it's definitely not going to be me.

On another note: Talk to your family, friend, especially your dad. I can feel the weight of putting it off in my hands as I read your letter. (And I hereby acknowledge that I am a hypocrite, who should definitely take his own advice)...

Chapter Thirteen

Since bodies were off the table—literally—Mercy was determined to make Zeddie fall in love with undertaking via the gorgeous sweet chestnut she had handpicked at the lumberyard. How could anyone resist that grain once it was finished? And yet Zeddie did not share in Mercy's enthusiasm as he helped her cut and glue and nail and saw, while watching the parts come together made Mercy's heart sing.

"You have to be careful when you're nailing it. Chestnut splits easily," she told her brother, hovering over his shoulder as he readied his hammer over a nailhead.

Zeddie glanced at the clock and set both hammer and nail on the worktable next to the boat. "Lil and Danny are due back today. I should head home to make dinner."

"It's three o'clock. Are we dining at senior hour?"

"Good food takes time."

"So does a good boat."

"You know I don't give a shit about boats. And neither do dead people."

Zeddie's snappish response made Mercy's eyes sting with hurt. "Well, the living give a shit, and our boats mean something to them. Why can't you see that?"

He waved his arm, a big sweeping gesture indicating not only the boatworks, but Birdsall & Son and everything the family business stood for. "Why can't *you* see that this is never going to be for me? I know what you're trying to do here, and it's not going to work."

"You've never given it a chance."

"I was never given a choice, and neither were you. This place is wringing the life out of you. How many hours of work are you putting in every week?"

"I..."

"Lil calculates it at seventy to eighty. Seventy to eighty hours of your life, every week, doing this. Is it worth it?"

"Yes," Mercy insisted, and she meant it. She meant it with everything she was.

"Well, it's not worth it to me. I've got an apprenticeship in Argentine, starting next month. I'm studying under the chef at Proserpina's. After my two-year apprenticeship, I'm going to open my own restaurant."

He might as well have spoken another language for all Mercy could understand him. "What?"

"You keep asking me what I plan to do with my life. There's your answer. I'm going to be a chef."

"A chef?"

"Yes."

Mercy's lungs stopped working properly. She imagined herself crawling into the nearly finished boat in front of her and slowly running out of air as her brother sealed her inside, hammering in the nails of her doom.

"Is this a paid apprenticeship at least?"

Zeddie breathed out hard and folded his arms. "No. I'm lucky she was willing to take me on at all."

"So Birdsall & Son is going to finance the 'Son' while he abandons ship? That seems fair." Mercy grabbed a shop towel off a sawhorse and hurled it at her brother. Zeddie threw it on the ground and headed for the door.

"We are not finished, Zeddie!"

"Yes, we are. I can't argue with a brick wall."

Mercy stomped after him through the boatworks door in time to see Pop greeting Lilian and Danny as they got out of the delivery duck at the dock.

"There's Pop, Zeddie. Go ahead. Tell him to his face," Mercy shouted. "Tell him how he spent his hard-earned money to send you to school so that you could study ancient Medoran philosophy."

Zeddie's lips went bloodless as Pop asked, "What?"

Danny froze on the edge of the dock. "I'm going to go check on the...uh...the thing...with the..." He murmured something about oil and axles as he fled the scene to return to the safety of the autoduck.

Zeddie's eyes blazed at Mercy, but that didn't stop the hot words that sparked off her tongue. "Tell him how he's supposed to let you freeload off him for the next two years so that you can learn how to cook. Tell him Birdsall & Son is only Birdsall now."

Pop frowned, but in hurt rather than anger. "Is this true?"

Zeddie's bottom lip quivered. He nodded.

"I have to pee, but I don't want to miss any of this," said Lilian.

"Now's not the time for joking, honey," Roy chastised her.

"I'm not!"

Pop returned his attention to Zeddie. "Why didn't you tell me?"

"I knew you'd be disappointed."

"You've got that right."

Zeddie bowed his head and sniffed hard.

"And you." Roy turned on Mercy. "You knew about this, but you didn't say anything when I got that buyout offer from Cunningham?"

"You're mad at *me*?" Mercy protested, but Zeddie had heard

the words of his salvation, and there was nothing Mercy could do but watch as the situation got away from her, like an unbridled equimaris making a break for the sea.

"Buyout offer? What buyout offer?" Zeddie demanded.

Lil piped in with equal enthusiasm. "How much are we talking about here? Can we make a counteroffer? Ugh, Mother of Sorrows! Can you all please pause so I can pee?"

"We don't need Cunningham's money," Mercy insisted.

"I beg to differ," Zeddie snapped. "I can't believe you, Mercy. This offer is my freedom. And yours, too, for that matter."

"But my whole life is here!"

"Because Pop made it your life. And mine."

"Hey, now. That's not fair," said Roy.

"Fair? Was it fair that you assumed I wanted to follow in your footsteps? Was it fair of you to decide my whole life for me? And look at what you've done to Mercy! She's thirty years old and stuck in the same life you foisted on her when she was seventeen! How is any of that fair?"

Zeddie's words rang through the dock, and then he stood there, quivering, as tears of rage slipped down his cheeks.

"Zeddie," Mercy began, but he cut her off.

"It's true."

"He's right," said Lil.

"It isn't true!" cried Mercy, stomping her foot, though she knew it was childish. "And you have no right to speak for me! None of you do!"

Zeddie's eyes narrowed to cold slits as a ghastly smile spread across his face. "Say, Mercy, get any more letters in the mail from your 'friend' lately?"

Mercy's stomach dropped. She shook her head at Zeddie, but it was too late.

"What letters?" asked Lilian. "What friend? What's going on? And please, dear gods, I really have to pee."

"Oh, didn't she tell you? Mercy has a boyfriend. They've been writing letters to each other. Right, Mercy?"

Mercy strangled her brother with her eyeballs. "He's not my boyfriend, and you had no right to tell them—"

"What boyfriend?" Pop asked.

"He's a pen pal. It's nothing. I've never even met him."

The second the words departed her mouth, she wished she could reel them back in. Her stomach dropped a few more inches.

"You're writing letters to a complete stranger?" Pop asked in his very best Concerned-Father Voice.

"No! I mean, sort of, I guess, but—"

Lilian cringed. "Oh, Mercy, honey. I thought Nathan was bad, but now you're dating a guy you haven't met?"

"We're not dating!"

"He could be an axe murderer for all you know. Or some sniveling Old Gods acolyte."

"No, he isn't!"

"How would you know? You've never met him."

And now Pop put on his guilt-inducing Disappointed-Father Face. "You keep Zeddie's secret from me. You waste your time writing to the gods know who. This isn't like you. Where is your head, muffin?"

Mercy took in her sister's condemnation, Zeddie's glaring resentment, and her father's worry-worn face. They all thought they knew what was best for her, but had any of them bothered to ask her what she wanted, what would make her happy? Had any of them so much as scratched the surface, or did they all assume she would go on as she always had, putting everyone else first without contemplating the toll she paid for it?

Mercy matched Zeddie's quivering posture of outrage. "Where's my head? My head is right here on top of my neck, thinking that there's at least one person in this world who cares about who I am and what I want. And he's not under this roof at the moment."

With that, she fled for the stairs.

"Unbelievable," said Lilian, as if she had earned the right to her long-suffering tone. "I'm going to the bathroom."

"Hey! Lil's pregnant!" Mercy shouted from halfway up the stairwell. "There! Done! No more secrets!"

Her feet thundered the rest of the way up to her apartment, but the sound didn't cover her sister's indignant reply.

"Mother of Sorrows! Thanks a lot, Mercy!"

Mercy made her way to temple on Allgodsday morning, arriving at ten o'clock on the nose, when the votaries opened the heavy oak doors. She hoped to get in and out before any of her family showed up, since she was in no mood to confront them. So far, so good.

She walked down the center aisle to the skylight at the apex of the temple's roof. The great arched ceiling above her was painted like the night sky, the altar of the gods who had come before, their stars shining in the darkness. The skylight was a symbol of the Unknown God, the Void Beyond the Sky who came to know theirself, and who gave that self-awareness to the world. A sense of peace fell over Mercy as she stood in the sunlight streaming downward.

When she was small, her mom used to read *A Child's Book of the Gods, Old and New* to her and Lilian and, later, to Zeddie. Mercy could still hear the cadence of her mom's voice as she read through the pages. The words brought her closer to the memory of her mother, and her mother's memory, in turn, brought her closer to the gods.

First, there was the Void. The Void became aware of theirself, the first and most powerful of all gods, the Unknown. They created others, children made from pieces of theirself. The children wanted to be like the Unknown God, so they created their own children, more gods, but weaker than their parents, and so on.

Eons passed. The first gods slowly tired of existing, and they vanished, leaving nothing but pinpricks of light as a memory of who they had been. Their children created the sky as an altar to their parents' memories, and when they, too, tired and faded, they became stars in the sky as well. Only the Unknown God remained eternal, rejoicing and mourning each generation of their family as their children and their children's children came and went.

Over time, the children of the children of the children of the children of the Unknown God were so diminished that they could not make more gods. Instead, they hung the sun in the starry altar of the sky and made the world to go around it. They created land and seas and all the living things that dwelled there. Finally, three of them made children of their own, crafted from the land and sea. These children looked and spoke and felt like gods, but their beginnings and endings came one atop the other. One mother gave her children the gift of sorrow so that they would know joy. One mother gave them the gift of fortune so that they would know hope. And one mother gave them the gift of wisdom so that they would know their end and, therefore, appreciate their life.

Admiring this creation, the siblings of the Three Mothers gave people more gifts: streams for fishing, woods for hunting, fields for planting, hearths for food and warmth. All of this pleased the Unknown God, but many of the older gods grew jealous of their offspring's creation. They wanted humanity's devotion, too, but they bought mortal praise with cursed gifts: power, war, famine, greed, envy, fear. This is how the Old Gods became most valued in the eyes of humans, and the more people prayed to them, the more powerful the Old Gods became. People forgot about the Mother of Sorrows and the Bride of Fortune and Grandmother Wisdom, and they took for granted the streams and woods and fields and the hearth. They prayed to the Old Gods alone out of fear—fear of war, fear of starvation, fear of loneliness and despair.

The Unknown God took pity on the people that their children's children's children's children had created, and while mortals could not be divine, the Unknown God gave them each a piece of theirself—the soul—and asked three of the New Gods to fashion a way for these pieces of theirself to return to them. One god set souls free of their bodies when it was time to go home, and he returned their flesh and blood to the earth. One god made the Salt Sea as a path from the world of the living to the Void Beyond the Sky. And one god took his place beside the door of the House of the Unknown God to usher every soul inside. These are the Three Fathers: Grandfather Bones, the Salt Sea, and the Warden.

Eventually, the New Gods rose up against their parents, a war so fierce that it fractured the land and created the islands of Cadmus as we know them today. And because the New Gods could not put an end to their parents, they created Tanria, a prison on Earth. Over time, the Old Gods lost the will to go on and begged the Unknown God to let them take their place as stars on the altar of the sky, like their parents and their parents' parents before them.

The Warden came then and cut a door into the Mist of Tanria to let them out, and he sealed it shut behind them. Grandfather Bones made them a boat and sailed the Old Gods across the Salt Sea, where the Unknown God forgave them and welcomed them home and set them on the altar of the sky.

There are still war and greed, envy and fear, and all the dark, sad things that the Old Gods put into the world. Once those things entered our hearts, there was no removing them, even if the gods who created them are long gone. All we can hope to do in our short lives is to live well and honor the gifts our Mothers and Fathers and the New Gods gave us, and willingly return to the Unknown God when we sail the Salt Sea, and Grandfather Bones returns our body to the earth, and the Warden opens the door to our home in the Void Beyond the Sky.

Mercy stood below the skylight, contemplating the vastness of the Unknown God and the smallness of her earthly worries, before she chose an alcove for prayer.

As a motherless child, she usually prayed at the altar of one of the Three Mothers. Today, however, she made her way to the alcove of the Warden—the god of doorways, of exits and leave-takings and endings. His icon showed a two-faced deity, a being who gazed both inward and outward. She had loved all the colorful illustrations in *A Child's Book of the Gods, Old and New*, but the Warden's picture had been her favorite. She loved the way he opened the door to the House of the Unknown God as if it led to an interesting new beginning as much as an ending. Mercy placed one of Zeddie's leftover mini soufflés on the god's altar and hoped the Warden knew what a sacrifice it was. Those things were delicious. Then she lit a candle and took a seat in one of the pews.

A door is closing, and I'm not sure how to find a new beginning once it does, she told the god in her mind. *If you have any guidance on this one, I'd appreciate it.*

Mercy sensed someone sit down beside her. She turned to find Lilian gazing up at the death god's icon.

"The Warden? Interesting choice."

Mercy shrugged, and the sisters sat in silence. After a few minutes passed, Lilian asked, "Why didn't you tell me or Zeddie about that offer?"

Mercy stared at the forlorn soufflé on the altar and shrugged again.

"Because you knew that if Pop found out about Zeddie and me, he might decide to take it?"

"That sounds about right."

"That's not fair to him. Or to Zeddie. Or to me and Danny. It's not your decision to make alone. And if you think about it, it's not fair to you either. Your entire universe revolves around the business, but there's more to life than dead people."

"I know, but..." Mercy gazed at the Warden's two faces. As a death god, he looked toward the future and toward the afterlife, but as the god of introspection, he looked inwardly with his second set of eyes. "That doesn't seem like such a terrible thing to me."

Lilian seemed as if she might say more. Instead, she changed the subject entirely. "Want to go key shopping after this?"

It felt like forgiveness, and Mercy's lips curved up. "For the baby?"

"Since someone let the cat out of the bag, I may as well start thinking about a birth key."

Mercy's brief smile turned into a grimace of regret. "Sorry about that."

"I was going to tell everyone this weekend anyway. It's not like I can hide it anymore. But you're still a jerk."

That was definitely Lil's brand of forgiveness. Mercy kissed her cheek.

After Lilian made her offering to the Bride of Fortune, they walked arm in arm up Main Street to Mimi's Gift Shoppe.

"So, these letters," Lil said as they sidled to the glass display case, where gold and silver keys shone on a bed of blue velvet.

"Oh boy."

"I can't believe you didn't tell me about it."

"There's nothing to tell."

"You are a lying liar who lies. Start from the beginning."

It came as a relief to tell Lilian about her secret friend, as if simply acknowledging the man's existence made him real. By the time Mercy finished, Lil had narrowed down the key choices to three.

"You really like this guy," she surmised, saying the thing that Mercy would not let herself think. But there was no denying it, especially when Lilian saw through her no matter what she said.

"I know that probably seems stupid," she admitted.

"To be honest, yeah, it does. It's easy to like someone on paper, but that's because you can curate yourself for him, and he's doing the same thing. You two don't know the first thing about each other."

"But we do," Mercy said. And then she thought of all the banalities she kept out of her letters, the boring details of everyday life that formed a huge chunk of who she was.

"This whole thing is a bad idea," Lilian continued, moving one of the keys to the reject pile. "If you're lonely, find someone in reality."

"It's like you said; I've been taking care of you and Zeddie and Pop and the business for years, and I don't regret it. But those letters? They're the one thing in my life that's for me."

"I get that. But letters are made of paper, and that seems like a pretty flimsy foundation for a solid relationship to me. So either meet this guy in the flesh and find out if he's a decent human being, or move on."

They both turned their attention to the two keys remaining on the counter, one of which would be consecrated when the baby was born.

"This one," Lilian declared, holding up the winner. It wasn't the one Mercy would have chosen, but Mercy wasn't the one having a baby.

"That one," she agreed.

When she got home, she sat at her desk, which had once belonged to her mother, and took out a pen and a sheet of stationery. *Dear friend*, she wrote, but got no further. She thought of her prayer to the Warden, and she looked to the door of her apartment for inspiration. If her life had run a different course—if Mom were still alive, if Nathan had never cheated on her, if Zeddie had wanted to be an undertaker, if a million other things had or had not happened—there might have been an altar there beside it, a place for a new family with new keys and new beginnings. She expected her hand to shake with nerves as she set pen to paper again, but it was remarkably steady.

I think we should meet.

Chapter Fourteen

Hart was stretched out on a cot in the barracks, his long legs crossed at the ankles, his feet hanging off the end, his head propped up against the wall as he read an interlibrary loan book—*The Almost War of Lyona and Medora, and the Much-Maligned Purpose of Governance in the Early Federation*—by the light of the early evening sun eking in through one of the small windows.

Duckers had made it through training, which meant that Alma could now assign Hart and his apprentice to a sector on the tour schedule. They'd be pulling the day shift in W-26 for the next week, while Banneker and Ellis patrolled in the evenings, which meant they'd stay in the barracks at night rather than camp out. Hart thought that Duckers would be thrilled by the prospect of interacting with marshals other than himself and sleeping in an actual building with a roof over his head, but his apprentice slumped on his own cot with an unread Gracie Goodfist comic in front of him, and he was being unusually taciturn. Hart should have enjoyed the respite from Duckers's incessant jabbering; instead, it was aggravating him to no end.

"You're not talking," he said over the top of his book. "Usually, you never shut up. What's the matter with you?"

"Have you ever heard of a drudge cluster, sir?"

Hart glanced over the top of the book to study Duckers's troubled mien. He should have seen this coming, but he found himself wrong-footed. He buried his nose between the pages again as painful memories flickered across his memory. "I'm guessing some old-timer scared the shit out of you with a harrowing tale?"

"This morning in the commissary, I asked Marshal Herd how he lost his ear, and he said he got caught in a drudge cluster eight years ago."

"Every veteran has some bullshit story about getting caught in a drudge cluster. And that's what it is: bullshit. They're inflating the numbers to make themselves look good—Herd especially—so don't worry about it."

"He said that drudges have been teaming up more and more lately, attacking people in groups of three or four all over Tanria."

"Ten or more drudges constitute a cluster. Three or four does not a cluster make. A single well-trained marshal can take out a handful of drudges without too much trouble."

"Have you ever been caught in a cluster?"

Hart gave up on reading. He tucked the worn leather bookmark Bill had given him eons ago between the pages, set the book aside, and answered Duckers's question with another question. "Have you noticed that no marshals are assigned to Sector 28?"

"No."

"Well, they're not. It doesn't even have a station designation. Know why?"

"No, sir."

Hart consulted his pocket watch, which had belonged to his grandfather, and decided there was time enough before sunset to reach the boundary line of Sector 28. "Saddle up, and I'll show you."

Less than an hour later, he led his apprentice on equimarisback to a ridge overlooking a ravine directly below and a wide meadow in the distance. At the center of this field stood a whitewashed two-story farmhouse that Hart knew his apprentice could not see, just as no one but Hart could see the souls of the dead floating around it.

"This is the western boundary line of Sector 28. There have been five honest-to-gods drudge clusters reported since Tanria's opening twenty-five years ago. One was on that ridge to the southeast. A marshal died that night. Another was in that gully. Two marshals went down. One was against the cliffs down there. Every marshal involved died, so we don't know for sure that there was a drudge cluster that day. One was in those trees to the northwest. Everyone got away that time. And one was on that field. A good marshal lost his life that night."

Hart could recall with crystalline clarity Bill's anguished cries as the drudges tore into him, but he kept himself composed for Duckers's sake.

"Every drudge cluster has happened within a two-mile radius of that meadow, so don't get any closer to it than you are now, and you'll be fine. Got it?"

"Yes, sir."

"Good." He reached out and patted Duckers on the back and was gratified to watch the load lighten from the kid's shoulders.

The sun set as they rode to the barracks, and the Painter coated Duckers's face in warm light, making him appear younger than usual. An affectionate pang shot through Hart's chest, and he wondered if Bill had felt this way about him. Back then, he had thought of his mentor as if Bill had been born a middle-aged man, with a complete and perfect understanding of the world. Now that Hart had an apprentice of his own, he couldn't imagine that he exuded that kind of unquestionable expertise. And yet he couldn't help but wonder if Duckers thought as highly of him as he had thought of Bill.

Bill, who had left a wife and a child in Honek and had never mentioned them to Hart.

By the time they returned to the barracks and stabled the equimares, he was mired in memories of his mentor, a reminder that he could push away the past from time to time, but he'd never truly outrun it.

"Have you ever been to Sector 28, sir?" Duckers asked as Hart fried up eggs for dinner on the old woodstove. Hart was tempted to lie, but the thought of being dishonest with Duckers didn't sit well with him.

"Yep. In the early days of the marshals, before we knew better."

"You didn't answer my question before. Have you ever seen a drudge cluster?"

Again, Hart was tempted. Sorely tempted. But his hesitation answered Duckers's question without his having to open his mouth. No point in denying it now.

"The drudge cluster on the meadow. That's how I lost my first partner."

"Dang, sir. Sorry." There was a note of admiration in Duckers's voice to go along with his condolences. Hart knew he didn't merit it.

"It was a long time ago." Hart gave his full attention to the eggs and hoped Duckers would take the hint and stop talking about drudge clusters.

He didn't.

"Why are drudges more dangerous there?"

"No idea." This time, Hart lied without hesitation. He'd never even told Alma about the house and the souls or what had happened the night Bill died. He plated the eggs with some beans and toast, but his worst memories lingered, haunting him, robbing him of his appetite.

"Now you're the one not talking," Duckers pointed out as they sat down to eat.

"I never talk much."

"Yeah, but your not-talking is extra mopey tonight."

Hart was saved by Bassareus's bellowing outside. "Knock, knock! Mail delivery!" The nimkilim stepped into the barracks, the earring glinting in his tall ear. "Three for the kid, and one for you, loser."

Hart's heavy heart lifted as he took his friend's letter from the rabbit's paw, while Duckers got out coins from the tin where they kept the tip money and poured Bassareus a cup full of whiskey.

"Extra tonight, right, sir?" he asked Hart, referring to their special arrangement wherein they bribed the rabbit to come back the following night to pick up any letters they wanted to send, since there weren't any nimkilim boxes inside Tanria.

"Yep," Hart answered as he loosened the flap of the envelope. He loved this moment, the anticipation before finding out what his friend had to say to him, the silky sound of good paper sliding free, the rustle as he unfolded the letter, the first view of cursive dancing its looping slant across the page.

And then he read the first two lines.

Dear friend,

I think we should meet.

Hart's ears started ringing as the meaning of his friend's words sank in.

"You okay?" Duckers asked him, adding "sir" as an afterthought.

"Fine."

"Your eggs are getting cold."

The thought of eating his cold eggs nauseated him. He stood so abruptly, he knocked over his chair. "I'm going to take a piss."

"Sure you are."

Gods, he knew he was in trouble when a nineteen-year-old could see right through him. He stepped outside and read the letter in the scant light after sunset.

Dear friend,

I think we should meet.

I know it may not be possible if we discover that we live miles or oceans apart, and if I'm being perfectly honest, there's a part of me that doesn't want to meet you in real life, that wants to go on presenting my best self to you on paper. But I'm beginning to wonder if a relationship made of letters makes us little more than paper dolls. If we are going to be friends—true friends—shouldn't we know each other as people, with all our faults and foibles included?

It may be that you don't want to meet me in person, and believe me, I would understand if you don't. But if you do . . .

Honestly, I don't know how to finish that sentence, so I won't.

Sincerely,
Your friend

"Troubles with your broad?" Bassareus's voice cut through Hart's spiraling panic. To Hart's consternation, the rabbit hadn't left yet and was lounging in one of the deck chairs outside the barracks, savoring his whiskey.

" 'Broad'? Who talks like that?"

"Messengers for the Old Gods who find themselves relegated to a life of miserable mail delivery for eons until they disappear and maybe—*maybe*—become stars in the night sky?"

"Right." Hart dropped into the chair beside Bassareus.

"Those were the days, when the Old Gods lived it up and let you say whatever you wanted."

"Sounds like an enlightened time."

Bassareus sucked his enormous front teeth. "What's wrong with you? You're pissier than usual, Pissy Pants."

Hart clutched the letter and thought, *What the fuck*. If he didn't have any human beings to confide in, he might as well pour his heart out to a nimkilim. There was nothing to lose here, because Bassareus wasn't a part of his life.

Was he?

Hart held up the letter. "My friend wants to meet."

"So? That's a good thing, isn't it?"

"No. What if she doesn't like me in real life? I'm not exactly Mr. Warm and Fuzzy. Even you can't stand me, and you're an asshole."

Bassareus preened, slicking back his ears. "Thank you very much."

"Or what if she sees what I am and it makes her feel...I don't know...Or worse, what if she can *only* see this?" He pointed to his unnatural gray eyes.

"So you've never met this bird before?"

"No. That was kind of the point."

"Sounds point*less* to me."

Hart opened his mouth but found that he had no easy answer.

Bassareus nodded. "So basically, you want a girlfriend without having to put in the work of being a decent person in her presence. You can paint the best possible picture of yourself on paper and call it good."

"No, we're one hundred percent honest with each other."

"Oh, so she knows that you're a grumpy-ass demigod, marshaling Tanria?"

Hart shifted in his chair. "No."

"So she doesn't know you at all. And what do you know about her?"

Here, Hart perked up. "She likes music and romance novels and cake. She's smart and funny and—"

"And you know next to nothing about her. Point. *Less.* This?" Bassareus reached over and crinkled the paper in Hart's hand. "Is some flimsy-ass shit."

"Knock it off!" Hart tugged the letter out of the rabbit's paw.

"Quit being a fucking coward and meet her."

The nimkilim's blunt words twisted Hart's innards like the key of a windup toy.

"What if it doesn't work out? What if we stop being friends?"

"Then you can stop dicking around with letters and find a real person in real life to date." Bassareus's beady eyes softened. "You keep asking what if this bad thing happens or that bad thing happens? How about, what if you two hit it off? What if she's the love of your life, dumbass? Thought about that?"

It was as if the rabbit had let go of the windup key and set Hart's inner mechanics spinning. He swallowed and nodded.

"Then go meet her, 'cause you've only got one life to live. May as well make the most of it." Bassareus smacked him on the shoulder as if they were friends, and grinned at him, revealing his broken tooth, before he walked away to finish his mail route.

"I may have only one life to live, but who knows how long it's going to last?" Hart asked, but in a voice pitched too low for anyone to hear him but himself.

And how much of that life are you going to spend alone, you poor pitiful bastard? his own mind responded.

With these uncomfortable questions pricking him from the inside, he returned to the barracks, where he found Duckers sitting on a cot, smiling over a letter from Zeddie, oblivious to Hart and the raging firestorm of emotion inside him. Hart got out paper and pen from his pack and sat at the table, pushing aside his cold eggs and beans.

"I am taking advice from a drunk rabbit," he marveled under his breath as he began to write his reply to his friend.

Chapter Fifteen

As she hummed under her breath, Mercy wished for the millionth time that there was room for a gramophone in the boatworks. She longed for music to drown out the deafening silence that had overtaken Birdsall & Son, Undertakers. The Birdsalls did not argue often, so when they did, they did so badly. Mercy had patched things up with Lil before her sister and Danny left on the delivery run Sorrowsday morning, but Pop continued to fume in his office, refusing to speak to her, and Zeddie had stopped coming into work altogether. A pall that had nothing to do with death hung in the air.

Such was the mood when Horatio arrived. Mercy knew better than to expect a reply from her friend on Saltsday when she had sent her letter on Sorrowsday, but she was disappointed all the same when no response from him arrived. Instead, Horatio handed her a thick envelope embossed with the Cunningham's Funeral Services logo, addressed to her personally.

"Ugh," she told the nimkilim as she plunked a silver coin onto his outstretched wing.

"You are most welcome, darling, I'm sure," he huffed before flitting off. Mercy could tell that she had offended him and would have to spend the next week buttering him up to make him civil again, but she couldn't bring herself to care. She tore into Cunningham's envelope and read the note card inside.

Dear Mercy,
I hope you will do me the honor of joining me for a cup of coffee at my office this afternoon at 2:00. In addition to enjoying the pleasure of your company, I should like to bend your ear regarding an important matter of business.

Yours sincerely,
Curtis Cunningham

Mercy debated the pros and cons of accepting the invitation throughout the morning as she delivered Mr. Tomlinson's boated remains to the temple, stood respectfully in the foyer during the funeral, and wheeled him to the duck to take him to the shipyard for the burial service. On the one hand, she suspected Cunningham was setting a trap for her. On the other hand, she'd rather find out exactly what the Other Undertaker had up his sleeve so that she could plan Birdsall & Son's counterattack.

And so it was that at one forty-five in the afternoon, she cleaned herself up, traded out her coveralls for a dress, and sneaked out the front door, which was easy since Pop wasn't talking to her anyway. As she walked up the boardwalk to Cunningham's Funeral Services, she whispered a prayer to the Three Fathers, with promises to steal Zeddie's next batch of profiteroles and offer them on all three altars if they would have her back during this meeting. Soon enough, she found herself seated in a plummy leather chair across from Curtis Cunningham, the acreage of his gleaming mahogany desk stretching between them.

After a blessedly brief round of small talk and niceties and the offer of coffee, Cunningham got down to business, leaning back in his plummier leather chair and steepling his fingers. "Roy has been remarkably silent in regards to my offer. He did *receive* my offer, did he not?"

"Yes, Mr. Cunningham, he has your offer in hand," Mercy said curtly, irritated by the insinuation that she was trying to hide the letter from her father and more irritated by the fact that she had, in fact, hidden it for quite some time from her siblings.

"And has a decision been reached?"

Mercy decided to toss aside the veneer of formality. "Ask Pop, Curtis. He's the one who owns the business, not me."

"I'm not asking the person who owns the business. I'm asking the one who *runs* it."

Mercy offered no reply, but Cunningham, who had nothing to lose, felt free to continue, his tone light and chatty as he took up his hefty silver pen and began to play with it like a cat toying with a mouse.

"In the absence of a reply to my offer, I have decided to speed along your response for you."

Mercy couldn't shake the feeling that Cunningham was about to press a button under that behemoth of a desk and open a trapdoor beneath her chair. He slathered a kind, paternal smile across his pale, handsome face as he continued.

"Which is why I feel you should know that I've secured a deal with the Afton Lumber Company. In exchange for exclusive rights to all lumber appropriate for the construction of our handcrafted line of funereal boats, Cunningham's Funeral Services will offer all its workers an extremely attractive line of prepaid packages at a thirty percent discount."

Mercy sat up, splashing coffee onto her lap and burning her thigh. Afton was the sole supplier of lumber on the western border. If Birdsall & Son lost access to their inventory, she would have to source materials from the other side of Tanria or possibly overseas. The cost of transport alone would sink them. She set the cup on Cunningham's desk and willed it to leave a ring in the wood.

"You can't do that," she said as calmly as she could.

"It's already done. The new arrangement will go into effect next calendar year, as will Cunningham's complete control over the lumber market of western Bushong."

"That's a monopoly. We'll take you to court."

"Oh? Do you have a lawyer on retainer? Because I do."

Mercy slowly deflated into the ostentatiously expensive leather of her seat. The Birdsalls barely kept their books in the black. They couldn't afford a lawyer, and they most definitely couldn't afford to lose their primary supplier.

Cunningham leaned forward with faux concern, resting his forearms on the desk. "Mercy, you did your best, and I'm so proud of you for what you've accomplished. You always were a good girl. But Birdsall & Son won't survive this. If you go out of business, where will you be then? Or your father or Zeddie or Lilian? Take the money, sweetheart, for their future and for yours."

Despite the coffee stain on her skirt, Mercy rose from the chair with as much dignity as she could muster. "I'm not a 'good girl' or a 'sweetheart,' Curtis, and you don't have the right to be proud of me, especially since I know we wouldn't be having this conversation unless you were terrified of me. Which you should be. Now if you'll excuse me, I have a business to run."

Her burst of bravado had abandoned her completely by the time she stood on the boardwalk outside Cunningham's Funeral Services. Her walk back to Birdsall & Son seemed far too short, but she was unwilling to hide the truth from her father again. She knocked on the door to his office and was answered with a gruff "What is it?"

She opened the door, but Roy refused to acknowledge her. "I spoke with Curtis Cunningham. He's come to an agreement with Afton Lumber. We're going to have to source our wood from another vendor."

She watched as her words sank in and understanding overtook

her father's face. He cleared his throat, but he said nothing. Since neither Curtis Cunningham's offer nor his arrangement with Afton Lumber changed the fact that Mercy needed to wrap and salt at least two more bodies today, she returned to the boatworks and left her father to stew at his desk. Pop locked up and went home without popping in to say goodbye.

Mercy doubted she was going to be welcomed at the family dinner table, especially with Lil and Danny gone, so she dragged herself upstairs and made a plate of subpar macaroni and cheese for the second night in a row, after which she drank too much wine and dove into the romance novel that she had checked out from the library. She had hoped that the steamy bits would distract her; instead, she wound up feeling her own lack of steam acutely. Tossing the book to the side, she turned out the light and slept fitfully, with Leonard snoring beside her.

The following morning, Mercy opened the front door before Horatio had a chance to knock, and greeted him with a mimosa. It was made with the overly sweet sparkling wine of northern Bushong, but there wasn't much she could do about the unavailability of a decent vintage in the wilds of the Tanrian border towns.

"I'm sorry I was short with you yesterday," she told him as she handed him the flute.

The nimkilim sniffed, but it was a forgiving sniff. He accepted the proffered glass and took a delicate sip. "Orange juice does mask a world of evil, doesn't it?"

At least there was one being in this world besides Leonard who wasn't furious with her.

"Thank you," said Mercy.

"Prepare to double your gratitude," he said with a wink as he handed her the letter she had been anticipating on pins and needles. Her squeal of delight was so high pitched that Horatio drawled, "Do be careful, or you'll wind up with a pack of feral dogs scratching at your door."

Mercy tore into the envelope as Horatio waddled out the door.

Dear Friend,

We are always honest with each other, so here it goes: I want to meet you. Very badly. But I am also terrified to meet you, not because I worry that I won't like you (I'm certain that I will) but because I worry that you won't like me. I suspect that I make a better paper doll than a human being, and I feel very strongly that you deserve a friend more worthy of you than I am in reality. Are you sure you want to meet me? The grouchy, doesn't-know-how-to-live-a-little me?

Best,

Your Friend

P.S.—I live in Bushong.

P.P.S.—Telling you that much makes me break out into a cold sweat.

Bushong. All this time, they had been inhabiting the same island and never knew it. Mercy wasn't sure that she believed in fate, but this was beginning to feel like something that was meant to be. She raced up to her apartment to write her reply.

Chapter Sixteen

Dear friend,

I'm terrified, too, and I'm also worried that you won't like me when you meet me in person. That's only natural, isn't it? And would you want to be friends with a self-centered jerk who assumes everyone loves them anyway? Of course you wouldn't, and I wouldn't either.

Anything worth doing in this life requires a leap of faith, and I have faith that our friendship can exist beyond these letters, despite all the faults and weaknesses of our flesh-and-blood selves, which is why I want to meet you, to know you better. Let us be brave.

Sincerely,
Your friend

P.S.—I also live in Bushong!

Dear Friend,

For you, I will be brave.

Are you free next Wardensday? There's a place

in Mayetta called the Little Wren Café. I can be there by 7:00 PM.

Can you read this? My hand is shaking so badly I can hardly hold the pen.

Your Friend

Dear friend,

Next Wardensday, 7:00 PM, at the Little Wren Café in Mayetta it is. I'm so excited to meet you! I'll wear yellow, so you'll be able to spot me easily.

Yours giddily,
Your friend

Dear friend,

I'll be there, but I won't be wearing yellow. My entire wardrobe is a.) very limited, and b.) extremely drab. You can tell me to live a little when we finally meet. In person.

Your Friend

P.S.—I have mentioned that I am terrified, right?

Chapter Seventeen

Each day that brought Wardensday closer made Hart's nerves ratchet higher. By the time Wisdomsday rolled around, he had no patience left to spare for poor Duckers, which was why he went apoplectic when he spied the wad of wrinkled paychecks in his apprentice's open rucksack.

"You have got to be kidding me. What the fuck, kid?"

Duckers winced. "Yeah, I was going to get to that."

"Sometime this decade?"

"I mean, sure. Of course."

"You do have a bank account, correct?" When Duckers bit his lip, Hart repeated, stridently, "Correct?"

"My mom's going to help me set one up whenever she can get away for a visit."

"If you haven't cashed your paychecks, how did you buy a prepaid funeral package?"

Duckers bit his lip again and scraped the toe of his boot through the leaf litter at his feet.

"You're dating an undertaker!" said Hart. He was about to unleash a steady stream of exasperated profanity when he realized that a branch of Federated Banking was located in Mayetta. If he took Duckers to open a bank account tomorrow, he could send him on his way to buy a prepaid funeral package and ID key at Birdsall & Son, which meant he could get his apprentice out of the way early and give himself enough time to get ready for dinner. It was as if the clouds above had cleared and a ray of sunshine were blazing directly upon his head, with "The Hymn of the Bride of Fortune" filling his ears. He was almost giddy when he dragged Duckers by the shirt collar into Alma's office the following day.

"What's up?" she asked.

Hart held up the uncashed, undeposited paychecks. "This child has no bank account."

Alma burst out laughing.

"Ha ha. Very funny," Duckers muttered.

"Mind if we head out early to get this dipstick set up?"

"Hey!" Duckers protested.

"You got it," said Alma.

Hart succeeded in keeping a stupidly happy, telltale grin from spreading across his face. Now he was free to fret about his rendezvous with his soon-to-be-known friend for the next seven hours. Those seven hours did not, however, pass uneventfully. Duckers dawdled at the station after lunch, comparing notes with another apprentice over three helpings of cake, until Hart began to worry he'd have to take the kid out of there at rapier-point. When they finally did hit the road, Hart's autoduck blew a tire fifteen miles outside of Mayetta, setting them back more. And the process of getting Duckers's bank account set up took a full hour longer than Hart had anticipated. By the time they got to the hotel, it was well past six o'clock.

As Duckers preened in the hotel room mirror, Hart tried to examine his own appearance without *looking* like he was examining his appearance, and failed miserably. He finally gave up and butted Duckers out of the way so that he could stand in front of the mirror like a normal person getting ready for a . . . what? A meeting? A get-to-know-ya?

A date?

Hart assessed his reflection, studying the harsh lines of his face and the startling paleness of his irises. His efforts at combing down his messy blond hair did nothing to improve or soften his appearance.

She wasn't going to like him.

"Everything okay, sir?" Duckers peered over his shoulder at Hart's reflection. The kid had never asked him about his eyes or his parents or what it was like to be a demigod. He'd simply taken him as he was, and all of a sudden, Hart was incredibly grateful for it.

"I need a favor," he admitted.

"All right. What?"

He pulled his watch from his pocket. Six fifty-six.

"Come with me." He took Duckers by the arm and pulled him into the hall, locking up the room behind them.

"But I'm going to see Zeddie."

"This won't take long."

Hart ushered a moderately resistant Duckers out the front door of the hotel and one block over to the Little Wren Café, arriving at seven o'clock on the nose.

"Okay. What's this favor?"

"I need you to look through the window and find a woman dressed in yellow."

"Okaaay. Why am I doing this?"

"Just do it."

"Not unless you tell me what's going on."

"It's none of your business." Hart resisted the urge to loosen his collar.

"That whole bank account thing was a cover, wasn't it? You're here to meet a woman."

Hart said nothing, but Duckers's whole being lit up with amusement.

"It's your letter-writing 'friend,' isn't it?"

"Fine, yes. Now would you look?"

"Because you want to know if she's ugly so you can ditch her?"

"No!"

Of course, it had occurred to Hart that this woman might not be physically attractive, but the truth was that he was far more worried about getting ditched than being the ditcher.

"I can't believe you dragged me here to case the joint for you, you big chicken!" Duckers tucked his hands into his armpits and flapped his elbows. "Bock, bock, bock, BOCK! Who's a big chicken?"

Mortified, Hart pushed him none too gently toward the window. "Just look."

"I'm on it." Duckers made a show of flapping his elbows as he waddled up the front steps of the Little Wren Café to peer into the restaurant's picture window.

"Do you see her?"

"Give me a sec."

"Well?"

"Would you calm your—oh my gods."

The sinister glee in that *oh my gods* filled Hart's veins with dread. "What?"

"No way!"

"What?" he begged.

When Duckers spun around, he had pure, unadulterated joy painted all over his face. "Haaaaaaa!" he cackled so loudly the sound echoed off the neighboring buildings.

"Shh!"

"Ha ha ha! This is the greatest day of my life!" crowed Duckers.

"So help me gods, I'm going to throttle you. What does she look like?"

"What would you say if I told you she looks a lot like Mercy

Birdsall?" Duckers answered, traipsing down the steps in a series of jovial hops.

"I would say kill me now."

"Mercy's pretty, sir. You have to admit that."

"I most certainly do not."

"Well, if you don't find Mercy Birdsall attractive, you're not going to like this lady."

"Really?"

"Yeah. Because she *is* Mercy Birdsall! BOOM!" Duckers danced in triumph in front of Hart. "Who was right? I was right!"

"What?" The boardwalk seemed to spin like a carnival ride beneath Hart's feet.

"Your pen pal is the one, the only Mercy Birdsall of Birdsall & Son, Undertakers. Who. You. Like." On each of the last three words, Duckers poked Hart in the chest over the hollowed out spot where his beating heart should be.

"No," Hart breathed, his lungs deflating.

"Yes."

"That can't be right."

"See for yourself."

Hart's ankles and knees went rubbery as he made his way up the stairs and peered through the window. There was Mercy, wearing the same bright yellow dress she'd worn the day he'd walked into Birdsall & Son over four years ago. She sat toward the back, craning her neck, glancing eagerly about her. He had never before seen her with her hair down. Now the dark locks curled about her shoulders, glinting auburn where the candlelight hit it, and for one instant, he forgot that he couldn't stand her. He could think only about how lovely she looked.

And then reality sank in like the teeth of a feral dog.

All this time, he had been writing letters to Mercy Birdsall. Mercy, with her *Hart-ache* and her insults and her fake dimples, as if she were thrilled to smile in the face of death. Had she known it was him all along? Was this a sick joke? The cruelty of it made his chest burn from the inside. Hart's whole body went so rigid he could barely bring himself to go down the stairs. His boots hit each tread with a heavy *clunk*.

"Aren't you going in?" Duckers asked.

"Nope." Hart continued to walk in the direction of the hotel.

"You're standing her up?" By now, Duckers was meeting him stride for stride, talking at his shoulder.

"Yep."

"At least go in there and come clean so she's not waiting around all night."

"Weren't you going to take the autoduck to Eternity? Better get going."

"Sir." Duckers put out a hand to stop him, but Hart jerked away.

"Don't tell anyone about this, not Zeddie, not . . . *her*. No one. You don't breathe a word of this ever. Promise me."

"With all due respect, sir, you're being a dick."

Hart had steel to spare this evening, and he sank all of it into the glare he unleashed on Duckers.

"Fine. I promise. Happy now?"

No. Hart was not happy. He was the opposite of happy. He turned his back on Duckers and walked away, but behind him, he heard his apprentice shout, "Bock, bock, BOCK!"

He kept walking anyway, listening to the familiar squeal of his autoduck's front door as Duckers got in and slammed it shut. The engine turned over, and the wheels susurrated in reverse before Duckers pulled away down the paved main street of Mayetta. And then Hart was alone on the boardwalk and alone inside his skin.

He couldn't make the friend in his letters match up with the woman who had spent the past four years sniping at him from behind the counter of Birdsall & Son. It had to be a malicious prank. Somehow, some way, Mercy must have found out he had written that first letter and had toyed with him, tricked him, lured him here to make a fool of him. She hated him this much.

Or could he have been wrong about her? Could Mercy Birdsall have written the words that Hart had read so many times he had committed them to memory? Could she have poured her heart out to him without knowing who he was?

Could she have liked the man she had met in his letters?

The image of Mercy sitting by herself in the Little Wren Café filled his mind. He saw her watching the door, hopeful, her yellow dress bright in the atmospheric dimness of the restaurant, her shiny hair skimming her shoulders, her glasses glinting in the candlelight. Hart was almost certain her letters were a horrible gag, but there was a chance, however slim, that Mercy was anxiously waiting for her friend to show up.

Guilt percolated inside him, filling him up. No one would describe Hart as "nice," but he wasn't cruel either. If the letters weren't a joke, if they were genuine and true, he couldn't leave her there, believing that her friend had stood her up.

He had to face her.

A pitiful mewl of self-preservation escaped his throat, but his morals compelled his feet to deliver his body to the Little Wren Café. He willed a mask of disinterest over his face before he pushed in the door and stepped inside. A bell over the lintel announced his entrance, and Mercy looked up.

And it was exactly as it had been the day they met, with Mercy like sunshine personified in her yellow dress, and every thought Hart had ever had in the course of his life emptying out of his brain and vanishing into thin air.

His feet kept moving, and each step that brought him closer to Mercy made her big brown beautiful eyes go wider and wider behind her glasses, and then he was standing over her, and one thought finally took shape in his brain: *I think I want this to be real.*

"No," she breathed. "No, no, no. What are you doing here?"

He knew that he needed to say something, but Mercy had injected the word *you* with enough vitriol to rust a hole in a tin roof, and he couldn't find a word in his head to save his life.

"I can't—can*not*—deal with you right now, Hart-ache. I need you to not be here."

But he had arranged to meet her at the Little Wren Café on Wardensday at seven o'clock, hadn't he? And here he was, albeit a few minutes late. But as Mercy tilted her head, staring past him toward the door, he understood that she could not entertain the idea that Hart Ralston was the man behind the pen. And somehow, that was worse than the notion that this had been a joke to her.

"Hello, Merciless," he said, a hard lump in his throat making his voice gravelly.

"I have an important thing tonight, so can we not do this? Please, leave me alone."

Feel free to never come back again, she told him in his memory.

Hart scanned the restaurant full of happy people having happy conversations and living happy lives, and he wanted to light the place on fire. He fixed a nasty smile onto his face. "Pretty crowded tonight. Mind if I join you?"

"Yes. I mind."

She pushed her purse toward the opposite place setting, trying to save the seat for someone who had already arrived. Whether she knew it or not, that chair was meant for Hart, and he sat in it.

"Excuse me—"

"You're excused."

"I'm meeting someone who is not you."

A bitter laugh pulsed through his throat as he pulled his watch from his pocket. "At seven ten? Seems like a strange time to meet. Are they late?"

"None of your business, and I'll thank you to vacate that seat."

A waitress stopped at the table and asked Hart, "Can I get you anything?"

"No, he's going on his merry way," Mercy answered for him, her eyes doing their level best to flay him alive from across the table.

"Why, yes, thank you. I'll take a cup of jasmine green tea," Hart told the waitress, deliberately giving himself away with his drink order. Mercy failed to notice. She was too busy killing him in a variety of violent ways in her imagination.

"Leave," she said, seething.

Hart crossed his ankle over his knee, as casual as you please, when every muscle, vein, and bone in his body felt as if it were screaming in rage. "Tell you what. I'll keep you company until your friend comes along."

"Why would you want to keep me company? You hate me as much as I hate you."

Hate. He could almost see the word written across his white shirt in a blood splatter.

"*Hate*'s a strong word, Merciless. Do you really *hate* me?"

Say yes, Hart begged her in his mind. *Lay into me so that I can hate you, too.* But the front door opened with a chiming of bells, and Mercy looked past Hart with a hopefulness that sliced him from his guts to his throat. He turned toward the door and saw what Mercy saw, an elderly couple asking for a table. He turned in time to watch her sag with disappointment.

"Not your friend, I take it?"

Pointedly ignoring him, she reached into her purse, pulled out a book, and pretended to read. With each second that she refused to see him for who he was, a thunderous wrath built in his chest. He wanted her to hate his letter-writing self as much as she hated his flesh-and-blood self. He wanted to obliterate any foolish hope she'd been cherishing about her *friend*, the same way she was destroying his now. And then he could go back to the way he'd been before he'd ever set pen to paper and slid a ridiculous confession into a nimkilim box.

He checked his watch again. "If your friend was supposed to meet you at seven, they've gone from being mildly late to very late. Pretty soon it will be egregiously late."

"Mind your own business."

He examined the spine of her novel. "*Enemies and Lovers*, huh?"

"It's a classic, but I'm sure you're one of those men who've never read it because you believe it's a drippy romance novel that tries to pass itself off as great literature."

That was exactly what he thought of *Enemies and Lovers*. "Touché."

"Gods forbid you read a love story and experience personal growth as a result."

"Ah yes. Nothing says personal growth like Eliza Canondale, wasting away under her father's misogynistic roof, waiting for her demigod hero to sweep her off her feet."

"I thought you've never read it."

"I haven't, but I don't live in a cave."

"Don't you?"

She may as well call him a pathetically friendless loser again.

The waitress appeared at his side, setting his order down before him. "Your tea, sir."

The steam billowed between them as Mercy leaned in, alight

with fury. "I'll have you know that Eliza Canondale takes control of her own life and requires no rescuing. And let me assure you that you only wish you had Samuel Dunn's strength of character."

"And what kind of character does your"—Hart checked his watch again—"egregiously late friend have?"

"My friend has more decency in his pinkie finger than a brute like you could dream of."

Hart took a delicate sip of tea with his pinkie in the air to demonstrate his complete lack of brutishness. Mercy huffed as he set the cup on its saucer with a musical *clink*.

"Maybe there are things about me that would surprise you, Merciless, if you bothered to scratch the surface."

How could she fail to recognize him when he was quoting their letters to her, daring her to know him for who he was? But Mercy snorted, oblivious to the truth sitting three feet in front of her.

"Please," she scoffed. "If I cut you open on my prep table, I'd probably find a rapier where a heart should be and a bleak, grim, depressing novel that no one but you could possibly want to read lodged in your appendix."

It was as if Mercy had grabbed the blunt knife from her place setting and filleted him with it. He had come here tonight to do the right thing, only to find himself wounded and bleeding. He bared his teeth like a cornered animal when he spoke again. "And this friend you're waiting on is a bighearted, soulful paragon of human decency?"

"Yes, he is. He's kind and smart and funny and thoughtful—"

"And apparently he's invisible, because you sure as shit don't see him here."

Mother of Sorrows's tears, he might as well be wearing a sign that said *I'm your secret pen pal, Mercy!* with an arrow pointing at his face.

"What do you care, you self-serving, prickly, glowering nightmare of a man. Oh, excuse me, *half* man, because who knows where your other half came from."

That barb shredded him so thoroughly, Hart could barely breathe.

"How very precise of you," he said in clipped syllables, feeling as if she had run him through with his own rapier.

The front bell rang again, and Mercy's eyes darted to the door, where three women came in together. This time, a tear slid down her cheek, salt water that stung all the gashes she had carved into Hart. "Go, okay? Leave me alone."

"Gladly." His voice was chilly, but his insides were a conflagration. He took one last sip of tea before heading for the bar, where he paid for Mercy's drink as well as his, a parting shot accomplishing he knew not what.

In his hotel room, he lay spread eagle on the bed without bothering to pull down the coverlet. His friend who, as it turned out, was not his friend at all, had told him he had a rapier in place of a heart, and maybe she was right. It was stabbing him in his bleak, grim, depressing novel of a soul.

Chapter Eighteen

On Allgodsday, Mercy argued with Lilian.

Allgodsday was, of course, Mercy's day off, but it was also the only day of the week without mail service. She didn't know how she was going to make it through the day without her friend's letter explaining why he wasn't at the Little Wren Café last night. Because that letter *would* arrive. Tomorrow morning. She was certain of it.

She went to temple and once again sat before the icon of the Warden.

Mom used to say that when the Warden shuts a door, he always opens a window, she prayed to him, *but it feels like you've closed at least two more doors on me since the last time I was here. I don't mean to complain, but if you could point me toward a window or two, I'd be very grateful. Also, Zeddie's not talking to me, so I haven't been able to get my hands on his baking. The toaster pastry was the best I could do this morning, I swear.*

The god's two faces gazed ahead and behind, and it seemed to Mercy that the last place he was looking was at her.

She made it in and out of temple without running into a family member, but it was hardly surprising when, shortly after she returned to her apartment, she heard the front door open, followed by her sister's determined footsteps up the stairs.

"I can't believe you missed dinner last night," Lil declared when Mercy let her in. "It was delicious, by the way. Zeddie got his mitts on imported sole fillets. I don't usually like fish, but that sole was the best thing I've ever eaten. How does he do it?"

"No idea. Good for Zeddie. I'm beside myself with joy that he's found his calling," Mercy said flatly as she offered her sister a foil packet containing two jelly-filled pastries, the only breakfast-like substance in her apartment.

"So where were you?"

"I had a date, kind of," Mercy admitted.

Lil shrieked. "With who?"

With whom, Mercy thought, her mind filling with her absent friend's familiar handwriting to correct Lilian's grammar. It sank her spirits lower.

"Was it the letter guy? Why didn't you tell me this the second you opened the door? I want details!"

"He couldn't make it." Mercy took a bite of her pastry, and it crumbled in her mouth like sawdust. She didn't know why she kept buying them. They were always such a disappointment.

"He stood you up?"

"He couldn't make it," Mercy repeated.

Lilian's pupils dilated into pinpricks of outrage, but Mercy didn't want her to be mad at her friend; she wanted her sister to direct that anger toward its rightful target.

"And then Hart Ralston saw me sitting alone and sat down at my table and was his usual horrible, insulting self!"

Gallingly, Lilian fanned herself with the foil wrapper. "I don't think I'd mind if Marshal Ralston sat at my table."

Mercy blinked at her, stunned by her sister's treachery. "He's pure evil."

"In a very nice body."

"Lil!"

"I know you hate the guy, but I never thought he was that bad. A bit gruff, maybe. Lots of demigods are. Probably sick of the way most people fawn all over them. He was always polite to me." Lilian had already polished off the first pastry in the packet and now tore into the second as if she were taking a bite out of Hart Ralston's impressive backside.

"Go ahead. Join the Hart-ache Fan Club. He never decided to loathe you for no reason."

"Don't you think it's weird, the way you two instantly hated each other? What demigod in his right mind wouldn't fall for you?"

"Who said Hart Ralston is in his right mind?"

"And I can't for the life of me figure out why you wouldn't swoon over a smoking hot marshal."

"Are you serious? Don't make me barf up my extremely disappointing breakfast."

"All I'm saying is that a tall, single, and extremely attractive Tanrian Marshal who is standing before you in the flesh sounds a lot better than some letter-writing weirdo who stands you up."

"For the last time, he couldn't make it!"

"Forget it. Sorry." Lilian threw up her hands as if she were the one who deserved to be exasperated. "I came here to talk to you about Cunningham's offer, anyway."

Mercy buried her face in her hands, muffling her voice as she answered, "Then you can turn around and leave, because I am not in the mood."

"Well, when are you going to be 'in the mood'? Because this is a decision that involves all of us. It's not yours to make alone."

Alone.

Maybe Mercy had more in common with her absent correspondent than she had initially thought. In many ways, alone was exactly what Mercy had been for years, and it seemed blisteringly unfair of the gods to allow the future of the family business that she had single-handedly kept up and running to be decided by committee.

She let her hands fall away from her face and snapped, "Yeah. Got it."

"Fine. Be that way. But when Danny and I get back next week, we're having this out once and for all."

Lilian dusted the crumbs off her baby bump for Leonard to lick up, and let herself out. Mercy spent the rest of the day with a sinus headache and a mediocre novel.

It was, by far, her best day of the week.

On Sorrowsday, Mercy argued with Steve Coopersmith, the lot manager of the Afton Lumber Company.

When Mercy first took over Birdsall & Son's clerical work after her mother sailed the Salt Sea, the family business could afford to pay for delivery from Afton. But the more Cunningham had cut into their business, the more corners Mercy had had to cut. Birdsall's had long since switched to picking up their order. Ever since Pop had his heart attack and couldn't join her anymore, Mercy had had to sweet-talk one of the foremen into helping her load the wood into the hold of the duck. Today, it was Steve.

She decided to test out Cunningham's threat by handing Steve her lumber order for the next two months. Despair set in as she watched him shuffle his feet and rub the back of his neck.

"Thing is, Ms. Birdsall... um... I'm afraid we won't be taking any more orders past the first of the year."

"So it's true. Ms. Afton is selling exclusively to Cunningham?"

"Sorry."

Mercy knew that Steve had played no part in this, but she was livid at Afton Lumber, and right now, the face of Afton Lumber was Steve Coopersmith, whose long, dark mustache drooped in response to her indignation.

"Birdsall & Son has been a loyal customer for over twenty

years. We were in the Tanrian funeral business before Cunningham set up shop, and we've always paid our bill."

Steve cleared his throat. "Late."

"But paid! And now you're selling to Cunningham and no one else? How is that fair? Have you bothered to consider what this is going to do to the rest of us on the western border?"

"It's not up to me." He flipped through the pages of his clipboard as if there were something of burning importance there.

"But did you stand up for us when Ms. Afton told you about the deal with Cunningham?"

"No, I did not."

"Why?"

Steve gave up the ruse and met her eyes over the clipboard. "Because I've got three kids I'd like to send to college, and if I can recoup some of the money I shelled out for a prepaid funeral package, you better believe I'm going to do it."

"We'll match Cunningham's offer," Mercy promised him, inwardly cringing at the note of desperation in her voice. "And tack on an extra five percent off."

"Can you afford that?"

She did the math in her head. It wasn't pretty. "Probably?" she said.

Steve gave her a pitying look. He meant to be nice, but really, it was the nail in her cutter. "There are other lumber companies."

"On the eastern border. We're not going to be able to cover the cost of shipment."

"That's your problem, not mine. I'm sorry. Now, if you'll excuse me. I have a business to run, and last time I checked, you do, too."

"But for how much longer?" she called after him and was gratified by the shameful hunching of his shoulders as he walked away.

On Saltsday, Mercy argued with her father and her brother.

With Cunningham's threats verified by Afton Lumber, she was in a vile mood, so when Horatio delivered a stack of bills with nary a letter from her friend in sight, she felt like her skin might crack from the frustration building inside her.

Why didn't he write? she asked the Bride of Fortune over and over as she salted and wrapped two bodies for delivery and five for the burial pits. *Why? Why? Why?* By the time she caught Pop following Zeddie and a tray of freshly baked chocolate croissants into the kitchenette, she was ready to blow.

"Dr. Galdamez said no more coffee!" she screeched, yanking the carafe from his hand and staining the tiny yellow flowers of her blouse with a splatter of caffeine. "And the pastries!" She grabbed one from his plate and slammed it on the tray from which he had plucked it. "Will!" She took another croissant and did the same, sending shards of buttery lamination scattering across the counter. "Kill you!" She grabbed the remaining croissant and chucked it back where it came from, making a bigger mess than the one Roy had created by putting them on his plate to begin with.

"Easy now, muffin."

"Don't tell me 'easy now,' and don't call me 'muffin'! This is a place of business! Start treating it like one!"

"You can't talk to Pop like that," Zeddie told her.

"And you!" Mercy turned on her brother, pointing an accusatory finger at him. "You were supposed to help me stop Pop from doing things like stuff his face full of coffee and pastries, and here you are, encouraging him!"

"Stop worrying so much, m—" Pop stopped himself, took a breath, and continued. "I can take care of myself."

"Can you? Can any of you? Because I've been taking care of everything and everyone for thirteen years."

"Except yourself," Zeddie muttered.

"Why are you here? Don't you have something fancy and useless to cook?"

Zeddie's eyes brimmed with tears. "You know what? Since you don't respect what I want to do with my life, you don't get to eat what I make."

He picked up the tray of croissants and stalked out of the building.

Mercy stood still as a statue. She was afraid that if she spoke or moved or breathed, she would dissolve into a weeping puddle. Roy caved and put a heavy arm around her shoulders. After two weeks of the silent treatment, that single gesture broke open the floodgates inside her, and she burst into tears.

"Who needs him?" she wept, and the sad truth was, she didn't need Zeddie, not when it came to running Birdsall & Son. What she needed was someone, anyone, who could pick up the slack around here.

But one of those chocolate croissants would have been nice, too.

She blew her nose, pulled herself together, and asked her father the question she had put off for too long. "Are you going to sell?"

His eyes drifted. As far as Mercy was concerned, he should have taken in every aspect of the building and the business it represented: the dock, the boatworks, the office, the lobby, the stairs leading up to Mercy's apartment—everything he had worked so hard to build over the past two decades. Instead, he stared at the front door, gazing longingly after an absent son who was probably halfway down Main Street by now.

"Honestly, muffin, I can't think of a single reason not to sell."

She felt like he had grabbed an awl from the boatworks and was now burrowing a hole into her heart with it. She slipped out from underneath his arm. "So Zeddie is a reason to keep the business going, but I'm not?"

"The business has been a burden on you long enough. You deserve better."

"Well, I'm so glad you're the expert on what's best for me. You and everyone else."

She didn't give him a chance to reply. She marched to the boatworks. Whatever Birdsall & Son's future held, today, she had work to do.

On Fortunesday, Mercy argued with herself.

I'm going to write to him.

No, you will not.

What if something's wrong? What if he's lying in a ditch, mortally wounded?

What if he decided you aren't worth it?

I need a friend right now.

Then find one in reality.

But—

Have some pride, Mercy.

Pride? What pride?

She wrote the letter.

On Bonesday, Mercy argued with Horatio.

"Had another dreadful night, did we?"

Mercy gave him a withering look. "I like you, Horatio, but sometimes I loathe you."

"My, my. Quite dreadful, then."

She took the proffered bundle of envelopes. "I slathered on makeup this morning, so I know for a fact that to all outward appearances, I do not have bags under my eyes."

"Not that mortals can see, no."

Mercy growled as she flipped through the mail, each bill crushing her hope.

"Oh now, don't mind a bitter old nimkilim, although you, too, would be insufferable if you had been demoted to a position of common postal carrier after centuries of delivering messages for the most divine beings in the universe. Do you have any idea how awful it is to be an immortal of such discerning tastes and to be cast upon the wilds of Bushong?"

"I like it here. It's unpretentious."

"What is there to admire about a lack of pretension?" Horatio shuddered.

Ignoring the slight on her town, Mercy slapped the disappointing mail onto the counter and declared, "There's been a mistake."

"How do you mean?"

"I should have received a certain letter by now. Did you lose it?"

Horatio pressed the tips of his wing feathers to his heart. If he'd been wearing pearls, he would have clutched them. "My little button, when it comes to fashion and mail delivery, I am infallible."

She did not tip him.

On Wisdomsday, Mercy argued with Nathan McDevitt.

Sort of.

She went to city hall to pay her stupid drudge-drill violation before she wound up with a late fine tacked onto it. A familiar voice called her name in the vestibule, the two syllables bouncing off the marble floor and counter, and there was Nathan, his silver deputy's badge winking on his vest. He came at her so fast that Mercy thought he was going to hug her, and she recoiled. He pulled up short, started to extend his hand, then wiped it on his pant leg.

"Hey," he said.

"Hey."

"What are you doing here?"

She clenched her jaw in irritation as she held up the ticket between two rigid fingers, and was taken aback when he snatched it from her hand.

"I need to pay that!"

"No, you don't. I never filed the paperwork." He tore it in two, shoved the pieces into his pocket, and glanced around furtively. The first ray of light indicating that this perfectly awful week might end on a happy note seemed to shine through the large front windows of city hall. Nathan kept his hand in his pocket and bunched his shoulders up to his earlobes, which were turning pink.

"I'm sorry. I was a real jerk that day," he said.

For a full month after she had found out about Nathan's cheating on her, Mercy had longed for him to come knocking on her door, groveling, apologetic, pathetic with longing. She wouldn't exactly describe him as groveling or pathetic with longing at the moment, but it was nice to receive an apology, for the ticket at least. She didn't know what to say.

His cheeks went as pink as his earlobes, and he gave her a wry smile. "No, no. Don't argue with me on this. I was a complete jerk, and I won't hear your objections."

"Thank you," Mercy said with a small laugh.

They continued to loiter in the vestibule, neither of them knowing where to look. By now Nathan's entire face was pink. Finally, he swallowed and said, "I miss you."

Good gods, how long had Mercy yearned to hear those words? And yet now that they had been said, she floundered, unsure of how to feel or respond.

"Any chance I can buy you a cup of coffee?" he asked.

Ah, she thought, *he's angling for something.* But then she realized that the thing he was angling for was her, and wasn't that what she had been longing for? She recalled Lilian's advice about focusing on the man before her in the flesh rather than her letter-writing friend, who remained silent. At least Nathan was better than the "tall, single, and extremely attractive Tanrian Marshal" her sister had been talking about.

"Okay," she agreed.

Nathan pulled his hand from his pocket but didn't seem to know where to put it. "Really?"

"Yeah, sounds good. Where to?"

His grin straightened, and he looked less like a weasel than usual. "I need to finish up a couple of things and clock out, but I can meet you in an hour. The Salt and Key?"

"See you there."

As she made her way to the Salt and Key to wait for Nathan, Mercy couldn't help but notice that she wasn't as happy about this change in circumstances as she ought to be.

Since she still had her copy of *Enemies and Lovers* in her purse, she got it out to read while she waited. Mercy had brought it with her to the Little Wren Café on Wardensday evening so that she could loan it to her friend, and she had planned to ask him what his favorite book was, and they could have gotten to know each other better through the books they loved. But her friend hadn't shown up, and now she had to figure out how to disassociate her favorite novel from a certain abhorrent Tanrian Marshal.

She flipped to one of the most famous scenes, the part where Eliza Canondale first realizes that Samuel Dunn is more than what he seems. Soon enough, Mercy was sucked into the story, the café disappearing around her as she lived and loved through the characters' eyes, which was why Nathan's arrival took her by surprise, despite the fact that she had been expecting him.

"You never get tired of that book, do you? How many times have you read it?"

Without waiting for her answer, he handed Mercy a bouquet of daisies, which she accepted graciously, even though she had never understood the point of giving a woman flowers. Maybe it was because of her profession, but she had always thought it strange to hand someone a bunch of plants that were already well on their way to their ultimate demise. Then again, he was trying, and it was nice to see Nathan trying on her behalf.

"So how's your mom?" she asked him, which led him to tell her a funny story about how his nephew recently lured a raccoon into his mother's kitchen with a freshly baked pie. At least, Nathan thought it was hilarious. Mercy thought it sounded fairly traumatic. From there, Nathan told her how his father was doing booming business at the new general store he had opened in Herington, how his sister wasn't a very good mother, and how his nephew seemed to be turning out well regardless, a sentiment with which Mercy privately disagreed. He talked about some interesting cases he'd handled over the past few months and how he was anticipating his promotion whenever Sheriff Connolly finally got around to retiring. Mercy's part in the conversation consisted primarily of "Oh" and "Really?" and the occasional (admittedly fake) "Ha ha ha!"

As she listened to Nathan talk about his job, she thought of her friend, of all the questions he had asked her about herself, how he had wanted to know as much about her as she wanted to know about him. Nathan hadn't so much as asked, "How are you?"

And he did resemble a weasel.

"Listen, Merc, I know this has been a long time coming, but I'm sorry about... well, about lying to you."

The air left her lungs in a *whoosh*. The hurt and humiliation of his cheating on her still rankled her, but if Nathan was ready to clear the air, she was glad to get it out of the way.

"Cheating on me, you mean?"

His face went from pink to scarlet. "Yeah."

"And for blaming it on me because you were lonely when I had to spend so much time taking care of my father after he almost died?"

He nodded slowly. "That, too."

Mercy considered him as he squirmed in his seat, nervous and jittery but earnest. She could see he meant it.

"So, apology accepted?"

"Yes. Apology accepted."

He laughed and ran his hands through his sandy hair. "Gods, what a relief! All these months, I didn't know what to do or say. You have no idea how hard it's been for me."

Mercy let loose an incredulous guffaw. "I might have had an inkling."

"This is great! Together again! What time should I pick you up tomorrow night?"

"Tomorrow night?"

"The Founders' Day party. It's a date, right?"

Mercy realized that he seemed to be confusing her acceptance of his apology with a welcome mat back into her life. The awkwardness was so visceral, it seemed to pull up a chair and order a drink.

"Nathan, I appreciate your apology, but I don't think we were meant to be."

"What are you talking about? We're great together."

"We're not, and you deserve to be with someone who's better suited to you."

"We've had one cup of coffee, and you're already dumping me again?"

"Would we call this 'dumping'?"

He wadded up his napkin and made a show of dropping it on the table. "I don't get it, Mercy. What more do you want from me?"

"I want to be with someone who asks me how my day was, someone who finds what I have to say interesting. I want to be with someone who thinks that—I don't know—that I'm kind of special. That's all."

Nathan puffed his lips as if Mercy had uttered the most unreasonable thing he'd ever heard.

"Thanks a lot!" she said.

"I'm not trying to be mean, but come on. Life isn't like those fluffy books you read. People don't sit around mooning over each other. This is reality, and in reality, you find someone you like and that you're attracted to, and you get married and you have a family, and that's all there is to it. It's that simple."

Mercy sagged in her chair. Maybe Nathan had a point. Maybe she was reaching too high and wanting too much. Maybe it was time to lower the bar and readjust her expectations. It wasn't like the population of western Bushong was bursting at the seams with available men in general, much less available men who showed any inclination to go out with her.

Nathan took her hand. "So, what do you say? Are we on for tomorrow night?"

Mercy almost said yes. The word balanced on the tip of her tongue, ready to walk the plank. But then she remembered something her friend wrote in one of his last letters.

I feel very strongly that you deserve a friend more worthy of you than I am in reality.

Maybe he hadn't shown up because he sincerely believed that he wasn't good enough for her. Maybe he hadn't shown up precisely because he thought she was kind of special. Mercy wanted a man who thought she was worth something, and that man clearly wasn't Nathan.

"I don't think so," she told him. She took her hand back and stood up to leave.

“Well, ‘I don’t think so’ isn’t ‘no,’ so I’m going to hold out hope for us.”

Mercy shook her head and left, wondering why he’d bother to hope for something he didn’t seem to want very much.

On Wardensday, Mercy did *not* argue with Hart Ralston.

Chapter Nineteen

On the morning following his disastrous showdown with Mercy at the Little Wren Café, Hart lay like a slug on his unforgiving hotel room bed in Mayetta with the curtains drawn, waiting for Duckers to show up with his autoduck. He wanted very much to be unconscious and tried to spend the morning asleep. When that didn't work, he tried to read his newest interlibrary loan—*Rabble-Rouser: The Federated Government and the First President*—but his mind kept drifting to Mercy and their letters to each other and his suffocating disappointment. He tossed the book onto the side table and attempted to clear his mind of all thought, but turning off his thoughts transformed him into a pile of throbbing, painful, wordless emotions, when feeling anything was the last thing he wanted to do.

Checkout time rolled around without any sign of Duckers, so Hart was forced to remove himself from the hotel bed that felt more like his bier than a place of rest and wait for his apprentice at the Little Wren Café, the place he least wanted to be. The only available table for lunch was the one at which Mercy had sat the night before, waiting for a friend who never came. He couldn't bear to sit in the chair he had occupied, so he took her seat instead, watching people come and go through the front door, which was somehow worse. He ordered tea and forced himself to choke down a BLT, his irritation with his apprentice ballooning by the second.

The door chimes tinkled Duckers's arrival around one o'clock. His swagger through the restaurant indicated his unpardonable happiness. How could Duckers be so delighted with one Birdsall when Hart was livid with another?

"You look miserable," Duckers chirped as he sat down at Hart's table and plucked the pickle from his plate.

"Order your own lunch."

"I had a late breakfast of eggs benedict with prosciutto and a blueberry muffin. There are serious benefits to dating a man who cooks." Duckers finished off the pickle and dried his vinegar-coated fingertips on the tablecloth. "So, about last night—"

"I give zero shits about your love life," Hart said, cutting him off before taking a bite out of a sandwich he didn't want.

"I'm not talking about my love life, sir. I'm talking about yours."

"Don't have one."

"Whose fault is that?"

"Don't want one."

"Are you seriously not going to talk to—"

"So help me gods, Duckers, if you utter that harpy's name, I will rip your balls off."

Hart paid his tab, and he and his apprentice drove through the desert scrub to the West Station. When the squat adobe building came into view with the Mist of Tanria shifting restlessly behind it, Hart felt his shoulders ease. This was what he needed: to get back to work and take his mind off the nightmare he had left behind him in Mayetta. But his shoulders tensed all over again when he checked the week's assignment board and saw that Duckers had been given checkpoint duty, while the words *Report to the chief's office* were written next to his name.

"Are you in trouble, sir?"

"I highly doubt it," he told Duckers, but whatever it was, he was in no mood to do anything other than his job. Five minutes later, he rapped on the office door, stepped inside when beckoned, and asked, "What the fuck, Alma?"

"And a good afternoon to you, too, Marshal."

He dropped into the chair across from her. "Sorry. What the fuck, *Chief Maguire*?"

She folded her hands over a stack of papers on her desk, as smug as a kid with an ice-cream cone. "Are you familiar with Legislative Bill B27-TL5?"

"No. Should I be?"

"Legislative Bill B27-TL5 passed last week and is effective immediately. It states that any federal employee accruing more than two hundred vacation days must take the surplus. Do you know how many vacation days you have accrued in the past nineteen years, Marshal Ralston, federal employee?"

Hart had no idea how many vacation days he had piled up, but he had a bad feeling about this. "Well, I'd have to check my records, but..."

Alma held up one of the documents on her desk. "Two hundred and seven."

"So?"

"So enjoy your vacation."

Hart was aware that most people looked forward to taking a vacation, but as seven days with nothing to do stretched before him, the word itself spelled his doom.

"I don't want to go on vacation," he whined—literally whined.

"Tough shit. Have fun!"

Denial bubbled inside him. All he wanted to do was lose himself in his job, and now he was going to have nothing but free time to fill with thoughts of the disaster that was Mercy.

"You're enjoying this too much, you cruel, cruel woman," he told Alma helplessly.

"Vacations are for enjoying. Enjoy yourself for a week, all right?"

He levered himself out of the chair and grumbled, "Great. Thanks."

"Oh, believe me, it is my pleasure."

Hart left Alma's office and walked aimlessly through the station, winding up in the parking lot beside his autoduck. Maybe a vacation wasn't a terrible idea. Maybe getting away from the familiarity of Tanria and Eternity—and Mercy—and taking a long drive over the sea was the best way for him to get his head on straight.

He filled up the gas tank in Herington, picked up his holds at the library, and hit the road, driving west until he came to the Great Western Sea, after which he cruised up the coast for another hour before exiting onto Seaway 95, heading to the Inner Islands. There was hardly any traffic, and the Great Western Sea opened up around him. He draped his forearm across the open window and let the ocean spray cool his skin. If only it would soothe the burning inside him, this pernicious emotion he could not name with accuracy. Disenchantment? Regret? Whatever it was, it accompanied him like an unwanted guest in his passenger seat.

He arrived on LeHunt Island by late afternoon. The beaches here were rocky, so it was the least touristy of the Inner Islands, which was why Hart had chosen it as his reluctant vacation destination. Most of the island was a federal waterbird preserve, so at least he wouldn't have to worry about interacting with people. He could be alone with his turmoil in the tent he pitched inland.

As the sun set, he walked to the shore and watched the sea roll in and out, its whispered undulation like the heartbeat of the Mother of Sorrows. The infinity of gray-blue water reminded him of his friend's letter, how she had looked up at the night sky and felt a part of something bigger than herself.

It wasn't a friend who wrote that letter, he reminded himself with a fresh surge of the unnamed emotion he couldn't shake.

Mercy had gone to her father's house that night and had touched her mother's key with salt water on her fingertips. Hart had no desire to emulate her, but as he watched the waves billow in and out, feeling adrift in his own skin, he dipped his fingers into the salty water and touched his mother's key over his sore heart.

In the days that followed, he haunted the island like a ghost, wandering along the beach, letting the wind buffet him, tousle his hair, whip his shirt against his skin. He wanted to feel something—anything—other than the despondency that had taken hold of him and refused to let go. He tried to read, but he had neither the attention nor the appetite for books, and the more he was left to his own devices without his job to anchor his thoughts, the more his mind was free to go ferreting about the darkest places inside him. He had come here to escape from Mercy, but as the week trickled by and he did his best to push all thoughts of her to the side, he wound up slamming into his memory of Bill and all the remorse that came with it. He tried to grasp onto the happy times he had spent with his mentor, but as night crept in, it was Bill's death that gnawed at him in the darkness.

By Wisdomsday, he itched to go... home? But he had no home. He thought of the Mist swirling beyond the West Station and said to himself, *That shithole is your home. How sad is that?* Regardless, he had already packed his bag, preparing to drive back to Bushong early, when a nimkilim cleared her throat outside his tent and announced, "Mail delivery."

A letter! Hart thought out of instinct as he stepped outside, and then his knee-jerk hope came crashing to the ground as he remembered: *From Mercy.*

The nimkilim, a pelican in a starched white shirt, opened her beak and plucked the envelope from the stack therein, presenting it to Hart with an efficient flick of her wing. Hart was tempted to find out what would happen if he refused delivery, but the magnetic pull of a new letter was too ingrained in him to resist. He fished in his pocket for a tip and accepted the letter. The words *To: A Friend* were written on the front of the envelope as they always were, in the same graceful handwriting he had come to cherish.

He set the letter on his bare cot, sat on the other end, and stared at the unopened symbol of his unfinished business with Mercy. His whole life was like this letter, a series of goodbyes that never happened, a line from his past to his present that he could draw in his mind with a thick-nibbed pen from his mother to Bill to Gracie to Mercy.

He didn't need a vacation. He needed to put the past behind him once and for all.

Hart drove to Bushong and sneaked into Tanria, which is to say, he entered through the northern checkpoint rather than the West Station so that Alma wouldn't know what he was up to. He wasn't thrilled to discover that Saltlicker—his least favorite stallion—had wound up at the North Station and was the only mount available.

"Typical," he told the equimaris, who gurgled in surly agreement.

He rode south to Sector W-43, worried that he wouldn't be able to find Gracie's grave after more than four years, but as it turned out, he could never forget where he'd buried her. The stone cairn was still there, though not as tidy as he had left it. At least the untidiness was the result of the ground shifting over time, not scavengers trying to dig their way in.

He pictured his dog in his mind—her liquid brown eyes, her crooked ears, her mouth a smile outlined in black fur. He remembered the bristly texture of her fur beneath his hand, the way she snorted in her sleep, and his tears welled up, strong and fast. Out here, where no one could see him, he let them fly.

"Well, Gracie," he said with a sad, shaky laugh, "I was a mess before, but I've made a pig's ear of my life since you left me."

If she had been alive, she would have flopped down beside him and propped her head on his thigh and sighed as he stroked her between her adorable ears. He pulled a handkerchief from his pocket and blew his nose before patting the stones over Gracie's grave. It was not as hard as he had thought it would be to say goodbye to her, or rather, his farewell to his dog came with as much comfort as bereavement. He didn't anticipate the same catharsis for his next stop.

He remounted Saltlicker and rode to the ridge overlooking Sector 28 with nothing but the slap and suck of the equimaris's webbed feet against the pink mossy earth to keep him company. Below him, the whitewashed farmhouse with the blue front door sat in the center of a blanket of ruddy grasses and gray wildflowers, the house that no one but Hart could see. Dozens of souls—again, something no one else could see—drifted nearby.

He had known that he could see human souls long before he came to Tanria. By the time he was eight and watched his grandfather's spirit leave his body, he knew that he was different in a way that was somewhat good but mostly not so good. After that, Mom was all he had, the two of them living in the old house with the blue door in central Arvonia.

The same house that, inexplicably, stood below him in this field in the middle of Tanria.

When Hart was eighteen, and he and Bill had come across this field for the first time, when he saw his own house here in Tanria—a house that Bill could not see—he told his mentor everything, about the house *and* the souls. A year later, Bill died because of it. That was why Hart stood here now, overlooking the spot where he had watched Bill's soul depart his body.

Where he had done more than simply watch.

Hart did not think he was the offspring of one of the death gods. Most demigods displayed gifts that had nothing to do with their divine parent. Alma was a perfect example. Her mother was a water spirit, but her gift was the ability to start a fire and snuff it out again with her bare hands. And yet while Hart's parentage remained a mystery, his gift did not. He could see the souls of the departed, and once, he had watched one of those lights—Bill's light—open the door to that house in the middle of Sector 28 and go inside.

During his time with the Tanrian Marshals, Hart had saved many lives, but none of them counterbalanced what had happened to Bill. Everything about Bill was unfinished business, and Hart had no idea how to go about finishing it. He didn't think he could. All he could do was stand here and make himself stare at the spot where his beloved mentor had lost his life. Because of Hart.

The western sky turned orange, then pink, then indigo, but Hart stayed put, reluctant to leave this place for once. He picketed the stallion, taking pains to secure the reins so the stubborn asshole wouldn't abandon him to go off in search of water. Then he built his campfire and brewed a pot of strong black tea and heated up a tin of beans and ate some canned peaches, the same meal he had eaten with Bill countless times. He had said goodbye to Gracie, and he had at least tried to put to rest his guilt over Bill's death, albeit unsuccessfully. Now it was time to bid one more adieu.

He sat on his heels and dug around in his rucksack for the packet of letters, bundled together with twine. *A relationship made of letters makes us little more than paper dolls*, she had once written, and she was right. Their friendship had been nothing more than paper, and paper burned with ease. He held the letters over the fire and was about to drop them into the flames when he realized that Mercy's last letter remained wrinkled and unopened in his pocket.

Don't read it, he told himself. *Let it burn and be done with it.*

But he reasoned that he ought to bundle it in with the others so that he could toss them into the flames all at once. He undid the twine, meaning to do just that, but some force that was in no way related to his brain caused him to reach instead for the first letter Mercy had written to him. He read it, even though he already knew the words by heart.

Dear friend,

Apparently, I exist, because your letter has found me, although I don't know how or why.

It read differently this time. Now he heard Mercy's voice in his head, her musical manner of speaking, the way the words flew up and down the spoken register as if she were singing.

He read the next letter and the next, and Mercy filled his head like a symphony in a concert hall.

A tiny part of me does want to know where you work, what you look like, how old you are—you see, I refuse to lie to you—because those things are a part of who you are, too.

He couldn't stop himself. He was like a thirsty man with a fire hose. Every letter was Mercy's voice; Mercy's words; Mercy in a yellow dress; Mercy with sawdust in her hair; Mercy holding a mug of coffee (splash of milk, no sugar); Mercy, who had lost her mother, too; Mercy, who smiled at everyone but him.

I have faith that our friendship can exist beyond these letters, despite all the faults and weaknesses of our flesh-and-blood selves, which is why I want to meet you, to know you better.

He saw her sitting alone at a table, watching the door of the Little Wren Café, waiting for a friend who never showed up. Except he had shown up. She simply hadn't seen him.

And had he really seen her? For years, he had convinced himself that she was fake, that no one who worked with the dead for a living could be so alive and contented—that no one in general could put that much life and joy into the world—but these letters in his hands were real, and those dimples were real, and that woman who looked death in the eye but still found a reason to sing in the bathtub was real. And he wanted to know her better, no matter the faults and weaknesses of her flesh-and-blood self. He was beginning to believe that she didn't have as many as he had thought, while the gods knew he had more than enough faults and weaknesses for the both of them.

He pulled her last letter from his pocket and opened it.

Dear friend,

I have something to tell you: My name is Mercy Birdsall.

I'm very tall, and not in the willowy way. I have dark brown hair and olive skin and brown eyes, and I wear red glasses. My favorite color is yellow. I wear it a lot.

I'm an undertaker, or, at least, I have been for the past few months. I salt bodies and wrap them in sailcloth and sing the incantations over them. I build boats for the dead and send them where they need to go. I love what I do, helping souls find rest in the House of the Unknown God, and comforting the living in the process.

My father's name is Roy. My sister's name is Lilian. My brother's name is Zeddie. My brother-in-law is Danny. Lil is about to have a baby, and I'm so excited about it I can hardly see straight. I love them all more than anything in the world.

I don't know why you didn't come to the Little Wren Café last Wardensday, so now I'm trying to show you who I am the only way I know how, and you can decide for yourself what you think of me—the real me. Because I want to know the real you. Even if we can't meet in person, I want to know who you are: your name, what you do, what you look like, what you care about, who you love.

Forgive me if this sounds cruel or harsh or demanding, but if you can't bring yourself to tell me your name or to show your true self to me, please don't write back. Because anything less isn't true friendship.

Sincerely,
Mercy

P.S.—I miss you.

Hart stared at her name, at the way she put herself out there, risking the pain and rejection that might come along with it. Did he have the courage to stand in front of her and say, "This is who I am"? The prospect sounded terrifying. But then he read the postscript again, and it echoed inside him until he didn't know if it was Mercy's voice or his own saying the words.

I miss you.

He missed her.

He missed Mercy Birdsall, who had somehow, miraculously, become his friend.

He took out a pen and paper from his pack but put it away as quickly. Mercy deserved an answer, and a letter would no longer suffice.

Hart expected to toss and turn as he camped out under the stars with a pistol crossbow under his pillow, but he slept soundly. The following morning, he took one last glimpse at the field below and murmured "I'm sorry, Bill" before he packed up and rode Saltlicker to the portal at the North Station with the morning sun and the determination to finish some unfinished business lighting his way.

Chapter Twenty

It was an hour's drive from the North Station to Eternity, so Hart should have had ample time to consider what he wanted to say to Mercy. But by the time he turned off onto the exit, he was a nervous wreck, and the fact that there wasn't a parking space to be had anywhere near Birdsall & Son did nothing to assuage him. The reason for this predicament became clear when he saw the banner stretched over Main Street.

Mayor Ginsberg courteously invites you to celebrate
FOUNDERS' DAY: 25 YEARS OF ETERNITY!
Petting zoo! Equimaris rides! Barbecue dinner!
Dancing under the stars! Fireworks display!

Hart cursed his bad luck. If Birdsall & Son was closed, he'd have to wait until after his next two-week shift to talk to Mercy, which sounded like an excruciatingly long time.

He caught his reflection in the rearview mirror and rubbed the stubble he should have shaved off this morning. There was nothing he could do about it now, but he could at least comb his hair. He did his best to make himself presentable, and got out of the duck before he could lose his nerve.

The crowded boardwalk made him feel like a cow in a cattle pen on his way to the slaughter. The sounds of children squealing atop miniature equimares and the bleating of goats and sheep at the petting zoo added to the doomed-livestock effect. He'd barely taken three steps in the direction of Birdsall & Son when the city hall bell began to ring, and everyone around him froze. The cacophony of moments ago evaporated; all but the goats and sheep went silent.

"A drudge drill? Now?" a gangly boy whined, but his mother grabbed his hand and shushed him.

"It's not a drill!"

Shrieks and cries from somewhere down the street pierced the air, and Hart's years of experience in the Tanrian Marshals kicked in. He sprinted to his duck for his belt and strapped it on as he ran toward the commotion.

"No running!" someone shouted at him, but he paid no attention. Seconds later, he spotted the rogue drudge, badly decayed, shambling down Main Street on the next block, heading straight for a woman who stood on the curb outside Birdsall & Son, her yellow skirt like a bright beacon on the dusty street.

Mercy.

He surged forward, drawing the pistol crossbow from his belt. The drudge was seven feet in front of her when he took his first shot, knowing the odds of hitting its appendix were slim to none at this distance. It paused as if it were confused. Then it refocused its attention on her and limped closer.

Six feet.

Five.

It lunged.

"Please," Hart prayed to any god who would listen, and he fired.

The drudge jerked, then collapsed at Mercy's feet. Hart ran as fast as his long legs would carry him as the amber light of the soul that had possessed the body oozed out of the wound and soared toward Tanria.

Seconds later, Hart was standing over the drudge, unsheathing his rapier and jabbing down and down and down until he was beyond certain the thing was dead, and he rolled it away from Mercy with the heel of his boot. She stood unmoving in front of him, but her eyes were alive with terror, boring into his. The bell was still ringing when Hart dropped his weapons and reached for her, taking her face into his trembling hands.

"Mercy?" Her name was a sob in his mouth.

Her eyes drifted to the body in the street.

"Did it hurt you?" Hart asked her.

Begged her.

She met his eyes again and shook her head. Hart realized that he was touching her face, and snatched his hands away, his emotions a turbid mixture of embarrassment and fear and relief. He turned away from her to see if there were any more drudges on the loose, but Mercy grabbed frantically for his arm, as if she were terrified that he would leave her. He stiffened awkwardly beneath her touch, then placed what he hoped was a comforting hand over her chilled fingers. "It's okay. I promise."

Her face remained ghastily colorless, but she nodded and released him. He turned toward the street, taking in the slain drudge, the gawking onlookers, and two deputies running toward the scene. One of them put a possessive hand on Mercy's upper arm once he'd reached them, and said, "Mercy? What happened?"

Hart's vision went red. "You call yourselves deputies? How the fuck did you manage to let a drudge shamble halfway down Main Street?"

The second deputy panted over the corpse before he answered. "We've never had a drudge in Eternity before. We're nearly fifteen miles from the Tanrian border. I don't know how it could have gotten here."

The first deputy was calmer and more professional, but he still had his hand on Mercy's arm. Hart stared at the spot where skin met skin and felt very strongly that this man needed to stop touching Mercy. Now. He gritted his teeth as Deputy Handsy explained the situation.

"We had a report that there was a drudge on the loose at Clem Crenshaw's farm, a half mile outside of town. A rogue drudge sighting around these parts generally turns out to be a drifter or a kid playing a prank, but we always take this sort of thing seriously."

"It was a drudge, right there in Crenshaw's cabbages!" the other deputy cut in. "Dead as dead can be, waltzing around in broad daylight!"

"We took it down, then went to Cunningham's to arrange for its collection. But we got the appendix. I know we did."

"Obviously, you didn't," Hart snapped, his tone so sharp he was surprised the men weren't bleeding.

By now, the sheriff had jostled his way through the crowd. "Brewer, McDevitt, get this cleaned up, and then you can explain yourselves in my office," he ordered his deputies.

"And the body goes to Birdsall & Son, not Cunningham's," Hart added.

Out of the corner of his eye, he saw Mercy put a hand to her cheek and sway on her feet. He caught her under the elbow before her knees gave out, since Deputy Handsy wasn't paying attention and nearly let her fall over. "Hey now, Merciless, you're all right," he told her softly.

"That... It... And I was..." Her words sounded like they were being pressed through a laundry mangle.

"Come on. Let's get you inside."

"I'll take her," the man with his hand on Mercy volunteered, and Hart wished there were dragons in Tanria so that he could chop off this incompetent asshole's arm and feed it to one of them.

"No, *I'll* take her. *You* do your job."

The man shrank away, leaving Hart free to usher Mercy home.

"You're going to have to file a report, Marshal," the sheriff called after him.

"I'll be down after I see to Ms. Birdsall."

He didn't wait for permission to escort her to the front door of Birdsall & Son, which was blessedly unlocked. He got her into the lobby and deposited her into one of the armchairs. Leonard hopped off the neighboring chair and leaped onto her lap.

"Mr. Birdsall?" Hart hollered as he pushed the dog to the floor.

Roy Birdsall stuck his head out of the office, his glasses propped perplexingly on top of his eyebrows, and Mercy burst into tears at the sight of him. Hart nearly dropped to his knees to comfort her, but then he remembered that he had no right to do any such thing, and Roy beat him to the punch anyway, his knees popping as he knelt beside his daughter.

"Muffin, what happened?"

Not wanting to be an interloper, Hart made his way to the kitchenette and made himself useful. He could hear Mercy spilling the whole story in a sob-filled storm to her father as he put on the kettle and dug through the well-ordered cabinets. He found a mug, a tin of black tea, a jar of honey, and a bowl of lemons. Leave it to Mercy to keep lemons on hand in case a squeeze in a cup of tea or a glass of water might bring someone comfort.

He could not erase the image of her standing on the curb, her lemon-yellow skirt fluttering in the wind as he fired the second shot the moment he thought he had already failed.

The kettle began to whistle.

Pull it together, he told himself, gripping the edge of the countertop. When he was steady enough to take the kettle off the hob, he poured the steaming water over a tea bag, after which he stuck his head into the lobby, directing his gaze at Roy.

"Birdsall, got any whiskey?"

Roy glanced guiltily at his daughter before answering, "My desk in the office. Bottom drawer, at the back."

Hart's hands wouldn't stop shaking. Thank gods he had something useful to occupy them. He found the illicit whiskey bottle and poured a healthy dollop into the steaming cup of tea and honey and lemon juice in the kitchenette, Bill's recipe for "medicine." Hart was tempted to pour two or three fingers of whiskey for himself but thought better of it. Mercy was the one who needed comfort right now, not him.

He brought the cup into the lobby and helped Mercy to wrap her fingers around the handle, making sure she had a good hold on it before he let go.

"Drink up, but take it slow," he advised her, his voice alien and calm, mismatching the cyclone inside him.

"Oh!" she cheeped in surprise after the first drink. Hart watched the color seep back into her cheeks and lips with each sip, but then he had to resign himself to the fact that he no longer had a legitimate reason to stay. He would have to come clean about the letters another time.

"I'll get out of your hair. You're all right?"

"Honestly, I'm not sure," Mercy answered weakly. For the first time in over four years, Hart saw something other than hate in her eyes, which made his chest bloat with a painful yet oddly pleasant ache.

"You will be," he assured her, and he left before Roy felt the need to creak to his feet or shake his hand.

Hart felt jittery as he headed for city hall to find the sheriff's office. He needed to file a report about the drudge incident, but every stride that took him away from Mercy felt like a step in the wrong direction. There was nothing for it, however, so ten minutes later, he sat across from Sheriff Connolly at a dinged-up metal desk, jiggling his feet, wishing he could be alone with his thoughts for a few minutes. He answered the sheriff's thorough questions and was unspeakably relieved when the man finally set down his pen and said, "I think I've got all I need, Marshal. I'll be in touch if I have more questions for you."

Hart practically shouted "Thank you" as he leaped to his feet to escape.

The sheriff got to his feet, too, and shook Hart's hand, but he didn't let go right away. "How do you like marshaling?"

"It's a living." Hart glanced down at the Handshake That Would Not End.

"Is it? A living? Because it seems to me there's a lot of dying involved." The sheriff released his hand, and when he spoke again, his tone was casual and chatty. "Around here, we deal with petty theft, grievances, public safety, that kind of thing, but our primary focus is on service to the community. We work reasonable hours. Our deputies go home at the end of their shifts and spend time with their friends and family. Don't suppose you'd consider a move from federal to local law enforcement?"

So this was recruitment. It felt strange to be courted, but at least it was a welcome distraction from the confusion and fluster of his heart. "Hadn't crossed my mind," Hart said.

"Your experience would be welcome here, and you could do a lot worse than settling down in a place like Eternity. You think about that." The sheriff slapped Hart on the shoulder in friendly dismissal.

"I will. Thank you."

By the time Hart stepped out into the glaring sunlight, his boots clomping on the boardwalk, he didn't know which way he should be heading. The fact that another drudge had escaped Tanria, probably through a pirated portal, should have inspired him to return to the station to investigate, plus he needed to get ready for work in the morning. But he badly wanted to see Mercy before he left, wanted to talk to her one more time, wanted to make sure she was okay. And as he read the banner advertising the Founders' Day celebration, he was pretty sure he knew where he could find her tonight.

A sudden wave of nausea overtook him. He turned and stumbled through the city hall lobby again and careened into the men's room. The faucet handle squeaked as he turned on the tap. He cupped his hands under the stream and splashed cold water on his face until the nausea subsided, and he turned off the tap with another rusty squeal. The hand towel he clutched to his face smelled faintly of bleach, but he kept it there longer than was necessary, because he already knew what he would see in his reflection in the mirror over the sink. He hung the towel on its peg anyway and looked himself in the eye. There it was, a truth so evident that it may as well have been painted on his forehead in red letters.

He was helplessly, boundlessly, stupidly in love with Mercy Birdsall.

Chapter Twenty-One

A near-death experience was all it took to make Mercy's family forgive her for keeping secrets, as Zeddie illustrated when he tackled his sister on her settee.

"Get off her, you oaf!" Lilian scolded him, only to crush Mercy herself as soon as she'd shoved their brother onto the floor.

"I think they're glad you're alive," said Danny, eating a slice of the coconut cake that Zeddie had brought over.

"I won't be alive for much longer if Lil doesn't get her pregnant butt off me."

"Is that a fat joke? Rude."

Normally, the Birdsall family would gather at Pop's house for a special occasion—such as a celebration of the fact that Mercy had not been murdered by a drudge—but today, everyone came to Mercy, crowding into her apartment like sardines in a can. She thought of her friend lamenting the fact that he was lonely, when at this moment, she wanted nothing more in the world than to be alone. While every Birdsall but Mercy ate cake and filled the small parlor with talking and laughter, she sneaked into the bathroom for respite. Sadly, Pop's prostate had demands, and soon enough, he was knocking on the door and asking, "Almost done in there, muffin?"

The second she came out, Lil sidled up to her as Danny and Zeddie discussed various ways to prepare egg dishes. "How does it feel to have your life saved by your nemesis?" she asked, arching an eyebrow suggestively as she jabbed a huge bite of cake into her mouth.

"I haven't given it much thought," Mercy lied. In fact, she could think of nothing else. Her brain was now entirely dedicated to the expression on Hart Ralston's face when he'd reached her, the intensity that had been drawn in every line and muscle, the way he'd touched her cheeks, his fingers hot against her skin. It was as if he had ceased to be Hart-ache and had become someone else entirely.

It was all so disorienting.

"I don't think I'm up for the Founders' Day party tonight," she told Lil.

"Pish. It'll get your mind off everything. Dr. Lilian says so."

"Dr. Lilian" was relentlessly persuasive, and after a half hour of her sister's wheedling, Mercy caved and let her family drag her across the street to the festivities. But while the Birdsalls arrived as a group, they quickly scattered to the winds. Pop was immediately summoned to sit at the table with the men who argued about sea polo without ceasing. Zeddie threw his arms around two friends from school and whisked them away to the bar. Lilian and Danny headed straight for the buffet table, where Danny held two plates so that his wife could heap a staggering amount of fried chicken and potato salad onto them. Abandoned and alone, Mercy was defenseless against her neighbors and acquaintances, who stopped her every step along the way to the buffet table, begging her to recount the drudge attack again and again. If "Dr. Lilian" had believed that being here tonight would take Mercy's mind off her near-death experience, she had sadly misdiagnosed the situation.

Eventually, Twyla Banneker came to Mercy's rescue, handing her a paper plate loaded with food. "I'd ask you how you're doing, but I suspect half the town has already made you recount every harrowing detail of your ordeal."

"That about sums up my evening so far."

"I sent Frank to get you a drink and told him that he wasn't allowed to talk to you about anything other than the weather."

"Bless you."

Twyla Banneker and Frank Ellis were Mercy's favorite marshals. Middle aged and down to earth, they were partners in Tanria and next-door neighbors in Eternity, the sort of best friends who came as a matching set, as if they were attached by hyphens: Twyla-and-Frank.

Mercy tucked into her pasta salad as she awaited her drink, but nearly choked on the macaroni when she noticed Hart Ralston's unmistakable form looming at the edge of the gathering. Her mind whirred into a panic. Should she talk to him? Thank him? Hide under a rock? Hug him? No, she definitely should not hug him, although she wanted to, which was strange and unsettling.

As she contemplated how to handle a post-drudge encounter with the man who had saved her life, she caught sight of Zeddie inching toward him. A second later, her brother pounced on her savior and hugged him around the waist, and Hart went rigid as a flagpole in Zeddie's embrace.

"Oh my gods," Mercy said, setting her plate on a table as her appetite ran for the hills. She watched in horror as her father and Lil materialized out of the crowd to join her brother in humiliating her. Lilian pulled Zeddie off Hart so she could get in her own hug, while Pop grabbed the marshal's hand and pumped it like an autoduck jack. Hart looked horrified, as if a cluster of drudges had attacked him rather than the Birdsall family.

Twyla cackled. "I'm sorry, but Hart Ralston's face right now is priceless."

"This is so embarrassing, it's almost physically painful."

"Bless his heart, he stands out like a red velvet dinner jacket at a funeral. No wonder he never goes to parties. I'm shocked to see him here, honestly."

Mercy couldn't bear to watch one more second of the mortifying scene playing out on the other side of the Founders' Day celebration, so she turned to Twyla. "What's he like? I mean, when he's on duty. Does he get along with the other marshals?"

"In a manner of speaking. He's not what you'd call friendly, but he's excellent at his job, the sort who's always got your back. People respect him."

"I'm glad he had my back today," Mercy admitted. It was an unexpected relief to say it out loud, like fessing up to a mistake.

Frank arrived and declared "Beautiful weather we're having" as he handed Mercy a glass of lemonade, making her laugh despite her family's exuberant fawning over Hart.

"Thanks, Frank. Cheers."

"Oh no," said Twyla, frowning over Mercy's shoulder. "Liz Brimsby is heading this way. Ask her to dance, Frank, before she corners Mercy again."

Frank handed Twyla his drink. "I'm a wonderful human being," he informed her.

"You truly are."

He slapped a smile on his face and made the interception. "Lizzie, darlin', cut a rug with me."

Liz took his arm with a delighted giggle. Half of the over-forty population of Eternity was in love with Frank Ellis and his long silver-streaked black hair, but he had no clue.

"And now Bob and Eugene are edging this way," said Twyla. "You poor thing, they're like sharks circling blood in the water. I'll take care of this. You go hide. Once people have had a few more drinks, I'm sure they'll leave you alone so you can enjoy the party in peace."

"Thanks, Twyla."

"You bet." Twyla stepped between Mercy and two of Eternity's biggest gossips so that Mercy could make a run for it. "Is that your apple pie on the buffet table, Eugene? I swear, you make the flakiest crust."

Mercy abandoned her lemonade and feigned a course for the ladies' room, which allowed her to abscond unnoticed to the outer limits of the park behind city hall, where the party lights didn't quite reach. She sat on a picnic table, rested her feet on the bench, and drank in the serenity of being quiet and alone for however long it lasted.

It didn't last long, because five minutes later, Hart Ralston crossed the park and found her where she sat in the shadows. Bizarrely, he was the one person whose company she didn't mind at the moment, even though the air crackled around them with visceral awkwardness.

"Hi," he said, standing so high over her seated position that she practically had to lie down on the picnic table to see his dimly lit face. The man's height never failed to stun her. She thought she knew how tall he was, but then she'd see him in the flesh and think, *Mother of Sorrows, he's tall.*

"Hi," she answered, feeling more like a gawky fourteen-year-old than a full-grown woman.

He tilted his head toward the party. "I wanted to talk to you over there, but I couldn't get anywhere near you."

"Because half the town mobbed me?"

"And the other half mobbed me."

"The other half being my family. Sorry about that."

"No worries."

Mercy knew she ought to say something, but her mind wouldn't stop reliving the events of the morning: the drudge, Hart's face, the feel of his hands on her cheeks, the way his fingers had wrapped around hers until he was certain she had hold of the cup. She didn't know what to make of it. Of him.

"Anyway," he said, "I thought I ought to check on you before I head back to Tanria. Make sure you were all right."

"I am. Thank you."

He nodded.

"Are you here for the party, then?" She inwardly cringed at her feeble attempt to make small talk.

"Sort of."

"No offense, but you don't strike me as the partying type."

It wouldn't be accurate to say that Hart smiled, but his lips quirked up, and the corners of his eyes turned to crow's feet, a hint that some form of happiness or humor resided within him.

"There's a reason I'm over here and not over there," he said.

She tried to smile at him, but it came out more like a grimace. Hiding under a rock was beginning to sound like an excellent idea.

Hart batted the spiky seedpod of a sweetgum tree with the side of his boot. "I was on my way to see you today when the drudge got loose."

"To drop off a body?"

"No. I wanted to apologize for that night at the Little Wren Café. I was an ass to you, and I'm sorry. And I was an ass to you the last time I dropped off a body. And most of the times before that, too, so... I apologize. For all of it."

This was the second unexpected apology she had received in the past thirty-six hours, but unlike Nathan's, Hart's regrets didn't seem to come with any strings attached. Once again, her perception of the universe turned on its axis.

"I haven't exactly been a ray of sunshine to you either," she admitted. "Besides, I should be groveling at your feet in gratitude right now."

Hart toyed with the sweetgum ball at his feet. "Just doing my job."

"Well, it's a terrifying job."

"You get used to it."

"*You* get used to it."

He stiffened.

"That wasn't an insult," Mercy amended. "I'm trying to thank you. So thank you."

"You don't have to thank me. Trust me."

"Too bad. I'm thanking you anyway. I can't believe you do that for a living. I definitely couldn't."

"Most people couldn't do what you do either."

She could tell he meant it as a compliment, and it made her face flush.

"There's something else." His voice cut off, as if he had intended to add more words to the end of the sentence.

"Something else?" she prompted when the proposed *something else* wasn't forthcoming.

"Would you like to dance?" he blurted.

She gaped at him in disbelief, the heat of her cheeks expanding down her neck.

"You want to dance?" she asked, because she was certain that she hadn't heard him correctly.

"Yep."

"With me?"

"If you want to."

"Who are you, and what have you done with my Hart-ache?"

He kicked the sweetgum ball and watched it bounce off the trunk of a tree. "I guess that's a no."

But Mercy was not about to lose the opportunity to dance with a man who was taller than she was, especially one who had made sure she didn't die that day. "You guessed wrong. That was a yes."

The crow's feet reappeared, and Mercy suspected that he was biting the inside of his cheek to stop himself from smiling, which was, if she was being perfectly honest with herself, endearing. He held out his hand, and she took it, willing her palm to refrain from pumping sweat into the spot where she was joined to him as he pulled her to the outskirts of the dance floor. She couldn't remember the last time a man had held her hand—Nathan wasn't a fan of the practice—and she had forgotten how much she enjoyed the touch of masculine sinew and bone and skin.

The band was playing a love song, the peppy sort, with the plunking rhythm of a banjo and the joyous tinkling of a piano in a major key and the drums pounding out the beating of a heart in love. Hart put his hand on Mercy's waist—firm and solid, warming her skin through the thin fabric of her blouse—and he guided her into an easy two-step, a thousand times more graceful than she would have expected for a man of his height. He spun her out and turned her back into him, and now he was holding her closer. A shocked laugh burbled out of her.

"You're a good dancer!"

"Surprised?"

"Very!"

"Maybe there are some things you don't know about me, Merciless."

He turned himself behind her back, sliding her from hand to hand in front of him.

"Am I crazy, or are we having fun right now?" she marveled.

"I'm not really the fun type."

"The jury is still out on that. Would it be inappropriate of me to thank you for being taller than I am?"

Something resembling a laugh escaped his mouth. "Not at all. Thank you for being tall enough for me to dance with you on my feet rather than on my knees."

"Was that a joke? Do I spy a smile on your face?"

He was definitely biting the inside of his cheek now. "Nope."

"Your mouth turned upward for half a second. I saw it."

"Probably indigestion."

"Or evidence of mild joy. Someone hand me a paper bag. I'm hyperventilating from the shock of it."

"You're not helping your 'Hart Ralston is fun' argument here."

"Then prove me wrong."

His face broke into a grin so genuine and surprising that Mercy felt as if someone had shaken up a bottle of root beer and opened it inside her in a fizzy explosion. His eyes glinting with mischief, he backed his way toward the middle of the dance floor, shaking his hips from side to side as he pulled Mercy with him.

"I can't believe what I'm seeing!" she laughed. *And wow, those hips*, she thought as he spun her out into a basket-whip step.

Right into the arms of Nathan McDevitt.

"Whoa there, tiger," Nathan said as he caught Mercy and gave Hart a smile full of strained bonhomie, reaching out to shake his hand. "Marshal Ralston, I didn't get a chance to thank you for saving my girl earlier today."

"Your girl?" Mercy said, indignant, but neither of the men seemed to hear her.

Hart's grin vanished. He had had no problem laying into Nathan over a drudge on Main Street, but now that Mercy's ex-boyfriend had rudely interrupted their dance, his demeanor drained of self-assurance. "Oh. Right. Sure thing."

"I'll take it from here, Marshal," Nathan told him, and then he whisked Mercy off to the other side of the dance floor.

"What do you think you're doing?" she protested.

"A marshal, Mercy? They're not exactly known for healthy, long-term relationships."

She pulled herself free of his grasp. "What's it to you? I am not 'your girl.' We are not dating."

"Well, I don't think you're dating Ralston either, because I've never seen a man exit a dance floor that fast. I'm here, and he's gone, so what are you going to do? Make a fool of yourself and go running after your demigod hero?"

The music blared, and couples laughed and danced around her, but from Mercy's perspective, the world stilled. She tallied up Hart's words and actions over the course of the past several hours, and none of them figured into the man she had summed up over four years ago. Today, he had come to her rescue, escorted her home after a drudge nearly killed her, made her a cup of doctored tea, and asked her to dance when he found her alone at a party, after tracking her down for the specific purpose of apologizing to her.

It was the apology that rattled her the most, that made her wonder if she'd never had him figured out at all. She had called him arrogant the day they met, but an arrogant man apologized to obtain absolution. A *good* man admitted his errors and expected nothing in return. Now Mercy had a burning desire to find out whether or not Hart Ralston was a good man.

"You know what? Running after my demigod hero is exactly what I'm going to do," she told Nathan, and throwing caution to the wind, she bolted from the dance floor.

"But—but, Mercy!"

"And I hope you don't get that stupid promotion!" she shouted over her shoulder as she left.

Chapter Twenty-Two

She ran toward Main Street, the clicking of her heels growing louder the farther she got from the noise of the party, until she skidded to a stop on the boardwalk and spotted Hart's shadowy, lanky silhouette. *Up*hill. Of course.

"Infuriating man," she muttered as she hoofed up the boardwalk, pathetically out of breath within seconds.

He turned toward the sound of her clacking shoes, but by the time she reached him, she was breathing too hard to speak.

"What's wrong?" he said, and Mercy caught a glimpse of the concern and alarm she'd seen when he'd taken her face in his hands after slaying the drudge that morning.

"What's wrong?" She threw her hands into the air and panted. "You rescue me from a drudge, but you ditch me on the dance floor with that weasel?"

"I thought he was your boyfriend."

"*Ex*-boyfriend."

"Oh." He considered this. "He does resemble a weasel."

"He *is* a weasel."

"Sorry." Hart stuffed his fists into his pockets and wore a face as guilt ridden as Leonard's that time he managed to get onto the kitchen counter and eat the last two fancy chocolates left in the box that Pop had given her for her twenty-ninth birthday.

"What is happening here? One minute you hate my guts, and the next minute, you're dancing with me like we're..." She waved her hand at him as if whatever she wanted to say was written all over the front of his shirt. "Why are you being nice to me all of a sudden?"

"Maybe the better question to ask is, why were we so mean to each other to begin with?"

"I don't know!" Her voice was so shrill that a dog barked in the distance.

Hart frowned at the toes of his boots, and while Mercy didn't know what exactly she had intended to do once she had caught up to him, she was fairly certain this was not it. She tried a more peaceful tack.

"Do you like cake?"

Hart blinked at her. "Cake?"

"Coconut cake."

"Yes?" he answered doubtfully.

"Oh, good. I was afraid you were one of those horrible men who don't have a sweet tooth and never eat desserts."

"I am horrible, but I like cake."

Mercy clutched her skirt, as if the cotton could infuse her with bravery. "Would you like a slice of coconut cake?"

"Is this a hypothetical question?"

"No, there's a literal coconut cake waiting for me at home. Zeddie brought it over to cheer me up this afternoon, and I haven't had any yet."

"You're inviting me over for cake?"

"Yes."

"Now?"

"Yes." Mercy's poor skirt was going to be as wrinkled as her great-aunt Hester by the time she was through with it.

Hart's shy reticence made inexplicably fluttery things happen behind Mercy's breastbone. "All right," he said, and the flutter inside Mercy's chest burst into applause.

They walked for half a block in silence. The will-he-kiss-me-at-the-door frisson of a first date wafted around them, when, obviously, this had never been and never would be a date, and the whole point was that he was coming inside for an innocuous slice of cake anyway.

"Where did you learn to dance like that?" Mercy asked him.

"My mom."

Mercy clamped her lips against the urge to laugh.

"What? Did you think the Three Mothers chucked me onto the earth, fully formed?"

"Kind of?"

Another one of those gusty laughs burst out of Hart's mouth, inspiring the fluttering applause in her chest to turn into a standing ovation.

"Are you close to your mom?"

"I was."

The applause died.

"Sorry."

"It's all right. You didn't know."

They arrived at Birdsall & Son, and Mercy rushed to unlock the door before the uncomfortable kiss-at-the-front-door weirdness got any weirder.

"I need to let Leonard out. Prepare yourself."

"Duly noted," he said, an increasingly intoxicating sense of humor lacing his words. He stepped across the threshold, an act that struck Mercy as intimate, the movement from outside in. Granted, it was the lobby of an undertaking business, but she felt swoony as she watched him hang his hat on the coatrack and run a hand through his hair to neaten it.

It's an innocent slice of cake, Mercy, she reminded herself as she clicked upstairs in her kitten heels and opened the door to her apartment. Leonard bolted out, his paws hammering the stair treads. Mercy balanced the cake stand, two plates, two forks, and two napkins in her arms and made it downstairs in time to see Leonard running excited circles around her guest. Unbothered, Hart gave the dog the wide grin Mercy had been trying to coax out of him for the past ten minutes as he caught Leonard and squished the dog's jowly face.

"I'm not sure which of you is more besotted," she said. She let Leonard out the front door, and Hart stood next to her, his presence like an oven, the heat of his body radiating off him. Mercy resisted the urge to fan herself as Leonard finished his business, trotted inside, and settled onto one of the green velvet armchairs. She cut two slices of cake, setting one plate on the customer side of the counter for Hart and moving behind it with her own slice to face him as they ate. He stood up straighter after his first bite.

"Zeddie made this?"

"Shocking, isn't it? He's got an internship at a fancy restaurant in Argentine. He's going to be a chef."

Hart squinted in confusion. "What about Birdsall & Son?"

"Curtis Cunningham has offered to buy us out. I think Pop's going to take it."

"But what about you?"

His concern on her behalf sent an electric zing of gratitude bouncing around her insides like a pinball. "Yes. Exactly. Thank you for asking. Because do you know what? You're the only person who has asked that question: 'What about you, Mercy?'" She shook her head and scraped a bit of stray frosting onto her fork. "Pop and Zeddie and Lil keep saying this is what's best for me and that it's time for me to move on with my life. But I don't want to. I admit that running the office isn't my ideal career, but I do love building boats. I love performing the funeral rites. I love being able to bring some sense of peace and closure to families in mourning. I love being an undertaker."

"So why can't you do that?"

"Undertaking has always passed from father to son, not father to daughter. Besides, there's no one else who can run the office. So if Zeddie doesn't want to be an undertaker, and my sister and her husband aren't going to be running delivery anymore, that's that. It's over. And it's not like there's another undertaker out there who's going to hire a woman, especially one who hasn't gone to trade school."

Mercy set her fork on her plate in defeat. This was the first time she had managed to articulate what exactly it was that bothered her about selling the business, and it left her with a sadness that settled into her bones. She was thankful that Hart didn't try to cajole her out of it. He watched her, waiting for her to go on.

"Pop deserves to retire, and Zeddie shouldn't have to give up his passion for a career he doesn't want. Lilian and Danny have their own lives to live. I would never in a million years expect any of them to give up their hopes and dreams for me. But my whole life, I've done what's best for everyone else, and I never minded it or begrudged my family anything. Now, for once, there's something *I* want, and it feels like there's no one in my corner."

Hart ate a ruminative bite of coconut cake. "I'm sorry. That's a shitty situation."

"It is. Thank you."

"I'm known for my eloquence."

Mercy burst out laughing, and an honest-to-gods smile spread across the severe lines of Hart's face in response, making his pale eyes light up. She had always thought of those eyes as cold and reptilian, but here, in the gaslight of the lobby, everything about him softened and warmed. As she regarded his strange eyes, she itched to ask him a question that was none of her business.

He cut off another bite of his shrinking dessert with the side of his fork. "You are dying to ask me which god is my dad, but you can't figure out how to phrase it without being rude."

Mercy was glad that her complexion didn't lend itself to blushing. "How did you know?"

"You have the Which God Is It? Face. I've seen it a million times."

"Sorry."

Hart shrugged off her embarrassment. "It's all right. The answer is that I have no idea. He told my mom his name was Jeff."

"Jeff?"

"Jeff." One corner of Hart's mouth veered skyward in irony.

"That seems so... not godlike."

"He left my mom high and dry. That doesn't seem very godlike either."

His tone was light, but Mercy sensed that his life as a demigod—with people gawking at him and wanting to know if he had any special powers—most certainly wasn't.

"I didn't ask that question aloud, and yet I managed to put my foot in my mouth," she said.

"Sure did."

That one-corner-up smile was starting to make her light-headed.

"Well, I've already got one foot in, so I may as well stuff in the other." She put her elbows on the counter and leaned in, and even in the dim light, she could see his cheeks go pink.

"Mortal or immortal?" he guessed.

"Do you read minds?"

"I don't know. If I'm mortal or..."

"Really?"

"Only one way to find out." Again, his tone made light of it, but his eyes were bottomless.

Mercy tried to wrap her brain around the idea of immortality. "So you have no idea if you're going to live forever unless you..."

"That about covers it. They say everything comes to an end except the Unknown God, if you believe in that sort of thing, but an eon is a long time, so..." He had a tiny smear of frosting stuck in one corner of his mouth, and it made him seem so human and vulnerable.

"That must be lonely."

"I guess."

"I'm sorry. I put that badly. I mean..."

Mercy reached across the counter to touch his wrist, the place where bare skin peeked out from under his sleeve, and she could have sworn that a spark flew out on contact, like flint hitting steel. She resisted the urge to tear her hand away as she spoke.

"I face my own mortality every day. I can buy a fabulous blouse from a mail-order catalog, cook a terrible dinner, and go to bed with a good romance novel, but when I send the dead sailing across the Salt Sea, I know that the new blouse and that terrible dinner and a good romance novel won't mean a thing when I'm gone. And honestly, it's a comfort. It's something that links me to everyone around me, no matter who they are. Most people seal themselves off from death, but that doesn't change the fact that we're all joined together by this single thread. But you..."

He rolled his napkin between his fingers. "Go on."

"That's it, isn't it? You could go on and on, and everyone you'll ever know or love will grow old and die, but you'll still be here. It'd be like reading a book that doesn't end. No matter how good the story is, you want it to be over at some point. For everyone else, death is a question of when, not if, but for you, it's the opposite: if, not when."

He finally met her gaze, his face unshuttered, and she saw that while most people were scared to die, Hart Ralston was afraid to live.

"Thank you," he said.

"For what?"

"For getting it."

They stared at each other across the counter, and Mercy thought he really might kiss her. Her breathing shortened at the thought, and her lips went plump with expectation.

Did she *want* Hart to kiss her, though?

The second she thought the question, the answer came roaring up from every nook and cranny of her being: *Yes. Please, dear gods, yes.*

His eyes fell to the place where her fingertips touched his wrist, and Mercy pulled her hand away, as if he might not notice that she'd ever touched him, when the heat of his skin still sang in her fingertips.

"Do you make terrible dinners on purpose?" he asked her.

Humor. Thank the Trickster for humor.

"Only when I cook."

He rewarded her with the one-corner grin and crow's feet. "Good thing Zeddie's going to be a chef, then."

"Indeed."

"Well, my compliments to him on the cake." He stared at his empty plate, and Mercy understood that there was no longer any reason for him to stay. "I should probably get going. Early shift tomorrow."

"On Allgodsday?"

"Drudges and poachers aren't too particular about days of the week."

"Right."

He went to the coatrack to get his hat, and Mercy came out from behind the counter to walk him to the door. There was something growing and changing between them, as fragile as glass, and Mercy worried that if he left now, it would break irreparably, but her mind emptied, unable to think of a single excuse to keep him there.

"Thanks for inviting me in, Merciless." The nickname sounded fond rather than insulting.

"Thanks for eating cake with me, Hart-ache."

He stood at the door, clutching the brim of his hat, looking very much as though he had something more to say, and yet his mouth remained silent.

"Wait—you have some frosting there," Mercy told him, indicating the spot on her own mouth.

He wiped the wrong corner with the pad of his thumb, and the combination of his embarrassment and the touching of his thumb to his lips was the sexiest thing Mercy had ever seen in her life.

"No, other side," she murmured, mesmerized by his mouth.

"This is all part of my debonair charm," he told her once he was free of frosting.

"Yes, exactly what I was thinking."

She realized that he was eyeing her lips, too, and she felt as if she were standing on the burner of a stove with the flames licking up all around her.

"Well. Thanks again." He hovered at the door with his hand on the knob.

"Hart?"

It was the first time she had called him by name to his face without adding "ache" onto the end of it. They were standing so close to one another that she could see his chest move as he breathed.

"Yep?"

"I think I'm about to do something stupid."

"Okay."

Mercy stood on tiptoes and kissed the corner of his mouth on the exact spot where the frosting had been. She pulled away and watched him as he gawked at her and said nothing, and his silence screamed around her until she couldn't take it anymore.

"Well? Say something."

"I'm still waiting for you to do something stupid."

Mercy's heart shot off like a champagne cork as Hart leaned into her, still clutching his hat.

"May I k—"

"Yes, please."

He lingered an inch from her face, as if he needed to work up the courage, before he pressed a soft, sweet kiss to her lips. It was over too soon, but then she heard his hat hit the floor as he reached for her with both hands, his fingers uncurling against her cheeks, and he kissed her again, his lips sliding against hers, sensuous and savoring. She pulled off her glasses and let them dangle from her fingertips in time for him to open the kiss wider, his tongue velvety and tasting of sugar and coconut. She wrapped her arms around his neck and pressed him between her body and the door, and her toes curled when he uttered a helpless, guttural sound that reverberated through his chest and vibrated into hers. He pulled her in closer, his body heavenly everywhere they touched.

Mercy had never in her life experienced a kiss so good that she couldn't stand on her own two feet, but now Hart Ralston was kissing her boneless, and she hung from his arms like a rag doll. He sucked her bottom lip into his mouth and bit down, not hard enough to draw blood but with enough force to send an urgent message straight to the growing tension between her legs.

Their lips parted, and Mercy sucked in air as she stared into Hart's huge, unfocused pupils.

"Sorry," he gasped. "That was... I shouldn't have—"

But Mercy didn't want his apologies. She wanted him to feel as unmoored and heady and ebullient as she did. She kissed him again, this time with a depth and tenderness that placed a chunk of her own vulnerability on the line like a dare. The decadent movement of his lips against hers, the gentle stroking of his hands on her back, the sharp uptick of his arousal against her thigh clearly signaled that she had made her point.

She broke off the kiss to whisper, "Come upstairs."

Chapter Twenty-Three

Upstairs.

Upstairs meant Mercy's apartment, Mercy's bed, Mercy's naked body held against his own. Her breasts, her hips, the smooth skin of her thighs and the sweet promise nestled between them. It meant his body, his heart, his painful fragility offered up and laid bare before her.

She waited for his answer. Without her glasses on, her face seemed exposed and defenseless.

He needed to tell her about the letters, but how could he fess up now, when she wanted him—not his letters—*him*, exactly as he was?

Her hair was mussed, with dark tendrils falling down around her neck. He curled a lock around his finger and reveled in the sensation of the thick, coarse texture against his skin.

"Are you absolutely sure about this?" he asked her, his voice hushed as if he might shatter the moment if he spoke too loudly, pushed too far, asked for too much.

She spoke her answer against his lips. "Yes. Very."

He pressed his forehead to hers, and because it would be absurd to tell her that he loved her, he poured everything he felt into one word: "Mercy."

And then they were kissing again, her body pressing his to the door and his ecstatic erection answering back. His lips skimmed an indulgent path down her neck, following her fingers as she undid the tiny buttons of her blouse, one by one, revealing a plain blue satin brassiere, an undergarment that was more practical than alluring, but as far as Hart was concerned, it was a million times sexier than all the lace in the world. He kissed his way along the line where cups met skin, blazing a trail of heat and want across the top of her breasts.

She took his face in her hands and brought his lips back to hers, smiling against his mouth. "Upstairs," she said, and this time, it was not a question. She twined her fingers with his and tugged him up the steps as her glasses dangled from her other hand. They were five steps from the apartment door when Hart couldn't stand it and reached for her, his hands sliding down her backside, pulling her into him as he kissed her again and again, his knuckles brushing the railing behind her in the narrow stairwell.

"We're almost to the top," she laughed.

"It's too far." He spoke the words against the warm, salty skin of her neck.

"You'll make it."

He wasn't so sure, but she managed to drag him into the apartment.

Leonard padded into the parlor after them, settling himself on a piece of furniture Hart couldn't be bothered to notice, not with Mercy before him, kicking off her shoes, lit by the light of a single lamp, her blouse open, her big eyes dark, her full bottom lip clenched nervously between her teeth. Now that he was standing in her apartment—her home—he was shy and nervous, too.

He nodded toward the glasses in her hand. "Can you see without those?"

"Only things that are up close."

He leaned in, inches from her face. "How close?"

"Hmm. Closer."

She was so tall that he barely had to bend his head for his lips to hover an inch above hers. It was excruciatingly satisfying. "Now?"

"Not quite." She stood on tiptoe, and her lips brushed his, featherlight. "There."

Hart was a match, and that kiss sent him flying across the striker to set him alight. He had enough wherewithal to take the glasses from her hand and set them carefully on the nearest surface—again, he had only the barest understanding of his physical surroundings with Mercy's bare cleavage outshining everything else in the room like a beacon of hope in a dark world—before he let himself loose and kissed her as if air were not necessary to her survival.

His hands roamed from want to want: the roundness of her hips, the curve of her ass, the valley of her waist, the why-is-there-still-clothing-here? temptation of her not-yet-naked breasts. As he removed the blouse and unclasped the brassiere, she tried to relieve him of his shirt, but he was too occupied by the perfection of her naked chest to be of assistance to her.

"Would you take this off?" she demanded, exasperated, tugging on his sleeve.

"Little busy at the moment," he murmured into her skin as he slid his lips down to her left breast. He drew the rosy brown tip into his mouth, his mind going blank with pure want. She gasped and buried her fingers in his hair and clutched him to her, and honest to gods, he had never been so turned on in his life.

"Take off your clothes before I strangle you," Mercy said with a huskiness that made Hart's erection stand up and cheer.

He massaged the fullness of one breast with his hand, feeling her nipple pebble against his thumb, as he swept his tongue over the soft, heavy underside of the other. She whimpered, and Hart grew drunk on the sound of her pleasure.

"Fucking magnificent," he whispered before he kissed his way down the velvet skin of her stomach until he knelt before her, unzipping her skirt and sending it cascading to the floor. He unclipped her stockings from the garter belt and slowly unrolled each one down her long, shapely legs, luxuriating in the sound of her ragged breathing. He helped her shimmy out of the garter belt, leaving Mercy in nothing but her panties.

"They're not very sexy," she said as if she needed to apologize.

The words *not* and *sexy* in combination made no sense in Hart's sex-fogged brain. He gazed into the expanse of pale pink satin stretched across Mercy's abdomen and the narrow band of delicate lace at her waist that met in the middle with a tiny bow, as if Mercy was a gift he got to unwrap. He looked up at her in confusion. "What's not sexy?"

"The boring underpants. If I'd had an inkling this was going to happen tonight, I would have worn something skimpier."

"You could wear a paper bag. As long as you're taking it off, that's all I care about."

And to prove that he meant every word, he peeled off the last of her lingerie, helping her step out of it as his eyes drank in her nakedness. He kissed her navel, the tip of his tongue dipping into the depression. Then he dragged his lips and tongue downward slowly, enjoying the anticipation before he reached his destination.

Mercy gasped. "You don't have to if you don't want to."

Again, he looked up at her in wonder. "There is literally nothing that I would rather be doing. May I?"

"Okay," she said with a grin that managed to be both shy and lascivious. He obliged, tasting her and soaking in the moans of her approval like good soil drinking in the rain.

She tugged on his hair, and he obeyed, skimming his teeth up her body until his mouth met hers. She pulled away long enough to suggest "Maybe in the bedroom?" with a nod toward a darkened doorway as she stroked him over the thick fabric of his dungarees. Desire shot through him, so strong his vision went white.

"Do you want to get in there on your own two feet, or do you want me to sling you over my shoulder and carry you in?"

Mercy's pretty eyes lit up, and she bolted for the bedroom. He chased after her, laughing as he caught up to her by the side of the bed, and he drew her into his arms. He kept his mouth on hers as much as he could while removing his clothes at the same time. She stepped into him, her nakedness pressed against the length of his, her body fitting into his body. He cast aside the nagging belief that this would not—could not—last. All he wanted to think about was the perfection of this one moment in time. She took him by the hands and drew him down with her onto the mattress and kissed him hard, and he kissed her in return, their bodies tangled together, moving in rhythm.

"Tell me what you like," he whispered.

"Everything. Everything you're doing," she answered breathlessly.

They touched and stroked and kissed and nipped. He maneuvered himself behind her and curled his body around hers and slid his hand between her legs, making her inhale sharply and buck against him.

"Show me what to do," he said into the soft skin behind her ear, and she moved her hand over his, guiding him into the rhythm she liked, the pressure, the places that felt best. Her breathing grew ragged as their fingers worked together. Mercy ground her backside deeper and deeper into Hart's pulsing need, and he nearly spilled over when he felt her release, her body convulsing in waves against him.

She rolled over to face him, and she reached between them to take him in hand. A cry of feral bliss tore free of his throat.

"Serves you right," she told him, her hand working miracles.

"Any more of this and I'm going to beg for mercy," Hart rasped.

"Oh, I like the sound of that." She kissed him, scraping her tongue against his teeth.

"I have a condom in my wallet."

"Too far away." She reached past him to fumble through the drawer of her bedside table, and Hart used the opening to lavish her breasts with the attention they deserved. She groaned as she tore into the foil packet.

"Can I put it on?" she asked.

"Gods, no. If you touch me again, I'll shoot off like a fireworks display." He snatched the condom from her hand and unrolled it carefully down his hair-trigger shaft.

Without warning, an explosion cut through the air. Hart and Mercy both startled as the first fireworks of the Founders' Day party sent red sparks flying through the night sky beyond the bedroom window. When their eyes met, they burst out laughing.

"Make me see fireworks, Marshal Ralston," Mercy challenged him, nudging his leg with her foot as their laughter died down, and Hart felt suddenly uncertain.

"How should we . . . ?"

In answer, Mercy lay down on her back, her loosened hair spreading dark shadows across the pale pillowcase as she spread her legs for him, a gesture so trusting and intimate that Hart felt the urge to cry.

"Are you sure?" he asked, his voice gruff. "I don't want to crush you."

"I'm a big girl, Hart-ache. I'm hard to break."

He wondered if she knew how true a statement that was. Hart was the fragile one, while she was strong in all the ways that mattered.

He took the chain from around his neck—he didn't want to

batter Mercy in the face with his keys—and set it on the table next to the bed. He positioned himself on top of her, kissed her softly, and nuzzled the line of her jaw before he slid into her, pausing once he was inside to sear the sensation into his memory. Then he moved, and she moved with him, a dance of two bodies. The fireworks crashed overhead, unheeded, until Hart let go at last and lost himself inside her.

Chapter Twenty-Four

Mercy pulled a men's undershirt and a clean pair of underwear from her dresser before she rushed into the bathroom. It was one thing to have spontaneous sex with a man she barely knew; it was quite another for him to get an eyeful of her naked body after the lust goggles had been removed. She cleaned herself up, put on the shirt and panties, and stared at her reflection as she brushed her teeth. Her lips were kiss swollen, her hair a mess. She took it down and brushed it out, continuing to marvel at the face in the mirror of a woman who'd just had mind-blowing sex with Hart Ralston.

I know I asked you to open a window, but wow, she prayed to the Warden. Upon further consideration, she added, *Thank you? I think?*

The memory of Hart's tongue slathering attention on her burned through her body.

Thank you, she told the Warden, more definitively.

She heard Hart moving about in the next room. Based on her experience with other men, including with Nathan, she expected to find him dressed and ready to go by the time she got out of the bathroom, so she was surprised to see him sitting on the edge of the bed, wearing nothing but his boxers, his undershirt, and the keys he had taken off before he...

Before he fucked you until you were howling his name, her memory supplied for her.

She turned down the bathroom light but stayed inside the frame, leaning against the jamb. "Are you staying?" she asked, getting right to the point.

"Do you want me to stay?"

"Most people don't feel comfortable here."

"Why?"

"There's a well full of dead bodies in the basement."

"Do the dead bodies usually come knocking on the door in the middle of the night?"

She laughed nervously. "Not usually."

"My old mentor used to tell me that 'there's more to fear from the living than from the dead.' So." He swallowed so hard that she could hear it from halfway across the room, and she realized that he was feeling as raw and timid as she was. "I'd like to stay, if you want me to."

"I do."

"Then I'll stay."

He scooted back to give her room. She got into bed beside him but shrank away when he reached for her. "It's okay. You don't have to."

He shrank away, too, as if he were a schoolboy about to get his hand smacked by the teacher's ruler. "I don't have to what?"

"Cuddle."

He propped himself up on his elbow and studied her. "What kind of assholes have you been dating?"

"Very big assholes. You met one tonight."

"They're weasels, the lot of them. What would *you* like to do?"

"I'd like to cuddle. A little," she admitted.

"Then come here."

He drew her into his arms, but she couldn't seem to relax. "Everyone knows that cuddling gets hot and uncomfortable after two minutes," she informed him.

"Then if either of us gets hot or uncomfortable, we'll desist, and no hard feelings. Deal?" He spoke the words into her hair and stroked her arm, finally convincing her that maybe, possibly, there were men in the world who liked to cuddle. She nestled into the soft cotton stretched over his shoulder and surreptitiously enjoyed the lingering aroma of his bath soap.

"Deal."

She tried to breathe without making noise and to exhale on him in a way that wouldn't be weird or gross. After a minute of near asphyxiation, Hart spoke up, his voice rumbling in his chest, vibrating against Mercy's cheek. "I think I should tell you that this bed is the greatest thing that has ever happened to me."

She grinned, although he couldn't see her face. "This is a sad confession."

"I mostly camp out in Tanria or sleep in barracks or, when I have to take a body into town, in a hotel. Camping out is actually the best of those options. The world is not built for giants."

Talking seemed easier than cuddling, so Mercy pushed herself up and looked down at him, liking the way his face softened in the glow from the gas streetlight that filtered in through her lace curtains. "Can I ask you something?"

He tucked a strand of hair behind her ear. "Is that really a question?"

"How old are you?"

"Turned thirty-six last month."

Mercy nodded, mulling over the math in her head.

"Older or younger than you thought?"

"About on the nose. But you've been with the Tanrian Marshals for ages, haven't you? You must have been a baby when you joined up."

"I was sixteen. My aunt took me in after my mom died, but she had her own family and her own life, and I was a mouthy teenaged boy who'd lost his mother. The Tanrian Marshals seemed like a good idea to all of us at the time, and frankly, it was. My mentor was a man named Bill Clark. He was good for me, got me in line. He was the father I never had, you know?"

The bittersweet tone of his answer made Mercy ask, gently, "I take it Bill is no longer with us?"

"Correct."

"I'm sorry."

"Comes with the territory."

"That doesn't make it easier."

"No, it doesn't."

So Hart's divine father had never been a part of his life, and he'd lost the only father figure he'd ever had. Mercy wondered what on earth she would have done if her father hadn't been there for her—for all of them—when her mother died, even when he was hurting so badly himself. She had been frustrated with Pop lately, but Hart's story reminded her how much she had to be grateful for, and since he had offered up a chunk of his past, she decided to give him a piece of her own story.

"My mom died when I was seventeen. She had cancer, but she wasn't sick very long, which was a blessing, I guess. Pop was devastated. We all were. Still are. But, you know, you learn how to live with it."

"I know," Hart said, and it was nice to talk to someone who truly understood what it meant to lose your mother at so young an age. "So you were seventeen, but you had to run the office and help raise your sister and brother, too?"

"I didn't *have* to; I *got* to." She toyed with the chain around his neck. "Why do you have two keys?"

He didn't answer. He simply watched her as she fingered the keys, an act that was beginning to feel more intimate than sex. Then she read the engraving on the ID tag, and her eyes narrowed.

"Cunningham's? Seriously?"

"In my defense, I bought their cheapest package."

"Their cheapest package is still price gouging. I'm ashamed of you." She dropped the key like a hot brick but fingered the second with greater care. "This one looks like a birth key."

"My mom's."

"Shouldn't it be on your altar?"

"Don't have one."

"How do you not have an altar?"

He squirmed in reply.

"Hart, where do you live?"

"I don't have an address per se, but it's more from choice than out of necessity." He tried to make light of it, but Mercy wasn't buying it.

"You don't have a home?"

"I work a lot. There's no point."

"Hart!"

"Mercy!" He imitated her shocked tone, bringing an exasperated smile to her face. She shook her head and snuggled into him. It felt more natural now.

"So where's your birth key? Who has it?"

"Alma Maguire."

"Your boss?"

"We used to be partners, and she's more family to me than my aunt."

Mercy could hear years' worth of loneliness attached to that one sentence. They settled into a comfortable silence after that. Mercy traced drowsy circles on Hart's chest with her fingertips, and Hart did the same on her back. She hovered over the precipice of sleep when he whispered, "Mercy, I... There's something..."

She lifted her head, waiting for him to say more, and when he didn't, she kissed him instead, light and soft and tender.

He gave in, rolling onto his side, drawing her close, kissing her as if it mattered that she was Mercy, and no one but Mercy would do.

"I'm sorry, but all this cuddling has made me hot," Mercy told him as she hitched her leg over his hip.

"You were hot to begin with." He bit her earlobe and leaned back to give her a flirtatious smirk, which quickly dissolved into a moan when Mercy reached for him past the waistband of his boxer shorts. He gazed at her through the sex-dazed slits of his gray eyes, and she smiled wickedly at him.

"No hard feelings?" she said.

"Oh, there are hard feelings. So many."

This time, there was no awkwardness afterward, and Hart must not have been hot or uncomfortable, because Mercy drifted off to sleep in his arms.

The gray light of dawn leaked in through the lace curtains as Mercy surfaced from sleep to waking, slowly sensing herself in Hart's arms. She felt pleasantly weightless, as if she were suspended in air, hanging in this pocket of perfect time.

And then Hart said "Fuck" and sat up so suddenly that he nearly toppled her out of bed.

She blinked at him blearily, knowing that her hair was a frizzy mess and her face sleep-rumpled. "Everything okay?"

"Sorry. I think I'm extremely late for work. I'm supposed to be there by seven thirty."

Mercy fumbled for her glasses, and then she remembered that Hart had set them down she knew not where last night before he had undressed her. She squinted at her bedside clock. "It's six forty-seven," she told him as she mentally calculated where he was, where he was supposed to be, and how little time he had to breach the distance between the two.

"Fuck!" He laughed with a self-deprecation that Mercy could eat with a spoon.

She had worried this would all seem like a truly horrible mistake in the morning light, but as she watched the human-shaped blur that was Hart get on hands and knees to search for a rogue sock under the bed, she couldn't shake the sensation that they might be... dating?

"Sorry to make you late," she told him as he shrugged into his wrinkled shirt.

"You." He came to the side of the bed and bent down to kiss her as he fumbled with his buttons. "Have nothing to be sorry for. Can I take you out to dinner when I finish this tour?"

Definitely dating!

"Yes, please," she said, resisting the urge to jump on her bed like a three-year-old. "When will that be, exactly?"

"The Wardensday after next."

"Two weeks?"

He paused with one leg in his pants. "I can't tell you how much I wish it were sooner."

"It's not your fault. You've got to put food on your nonexistent table."

"I'll have you know that the Tanrian Marshals supply tables in the barracks. We're not barbarians."

"Would you be willing to write to me in the meantime?"

He was smiling as he opened his mouth to answer, but a strange expression came over his face, and he suddenly seemed to find that the buckling of his belt required his full attention. "There aren't any nimkilim boxes inside Tanria. Something to do with the Old Gods."

"Oh."

She'd have to go two weeks without a word from Hart, when she had hardly started dating him to begin with. The urge to jump on the bed disappeared.

Mostly dressed now, he bent to kiss her again and again. The third kiss indicated that he was not inclined to leave, but he pulled back anyway. "Wardensday after next," he promised her.

She got to her knees on the mattress, put her hands behind his neck, and pulled his mouth down to hers, and for a while longer, she made him forget about Tanria and his job and the time and anything else that wasn't her.

Chapter Twenty-Five

Hart was late for work.

Very, very late.

He could not possibly care less.

Chapter Twenty-Six

As Mercy walked up the front steps of Pop's house, she felt like she was girding herself for battle. While her family had cosseted her yesterday, there was only so long a drudge attack on Main Street could put off the inevitable. She was certain that Lilian would get down to brass tacks about Cunningham's offer at dinner tonight, and Mercy wasn't sure she'd be able to come out and say what she needed to say without bursting into tears. The words had come pouring out of her when she talked to Hart last night. Why couldn't she do the same with her family?

Hart.

Last night.

She felt herself flush from head to toe.

It would be nice if he were here beside her instead of risking life and limb to fight drudges in Tanria. She had never given much thought to what marshals actually did, but now that she was dating one—wasn't she?—it gave her heart palpitations thinking about it. She imagined him standing quietly at her side, sliding his fingers between hers. That seemed like a very Hart thing to do. She had been dating him—probably dating him?—definitely dating him—for less than twenty-four hours, but there were already things that seemed very Hart to her. The way he fiddled with the brim of his hat when he was nervous. The way he tried so hard not to smile or laugh, as if he were afraid of joy. Or the thoughtful way he made his side of the bed before leaving this morning.

Right after he demonstrated yet again what his tongue could do between her legs.

She would have to pour a pitcher of ice water over her head to get through dinner, or else Lil was going to see right through her.

Mercy took a deep breath and went in. The usual explosion of talking and laughter hit her like a wave as she touched salt water to her mother's key. "Wish me luck."

Lilian accosted her seconds later. "How are you? You left without a word last night. We've been worried."

"I'm fine. I was exhausted after everything yesterday, so I went home early."

AND HAD SEX WITH HART RALSTON, Mercy's mind screamed so loudly that she was worried her sister could hear it. She brushed past Lilian, saying, "Hey, Danny, how about some wine."

Danny handed her a glass of shiraz with condensation frosting the sides. Mercy took a gulp beneath her sister's shrewd gaze and choked when the wine went down the wrong pipe. She attempted to pay attention to Pop's tirade on equimaris bloodlines in sea polo, while Zeddie put the finishing touches on dinner and made the occasional crack about the Paxico Penguins—Bushong's rivals—to get a rise out of his father. Mercy sat beside Lilian, observing how deftly her brother-in-law smoothed Pop's ruffled feathers. "Danny is the literal best," Mercy said.

"He's nice and all, but people who leave globs of toothpaste in the sink are barred from literal-best-dom. You, on the other hand, really are the literal best... which is why I know you're going to put on your big-girl pants tonight so that we can discuss Cunningham's offer."

"Yes. Absolutely," Mercy agreed. But as she rose from her seat to help Zeddie carry in the dinner dishes, Lilian put a hand on her arm to stop her. "Don't think I'm letting you escape without talking about a certain Tanrian Marshal, Little Miss He's-Pure-Evil. I saw you cutting a rug at the party."

In her mind, she could hear Hart's laughter-laced *Fuck*. She glanced at Pop, who was too busy holding forth on the finer qualities of the left and right drivers of Bushong's sea polo team to have heard Lil.

"Later," she hissed and went to help Zeddie. She wasn't ready to talk about what was happening between her and Hart, as if putting it into words would make it slip between her fingers like water. Besides, she had other, more pressing issues to focus on tonight. After Pop led them through prayers of thanks to the Three Mothers, the Three Fathers, and the Hearth, Mercy cleared her throat.

"I have some things I need to say."

She waited until she had everyone's attention before she continued, her knees bobbing nervously under the table.

"First of all, I'm sorry that I've been short tempered with everyone. Zeddie, I haven't been supportive of your career choices, and that's not fair of me. You should follow your bliss, especially if it results in me getting to eat chocolate croissants and lobster tails."

"Not together, though," he joked, but a relieved smile spread across his face.

"Lil and Danny, I had no right to go spilling your news." Mercy decided to take a page from Hart's book and added, "I was an ass."

"It's okay," Danny said at the same moment his wife answered, "You were a total ass, but I love you anyway."

"And, Pop, I'm sorry that I haven't been able to put into words what I've been needing to say all along. So here it goes: You've always thought that Birdsall & Son is a burden to me, that it's stopping me from living my life. You've all been telling me that. But what you don't seem to understand is that Birdsall & Son *is* my life. I admit that I didn't see myself running the office forever, but ever since we switched places, Pop, I've loved going to work every day. I want to be an undertaker, and if we sell the business, I'm going to have to stop doing the job I love. So that's why I've been so crabby about it."

"Muffin—" Pop began, but Mercy held up a hand. If she didn't make it through this speech now, she might never again muster the courage.

"I'm not saying that any of you need to give up something for me. Lilian and Danny, you have every right to stop traveling and settle down to raise your family. Zeddie, I want you to cook and bake and do the things that make you happy. Pop, you have earned the right to retire and sit around reading those Arvonian adventure novels you enjoy so much. We're a family, and I love you, which is why I think you should know what's in my heart, even though I know we're probably going to have to sell the business. That's all."

Mercy reached for her glass and took a fortifying gulp of wine, swallowing the giant lump in her throat along with it.

"Aw, Merc," Zeddie said with a soft sympathy that made the lump return with a vengeance.

"Don't you dare make me cry."

Pop reached across the table to put his big hand on Mercy's. "I've always felt terrible about how much you've had to take on, and from such a young age. I thought you *wanted* to move on at some point."

"Well, I don't," said Mercy, her voice going alarmingly wobbly. "But I will if I have to."

Lilian put both hands on the table like the head shareholder at a business meeting. "Stop being so drippy, everyone. We can fix this, can't we? Merc, what if I ran the office so you could build the boats?"

Mercy was dabbing her eyes with her napkin but stopped when Lil's words sank in. "Do you *want* to run the office?"

"Why not? It's a million times better than teaching math to a bunch of little shits again, plus I'd get to work with you every day, which would be great. And I'd bet all the beer tokens of the Redwing Islands that my darling husband would much rather stay home with the baby than work some office job every day."

Danny sat up straight and unfurled a wide grin. "Works for me!"

"There. Problem solved. So now all we need is a new delivery driver, and Birdsall & Son stays in business. Birdsall & Daughter? What are we calling this joint now?"

Mercy and Pop glanced at each other across the table.

"Did you tell them?" she asked him.

"No. I thought you did."

Lil looked from Pop to Mercy. "Tell us what?"

"It's not that simple. Cunningham forged an exclusive deal with Afton Lumber. We're going to have to find another vendor, which means the delivery costs are going to go through the roof. I don't think we can absorb the deficit and remain solvent for long."

Lilian slapped the table in outrage. "Is that legal?"

"Can we afford a lawyer if it isn't?"

"Lawyer, schmawyer," Zeddie piped in. "If you ask me, there's something shady going on that has nothing to do with boring-ass lumber prices. Obviously, you're doing something that's making Cunningham nervous, Mercy, so find out what it is and stick it to the man."

Mercy, Lilian, Danny, and Pop stared at Zeddie in stunned silence.

"What?" he said, defensive.

Lilian tilted her head, considering him. "That was...smart. What in the Salt Sea, Z?"

He picked up a stray pea from his plate and, using his spoon as a catapult, fired it at his sister.

Ignoring them, Pop rose from his seat. "Then it's settled. I'm not selling to Cunningham. We'll figure out a way to keep our doors open." He took his wineglass and held it up. "To Mercy's future."

"To Mercy's future," everyone else agreed.

Lil patted Mercy's arm and said, "Don't you worry. We're going to make this work."

Mercy burst into tears of gratitude.

And Lil was so caught up in strategizing ways to keep Birdsall & Son in business that she forgot to ask Mercy about that dance with Hart Ralston.

It was the shushing of sandpaper that lured Roy into the boatworks the following afternoon shortly before closing. Mercy hadn't realized that he had crept in until he spoke up, pulling her out of her thoughts—a tug-of-war between Hart Ralston and Curtis Cunningham with an occasional digression to her silent pen pal—as she pressed the fairing plank to the frame to make sure it was flush.

"She's a beaut."

"Thanks," said Mercy, flushing with pride, but then she watched him in consternation as he picked up the tools from the pegboard that mirrored her own.

"What are you doing?"

"Helping out."

"But—"

"I know what the doctor said. It won't hurt my heart to fair a frame with my daughter."

Mercy watched him as he got to work, his hands knowing what to do without his having to think about it. Here in the boatworks, surrounded by wood and tools and the ceremonial accoutrements for the dead, he had the self-assurance she had come to miss dearly over the past year. She knew that a bit of sanding wouldn't overly tax him, so she got to work on the starboard side across from him, and they settled into a companionable rhythm.

"You were always a natural at this, took to it like a fish to water," he said after a while. "The Birdsalls have been undertakers in Bushong since long before Tanria opened. My pop taught me the ropes from the moment I could hold a hammer upright. He pinned his hopes for the future on me the way his father had pinned his hopes on him, but I never felt pressured or trapped. I wanted to do this. All these years, I've been pinning my hopes on poor Zeddie, when I should have seen it was you all along."

"I'm a girl, Pop. I couldn't see myself as an undertaker until a few months ago. Why should you? Why should anyone?"

"I should've seen it. Frankly, I'm ashamed of myself."

"Oh, Pop." She set her hand on the keel, as if it were her father's beating heart.

"You say, 'I'm a girl,' but the gods know you never had much of a chance to be anything other than a full-grown woman. And what a remarkable woman you are. The Three Fathers and the Unknown God will surely be honored to welcome you into the brotherhood of undertakers."

"Siblinghood?" she suggested, making a joke so she wouldn't start bawling.

"Siblinghood," Roy agreed, setting his big hand on top of his daughter's.

Mercy's whole body warmed with her father's approval. "What can I say? I learned from the best."

He patted her hand, then put his sander away. "We'll have to figure out what to call this place once you take over. You think on that. In the meantime, I'm heading home to see what the chef has cooking."

"Probably something Dr. Galdamez said you can't eat."

He came over to the starboard side to kiss her cheek. "Probably."

Chapter Twenty-Seven

The six days following Hart's exit from Mercy's apartment comprised a form of torture designed specifically for a besotted marshal who had to patrol Sector W-20 in the company of an apprentice who talked incessantly of Zeddie this and Zeddie that and "Are you sure there are no dragons in Tanria, sir?" All Hart could think about was Mercy, and how much he wanted to be in her bed, and how much he did not want to be stuck in Tanria, hiding his constant boner from Duckers. It came as a relief when the flare went up late Wisdomsday afternoon. At least now he had something to do other than miss Mercy.

His relief evaporated when he and Duckers galloped onto the scene. The flare brought them to the Ash Valley Heartnut Grove, where a handful of sap tappers were either scrambling up heartnut trees or firing off pistol crossbows from behind the trunks to fend off three drudges on the attack. Multiple drudges working in tandem was strange enough, but Hart also spied two more souls floating in the grove, as if they were standing by for a chance to infect a dead body. A drudge had already killed one of the sap tappers and knelt on the corpse as if it had slain the man for one of these lost souls.

"Oh, fuck, sir," said Duckers, gaping at the murdered man.

"I've got it. You take the one on the right."

Hart didn't wait to make sure Duckers followed his order—he

knew his apprentice well enough by now to trust him. He urged his equimaris toward the drudge crouched over the slain man, his mount's webbed feet slapping the earth as he drew the machete from the holster strapped to his back.

"Move!" he shouted at a pair of sap tappers who were trying to help their fallen comrade when it was far too late for that. They dodged out of the way in time for Hart to swing in and lop off the drudge's head. He circled around and slid off the equimaris to slice through the creature's abdomen. He missed the appendix, so he moved the machete to his left hand, drew his rapier with his right, and lunged, hitting the mark this time. The soul flew free, but one of the glowing spirit lights waiting in the wings darted in to take up residence in the newly slaughtered man. Hart was about to stab the slain sap tapper in the appendix when Duckers yelled, "Look out, sir!"

Hart sensed the third drudge at his back and rolled out of the way as his apprentice came barreling in, shooting his pistol crossbow and taking out the drudge with one shot. Before Hart could commend Duckers, the newly animated corpse grabbed Hart's ankle. Hart hacked off its hand with the machete, got to his feet, and dispatched the drudge with his rapier. He sheathed the machete but kept the rapier handy as he watched the lost souls—five in total—drift away from the grove.

The rescued sap tappers timidly approached the marshals, but Hart was more concerned about Duckers, who frowned down at the man who had been killed and reanimated and killed again. Hart cupped the back of his apprentice's head, something his grandfather did to him when he was sad or scared as a child.

"You all right?"

"Yeah. It's depressing, though."

"It is. I'd be worried about you if you *didn't* think it was depressing."

"Thanks, sir."

Hart rubbed the back of Duckers's head before sending him to fetch sailcloth from his pack so that they could cover the body of the sap tapper while Hart interviewed the witnesses. Once the marshals had everything they needed for the report, they sent the workers home to the Ash Valley barracks and got to work wrapping the remains.

"We need to enter you in some sharpshooting competitions," Hart told Duckers as he examined the drudge his apprentice had shot.

"Oh yeah? What kind of money can you make off that sort of thing?"

"Depends. What's my cut?"

"Point one percent."

"And after all I've done for you."

Duckers laughed. Hart had grown fond of making him burst out laughing like that. He nodded toward the cadaver the kid was wrapping. "Where's that one headed?"

"No tag. Yours?"

"Keyless."

"Mm-hmm."

Hart could hear the hopefulness in Duckers's voice. Birdsall & Son was one of the only drop-off sites for indigents, but surely the deceased employee of the Ash Valley Heartnut Grove would have a prepaid funeral package, so he decided not to get his own hopes up yet.

"This one's keyless, too, sir, in case you were wondering," Duckers offered a few minutes later, once he had started working on the third drudge. That left Hart with the remains of the man who had been killed today. As Hart suspected, he had a tag.

"This one's going to Faber & Sons," he told Duckers, doing a creditable job masking his disappointment. "Faber's is in Zeandale, by the North Station, and there's a Cunningham branch in the next town over where we can drop off the indigents."

Duckers gave him a sad-puppy face.

"What?"

"Can we please, please, please, please take the keyless bodies to Birdsall & Son?"

Hart was about to say no, but then he thought, *Fuck it. Professionalism is for people who are not in love with Mercy Birdsall.* What had he been thinking? Of course he was going to use this shameless opportunity to see Mercy again. But since he was not above messing with Duckers, he crossed his arms and said, "That's out of the way."

"I'll make your cut of my sharpshooting victories five percent."

Hart had no intention of ever letting his apprentice wind up in a sharpshooting contest, but he played along, shaking his head.

"Ten," Duckers offered.

"Twenty."

"You drive a hard bargain, sir."

Duckers held out his hand, and Hart pretended that he was being magnanimous when he shook it. "Birdsall & Son it is," he said with a fake sigh.

After they dropped off the departed heartnut-sap tapper at Faber & Sons, Hart expected Duckers to spend the drive to Eternity bouncing like a kid with a new rubber ball on his side of the bench. Hart's interior was certainly jumping up and down in excitement at the prospect of seeing Mercy again. Instead, Duckers tapped his fingers on the window frame in a manner that spoke of anxiety rather than joy.

"Out with it," Hart said. "What's eating you?"

"I still say that standing up Mercy was a shitty thing to do, and

I think you should come clean." Duckers closed his mouth and shrank away, as if he were awaiting a tongue-lashing. Hart would have laughed, except the fact that his apprentice expected sharp words from him made him feel like an asshole.

"I went to the Little Wren Café that night after you left," he admitted.

Duckers sat up straight. "You did?"

"Yep."

"And?"

Hart shrugged.

"Are you serious? Dang, you are a steel trap. Come on! What did she say?"

Self-serving, prickly, glowering nightmare of a man. Her words had cut Hart to the quick that night, but a week later, she had kissed the corner of his mouth and asked him to come upstairs.

"Nothing that wasn't true. The point is, it's sorted out, so you don't need to worry about it anymore."

"But you're going to be nice to her when we see her?"

"Of course."

Duckers's silence made Hart turn his eyes away from the road long enough to see his apprentice's cynical expression. He nearly drew blood biting his cheek so he wouldn't laugh.

"I'll be good," he promised.

He could not wait to be good to Mercy.

It did not occur to him to be nervous until he backed the duck up to the Birdsall & Son loading dock shortly before closing. He'd been so focused on how much he missed Mercy that he'd failed to consider that she might not be as invested in their blossoming relationship as he was.

"Don't we usually check in up front?" Duckers asked as he rang the dock bell.

Hart did usually go to the lobby first, but this time, he was here to see Mercy, not her dog, although he'd be happy to see Leonard, too. "This is faster," he said, and then the gate went up, and there was Mercy, dressed in a cotton blouse and a pair of denim dungarees that rendered her curves positively delicious. Her luscious bottom lip fell open in surprise, and Hart needed to get rid of his apprentice as soon as possible so that he could suck that lip into his mouth. If Mercy *wanted* him to suck on her bottom lip.

"Hi," he coughed, his inner critic adding, *Wow, setting her heart aflutter with that opening.*

"Hello." Mercy put a hand to her flushing cheek, which was adorable.

"We have three keyless bodies to drop off," Duckers chimed in, helpfully clueless.

"Three? My goodness." Mercy realized she was touching her cheek and removed her hand, which was also adorable. "Uh, right, bring them in."

"Is Zeddie around?" Duckers asked as Hart and Mercy stole glances at each other throughout the process of stowing the bodies on the lift in the boatworks.

"He's at the house. He doesn't start at Proserpina's until next week. I'm sure he'll be thrilled to see you."

"You go on," Hart told him. "I'll finish up here."

"Can I take the duck?"

"Sure." Duckers could drive it into a ditch tonight, for all Hart cared. He wanted his apprentice out of his hair.

"Sweet!" Duckers pointed a finger at his face. "Be nice."

"I'll do my best."

Mercy walked Duckers to the dock with Hart trailing a few steps behind, and they both watched him get into the autoduck and pull away.

"Sorry to show up announced," Hart said, his pulse ratcheting up as Mercy pulled down the gate. "I hope this is o—"

The second the gate clanged shut, Mercy grabbed him by his vest and pulled him into a hot, wet kiss that hummed through his body like a plucked guitar string.

"—kay," he finished breathlessly when she pulled away.

"Eh, I suppose it's all right."

He tried to keep his smile from splitting his face open as she wiped her lipstick off his mouth with her thumb.

Her thumb.

By his mouth.

He grabbed hold of it with his teeth.

"Oh my," she breathed, and then she pulled her thumb free, and her mouth was on his again. His hands traveled downward to her ass, pulling her into his hard need, and he moved with her gyrations, their rhythm heated and sinuous.

They paused long enough for Mercy to lock up, and then they were a tangle of limbs, their kissing frenetic, almost desperate. Once again, they succeeded in making it up the stairs, but not much farther. Hart had Mercy mostly undressed by the time they stumbled into her apartment. In a fit of horny illogic, she shut Leonard in her bedroom, at which point Hart pressed her against the closed door, tasting first her mouth, then every other part of her he had managed to unclothe, until Mercy could barely stay standing. She pushed him to the settee and straddled him.

"Why are you still dressed?" she demanded, exasperated, as she unbuttoned and unzipped his dungarees.

"Priorities."

He snaked his hand beneath him to pull the wallet out of his pocket and fish a foil-wrapped condom from inside, which he handed to her. Then he illustrated his *priorities* with his thumb and the first two fingers of his right hand. Mercy, not to be undone, took him in her grasp, as if it were a competition to see who could drive the other mad first. He hissed as she sheathed him with the condom, and grabbed her hips as she lowered herself onto him, letting her set the rhythm.

Hart fought to keep his eyes open as Mercy moved on top of him, watching him with equal heat as her glasses slid down her nose, and even that was sexy. His fingers curled hard into her flesh as Mercy slid her fingers between her legs and circled the mounting pressure of her exquisitely tight bud.

"Is this okay?" she gasped.

"Fuck yes, it's okay!" he half growled, half laughed, making a hysterical giggle bubble out of Mercy in reply.

He bucked beneath her, once, twice, and then Mercy's back arched in release. Hart held on for dear life as she rode out her pleasure. When he could take no more, he clamped his fingers on her hips as he thrust upward with a deep moan. Then he melted into the settee as if their coupling had removed his spine, and he gazed up at Mercy with glassy eyes.

"So, can I take you to dinner?"

Mercy's blouse was open and wrinkled, her brassiere unclasped and dangling off her shoulders, and the gods knew where her overalls had ended up. Her glasses, smeared with a combination of her sweat and Hart's, sat crookedly on her nose, and her hair snaked out of her scarf in riotous curls.

"Sure. Let me grab my purse."

Hart clamped his lips against the laugh pushing its way up from his lungs. Mercy narrowed her eyes at him and, without warning, reached down and tickled his stomach. No one had tickled Hart in his adult life, and he had been unaware until this second that he was still very ticklish. He squealed with helpless laughter as Mercy's fingers accosted him without... well... mercy. Tears of hilarity were streaming down his cheeks by the time she relented, and when he looked up at her for an explanation, she said, "Oh, good. You do have teeth."

The self-satisfied smirk on her face made his playful side—the one he'd thought long dead—roar to life. He grabbed her around the waist and tickled her until she was screeching like a peacock.

"Oh, good," he said. "You do have dimples."

Months ago, when Hart had slipped a letter into a nimkilim box at the West Station, he had felt as though he had a bundle of knots coiled in his stomach. With each letter from his friend and with each passing minute in Mercy's presence, those knots loosened, little by little, as if she were picking them apart with her capable fingers. He hadn't realized how tight his lungs were until Mercy gave him room to breathe.

Now he sat across from her at a nice restaurant—when was the last time he'd had a sit-down meal somewhere other than a greasy spoon?—sipping a glass of red wine—when was the last time he'd had wine?—as a fog of contentment covered him like a warm blanket.

"Probably shouldn't have ordered this," he said as he sipped from his goblet and set it down on the white tablecloth. The wine tasted heavy and velvety on his tongue and made him feel heavy and velvety, too.

Mercy snorted in disbelief.

"I don't drink much," he told her.

"How tall are you? Six six? Six seven?"

"Six nine."

"Pretty sure you can handle one glass of wine."

"All I'm saying is that it's a good thing you're driving tonight. I don't think I could get us home safely." He realized, too late, that he had uttered the words *us* and *home* in the same sentence, as if they belonged together. Worried, he studied her face, but she grinned at him, her face lit flatteringly by candlelight. Another knot inside Hart unraveled.

"I am growing very attached to the notion that Zeddie is going to apprentice here," Mercy said over her plate of sea skate braised in garlic butter, wine, and lemon juice with capers dotting the rich sauce. "If he wants to cook like this for me on a regular basis, who am I to argue?"

"So it's all settled?"

"Almost. Pop is going to hand the undertaking duties over to me, and my sister, Lilian, is going to take over my old office duties, which means we need to hire a new delivery driver. But then there's the matter of Cunningham's."

By the time she finished telling him about Cunningham's deal with Afton Lumber, Hart was ready to use Curtis Cunningham's head for target practice. The ID key around his neck weighed him down as he considered Mercy's options, which were few and far between.

She waved her hand in front of his face. "No. Nope. Turn that frown upside down. We're not going to worry about that tonight. We are having fun. Period."

Fun. When was the last time he had had fun? And then he remembered dancing with Mercy. And also having sex with Mercy, which was as fun as it was heartfelt. *Hart-felt*, he thought, unable to contain the inebriated giggle that popped out of his throat.

"You really are drunk after one glass of wine, aren't you?" Mercy asked, clearly delighted by the irony.

"A teeny-tiny bit."

Mercy bit her lip to contain her laughter at his expense, and because the wine had cast aside Hart's filter, he told her, "When you bite your lip like that, it makes me want to bite your lip like that."

"Cute little drunk Hart."

"Cute little sober Mercy with her cute fucking dimples."

Over dessert and coffee (Mercy) and tea (Hart), they traded funny stories. Mercy made him laugh so hard that tears sprang from his eyes when she told him about the first time she heard a dead body groan, as she'd helped their father load a boat into the old autoduck. She'd had no idea that a cadaver could make a sound, and it scared her so badly, she dropped her end of the boat, breaking open the stern so that the wrapped corpse within stepped on her toe. She then ran screaming all the way to the kitchenette, where she ate an entire package of store-bought cookies before her father came in to comfort her, at which point she got sick all over him.

Hart told Mercy about the time he caught a pair of big-game hunters who had come to Tanria to shoot dragons. They refused to believe him when he informed them that dragons didn't exist, and the only reason he managed to convince them to turn back was because a possessed possum had climbed out of a Tanrian violet oak and chased them. They tried to shoot it with their rifles, only to discover the hard way that New Gods–era technology didn't work within the borders of Tanria. The toothy, furry drudge shambled after them all the way to the portal, and Hart followed behind, enjoying the show with smug satisfaction.

He had never told that story to anyone before, mostly because he hadn't had anyone to tell it to, except maybe Alma and Diane, and he had stopped telling them much of anything. Sitting across from Mercy, laughing and tipsy and in love, he decided to visit them more often. Maybe he'd take a few vacation days here and there and give himself more time to be with the people he cared about. He had so many stories he'd never told anyone.

Hart was still buzzed after he paid the exorbitant bill. On the way to Eternity, he leaned his head against the window and watched Mercy drive. Unfamiliar emotions swirled inside him—tranquility, hope, expectation—and with the wine soaking into his brain, he didn't try to fight them. This thing with Mercy had already progressed well beyond the bounds of his imagination. Who knew how far they could go together? For once, anticipating the future was a comforting thought.

"Is it okay if I spend the night?" he asked before he sobered up enough to second-guess himself.

"Did you honestly think I'd use you for a nice dinner, then kick you to the curb?"

"I don't want to assume," he told her. "I don't want to push."

She kept her eyes on the road, but she was smiling. "Yes, I want you to spend the night."

"That's good, because I packed my toothbrush."

"I'd like to think you would pack your toothbrush no matter where you ended up."

"And deodorant. You are very special to me."

She laughed, and he knew then that he would never tire of the sound.

Once they reached Mercy's apartment, Hart put his toothbrush to work and his deodorant, too, to be on the safe side, after which he flopped onto the transcendent mattress and listened to the mundane sounds of Mercy getting ready for bed. With a stomach full of phenomenal food and the comforting routine of Mercy removing her eye makeup in the bathroom, a beautiful serenity encased him. His eyelids grew heavy. His breathing slowed. He could hear his own heart beating steadily in his chest. Mercy came into the bedroom and lay down beside him, snuggling into him.

"I wore you out, huh?" she said.

"Sorry." He was so relaxed that his lips barely moved.

"No need to be sorry. I'm one satisfied customer."

She brushed her nose against the skin of his neck, and he breathed a small laugh. "What are you doing?"

"I'm nuzzling you. You're very nuzzle-able."

"It tickles."

"Good."

She patted the hollow curve of his right shoulder. "This is my nuzzle nook now. Capital letters. Mercy's Nuzzle Nook."

He closed his eyes and inhaled the scent of her cold cream as she nestled her head into the real estate of his body she had claimed as hers, as if she didn't already own everything he was, body and soul.

"Works for me," he murmured, and he pushed aside the niggling worry that he was going to have to tell her about the letters at some point.

Chapter Twenty-Eight

In a way, Mercy was glad that her letter-writing friend had gone silent. She wasn't sure what she would tell him about Hart and how effortlessly he had integrated himself into her life, the way she had once imagined her pen pal might if they'd ever met. In the end, Lil was right: a tall, single, and extremely attractive Tanrian Marshal standing before her in the flesh was a million times better than a letter-writing stranger. However, the reason she was seeing Hart so often made her anything but glad.

"Fun fact: you don't need an excuse to come see me, so don't feel like you have to keep putting yourself in harm's way," she told him as she pried up the bandage on his shoulder. He and Pen had taken out five drudges near the Alvarez Ambrosia Bottling Company yesterday, and Hart had the wound to show for it. Now he sat on Mercy's bed in nothing but his boxers so that she could change out the dressing.

"It's not usually this bad," he said, facing away from her since Mercy was kneeling on the mattress behind him. "I've gotten clobbered by more drudges in the past three months than in the past three years combined, and they're all keyless. I don't know what's going on."

"And my well is full to bursting. Again."

Mercy frowned at the angry red gash on his skin, which was healing faster than it ought to. She suspected that the next time she saw him, it would be nothing more than a pink streak, if not gone entirely, like all the other scrapes and cuts she had patched up over the past few weeks. But since she knew that the prospect of immortality upset him—upset both of them, if she was being honest—she decided to finish bandaging the wound without comment. When she was finished, he turned and reached for her and pulled her onto his lap.

"I'm half tempted to tie you to the bedposts so you can't go back," she told him.

"I'm half tempted to let you."

"Bound to my bed in nothing but your underwear is probably not the best way to meet my father."

Hart startled, as if Mercy had poured a bucket of cold water over his head. "Is your father coming over here soon?"

"He's handing over some of his office duties to Lil this week. They'll both be downstairs around eight o'clock."

Hart looked at the alarm clock, which now read 7:42. "Fuck!" he cried. He nudged Mercy off his lap and scrambled for his clothes. "Fuck! Fuck! Fuck!"

Mercy put on her floral silk robe as she watched Hart panic. "Are you... Do you want to keep this a secret?"

"No, I... Do you?"

She hugged the robe more tightly around herself. "I don't like sneaking around, but my family is always up in my business, and Pop keeps harping on me about settling down. I'd hate to subject you to that, when everything between us is so..."

Hart paused as he was shrugging into the sleeves of his shirt. "So?"

"Perfect." It was a big word, right up there with *commitment* and *love*. She had reached so quickly for the *l*-word with Nathan. Too quickly. Inaccurately. She was not yet ready to utter it in Hart's presence, although she was beginning to think it in the private recesses of her mind.

She worried that her admission would scare him off. Instead, he rewarded her with his almost smile. Most men seemed to take up so much room, and here he was, six feet, nine inches tall, and the most unobtrusive person she'd ever met.

"Perfect," he agreed, and the word *love* grew bigger and louder in her brain. He zipped up his pants before he threaded his fingers with hers. "Your family is important to you, so if you want to tell them about us, go ahead. But if we are going to inform your dad that we're dating, I'd rather it be over a nice, wholesome dinner, not when I'm leaving your place first thing in the morning because I've spent the night worshipping at the altar of your glorious, beautiful, intoxicating pussy."

"Oh my," Mercy tittered, her cheeks heating.

"That came out more vulgar than I had intended."

Mercy did not find it vulgar. It was nice to be thought of as an altar, when every other man she'd dated had approached her with an attitude that suggested, *Meh, I guess you'll do.* She let the flaps of her robe hang open and relished the appreciative huff that came out of Hart's mouth as she pulled him closer. "Say that again."

"A nice, wholesome dinner," he drawled seductively.

Mercy laughed as she took his hand and guided his fingertips over her underpants, pressing his fingers into her, moving them with the pressure and rhythm she wanted.

"Fuck," Hart moaned. She relished the way she could render him helpless in two seconds.

"We have"—she glanced over his shoulder at the clock as she slid his hand inside her underpants—"fourteen minutes. I want you to worship at the altar of my glorious..."

"Oh, fuck," he whimpered as his fingers went to work, doing exactly what she liked.

"Beautiful, intoxicating..."

"If you say it, my soul is going to depart my body, I swear to the gods of death."

She unzipped his pants as her lips brushed his ear. "Pussy."

"Fuck, Mercy."

"That's the idea."

By 7:57, Hart was saying "Fuck! Fuck! Fuck!" again as he struggled into his clothes, but this time, he was giggling like a sex-sated teenager, and Mercy was as bad, cracking up as she fastened on her brassiere.

"When will I see you again?"

"Late Wisdomsday. I might not be able to get here until ten or later."

"You can show up at three in the morning, as far as I'm concerned." She took his face in her hands as soon as he had stepped into his boots. "Be careful."

"I always am."

"But now you need to be careful for me."

He went still and quiet in her hands, his pale eyes softened, and the word *love* expanded and grew heavy in her stomach. "I . . . ," he began, but he didn't finish whatever he was going to say. Instead, he pressed a kiss to her lips and promised "Wisdomsday, at the latest" before he tore down the stairs at 7:59, buttoning his shirt. Mercy followed close behind, tucking her blouse into her dungarees. They made it as far as the counter in the lobby when they heard the jingling of keys in the lock at the front door and Pop's and Lilian's voices outside.

"Back door! Back door!" Mercy whisper-shouted, and they were both snickering again as Hart changed course.

"Merc! Zeddie made the cutest mini quiches! You've got to try one!" Lil hollered from the lobby as Mercy and Hart made it to the dock. In their haste, they had left the apartment door open, and Leonard sprinted down the stairs, motivated by the prospect of dropped crumbs. His barking and antics covered the sound of Mercy letting Hart out the back door.

She already missed him.

And now she needed to face her sister, and her father, too. But whereas Pop was clueless, Lil was frighteningly observant, and Mercy felt as if she were wearing her two most recent orgasms on her face like bright pink lipstick. Until five minutes ago, she had believed that she did not like to be taken from behind. But then Hart had bent her over the settee...

Get your mind out of the gutter! she chastised herself as she made her way to the lobby, praying that Lil wouldn't notice Mercy's swollen lips.

"Good morning," she said brightly. *Too brightly. Take it down a notch,* she told herself.

Pop kissed her cheek in greeting, but Lilian dispensed with the pleasantries. She nodded at the coatrack and asked, "Whose hat is that?"

There was Hart's hat, left behind in his haste, the hat he had gripped for dear life the night their odd romance had taken off. "A marshal must have left it by accident." *Which is not a lie,* Mercy added in her head.

"Did I hear someone on the dock? It's awfully early to drop off a body, isn't it?"

"No worries. I handled it. Here, I'll take those."

Mercy relieved Pop of the platter of mini quiches and headed for the kitchenette. Pop went into the office, but Lilian followed Mercy, whose armpits went damp with alarm. Regardless of whether Lil was onto her or not, Mercy was ravenous, so she dug into a mini quiche without bothering with a plate or fork.

"These are amazing," she groaned.

"Your shirt buttons are off," Lil informed her.

Sure enough, her collar was two buttons higher on the right

than on the left. "Oh. Ha ha!" she laughed nervously as she brushed the crumbs off her boobs and got to work making herself presentable.

"Your hair's a mess. No scarf today?" her sister pressed as Mercy redid her buttons.

"Um, no."

Lil leaned in, squinting at Mercy's face. "Is that last night's mascara hanging out under your eyes?"

"Allergies? Make my eyes run?"

Lilian's face glowed with evil glee. "Whose hat is in the lobby, Mercy?"

She was caught, and she knew she was caught, and all she could do was flounder in the kitchenette like a landed fish. Lilian trotted to the lobby as fast as her pregnant belly would allow, and Mercy darted after her. Her sister grabbed Hart's hat off the rack and cried, "I know this hat! I've seen this hat! Where have I seen this hat?"

"Would you stop with the hat?" Mercy shot a glance at Pop's office door as she tried and failed to retrieve the hat from Lilian.

And then Hart walked past the front window, his long hand patting the top of his head as if he had realized at that exact moment that he had left his hat at Birdsall & Son.

"Oh. My. Gods," Lilian uttered before she turned on Mercy, her evil glee growing more evil and gleeful by the second. "Are you trying to tell me you got it on with Hart Ralston?"

"I'm not trying to tell you anything. You're yanking it out of me with brute force."

"Holy Three Mothers, how many times?"

Mercy wavered, a denial on her tongue, but she knew it would do her no good now. "How many times for him, or how many times for me? Because they're not the same, and I am definitely in the lead."

Lilian screamed in her face.

Pop poked his head out of the office. "Everything okay out there?"

"We're having girl talk, Pop," said Lilian.

Pop retreated posthaste to the office, probably assuming they were talking about periods or afterbirth, but to be on the safe side, Mercy ushered Lil to the kitchenette and shut the door.

"I thought Hart Ralston was persona non grata in Mercyland," Lilian said.

Mercy thought of the debacle at the Little Wren Café, when she had told Hart, *You hate me as much as I hate you*. She was ashamed of herself for how she had behaved that night, now that she'd gotten to know him for who he truly was.

"Maybe I changed my mind," she told her sister.

"How long has this been going on?"

"Since the night of the Founders' Day party."

"That was nearly three months ago! You've been holding out on me all this time?" Lilian smacked Mercy's arm.

"I'm sorry! I wanted to make sure it was an official thing before I told you about it. I haven't said anything about it to Pop yet either. You know how he is about me getting married."

"I'll be as silent as a shipyard. But can I say one thing?"

"No."

"Too bad. You love Hart Raaaaaaalston! Hart is your boooooooyfriend! You want to have Hart's baaaaaaabies!"

That was when Zeddie, of all people, sauntered into the kitchenette. Zeddie. Who almost never set foot in Birdsall & Son these days, yet here he was. When Lilian's taunt hit his ears, his jaw dropped. "Gods' tits! What?" he asked, but it was clear he needed no answer. Mercy propped her elbows on the counter and buried her face in her hands.

Lil grabbed a butter knife out of the dish drainer and made a threatening gesture toward their brother. "You tell Pop about this, and I cut you."

"Fine. But you can bet your ass I'm telling Pen. He is going to shit himself."

Lilian chucked the knife into the utensil drawer. "Your boyfriend is going to shit himself? Sexy."

"Why are you here? Did you show up for the specific purpose of tormenting me?" Mercy asked him.

"Pen and I were heading for the hotel to pick up Marshal Ralston, but he flagged us down on Main Street. Apparently, Hart 'Sexy Times' Ralston wasn't at the hotel last night, was he?" Zeddie cocked an eyebrow at his big sister as he swiped a quiche from the platter. "Anyway, I stopped by to grab a snack."

Mercy beat her head against one of the cabinets. Her secret was out, and like toothpaste squeezed out of a tube, there was no putting it back.

While Lilian wrested the books away from Pop in the office, Mercy got to work as the official undertaker of Birdsall & Son. They'd have to get around to changing the name of the family business soon, but in the meantime, Mercy had a well full of cadavers that needed tending. She decided to start with the keyless bodies that Hart and Pen had brought in the day before so that she could clear up space. As she brought the indigents out of the well and rolled them into the lift, she thought of Hart having to face drudges on a daily basis, a problem that was getting exponentially worse, based on her intake lately. The uptick was great for her bottom line, but it made her ill to think that she was making money off the problem, while Hart and Pen and all the other Tanrian Marshals risked their lives to keep people safe.

She cleaned, salted, and wrapped two bodies, doing her best

to focus on the incantations rather than let her concern for Hart consume her. As she dug the appendix out of the third body to make sure Hart and Duckers had sliced it—and they had—she noticed something odd. There was a strange ridge along the appendix, next to the wound. When she ran her scalpel underneath it, it peeled off, as if someone had stuck a paper-thin, flesh-colored patch to the small organ that housed the human soul. Beneath it was another hole gouged into the appendix, but there was no corresponding hole on the patch she had removed.

Mercy went ahead and finished preparing the body, but she paid closer attention as she worked on the last two. It was much harder to see on the next, but she found a similar patch stuck over a wound on the appendix of the fourth body, and the fifth body produced the strange patch on both the appendix and the exterior abdomen. The latter matched the skin so well, she didn't think she would have caught it if she hadn't been searching for peculiarities.

"What in the Salt Sea?" she wondered aloud.

Chapter Twenty-Nine

Knock, knock! Mail delivery!"

Hart got out the whiskey and poured a healthy splash into a cup as Bassareus stepped into the barracks.

"How you doin'?" The nimkilim raised his cup to both marshals before gulping it down. "Five for Mr. Popular and zero for the asshole."

Strange how the word *asshole* sounded like *friend* in the baritone register of a crass rabbit. Stranger still how much Hart was starting to like the nimkilim, maybe because "zero for the asshole" meant that Mercy preferred *him* him to secret-letter-writing him. It inspired a tip so generous that Bassareus broke into a genuine smile, his jagged tooth more childish than menacing for a change.

"Guess I'm coming back tomorrow night, Hart-throb."

"For the kid's letters. Now get the fuck out of here."

"That feels like a warm hug coming from the likes of you, ya big softy. See you tomorrow."

As he watched the nimkilim melt into the woods beyond the barracks door, Hart contemplated the once unfathomable notion that he really was turning into a big softy, a softy for whom Wisdomsday could not arrive soon enough. As Duckers read his letters, Hart stretched out on his cot with his newest interlibrary loan. His mind kept drifting to Mercy until Duckers cut through his pleasant thoughts with a voice so smug it sent a portentous finger along Hart's spine.

"Well, well, well."

Hart looked up from his book. "Well, well, well, what?"

"Fess up. I want to hear all about how I was right."

Hart tamped down a growing sense of vague foreboding. "I've got nothing to fess up to."

The foreboding went from vague to very specific when Duckers held up a letter scrawled in Zeddie's now-familiar exuberant handwriting. "All I know is that one of us is hooking up with Mercy Birdsall, and it isn't me."

Hart's mouth went dry. "Zeddie knows?"

"He overheard Mercy and Lilian talking about it. So it's true?"

"Her *sister* knows?" Hart was having trouble breathing.

"You clearly do not have sisters, because if you did, you would know that they tell each other everything. I mean, *everything*."

Lilian knew, and Zeddie knew, and now Duckers knew, and Roy Birdsall might know by now, too, and their knowing made the strange, beautiful, delicate thing between Hart and Mercy real and solid, something that could be broken. He and Mercy had talked about telling her family, but now that it had happened, Hart worried that it was too much, too soon. What if they didn't approve of him? What if they didn't think he was good enough for her? He shoved his hair out of his face with both hands and squeezed the sides of his head, trying not to panic. "Fuck."

"Ha! I was right! Say it!" Duckers was on his feet, dancing in victory.

"You were right," Hart said, feeling light-headed.

"Mean it!"

Hart had the wild urge to laugh. "You were right, okay?"

"About what, exactly?"

"About Mercy."

"I'm sorry. What about Mercy?" Duckers stood over him, leaning in, his hand at his ear.

"I'm in love with her."

It was as if a burden had been lifted off his chest, the words he had almost said to her yesterday freed from his heart and sent out into the universe.

"Oh, shit. Really?" Duckers's eyes bugged so hard Hart thought they might pop from their sockets, and his brief euphoria vanished.

"What the fuck did you think I was going to say?"

"Dang, sir, I don't know. I thought you were going to say that you like her, but you *love* her? Like, capital-*L* Love?"

"I swear to the Unknown God, you are a pox upon my soul, Duckers."

"So that's a yes?"

Hart thought of Mercy, beautifully disheveled after dancing with him, standing opposite him at the counter of Birdsall & Son with two slices of cake and more than four years' worth of misunderstandings between them. He thought of the ease with which she had swept the latter aside simply by talking to him and drawing him out, bit by bit, as if the man he was on the inside was worth knowing. He tried so hard not to smile he thought his face might break. Apparently, that was answer enough, because Duckers declared, "Told! You! So!"

Hart was grateful when Banneker and Ellis returned from their patrol, thereby cutting off Duckers's teasing. They hung their hats and sat down to dinner as Hart and Duckers headed for their equimares in the stable. Unfortunately, Duckers turned out to be a dog with a bone when it came to Hart's love life.

"So, like, you told Mercy about the letters that night at the café, right?"

Hart rubbed his stubbly chin and said nothing.

"Oh my gods. You didn't tell her." This time, it was an accusation, not a question.

"You worry about you."

Duckers flapped one elbow, performing a one-winged chicken dance with his left hand while his lantern hung from the right. "Bock, bock, bock!"

"Fuck off."

"You need to tell her, man."

"Last time I checked, my name was *sir* as far as you're concerned."

"Fine. You need to tell her, *sir*."

"And you need to shut your hole, *kid*."

Duckers shook his head as Hart saddled his equimaris. "I can't believe what a wimp you are. You slay the undead on a regular basis. Pretty sure you can handle telling that nice lady that you wrote her some love letters."

"What do you know?"

"I know I'm going to tell her if you don't."

Hart went as cold as stone. "I will fucking end your life."

"No, *you* will fucking end *your* own life miserable and alone if you don't tell her. Now. Like, *now* now."

If Hart was ice, Duckers was fire, grilling him with a truth he didn't want to hear but couldn't refute.

"I'll handle it," Hart relented.

"You'll handle it?"

"Yes. I swear. Don't tell her. Please."

Duckers leveled him with an ocular skewering that rivaled Alma's. "I like Mercy. She's a good person. So you better handle it. *Sir*."

Hart knew that Duckers was right. He needed to tell Mercy the truth, and soon, no matter what it cost him.

The problem was, it might cost him everything.

The only people residing in Sector W-7 were the employees of the Alvarez Ambrosia Bottling Company, who worked day shifts and barricaded themselves in their own barracks overnight. There were security guards on the grounds, but they were required by law to set off a flare to notify the Tanrian Marshals in the event of a drudge attack, which was why alarm bells went off in one corner of Hart's mind when he and Duckers heard a commotion near the Mist, more than a mile away from the Alvarez factory and storage cavern.

Silently, Hart drew his pistol crossbow and motioned for Duckers to do the same. They rode toward the tumult to find a brawl in progress, and since it was difficult to discern people from drudges at night, they stayed on equimarisback and went in for a closer look, lanterns blazing. Their light threw frenzied shadows against the uneven earth, and it took Hart a minute to distinguish five drudges from three living people, who appeared to be wearing the uniforms of Alvarez security guards. A pirated portal opened a hole in the Mist some distance behind them, and bizarrely, there were heaps of what appeared to be sailcloth piled all over the place.

"Have the flare ready for backup. I'm going in."

"I'm going with you."

"No, you stay here, and light the flare if things get ugly."

He didn't wait for an answer. He drew his machete and charged into the scene, chopping off the head of a figure he was absolutely certain was a reanimated corpse, then the arms of another drudge that was gripping a living man by his shirt. He hacked the head off one more of the undead with the machete before returning it to the scabbard at his back, sliding off his mount, and joining the melee on foot with his rapier drawn. He cut into the appendix of the armless drudge, followed by those of the headless corpses, as the living shot crossbow arrows at the remaining two drudges indiscriminately, which probably should have been a clue that something was more than usually wrong, but Hart was too preoccupied to consider it.

"Now, sir?" yelled Duckers, but Hart's attention was on the living people who were firing at will with no regard for his own well-being.

"Watch where you're shooting!" barked Hart.

He took out the last two drudges by the light of the lanterns strapped to the arching poles on his and Duckers's equimares as he barely avoided getting shot by the panicking humans. Once the five souls were dispatched into the night and only the living remained standing, Hart got a better look at the woman and two men standing in front of the portal. They wore the security uniforms of the Alvarez Ambrosia Bottling Company, but Hart didn't recognize them, and the fact that at least one of them had nearly shot him led him to believe he was dealing with something far worse than drudges here. There were several crime rings that had their fingers in Tanria, and the Alvarez plant was a tempting target since it sat close to the Mist. The Trickster knew the mob had plenty of access to pirated portals to get in and out of Tanria. If these three were mafiosi, Hart wasn't feeling so great about the fact that they had crossbows drawn, while he had only his rapier in hand.

"Thanks, Marshal. We can take it from here," the woman said, making no move to holster her weapon.

Hart played along, sheathing his rapier but keeping his hand near his pistol crossbow. "I need to get your ID tag numbers for the report," he said coolly.

No one moved or spoke.

"Tags, please," said Hart, his hand now on his sidearm.

One of the men began to ease backward toward the portal.

"Fire the flare, Duckers," Hart ordered without taking his eyes off the three people whose lives he'd saved.

"Sir?"

"Now!"

"Flare! He's got a flare!" cried one of the men, raising his weapon and taking aim at Duckers. Hart drew his pistol crossbow and squeezed the trigger, catching the man in his thigh as the flare hissed, then exploded above them.

"He fucking shot me!" the wounded man howled as he writhed on the ground.

"Put down your weapons!" Hart shouted at the other two, but it was too late. The woman pulled her trigger, and a shaft tore through Hart's left side. He staggered, trying to remain upright, despite the blinding pain, as the woman and the other man hauled their wounded comrade through the portal. They shut it down and pulled it off the Mist as Hart fell to his knees, his left side shrieking in agony. Duckers hopped off his mount and sprinted to him.

"I'm good," Hart told him as Banneker and Ellis came galloping in. He pressed his hand to the hole in his side, trying to get a feel for how much blood he'd lost.

"Sir?" Duckers crouched beside him.

"See? There's more to fear from the living than from the dead. You remember that," Hart told him, the same lesson that Bill had taught him long ago.

The world began to spin.

"Oh, fuck," he mumbled before he blacked out.

"How is he?" Alma asked Dr. Levinson outside Hart's room at the infirmary while he was supposed to be resting.

"Lucky. Most people would have wound up with sepsis with a wound like that, but he's healing almost as fast as Rosie Fox."

Hart felt as if every organ in his body had dropped to the floor beneath the uncomfortable hospital bed. Because Marshal Rosie Fox was an immortal demigod. Definitely, conclusively immortal.

"Ah," said Alma, and Hart knew her well enough to hear the unease in that one syllable. "Can I see him?"

"I suppose, but don't wake him. He needs rest."

Dr. Levinson led Alma into the room as she jotted down notes on Hart's chart.

"Well, look who's bright-eyed and bushy-tailed this morning," Alma said when she saw that he was awake.

"Some bed rest, and you'll be right as rain in a few days, Marshal," the doctor added.

"Great," said Hart, and realizing that his flat tone made him sound like an ingrate, he added, "Thanks."

"Can I have a minute with him?" Alma asked the doctor.

"Sure."

She waited until the doctor was out of the room before asking, "Ralston, why do you have to be Tanria's punching bag all the time?"

"You say that like I get shot every five minutes." His tongue felt thick and dry in his mouth, probably from the painkillers.

"I know you heard the Rosie Fox comment. It doesn't mean anything."

"It's okay. I'm fine."

Alma regarded him and tapped her fingers on the bed rail. He wasn't convincing either of them.

"Want me to leave so you can get some rest?"

"No, hold up. I've got something I've been meaning to say to you."

"All right. But if Doc Levinson gets mad at me, it's on you."

She pulled up a stool with a screech across the linoleum floor and helped him adjust his bed to a sitting position. "Shoot."

Hart stared at his hands in his lap, red and chapped against the pale blue of his hospital gown. They didn't look like the hands of an immortal.

"I hate that we've drifted apart these past few years. I'm sorry I let that happen."

"I'm sorry, too." She touched his arm, a gesture made more potent because it was Alma doing it. Her affection was rare, and more powerful for the rarity. "But I can't apologize for what I said about Bill. I'm not going to lie about the man to make you feel better."

"You have the right to your opinion, but there are things about Bill you don't know."

"Why don't you tell me?"

"I should. I will. But not now."

"Fair enough."

Hart extended his hand. "Friends?"

"Fuck you with your handshake." She pushed his hand aside and hugged him. It didn't help his wound, but it did wonders for his heart.

"Get off me, you sap."

She relinquished him and sat back on the stool. "Jerk."

"True. What were the perps who shot me trying to smuggle out of Tanria? Do we know?"

"The only thing we found on site was sailcloth, which is weird, but that's not your concern. I know this is going to make you cry, but the law requires that you take sick leave after being shot, at least a couple of days."

Hart's knee-jerk reaction was to protest, but then he realized that sick leave meant time with Mercy and the chance to come clean about the letters.

"Okay," he agreed.

"Okay? Just like that?"

"Yep."

She squinted at him. "What's got into you?"

He glanced around the room, at the floor, the window, the medical supply closet. Anywhere but at Alma's face. "I'm seeing someone."

"No! Really?"

"Really."

She scooted the stool closer, the linoleum beneath it crying abuse. "Is it serious?"

"Maybe."

She walloped him with a good-natured punch to the shoulder.

"Ow!"

"That didn't hurt, you big baby."

"May I remind you that I was shot?"

"Come on. The suspense is killing me. Who is it?"

He squirmed, but he couldn't wipe away the mawkish, bathetic grin taking over his face. "Mercy Birdsall."

Alma's aquamarine eyes went wide before she cackled.

"Shut up," he told her without an ounce of conviction.

"Oh, ho, ho! Shoe's on the other foot, isn't it? Working two-week tours sucks when you're head over heels, and now you see the light. I give it a month before you're begging me for a desk job."

"So I can take some time off?"

"You have to wait until the doc discharges you, but yeah. Because, as you pointed out, you were *shot*." She mussed his hair like she used to do when they first became partners. "Say hi to Mercy for me."

"Will do."

As long as Mercy didn't send him packing when he finally told her the truth, he thought, and his stupid grin vanished.

Chapter Thirty

If Hart was going down in flames, he intended to look his best for Mercy when he did so. He got a haircut and a shave, as well as two new shirts and a new pair of dungarees from the only men's clothier on the border that sold tall sizes, and he had his best boots shined to gleaming. He considered the purchase of a new hat as well, but given his proclivity for crushing it when he was nervous, and given the fact that he was already terrified to confess the truth to Mercy, he decided to save his money and abuse the hat he had left at Birdsall & Son.

In addition to these improvements, Hart was one key lighter. He had returned his ID tag and funeral package to Cunningham's first thing that morning. The receptionist pulled his file, sniffed at the cheap price tag, and handed him off to a junior associate, who couldn't have been older than Duckers. The young undertaker recited a canned speech, trying to upsell Hart on one of Cunningham's many embalming packages, even as he filled out the paperwork to process Hart's return. The place was an airless, joyless, soulless approach to death, and he couldn't understand why he'd chosen to patronize Cunningham's all these years. Maybe he'd found it easier to deal with mortality as a business transaction rather than face his own uncertain end.

He stopped by the bank and his lawyer's office, so it was late afternoon by the time he stood at the counter of Birdsall & Son, clutching a small paper-wrapped parcel in his sweating hands, his chest tight with nerves. He heard hammering coming from the boatworks, and he hoped that Mercy wouldn't wish to use that hammer on his face as soon as he told her about the letters. He took a deep breath, which did nothing to calm his raging jitters, and rang the bell.

To his consternation, it was not Mercy who answered the summons, but her father. If Zeddie and Lilian knew about Hart and Mercy, did that mean that Roy knew about them, too? Hart thought he might go into cardiac arrest as the man stepped behind the counter, but the affable smile on his face led Hart to believe that no one had clued him in yet.

"Good afternoon, Marshal Ralston. Dropping off a body?"

Hart wasn't sure that there was still blood flowing to his lips. "No, I . . . I'm . . ."

What was he supposed to say? *I'm here to see your daughter to tell her that I'm her secret pen pal and I'm hoping against hope that she won't hate me forever and might even want to have sex with me tonight?*

A furrow of confusion and concern dove between Roy's substantial eyebrows until Hart finally choked out the one true thing he *could* say to Mercy's dad.

"I'm here to buy a new funeral package."

"Well, now!" The affable smile returned—Mercy's smile, Hart realized. And the second he thought of Mercy, there she was, peering into the lobby from the hallway, her glasses sprinkled with sawdust.

"Pop, did you get the—" She saw Hart and bit her bottom lip, and his heart leaped out of his chest to go reside in hers.

"I've got it, muffin. Marshal Ralston is here to buy a funeral package from us."

This time, Mercy didn't bother hiding her grin. "Is he?"

"Come on in and have a seat in the office, Marshal."

Hart turned panicked eyes on Mercy as Roy clapped him on the shoulder and ushered him through the office door.

"Tea?" she offered, beaming at him.

"Yes, please."

"Now, remind me, are we updating a current package?" Mercy's dad asked as they took their seats on opposite sides of the desk. Hart set his parcel down on the empty chair beside him.

"No. I returned my package to Cunningham's. I'm here to buy a new one."

Roy's eyebrows shot up, taking the glasses perched on top with them. "I see. Thank you for your business."

Hart squirmed in his chair and nodded, and Roy spread out a brochure in front of him.

"We offer a wide array of handcrafted boats in three price tiers—I assume you're interested in purchasing a boat?"

Hart's old package stated that he would be shrouded in a simple sailcloth, cremated, and scattered on the outskirts of the shipyard. But if building boats was what Mercy loved, he'd put down the money to buy one. An expensive one. He scanned through the options and chose the model and corresponding wood with the highest price tag. Roy's eyebrows threatened to shoot right off his face, but he perched the reading glasses on the end of his nose and scribbled down Hart's selections.

"And would you prefer that your body be interred or cremated?"

"Cremated, I guess."

"Where would you like us to send the remains?"

It was one thing to tell a perfect stranger that he had no home and, therefore, nowhere to send his ashes. It was another to have to admit as much to Mercy's dad.

"You can scatter them on the shipyard."

"No headstone?"

Hart shook his head, and Roy's forehead creased, an expression that reminded Hart of Mercy's warm compassion.

"That's not very comforting to the loved ones you leave behind."

"Don't want to burden anyone with it."

Roy set down his pen. "Where are you from, Hart?"

It was nice to hear this fatherly man call him by name. Hart crossed his ankle over his knee and wished he had his hat to set on top of his leg. "Arvonia. I joined the Tanrian Marshals when I was sixteen, and I haven't been back."

"Got any family?"

"Not that I'm close with."

"Aren't you friends with Alma Maguire? She's your old partner, right?"

Hart thought of the last time he went to see Alma and Diane, the way they'd fretted over him in soft voices when they thought he was asleep and couldn't hear.

"Yep, we're good friends," he agreed.

"I've known Alma for a long time. I don't think she'd find scattering your ashes a burden."

Maybe Roy was right. Alma did have his birth key, after all, and she was going to have to figure out what to do with that if Hart died, so he nodded his agreement. "You can add her wife's name, too. Diane Belinder."

Roy picked up his pen to jot down both names in the appropriate box.

"Any instructions regarding your birth key or the keys of any family members in your care?"

"Alma Maguire is already in possession of my birth key. My mother's key should be sent to her sister, Patricia Lippett. I assume she's still living in Pettisville, Arvonia."

"Good." Roy jotted down the information as he continued to speak. "I do recommend that you keep your last will and testament on file with your final arrangements. It makes it easier on your loved ones when everything is in one place."

"I have that here." Hart reached into his vest pocket and retrieved the document, folded neatly into thirds.

"Excellent." Roy placed Hart's will into a manila file folder, along with the paperwork for his new funeral package. As he handed over the new key-shaped ID tag, he asked, "If you don't mind my asking, what made you cancel your order with Cunningham's and purchase your arrangements from Birdsall & Son?"

Hart had not anticipated this question. He uncrossed his legs and sat up, a clammy hand on each knee. If Mercy hadn't told her father about them yet, he didn't have the right to say anything, but at the same time, he was not eager to lie. Lying—or, at least, sins of omission—had caused him enough problems.

"I'm dating your daughter." His voice tapered to nothing at the end.

"I'm sorry, I didn't catch that."

Hart cleared his throat. "I'm dating Mercy."

Roy had printed *Ralston, Ha* on the file folder tab, but he froze, his pen clutched in his hand. A long pause sucked all the air out of the room before Mercy knocked on the door and stepped inside. She attempted to smile brightly as she set a steaming cup in front of Hart, but both men knew her well enough to see it for the nervous grimace it was.

"Everything all right?" she sang too cheerily.

"Of course. Thank you, muffin."

"Yep," Hart agreed, half tempted to cling to her ankle and let her drag him out of the office to safety.

"Well then." Another brutal silence stretched through the

room. "I guess I'll leave you to it." Mercy gave them both one last strained smile before she stepped out, closing the door behind her.

Roy's eyes met Hart's over the top of his reading glasses. Hart expected to find a sharp glint of disapproval therein. Instead, Mercy's father gave him an appraising look. "I know you saved her life, but I was under the impression that you two hated each other."

"It's definitely not hate."

"Huh. I'm gonna need a minute to adjust to this," he said gruffly, opening his desk drawer and pulling out the not-so-secret bottle of whiskey. He poured himself three fingers and held the neck over Hart's tea as an offer.

"I'm not much of a drinker."

"Good to know." Roy recapped the bottle, shoved it back in the drawer, and took a deep gulp. "No one tells me anything around here. I have three children, but you'd think I was the baby. So, you're seeing each other?"

"Yes."

"And it sounds like it's serious. Is it?"

"Yes. For me, it is. Although I'm not too sure I deserve her, to be honest."

"Good answer." Roy set his forearms on the desk and leaned in to study Hart, who was now experiencing heart palpitations. "Why don't you come over for dinner tonight?"

Here was the nice, wholesome dinner Hart had mentioned to Mercy, but as he watched Roy's huge hand dwarf the pen, he found the invitation daunting. He wasn't accustomed to fathers, and he wasn't sure how to act around Mercy's.

"Yes, sir. Thank you, Mr. Birdsall."

Roy held out his hand. Hart took it with trepidation, and his finger bones crunched alarmingly in the other man's grip.

"Call me Roy."

Chapter Thirty-One

Mercy tried to work, but it was hard to concentrate when she knew that Hart was in the next room with her father, buying a funeral package no less. Thank the Salt Sea she was midboat rather than midbody. She was measuring a plank to cut for the third time when both men showed up in the boatworks doorway.

"I believe Hart wanted to see you," said Pop.

Hart. Not *Marshal Ralston*. What exactly had they been talking about in there?

"I'm heading out for the evening, muffin. Have a good night."

"Good night, Pop."

Her father chucked Hart on the arm, and though Hart was much taller, he seemed to shrink, and his face went pale.

"See you tonight?"

"Yes, sir. I mean, Roy."

Pop's footsteps clumped down the hall and into the lobby, and the sound of the front door opening and closing followed. Hart remained in the doorframe, gripping a small brown paper parcel in his hands, his hair neatly trimmed, his face clean shaven, and Mercy was thrilled to discover that Clean-Cut Hart was every bit as handsome as Rugged Tanrian Marshal Hart. She raced across the boatworks and wrapped her arms around his waist. He bent to kiss her, but his lips were stiff.

"You're coming over for dinner? Did I know about this?"

"I unexpectedly got a few days off. Your dad just invited me." He disentangled himself from her arms and presented her with the parcel. "I got you something."

"You didn't have to get me anything."

"I wanted to. I guess flowers would have been better, but I thought this might be nice to have in your boatworks."

Mercy took the package from him and unwrapped it, revealing a small red metal box with a foldable crank on one side and a grid of tiny holes beside a gold dial on the other. "Oh! It's... wonderful! Thank you!"

"You have no clue what it is."

"None whatsoever," she admitted.

"It's a transistor."

Suddenly, the red metal seemed to glow like a sunrise in her hands. "Bride of Fortune, Hart! How does it work?"

"You crank it until it stops. Then you turn it on and spin the dial until you find a station you like. There are two stations on Bushong that come in loud and clear, and the Vinland stations are pretty strong, too. The volume is on the side here. It should last a good hour before you have to crank it again."

She jumped up and down like a kid getting everything she wanted on her birthday. She cranked the transistor, put it beside a can of paint on the shelf, and flipped the switch to *On*. The red box crackled to life, blasting static into the room. She turned the dial until she hit a station playing a song that was too twangy for her liking. She kept turning until she came to the familiar blare of a trumpet and the exhilarated thumping of a bass drum.

"I love this song!" she cried, and then she sang along, full throated, twirling her hips in time to the music. She didn't know the second verse, so she sang "I love this gift! This is the best gift ever!" in place of the lyrics. Hart laughed, but his gray eyes didn't light up the way they ought to.

"What's wrong?"

"I'm nervous."

"About dinner?"

"Among other things."

"Don't be. You have faced far scarier things in Tanria than my family."

The song finished and another took its place, a slow, sweet number.

"I know you're Mr. Fancy Feet, but do you think you can handle the old Sway in a Circle?"

"I'll give it my best shot," he said wryly, and Mercy decided that he was darling when he was wry. How on earth had she managed to detest him for so long? Everything he did now seeped inside her chest and took up permanent residence. She tucked her head against his shoulder as he guided her in a lazy circle to the slow, steady rhythm of the song. "You're perfectly Mercy-sized," she informed him.

"I'd like to think so." He spoke the words into her hair with that quiet, sexy laugh of his. She turned her face up and nuzzled the bare skin of his neck above his collar.

"Claiming the Nuzzle Nook outside the confines of your bed? Is that allowed?"

"I demand to have full and complete access to my Nuzzle Nook at all times."

"Mercy?" he said softly.

"Hmm?" She skimmed her lips down his neck, undid the top button of his shirt, and nipped his collarbone, savoring the way his breath stuttered.

"I should . . . I need to . . ."

She stepped back and regarded his tired, anxious face. "You really are nervous, aren't you?"

"That is putting it mildly."

"It'll be all right. I promise." She took him by the arms and gave him a reassuring shake before switching off the transistor. "Do you mind if I take a quick bath before we go over?"

"If it's a *quick* bath, then yes, I mind."

"Do you mind if I take a long, luxurious bath?" she amended.

"By all means. To clarify, I get to watch, right?"

"Sure, but are you up for hijinks? You look like you might be sick all over the linoleum."

"I don't think I'm up for hijinks right before the nice, wholesome family dinner. Doesn't mean I'm not going to enjoy the show."

As Mercy ran the bathwater, Hart retrieved her discarded clothes and folded them neatly, setting them on the edge of the vanity, an action that struck her as mind-blowingly thoughtful after years of picking Zeddie's dirty clothes off every surface of the house. She had already fallen for this man, and yet she couldn't seem to stop falling farther and deeper.

He sat on the bathroom floor, his back against the wall facing her, his long legs making giant triangles between them like an enormous cricket on the ceramic tiles. Leonard sat beside him, leaning his jowls against his beloved marshal's chest and snorting with joy as Hart pet him.

"This is even better than I thought it was going to be," he said as he watched her sink into the hot sudsy water.

"You've imagined yourself sitting on a cold tile floor, watching me remove five pounds of sawdust from my person while my dog drooled on your shirt?"

"Many times. You have no idea. Before I forget, Alma Maguire says hi."

Mercy's heart fluttered. If Alma was passing along her regards, that meant that Hart had told his best friend about her. Her cheeks were already warm and dewy from the bathwater, but the knowledge that Hart was owning up to dating her made half the blood in her body rush to her face.

"Tell her I said hello back."

"I will, but I hope we can hang out with Alma and Diane one of these days so you two can say hi to each other all you like in person."

He was prepared to take her along to meet up with Alma, who was practically family to him? This was getting serious, and Mercy, who had hated Hart from the depths of her soul a few months ago, was thrilled.

"Who's Diane?"

"Alma's wife. Gird yourself: She's going to hug you. A lot. If you ever meet her."

"I'm sure I will."

"I hope so."

Mercy was glad that she was in the bathtub; otherwise, she might be dancing a jig right about now. "Has this bath met your long and luxurious standards? Because I'm starting to wrinkle."

"Can't have that."

He helped her out of the tub, and now that the soapy water no longer covered her, she felt silly and self-conscious to be standing on her bath mat, dripping and naked, when he was fully clothed. She reached for the towel, but Hart beat her to it, patting her dry himself. It was sweetly chaste, the gentle way he tousled her hair and blotted the water from her skin. As he wrapped the thick terry cloth around her shoulders, Mercy shooed Leonard out of the bathroom and reached out to undo the buttons of Hart's shirt.

"Isn't your dad's house one of those classy no shirt, no shoes, no service kind of places?" he joked, but he leaned his long frame against the wall and watched her fingers work with smoky eyes, showing no inclination to stop her.

"You're always the one touching me. I want to touch you for a change."

She felt bold and vulnerable at once as she peeled back his shirt and slid it down his arms. She slipped her hands beneath his undershirt, pushing it up from the inside as she touched taut skin, ridged muscle, tickling hair…

"Mercy, I have to tell you—"

And a gauzy bandage wrapped around his torso.

"What happened?" she exclaimed, bunching up the undershirt to get a better look.

"It's nothing. A scratch."

"That's a big bandage for a 'scratch.' Why didn't you tell me?"

"In my defense, I've been very distracted since I arrived."

"Hart!"

He took the corners of her towel in his hands to bring her in close. "I'm all right, Merciless."

"You're not all right. None of this is all right. I'm scared every time you have to go back." She reached up and stroked his sharp cheekbones with her thumbs.

"Mercy, I need to…"

But she didn't want his words. She wanted his breath. She wanted his heartbeat. She wanted to feel the warmth of his living body, to know that he was alive and well and hers. She kissed him, and he kissed her in return with a tenderness that made her chest ache. Their movements were slow and soft as they made their way into the bedroom. He kept his forehead pressed against hers as he moved in and out of her, every movement of his body gentle and sweet. If Mercy had been unsure that she was in love with him before, she was certain of it now.

Chapter Thirty-Two

Now. Tell her now, thought Hart as they got dressed for dinner, but there was something he needed to straighten out before she kicked him to the curb. *If* she decided to kick him to the curb. *Please don't kick me to the curb*, he begged her in his mind. Aloud, he said, "I have a proposition for you."

Mercy raised an eyebrow, and although his anxiety jangled inside him, the gesture made him laugh.

"Not that kind of proposition."

"Okay. I'm listening." She stepped into her dress and turned, pulling her hair over her shoulder so that he could zip her up. This might be the last time he got to do something as intimate as zip her into a dress, a prospect that made telling her the truth even less alluring.

"What if I could help you? With the business?"

"How do you mean?"

She turned to face him, and he took her hands in his. "What if I hired a lawyer to help you fight Cunningham and Afton?"

"As in, you'd pay for the lawyer?"

He nodded.

"No."

That was a quicker and more decisive refusal than he'd been expecting. "Let me do this for you."

"Absolutely not."

"I have the money."

"Good. Keep it." She took her hands from his, and already, it felt like he was losing her.

"For what? I never spend it. And I..." *I love you,* he wanted to say, but he didn't have the right to tell her that, not until he came clean about the letters. "I care about you and what happens to you."

"I know you mean well, but this is my business. If I can't keep it afloat on my own, what's the point?"

"Think about it. That's all I'm asking."

Her mouth turned down, but it was out of exasperation rather than anger. "Okay. I'll think about it. But if my answer is no, you have to accept that. All right?"

"All right."

Now. Right now, he told himself when they took Leonard to play fetch at the park behind city hall to kill time before dinner, but it was so windy outside that he would have had to shout, and he didn't want to yell his confession at her.

Dear gods, now! his conscience begged him as he and Mercy walked together to her father's house with Leonard trotting at their heels, but she wove her arm through his, and he could not bear to risk letting her go yet. And then they were on the porch, and the front door opened, and Roy ushered them inside, and he had squandered the opportunity to say what needed to be said. Now he would have to survive a family dinner at the Birdsall house before he could tell Mercy the secret that sat in his guts like a ball of lead.

The first thing Hart noticed about the Birdsall house was that it was loud, and everyone seemed to be talking and laughing at once, and he couldn't figure out how so few people made so much noise. Roy kissed his daughter's cheek as they stepped inside, and he beamed at Hart as he shook his hand. "Glad you could make it."

"Thank you. I'm glad to be here." This was not entirely true, but Roy clapped him on the shoulder in a welcoming (and not a threatening) way, and Hart felt the stiffness in his spine ease. He followed Mercy to the family altar and watched her dip her fingers into the bowl of salt water and touch her mother's key. Then she pressed her fingertips over his chest, to the place where his own mother's key rested against his breastbone, and he understood then that if she broke things off with him once she knew about the letters, he would shatter, and there would be no putting him back together.

"They're here!" Mercy's sister, Lilian, shouted over her shoulder, and then she was hugging him around the middle, the way she had hugged him at the Founders' Day party, the way Diane had hugged him since he was nineteen years old, and he didn't dislike it, because he was fairly certain that she wouldn't be hugging him if she didn't think he was good enough for Mercy. He hugged her in return, albeit self-consciously.

"Have you met Danny yet?" Lil asked, taking Hart by the wrist and dragging him through the dining room toward the kitchen, where Zeddie was doing acrobatic things with onions and a large frying pan over the stove while a redheaded man leaned against the counter next to him.

"You must be Hart. I'm Lil's husband, Danny. Good to meet you." As Hart shook his hand, Danny leaned in and murmured, "They're terrifying, but you get used to them."

Lilian touched Hart's arm. "Are you nervous? Don't be nervous. Have some wine. Honey, pour Hart a glass."

Danny obeyed, getting a wineglass out of the cupboard. "I have been demoted from sous-chef to waitstaff. This one won't even let me mince the garlic anymore."

Zeddie scoffed from his place at the stove. "You call that mincing?"

"Hart's a lightweight," Mercy warned Danny. "Go easy."

Lilian took the bottle from her husband and filled Hart's glass to the brim. "Oh, this is going to be fun! Please, drink up on my behalf since I can't have any. You're so lucky you're not pregnant." Lil gasped theatrically and set the bottle down on the counter. "Are you?"

Hart did not require a mirror to inform him that he was blushing from head to toe. "Not the last time I checked."

Lilian burst out laughing. She looked nothing like her sister, but their laughter was the same. Danny pulled his wife into a hug and smushed her face against his shoulder to prevent her from embarrassing Hart further. "Forgive her. Her filter is flimsy."

"But you love me anyway," said Lil, her voice muffled against her husband's sweater vest.

"I do."

Salt Sea, thought Hart, *they're adorable. They're all adorable.*

Spending time with Mercy's family was a lot like going over to Alma and Diane's house, though much louder. There was a comfort in this home that eased into his bones. He no longer felt like an outsider by the time they sat down to dinner, and he didn't panic in the slightest when Roy started up a conversation with him over the scalloped potatoes.

"You said you're from Arvonia, right, son? Are you an Anemones fan?"

"Really, Pop?" said Mercy. "He sat down two seconds ago, and you're already grilling him on his sea polo preferences?"

But Hart had the bizarre urge to hug this big, burly man who called him *son*, and if Roy Birdsall wanted to talk about professional sea polo, Hart was game. "I was an Anemones fan when I was a kid, but I've worked in Tanria more than half my life, so I tend to root for the Bushong Giant Squids these days."

Roy's eyes went misty. He patted Hart on the back. "Good man. I like this one, muffin."

A warmth filled him that had nothing to do with the red wine he'd hardly touched. As he sat at the Birdsall family dinner table and watched Mercy's family joke and bicker and laugh, he realized that he was falling for them, too. If, by some miracle, he managed to keep Mercy in his life, he could be a part of this. He could have a family again.

A tendril of cowardly temptation eeled inside him. How terrible would it be if he never told Mercy that he was her secret friend? What good would it do to tell her about the letters now? None. He had so much to lose if he confessed, and everything to gain if he simply kept his mouth shut. Surely, he could convince Duckers to see it his way.

He had no sooner resolved to let his letter-writing past disappear without a trace than Zeddie, of all people, kicked off the process of destroying his life by raising a glass and declaring, "To Hart Ralston: the guy gets shot and almost dies, and shows up to a Birdsall family dinner two days later!"

The table did not respond with cheers. Roy, Lilian, Danny, and worst of all, Mercy gaped at him in various states of shock or alarm. In the pit of his stomach, Hart knew that this was very bad, although his mind hadn't pieced together exactly why.

Mercy turned on him. "You said it was a scratch! You were *shot*?"

"A little."

"How can you be shot 'a little'?" Mercy's voice hit operatic notes.

"It's healing fine, and I didn't want to worry you."

"Of course I'm worried about you! I can't believe you didn't tell me! And how did you find out about it?"

The last question was directed at Zeddie, and Hart realized that this was why he was completely fucked.

"I had a letter from Pen this morning."

"How can you have a letter from Pen? There aren't any nimkilim boxes in Tanria."

"Yeah, but he and Hart bribe their delivery nimkilim to pick up their mail."

Slowly, Mercy turned toward Hart, her face full of shock and anger.

"I...," he said but couldn't seem to get any further. Blood thundered in his ears.

"You told me you couldn't send letters from Tanria."

"That's not exactly what I said." The second Hart spoke the words, he knew they were a mistake, as evidenced by the ice daggers shooting out of Mercy's eyes and into his chest.

Zeddie sat down and leaned his head toward Lilian. "Hart's in trouble."

"Did he lie to you about something?" squealed Lil, before turning a fiery glare on Hart.

Mercy slapped the table. "None of you need to be involved in this conversation." She pointed her finger in Hart's face. "Except you. Come with me."

Hart could sense her fury and humiliation simmering like water in a teakettle as she got up and marched through the parlor and out the front door, which she slammed shut as soon as he followed her onto the porch. He held up both hands in surrender. They were shaking badly. He was going to lose her. He could already feel his joy slipping through his fingers like sand.

"Not a word out of you," she said. "I'm going to need the entire walk home to calm down enough to not strangle you."

Hart nodded meekly.

There was a scratching and whining at the door, and someone opened it wide enough to let Leonard out before shutting it. The dog was oblivious to the imminent destruction of Hart's life and bounded around him like a puppy.

The walk to Mercy's apartment was brutal but also far too short for him to compose a reasonable excuse as to why he'd lied about not writing to her from Tanria. Only the truth could save him now, and it probably wouldn't.

He followed Mercy and Leonard through the lobby of Birdsall & Son and up the stairs, but he didn't dare go farther into her home than the door, which he leaned against for support once it had shut behind him. Mercy walked to the open kitchen, took out a glass from the cupboard, filled it with water, and drank all of it, her back to him. When she faced him again, her eyes were no longer filled with fury. They were filled with hurt, which was infinitely worse.

"I don't understand why you would keep something like getting shot from me, or why you would lie to me about sending mail from Tanria. It makes me wonder what else you've kept from me."

"I know."

"Let's start with the part where you got shot. Why didn't you tell me?"

"It's probably easier to show you."

He unbuttoned his shirt and pulled up his undershirt to unwind the bandage, uncovering the pink pucker beneath. Mercy came over to study the wound, or the lack thereof. It didn't take a doctor to know that a pistol crossbow wound would not and should not have healed this quickly. Hart leaned his head against the door. He wasn't sure what he wanted to talk about less: this or the letters.

"The doctor wouldn't say it outright, but I think that arrow should have been a death sentence. And yet here I am." He spoke the words to the ceiling. It felt as if he were opening himself up to her with a crowbar.

She forgave him enough to run her hand up his torso until it rested over his heart, between his keys and his skin. "Do you have any idea how glad I am that it wasn't a death sentence?"

He wondered if she would be glad that he wasn't dead by the time this night was over. He took a lock of her hair and rubbed it between his fingers and thumb. "When I was seven years old, my grandpa took me to a circus in town. I was so excited to go, but one of the first things we did when we got there was go to the freak show. Almost everyone in that tent was a demigod. There was one woman in particular, an immortal who'd been alive for three hundred years. Thing is, her body kept aging. I remember thinking that she wasn't real—she didn't look human—but as I got up close, she opened her eyes. They were bright pink. I screamed and screamed, and Grandpa had to take me home, but those eyes have followed me every day of my life since."

Mercy tucked her head under his chin and held him in her arms. He had come to Eternity to fess up to the letters, but all of a sudden, he realized that he was about to tell her something else, something bigger. For seventeen years, remorse had sat on his chest like a boulder. Now he was about to push it off and send it rolling down a hill with no idea of the consequences. If Mercy didn't send him packing after this, she could forgive him anything.

"Can we sit down?" he asked her.

"Okay."

She let him lead the way. He took a seat on the settee and was glad that she sat next to him rather than across from him in one of the armchairs, where he couldn't touch her. He took her hand in his while he still could and said, "This isn't the first time I should've died but didn't. But I'm getting ahead of myself. I need to start at the beginning.

"I grew up on my grandpa's farm in Arvonia. It was just me and Mom and Grandpa. My grandma died before I was born, and Aunt Patty was already married by the time I came along. It was nice, a good place for a kid to grow up. But that's beside the point.

"One of my first memories is of seeing a light float across a newly planted cornfield. I remember asking my mom what it was, but she didn't seem to understand what I was talking about. I kept seeing them—these lights—and by the time I was six or seven, I realized that Mom couldn't see them, and Grandpa couldn't either. He died when I was nine—a stroke—dropped dead in the corn right in front of me. When I saw one of those lights come out of his body, I finally knew what it was I was seeing."

Mercy squeezed his hand. "You can see souls?"

He nodded. "I saw my mom's leave her body, too. How's that for an amazing demigod talent?"

In answer, Mercy stroked his arm with her free hand.

"There's more," he said, the pent-up words cramming into his mouth, eager to leave. "When I came to Tanria, I apprenticed under a man named Bill Clark, but he was more than my mentor. He taught me the ropes, but he also listened to me like I had something important to say, like I wasn't some kid who didn't know anything. He didn't want me to lose out on my education, so he got me a library card and humored me when I droned on about whatever I was reading—history, philosophy, astronomy, you name it. I was like a sponge in those days, and he took it upon himself to make sure I soaked up the right things. He had an incredibly strong moral compass, and he set an example of the kind of man I should try to be. Not that I've lived up to those standards."

Mercy nudged him. "Give yourself credit. I'm sure he'd be proud of you if he could see you now." Leave it to Mercy to think better of him than he merited. What he was about to tell her might change that opinion.

"I know there's some god out there who sired me, but Bill was my father. So when I got to Tanria and I noticed a bunch of souls floating around there—more than I'd ever seen in one place—I told him about it. And then I took down my first drudge, and one of those souls came out of it. So all those people who believe that the human soul resides in the appendix and that drudges are lost souls infecting a body? They're right."

"Can you tell where the lost souls are coming from?"

Hart shook his head. "I only know Tanria is full of them, the ones who didn't make it to the afterlife for one reason or another. I don't know why, but they're trapped there. When they find a dead body—or make one—they take possession of it. It's their way of being alive, in their own sad way. So you can puncture the appendix, but the soul flies free until it finds another body. If you kill a drudge outside of Tanria, it floats through the Mist and gets stuck all over again."

"I had no idea."

"That's because I never told anyone about it except Bill."

"But why?" Hart eased her brow's furrow of confusion with a gentle fingertip and traced the lines of her face, so beautiful in the dim gaslight of her parlor.

"There's nothing anyone can do about it. And I should know; I tried. We both tried, Bill and I."

"What do you mean?" she asked, her concern for him thickening the words. He reached for her, and she snuggled into him. *Please don't give up your Nuzzle Nook*, he begged her in his mind.

"Souls aren't the only thing I can see. There's a house in the middle of a field in the heart of Tanria, in Sector 28. No one else can see it, but I can. And those souls can, too, I think. Drudges tend to congregate there."

"Because they want to go in?"

"Because they don't want to go in. Because they don't want anyone to open that door."

"Is it... *a* house or *the* House?" she asked in hushed awe.

"I'm pretty sure it's *the* House."

She remained motionless in his embrace. The silence stretched on until, at length, Hart gave a bitter laugh. "And what's crazy is that it looks like my house—I mean, from when I was a kid, the house I grew up in on the farm. Looks exactly like it."

"This is incredible."

"I'm sure everyone sees their own home when they go to the House of the Unknown God, but I don't think you're supposed to see it while you're still alive. Lucky me."

"You think you're seeing your own door to the afterlife waiting for you in Tanria? I thought you were worried that you can't...?" Mercy's voice trailed off, but Hart knew how to fill in the blank.

"I'm not sure what it is or why it's there, but I do know that a lot of people wouldn't have believed me, wouldn't have listened to a kid. Bill did, and he also guessed it was the House of the Unknown God. In those days, we were still figuring out the best way to deal with drudges. A lot of marshals lost their lives on the job, people Bill knew, his friends. So he started to wonder what would happen if I went up to the house and opened the front door. Maybe the souls would go in. Maybe we could get rid of the drudges, once and for all. Maybe we could save lives."

Mercy's arm wrapped so tightly around him, he struggled to breathe, but he kept unreeling the story.

"I was nineteen when we decided to try it. We got about halfway between the tree line and the house when the drudges came, and I mean they came at us from every direction. I've never seen so many at once. Bill lit his flare and told me to get to the house while he held them off. So I did what he said. I took off running. Half of them chased after me. Gods, they were fast. Drudges are always so much faster than you think they're going to be. I had to stop and fight them off. When I looked back, there was Bill. He was badly outnumbered and bleeding, from his head, his arm, everywhere. He saw me hesitate, and when he shouted at me to keep going, when he stopped fighting long enough to yell at me, they...they buried him. I don't know how else to describe it. They piled onto him, and I couldn't see him anymore. He had told me to keep going, to get to the house, but I couldn't let him die like that. So I went back for him. I tried to fight off every single drudge that had piled onto him, but they tore into me, too."

"Oh, Hart."

"Let me say it. Let me get through it." He gripped her to him, so hard he was afraid he was hurting her, but he couldn't seem to stop. "I did it. I got them all, but more were closing in, and I didn't know what to do, because Bill was still alive. He was on the ground, and fuck, he was in such bad shape, Mercy. And he told me—he begged me—not to let them have him. So I...so I..."

"Oh my gods."

"So I made sure they wouldn't make a drudge out of him."

Mercy said nothing, and he wasn't sure he would have heard her if she had. He was far away, standing in the field, watching Bill's face contort in pain as Hart buried his rapier into his mentor's appendix.

His voice sounded flat and far away when he spoke again.

"The remaining drudges surrounded me, but I stood there and watched as Bill's soul floated to that house and opened the door and went inside."

"And you? What happened to you?"

Mercy slipped from his arms and gazed at him with every ounce of her kind, lovely empathy as a tear that Hart did not want to shed trickled down his cheek. With the story out of his mouth and released into the unknown, he knew that he'd break down completely if he looked at her now, so he stared past her to the darkened doorway of her bedroom.

"More marshals arrived on the scene, answering our flare. They fought off the rest of the drudges and got me to the infirmary. I recovered, but I shouldn't have. That place should have been my grave. That door was meant for me, but Bill was the one who went inside." Hart wiped his damp cheeks. "I should have gone back and tried to finish what we started—"

"No."

"But I didn't. I couldn't. I couldn't bring myself to go back there. The house is still there, but even now, I can't face it."

Mercy combed her fingers through his hair, her thumbs wiping at the steady leak of his eyes. "Don't you ever go back there. Don't you ever try to open that door again."

"If I had opened that door seventeen years ago, if I had done what Bill told me to do, he might be alive today."

"Or you might both be dead. You don't know if you're immortal, Hart. And you have no idea what's behind that door. And neither did Bill, for that matter."

"Don't you understand? I as good as killed him!"

"No, you didn't!" She grasped him by the shoulders, but he flinched from her sympathy—found it irritating, even—and moved away from her on the settee. She rubbed his arm, but he went rigid beneath her touch. He didn't deserve her comfort. He didn't deserve anything good, not when he'd taken everything away from Bill.

"Don't try to erase my guilt, all right? It's not going anywhere."

"I'm not trying to erase the guilt. I'm trying to place it on the rightful shoulders."

Her words sank in like venom. Because if the guilt didn't belong on his shoulders, there could be only one other person she meant. Irritation gave way to cold enmity, gripping his heart with icy fingers. He pulled away from her touch.

"Don't go there," he warned her, but Mercy wasn't having it. She was burning with anger, and that anger was aimed at Bill Clark.

"I don't care how much you loved the man. You were a kid. He was the adult. He was responsible for you and your well-being, but he asked you to risk your life. And for what?"

"I'm a marshal. He was a marshal. The whole job is a risk."

"Marshal or not, a grown man who asks a nineteen-year-old to do something stupidly dangerous is not a person with a 'strong moral compass.' "

"You didn't know him."

"Maybe I didn't, but I know this: Pen is nineteen. Would you ask him to open that door?"

"He can't see it."

"That's beside the point!"

Hart froze, a statue of icy rage, and since he refused to reply to her question, Mercy did it for him. "The answer is no, you wouldn't, because you do have a strong moral compass."

She was right. There was no earthly way Hart would ask Duckers to do what Bill had asked him to do all those years ago, and he hated her for understanding something he had failed to grasp. It was like the argument with Alma all over again. With one question, she had completely blown up everything he thought he knew about himself, about Bill, about the world as he understood it. He got to his feet and made for the door.

"What are you doing?" Mercy demanded.

"Leaving."

She raced past him and stood in front of the door, her arms folded. "Hart, talk to me."

"Why? So you can tell me the best person I've ever known was an asshole, when you didn't know him at all?"

"I'm not saying he was a bad person."

"Right, he simply lacked a 'strong moral compass.' "

"Those were your words!" Mercy put her hands to her temples and took a deep breath. When she spoke again, her voice was calm, but her anger vibrated beneath the surface. "Maybe I shouldn't have said it the way I did, but you need to understand that Bill's death was not your fault. He put himself in that situation. He put *you* in that situation. So no, I don't—and I won't—think well of him for that, whether I knew him or not. Look what it's done to you."

Her version of the truth slapped him hard. His jaw was so tight, he could barely push his acerbic response through the grim slash of his mouth. "Yep. I'm a real mess, aren't I?"

"Would you stop twisting my words around? I'm trying to help you."

"I don't need your fucking help."

He stalked into the bedroom in search of his pack, but Mercy followed him and stood in the doorway.

"Sure. You don't need anything or anyone. You've been doing dandy on your own."

Leonard's liquid eyes looked up from where he lounged on the bed, his jowls draped over Hart's pack, and he whined, a sound that echoed the pain and resentment welling up inside Hart. Because Hart had not been doing dandy on his own. That was how he'd wound up writing the words *I'm lonely* in a letter that found its way to the one person who could break him into a million pieces, the person who was breaking him into a million pieces right this minute as she trampled his memories of Bill.

"Don't leave like this," Mercy told him as he tried to slide his pack out from underneath Leonard, but the dog mistook the gesture for a game of tug-of-war. Now Hart had hold of the strap, while Leonard's jaw clamped onto the bottom of the sack. The dog growled playfully, his nubbin twirling with joy. Hart tried to yank his pack free, but Leonard's hold was firm.

"Let go," he demanded.

"Hart, would you calm down for a minute and talk to me?"

"Let go!" He tugged hard, and the strap ripped away from the bag. Leonard celebrated his victory, shaking the bag in his mouth as if it were captured prey, flinging the contents all over the bedroom floor. Hart's toothbrush. His comb. His deodorant. His clean shirt and underwear. His library book.

Mercy's letters.

Leonard continued to growl in delight, and yet a deathly pall came over the room. Hart watched in powerless horror as Mercy stared at the packet of letters bound together with twine, her own handwriting staring back at her.

To: A Friend.

Hart's rage of five seconds ago was gone, all gone. He couldn't breathe right, couldn't seem to draw in or expel enough air from his lungs. "Mercy," he said, his voice thin and high.

She turned on her heel, flung open the apartment door, and flew down the stairs.

Hart tore after her. "Mercy, wait!"

She raced into the office and turned up the gas sconce. Then she went to one of the filing cabinets and fingered the labels on the drawers, muttering, "Who have you brought in lately?"

Hart reached for her, but she jerked away. She yanked open a drawer and sifted through the file tabs. "Clayton, Coffindaffer, Córdova... Cushman!" She tore the file out and held it up for Hart to see, and the wrath painting her face curdled his guts. She slapped the file onto the desktop and opened it. There was Hart's handwriting on the report, the squared-off letters she must have come to know as intimately as he knew hers.

She glared at him and waited for him to say something. His rib cage felt too small for the expanding anguish inside him, but he couldn't think of a single thing he could say that would repair what he had broken between them by not telling her the truth.

"You knew," she fumed. "You've known since the Little Wren Café. And you said nothing."

He stared at the paperwork, wishing from the depths of his soul that he could somehow erase the evidence of his own hand.

"Look me in the eye," she commanded.

He did as he was bidden, and her tears of rage burned a hole in his chest. She was so livid that she shook from head to toe, her hair vibrating in a halo of gaslight.

"You made me think that you... and then you *slept* with me?"

"I can explain."

"No, you *could have* explained—past tense—but you didn't. Now you can't, because I'm not interested in hearing your excuses."

Everything was crashing down around him. He was losing her, all of her—Mercy and her letters.

"You have to believe me," he begged her.

She cut him off with an incredulous, bitter laugh. "I'm sorry, what? I have to believe you? Why? So you can find some other way to weasel into my pants?"

"I would never—"

"You would never what? Lie to me?"

Hart buried his face in his hands. He couldn't bear the hatred pouring out of her and into him. "I didn't mean to lie," he wailed into his palms, but she pulled his hands away from his face.

"Yes, you did! You meant it! Lies don't happen by accident. A lie is a deliberate choice."

"Mercy, please, I'm so sorry."

"I don't want your apologies. And you know what? I don't want you."

She hadn't yelled the words; she had spoken them with a cool precision that cut him apart. He stopped crying. He stopped feeling. He stopped functioning. He existed, and that was it.

"Don't you step foot in this place again," she told him, her voice as cold as the Salt Sea. "If you've got a body to deliver, you send Pen to do it. Do you understand?"

He couldn't think or speak. All he could do was nod.

"Now get out."

He couldn't remember leaving or closing the door behind him or getting into his duck. He drove for hours, and he had no idea where he was or where he was going. He had made it onto a two-lane waterway when the agony caught up to him. He pulled off to the side and floated in the middle of the sea. His tears came like sick, heaving out of him uncontrollably. He sobbed the way a child weeps, coughing and wheezing for air. He didn't know a grown man could cry like this.

Wrung out at last, he curled up in the cab and stared through the windshield at the frigid light of the stars, at the gods who had come and gone and been forgotten. He watched the sky spin overhead, and all he could think was the word *Heartbroken.*

Hart.

Broken.

Chapter Thirty-Three

Why do you want to work for Birdsall & Son?"

In the office, Mercy and Lilian sat across from their third interviewee of the day, a miner searching for a safer line of work outside the borders of Tanria. Mercy had high hopes for this one, given the debacle of the first two interviews, but when he directed an unctuous smile at her, her hopes quickly dwindled.

"Well, I have to say, ma'am, I like the view."

"Thank you. We'll be in touch," Lil said.

"I've only answered one question."

"And we have all the information we need. You can let yourself out."

"Damn women have no business in undertaking anyhow," he muttered as he left the office.

"How did Pop find Danny in this morass?" Mercy wondered aloud once they heard the front door close. Mercy had asked her sister to stay behind to help her with the interviews while Danny did deliveries, since they were going to be running the business together anyway, plus it seemed like a good way to force Pop to take a few days off. Now she felt like she was wasting Lilian's time.

"Maybe we should go to temple and leave a truly impressive sacrifice for the Bride of Fortune."

"'Dear Bride of Fortune: please send a woman to reply to our job opening for a new delivery driver, because men suck.'"

"Indeed they do."

Mercy had been doing a decent job of *not* thinking about a mendacious Tanrian Marshal every second of every day, but the mention of men's suckery made it difficult to sidestep her battered heart. She chucked her clipboard onto the desk and picked up the packet sent to her by the Quinter Lumber Corporation, which operated near the East Station.

"Why are you torturing yourself with that? We've done the math. The lumber rates are doable, but the shipment costs would sink us."

"They're the most reasonable offer we've had."

"That doesn't make it feasible. Even with the gains we're making on indigents, we can't afford it. We don't have the bargaining power of Cunningham's. They've got six locations. We're only us."

Mercy perked up, an idea taking shape in her mind. "But what if we did have bargaining power?"

"What do you mean?"

"Think about it. There are other undertakers operating around the West Station. Mayetta and Argentine both have undertakers, and I bet there's at least a couple up north that've been working with Afton. We're not the only ones affected by Cunningham's deal. If we form some kind of consortium with the others, maybe we can work out an arrangement with Quinter Lumber."

Lil chewed the eraser of her pencil. "It would depend on what kind of deal Quinter offered. I'd have to crunch the numbers, but yeah, it could work."

"Do you think they'll entertain the idea if it comes from a lady undertaker?"

"I don't see the menfolk coughing up a better plan, and you've been the interim undertaker here for a year without raising too much of a stir. Maybe us bordertownies are a more progressive lot than you think."

"It can't hurt to send out feelers. The worst thing they could do is say no."

Lil put the pencil out of its misery, setting it on the desk so that she could fold both hands over her pregnant belly. "I wish I could figure out why Cunningham wants to shut us down so badly. It's literally keeping me up at night. Well, that and the fact that this one here gets the hiccups at three o'clock on the nose every night and dances on my bladder from dusk till dawn." Lil patted her stomach. "But seriously, if you take our sales figures and inflate the numbers to match Cunningham's intake, plus the profit he's making off his ability to mark up the products he buys wholesale, plus the fact that he's cornered the market on embalming, I can't for the life of me see how our measly business cuts into his profits. Much as it pains me to say this, Zeddie was right. There's something shady going on here."

"Curtis Cunningham is Mr. Pillar of the Community. Even if he were doing something shady, I can't imagine we'd be able to do anything about it." Mercy deflated, putting her elbow on the desk and resting her chin in her palm.

"If Cunningham is doing his level best to get rid of us, it stands to reason that he's trying to shut others down, too. We should find out which undertakers have shuttered over the past year to see if they have anything in common."

"That sounds nice and all, but I have an overflowing well downstairs and four boats to build this week. I don't have time to be Mercy Birdsall, supersleuth."

"You should put that on your business card."

Mercy took off her glasses and rubbed at the headache blossoming in her forehead. Burying herself in work was what had prevented her from burying herself in heartbreak and misery these past few weeks. She was afraid to let her thoughts wander too far from the boatworks; they were likely to bump into topics better left untouched, such as how much she missed the man who'd lied through his teeth to her.

Lilian smacked her elbow. "Come on, humor me. Which undertakers have closed their doors fairly recently?"

Mercy closed her eyes and envisioned a map of Bushong and the border towns huddled around each of the four Tanrian Marshals' stations. She started north and worked her way clockwise, east, south, then west. "Estes Mortuary and Funeral Rites, Dresser & Knops, Bhathena's Funeral Services... That's all I can think of off the top of my head."

Lil jotted down the names and handed Mercy the list. "What do they have in common?"

Mercy longed to deal with bodies and boats rather than Cunningham's hostile takeover, but she put on her glasses and dutifully read through the list.

And a pattern emerged.

"Oh!" she cried, her pulse dinging through her veins like a bell. She flew to the file cabinet where she kept old financial records.

"Ladies and gentlemen, Mercy Birdsall, supersleuth, is on the case," Lil joked as Mercy pulled out the file on the Indigent Processing Grant and opened it on the desk. She riffled through the paperwork until she found the award letter that listed all the grant recipients: Bhathena's Funeral Services, Birdsall & Son, Cunningham's Funeral Services, Dresser & Knops, Estes Mortuary and Funeral Rites.

"Mother of fucking Sorrows, I knew it!" crowed Lilian over her shoulder.

Mercy shook her head in disbelief. "He wants a monopoly on the Indigent Processing Grant? It's got to be a pittance for him. He applied out of self-promotion, not for financial benefit."

"It isn't a pittance. Over the past six months, our indigent intake has gone up more than two hundred percent, and I'm sure it's higher for him. It's like saving coppers in a piggy bank. A few here and there doesn't amount to much, but if you fill up the bank, it adds up. I'm telling you, he knew the intake was about to increase exponentially, which is why he shut everyone else down. Shady!"

"How would he know that, though? It's not like he can get into Tanria to make the drudge problem worse. And who would make the drudge problem worse on purpose?"

"A shady asshole who stands to make a huge profit?"

"But how's he doing it?"

"How do you make the undead? With dead people. What does he have an unlimited supply of? Dead people!" Lilian slapped the desk to drive home her point.

"Yeah, but every body coming out of Tanria has a punctured appendix, so it can't be reanimated, not to mention the fact that someone would have to get all those cadavers past the checkpoint at the West Station."

"I'm telling you, Cunningham found a way. This guy hatched a nefarious plot to fill Tanria with dead bodies in order to swindle the government. That has got to be the least sexy evil plan ever."

Mercy leaned against the tall file cabinet, feeling wrung out. "I don't know, Lil. It seems pretty far-fetched to me."

"I think it's worth investigating."

"Maybe," said Mercy, but all of this talking and not working was making her feel again, and she was not in the mood to engage her emotions. "In the meantime, I'm going to send letters to anyone who might be willing to team up with us on lumber purchases, and then I'm going to buy copious amounts of chocolate, and then I'm going to put in serious overtime to get through the workload today."

"Solid plan, especially the chocolate part, but only if it also involves you buying me a blueberry muffin the size of my head."

As Mercy slipped the letters to the undertakers into the nimkilim box on Main Street, she had the familiar urge to write a letter to her pen pal, the same urge that had compelled her to write to him in the first place, the need for a friend. And then she remembered why she and Hart had broken up. She hated him for doing this to her, for ruining what they'd had together and destroying the letters in one fell swoop.

Hate*'s a strong word, Merciless. Do you really* hate *me?* he asked in her memory. She wished she could hate him, but she didn't. The sad truth was that she loved him, even if she was struggling to forgive him.

The same questions that cycled through her brain every night as she lay awake in her lonely bed somersaulted through her mind as she stood before the nimkilim box on Main Street: Why had he written the letters in the first place? Why had the nimkilim decided she was the recipient? Why had he humiliated her at the Little Wren Café, only to turn around and woo her a week later? How could he have slept with her when he knew the truth? How could he have let things between them go as far and for as long as they had without telling her?

She didn't bother to wonder if she would give him the chance to explain himself if he showed up on her doorstep. She knew that she would. The problem was that Hart had taken her at her word when she'd sent him packing. She had told him not to set foot in Birdsall & Son ever again, and he hadn't. Pen was the one who dropped off the bodies they secured, including indigents. Hart could have taken them to Cunningham's; instead, he was still making sure Mercy got the keyless bodies that he and Pen recovered in Tanria and, therefore, the money that came with them. Such thoughtfulness was infuriating, given the circumstances.

As Mercy walked up the street to Callaghan's General Store, she considered what it meant that, according to Lilian, indigent intake was up by over 200 percent. It followed that the drudge population inside Tanria had increased accordingly. If Lil's suspicions were correct and Cunningham had found a way to smuggle dead bodies with intact appendixes into Tanria, that put every marshal at greater risk. When she thought of the cuts and bruises she'd seen on Hart's skin during the months they'd dated, it made her blood boil. She might be livid with Hart, but the thought of him getting hurt or worse nagged at her without cease, particularly if Cunningham was increasing the drudge population on purpose.

Truth be told, she was worried sick about him, and not simply because of the physical perils of Tanria. She had refused to ask Pen how he was doing the few times they'd crossed paths since the breakup, but the last time she saw him at the house, Pen had volunteered his opinion without her having to ask.

"He's lost and miserable without you," Pen had informed her.

"He's got a funny way of showing it," she had muttered in reply.

She could reach out to Hart, but he was the one who had lied. He was the one who needed to explain himself. If he wasn't willing to swallow his pride and come after her, he didn't deserve her. And the fact that he apparently didn't feel compelled to beg her forgiveness was the reason why Mercy stalked the aisles of Callaghan's General Store to find a chocolate bar that would inadequately fill the emotional void inside her.

She also picked up a blueberry muffin the size of her head for Lil.

As she was paying at the register, she noticed a headline on the front page of the *Eternity Gazette*, smaller than the main headline—*Drudge on the loose kills two in Herington*—and tucked into the corner: *Cunningham awarded patent for miracle embalming patch.*

And *click*, everything snapped into place.

Pop had the *Gazette* delivered to the house every week, but Mercy forked over the change to buy a copy at the counter. She ran to Birdsall & Son as fast as her red canvas sneakers would carry her, threw open the door, and shouted, "Lil! I know how he's doing it!"

Chapter Thirty-Four

The grief Hart felt as he plodded through his days beside Duckers cut differently than the knife of losing his mother or Bill or Gracie. They'd been taken from him. They had gone to a place where he couldn't follow. But Mercy was alive and well and living in the world without him, and the reason he couldn't be with her was because he'd messed it up irreparably. He'd done this to himself, and now he couldn't undo it, and it was tearing him up inside.

He went through the motions, arresting smugglers and poachers, teaching Duckers how to pack sailcloth so that it didn't come spilling out of the pack, taking out drudges and watching their bitter souls float off into the winds of Tanria until they could infect someone else. At the end of each tour, Zeddie came to get Duckers at the station, while Hart returned to Tanria on his own to pick up overtime. It was always a relief to be alone with his sadness once Duckers was out of his hair, to drop the facade and simply be. But within a day or two, he ended up missing the kid more than he wanted to be by himself.

Maybe that was why, camped out in Sector W-26 on a solo night shift, he took out a pen and the stationery that had long since sunk to the bottom of his pack and wrote one last letter to Mercy. Months ago, he had told a friend with no name and no face that he felt better for having applied the weight of his loneliness to a piece of paper. It held true now, although he slid the letter into his vest pocket rather than a nimkilim box.

He thought he'd go back to the way he'd been before he fell in love with Mercy, but Mercy was the one who had made him see how years of worrying about his possible inability to die had resulted in a distinct failure to live, something he attempted to remedy now. When Duckers joked around with him, Hart found it in himself to crack the hard line of his mouth into a grin. When he sensed that he was spending too much time on his own, he went to Alma and Diane's for dinner or card games. He carried on pleasant conversations with the librarian who handled his interlibrary loans at the Herington branch of the Bushong Public Library. He did his best to live a little. The problem was that he wanted to live a little—or a lot, actually—with Mercy.

Which wasn't going to happen.

"Told you not to pick that one," Hart gloated, earning a glare from his apprentice. Things had come to a pretty pass when the world's most cheerful person, Penrose Duckers, could muster an honest-to-gods scowl, but after a day of chasing after Saltlicker, who kept running off in search of water, Duckers was worn to an exhausted nub, and his irritation was as electric as the scent of the imminent storm in the air. There was only one storm in Tanria, created by the old God of Wrath, zigzagging through this prison as it bounced off the misty walls, and it was heading their way, which did nothing to improve Duckers's mood.

Hart, on the other hand, was having no end of fun using Saltlicker as an educational opportunity. He thanked the Bride of Fortune for bringing him such joy when he badly needed it.

"I think we've learned a valuable lesson here, haven't we, Duckers?"

Duckers growled.

"In the future, you do what I tell you. Period. If I say, 'Pack two canteens,' you...?"

"Pack two canteens," Duckers answered flatly.

"If I say, 'You need to run drills with your rapier,' you...?"

"Drop everything I'm doing and run drills with my rapier."

"And if I say, 'Don't pick that stallion, because he's a pain in the ass,' you...?"

"Don't pick that stallion, because he's a pain in the ass, sir."

Hart was debating whether or not he should fix Duckers's picket when Bassareus arrived.

"Look at this sulking tit. What, does your pussy hurt, kid?"

Hart rubbed his forehead. "Thank you for once again personifying why the Old Gods needed to go."

Bassareus put his paw over his heart, and his face softened. "Aw. That's sweet."

Hart poured the whiskey while Duckers dug his letters out of his pack. He couldn't resent the kid for his happiness, but watching the letters go back and forth between him and Zeddie remained a brutal reminder of what Hart had lost. He blew out a miserable breath before he noticed that Bassareus was watching him. "What?"

The rabbit nudged his arm. "Been meaning to tell you, sorry about your girl. That's rough."

Hart wasn't sure what was more surprising: Bassareus's sympathy or the fact that Hart was touched by it. He nodded in gratitude. "Keep coming back for the kid. I'll tip."

The nimkilim had barely disappeared over the crest of a hill when Saltlicker tore free of Duckers's inept knot and made a run for it.

"Have fun," Hart told his apprentice, making it clear he had no intention of helping.

Duckers huffed and stalked off after his horrible mount, leaving Hart alone with his thoughts and his longing for the woman he'd lost.

There was a *boom* nearby, followed by a burst of orange light sizzling in the sky.

A flare.

From the same direction Duckers had gone.

An answering fear burst and hissed and sizzled inside Hart.

All thoughts of Mercy abandoned, he strapped on his machete and grabbed an extra cartridge of pistol crossbow ammo before mounting his equimaris and galloping after his apprentice. The flare dropped and blinked out as the mare tore through the trees, careening down a steep incline until her webbed feet splashed into the stream at the bottom of the ravine. With the water beneath her, she flew like an arrow, her nostrils flaring.

Hart saw Duckers's lantern in the distance, and a flash of lightning illuminated his silhouette ten yards ahead on the left bank of the stream, swinging his rapier like mad at not one but two shadowy forms. The stench of decay accosted Hart's nose above the clean scent of water and silt. With his heart thundering louder than the equimaris's feet, Hart gripped the mare with his knees as he drew the machete in time to mow down one of the drudges trying to murder his apprentice.

The mare shied and bucked in terror as the creature's head sailed past her flaring nostrils, and she tossed Hart ass-first into the water. Thunder pounded through the sky, sending the equimaris fleeing as the heavens opened. Rain poured over Hart in a punishing torrent. He jerked his head, trying to get his wet hair out of his eyes as he reached for the pistol crossbow holstered to his belt beneath the water's shifting surface.

Another blinding shaft of lightning flashed across the churning clouds, and Hart found Duckers again as the apprentice ran his rapier through the drudge that still had its head, but missed the appendix. Hart's lantern had gone with his equimaris, and now Duckers's light got swept into the rising water. Hart waited five agonizing seconds for his eyes to adjust to the darkness, then took aim at the dark shadow that was the drudge and fired, praying to the Three Fathers that he wouldn't hit Duckers by accident. The arrow sailed true, diving through the drudge's back, sinking into its appendix. It crumpled at Duckers's feet, sending its glowing amber soul flying into the night. Hart raced to the bank as fast as he could with the water sucking at his boots, but Duckers stabbed the headless yet animated drudge with a grunt, hitting his mark. By the time Hart reached him, the creature was down.

Another bolt of lightning sent shards of blinding light into the darkness, illuminating Duckers's terrified face.

"You all right?"

Duckers nodded as the light disappeared, and a roll of thunder shuddered across the landscape. The next bolt lit the sky, illuminating not one, not two, but many drudges, lining up along the ridge. Ten drudges constituted a cluster, and there were more than ten peering down at them, like falcons readying themselves to plunge at their prey. He and Duckers were nowhere near Sector 28, but that hardly mattered now. Every vein in Hart's body constricted with dread.

"Oh, fuck."

"Sir?"

"Move!"

Hart shoved Duckers ahead of him, holstering the pistol crossbow and unclipping the slingshot and flare from his belt. With the memory of Bill's death pressing upon him, he tried to light the flare as he ran behind his apprentice, but the wick was too wet to catch. He cast it into the water and pulled the pistol crossbow from his belt again. If anything happened to Duckers tonight...

Hart wouldn't let himself finish that thought.

"You call this moving?" he shouted over the storm. He pushed his apprentice from behind with his free hand, his right gripping his weapon. Duckers's rapier ticked like a metronome with the pumping of his arms as he ran.

Movement from higher up the western incline caught Hart's attention as he and Duckers charged through the ravine. He turned to see three more drudges stumbling down the hill to cut them off from behind. When he whipped his head to face forward, several more formed a wall along the stream in front of them.

"What do we do, sir?" Duckers's voice sounded like it belonged to a child. Hart stepped in front of him, barking orders, trying to sound calmer than he felt.

"Back-to-back. I've got the ones in front. You take the ones to our rear. Pistols first. Save the rapier for hand-to-hand."

"Fuck!"

"It's all right."

It was not all right. The stream was rising at an alarming rate, lapping their calves as it ate away the narrow banks on either side. Trapped in the bottleneck of the ravine, Hart knew that he and Duckers were fish in a barrel. It was Bill all over again, except this time, Hart was supposed to be the adult in charge, when he felt more like a scared kid. But then Duckers's warmth at his back reminded him of what he owed his apprentice.

"You're a good shot, Marshal. Don't panic. Take aim and fire. That's all you have to do."

"Yes, sir." Duckers's voice was a wet whimper as lightning cut a jagged scar across the sky. The accompanying thunder was the bell that signaled the beginning. The drudges leaped forward from both directions, and the fight began.

Hart got off five shots, but with no light to see by except the searing whiteness of lightning, he took down only two before the remaining four drudges were nearly on him. Instead of firing one last shot, he took those precious seconds to holster the pistol crossbow and draw both the rapier and the machete, the weapon of precision in his dominant right hand, the hacking blade in his left.

The next moments were a blur of jabbing, cutting, slicing, and chopping. Hart kept Duckers at his back at all times, even when he ought to dodge or feint. He might be immortal, but his apprentice definitely wasn't, so Hart did whatever he could to make sure that every scratch and grab and bite landed on his own skin, not Duckers's. A drudge got close enough to his left side to bite his arm. A burst of agony bloomed where teeth met flesh, tearing a hole in his shirt and sending blood oozing down his skin. He shoved hard, dumping the drudge into the rising water. It sputtered up, shrieking with an outrage that was cut short when Hart swung the machete and sliced into the creature's side, cleaving its rotting body all the way to the appendix. He ripped the blade out and sliced through the air in the opposite direction, hacking off the head of another drudge and skewering the body through the appendix with his rapier in the same breath.

All the while, the stream rose and swelled, tugging against Hart's knees, then his thighs, filling up the narrow ravine like a tap on full blast. He stumbled against the current as he lunged for another drudge, missing the target and leaving his right side vulnerable. The drudge scraped three gashes across the skin of his neck with jagged fingernails as it tried to grasp his throat.

Lightning blasted into a tree high up the ridge with an explosion of sound. The trunk splintered, sending the elm crashing down the ravine, straight toward them. Hart gored his drudge with his rapier and sent its soul into the stormy night, and then he grabbed Duckers by the back of his waterlogged jacket to pull him away from the oncoming tree.

A drudge hopped on his back, biting into the crook where his neck met his shoulder, sending a shaft of pain through Hart's body. He let go of Duckers and tried to twist out of its grip. The next thing he knew, Duckers was forcibly turning him, then ramming his rapier into the drudge so hard he ran the blade through the drudge's body and poked a hole into Hart's back. Hart cried out in pain, and Duckers shouted "Sorry, sir!" a second before the tumbling tree hit the water and knocked the kid into the current, sweeping him up in its branches and carrying him deeper into the heart of danger.

"No!" screamed Hart so loud he felt as if he were tearing apart the inside of his throat and his heart right along with it. The current slammed against his hips as the remaining drudges sprang at him, and there was no time to mourn or think. The world became a tiny, focused pinprick of survival. The rain poured down, and lightning spasmed into the darkness, and thunder shook the earth as Hart jabbed and sliced and dodged and lived and lived and went on living as he dispatched lost souls into the Tanrian night.

The water rose, and the rain washed his blood into the stream. He swung and missed, thrust and hit, and still the drudges came for him. If he was capable of dying, this was the way he was going to go. And if Duckers was dead and gone on his watch, he wasn't sure he could live with himself anyway.

Something in the water's current shifted, a force drawing Hart backward. He turned his head in time to see Saltlicker, gleaming in a flash of lightning, cutting against the current as the stallion headed straight for him. He dodged, trying to swim for the side of the ravine as one of the drudges caught the hem of his dungarees. With the last of his sapped strength, he kicked free and reached his long arms toward a sapling, pulling himself to shore in time for the equimaris to trample the drudges, sending half of them careening downstream. The stallion grasped another in its huge teeth and flung it into the water as if it were nothing but a stuffed toy. A bolt of lightning lit Duckers's face atop the equimaris, which made the inside of Hart's chest expand achingly with relief. From Saltlicker's back, the apprentice cut and skewered the remaining drudges until there was nothing left to fight. For now, at least.

"Think you can hop on, sir?" Duckers called down to him as Saltlicker trod the roiling water.

Hart's wounds sucked away at his strength, but the alternative was drowning, so he didn't have much choice. "Give me a hand," he yelled over the deafening stream.

Between the two of them, they managed to get him onto Saltlicker's back. By the time he got himself straddled across the stallion behind Duckers, all he could do was slump against his apprentice and try not to faint as they rode out of the ravine.

"I don't know whether to kiss you or shoot you," Hart slurred once they left the rain and the stream behind them, the water sloshing inside his ruined boots with the rhythmic canter of the equimaris.

"Are you talking to me or Saltlicker?"

"Saltlicker. I wouldn't kiss you in a million years."

Once they got to their campsite, Hart was barely clinging on. Duckers dismounted and tried to coax him off the equimaris. "We need to treat those wounds, sir."

The bite on the side of his neck was about three inches wide, but it felt as if it were taking up the entire left half of his body, and the one on his arm hurt so badly, he thought he might be sick, but he shook his head. "If I manage to get off this dickhead, I'm not going to be able to get back on."

"Are you hurt real bad?" Duckers asked as he unzipped his sleep sack and threw it around his mentor's shoulders.

"Not great. You?"

"Not great, but better than you."

Hart nodded. "We both need to get to the infirmary. Skip the barracks. Think you can make it back to the station?"

"Yeah. Can you?"

"Yep."

Hart suspected that was a lie, but he managed to stay on the back of the equimaris, shivering so hard his teeth rattled as Duckers rode through the night, all the way to the station and the infirmary.

Chapter Thirty-Five

When Mercy arrived at Pop's house to strategize next steps for Operation Takedown (Lil's moniker), she expected to be greeted with a glass of wine and a platter of Zeddie's tapas. She did not expect to find Penrose Duckers lying on the sofa in the parlor, his head propped up on a million pillows, his arm in a sling, and one of his eyes bruised and swollen shut, while her father snored in the recliner next to him.

"Pen! My gods! Are you all right?" cried Mercy as she knelt on the floor beside him.

"Yeah, but you should see the other guy."

She knew it was meant as a joke, but as far as Mercy was concerned, *the other guy* meant Hart. "What happened?"

"Got attacked by a million drudges."

Mercy gasped as Lil came into the parlor with a cup of tea for Pen.

"Here you go, sweetie," she cooed as she handed him the cup.

"Is that Mercy?" Zeddie called from the kitchen. "Tell her to let the invalid rest."

Pen smiled as much as his bruised lips would let him. "He's making me chicken noodle soup. Don't tell him, but Hart makes a much better version of this." He held up his teacup, and Mercy recalled with a bittersweet pang the way Hart's fingertips had brushed her skin as he placed a similar concoction into her hands.

She worried that he was hurt as badly as Pen, but that there was no one around to do the same for him.

As if he could read her mind, Pen said, "You gonna ask about him?"

There was no point in pretending. "Is he okay?"

"He will be. Probably. But he took a worse beating than I did, mostly because he made sure that the drudges got to him and not to me. He's staying at the chief's house until he heals up."

A sob of relief rose from her lungs, and she slapped her hand over her mouth to stop any more from coming up. *He's fine,* she told herself, remembering how quickly his pistol crossbow wound had healed, but the speed of his healing was and wasn't a comforting thought.

Pen gestured at her with his uninjured hand. "Look at you. You're miserable. And he's miserable. You're both miserable. Why don't you talk to each other? Dang!"

"It's not that simple." Mercy toyed with the fraying seam of the blanket over Pen's legs. "I do care about him. But he's a mess. And I can't fix him. And I shouldn't have to."

Pen mulled this over, nodding slowly. "For what it's worth, he's a lot less messy than he used to be. He's trying. Maybe you should hear him out."

Emotionally exhausted, Mercy let herself fall face-first into an empty section of the sofa cushions next to Pen's legs. Her glasses pushed painfully into the right side of her nose, but she couldn't bring herself to care.

"I'm not supposed to know about the whole secret pen pal thing, but I do, so let me say this: I think he didn't tell you about the letters because he was scared he'd lose you if you found out."

"He lost me because he *didn't* tell me."

Mercy still had her face buried in the cushion, but Lil, who was hovering over the sofa, didn't miss a beat.

"What letters? Wait! *The* letters? Hart Ralston was your anonymous friend?"

"Thanks, Pen," Mercy groused into the cushion.

Either Pen didn't hear her sarcastic tone, or he chose to ignore it. He pulled the curtain of her hair away from her face with his good hand. "Give him a chance."

There was a time when Mercy would have told him that she never wanted to see Hart's lying face again, but all it took to cure her of that notion was the thought that he (a) was badly hurt and (b) had almost died. She settled for whimpering into the sofa upholstery, which smelled an awful lot like Leonard.

Zeddie came into the parlor and clicked his tongue when he saw Mercy encroaching on his boyfriend's sofa territory. He nudged her off the furniture with a ladle. "Go away. You're tiring the invalid."

Mercy sat up and regarded Pen's bruised face. She could only guess how badly Hart was injured, and it lit a fire inside her. If her suspicions were right, if Curtis Cunningham was filling up Tanria with drudges so that he could make more money, if Pen and Hart and all the other marshals were in greater danger because of Cunningham, Mercy was done letting him get away with it.

"We've got work to do, Lil," she said through the grim set of her teeth.

"Ooh, are we plotting how to take down the man now?"

Mercy punched her fist in the air. "We are taking down the man!"

Pop snorted awake in his recliner. "Oh hey, muffin. I didn't hear you come in."

"I thought you said you were bringing doughnuts this time," Mercy complained as she watched the dock gate of Cunningham's Funeral Services through Pop's old travel binoculars.

"No, I said I was bringing my doughnut. For my hemorrhoids." Lil pointed at the pillow under her butt before turning to the sheriff's deputy sitting to her right. "Don't ever get pregnant, McDouchebag. It's the full-body experience from Old Hell."

"Thanks. I'll keep that in mind. Maybe don't call me a douchebag when I've agreed to help you out, though," Nathan McDevitt replied from the far end of the duck bench.

Mercy, who sat in the driver's seat, leaned over her sister's bulbous stomach. "Thank you for being here, Nathan. We appreciate it."

"Why did we bring him?" Lilian whispered to Mercy as if Nathan couldn't hear her, when he was literally crammed up against her in the autoduck.

"In case Cunningham's henchmen want to murder us when we catch them red-handed?"

"Yeah, all right. That makes sense."

Mercy and Lilian had cased Cunningham's for several days before they witnessed him loading cadavers into an unmarked autoduck in the alley late last Allgodsday night. It made sense, taking care of their criminal dealings on the one day a week when undertakers didn't work. No one would be around to witness their questionable deeds. Now it was the following Allgodsday night, and this time, they had brought law enforcement with them, also known as Mercy's ex-boyfriend. Leonard grunted on Nathan's lap. He didn't smush his jowls against the deputy the way he had slobbered over Hart.

"Does your dog have to sit on me?"

"Well, he can't sit on me," said Lilian, pointing at her belly. "There's no room. And Mercy's in the driver's seat."

Nathan sulked against the passenger-side door. "I can't believe I let you two talk me into this. You know this guy donates to orphanages and stuff like that, right?"

"And he dumps cadavers with patched-up appendixes into Tanria," said Lilian.

"I still don't get how that would work or why anyone would want to smuggle dead bodies into Tanria. It makes no sense."

Mercy had already gone over this with him twice. She stifled a sigh of impatience before she explained it once again. "Cunningham has developed special embalming patches to put over a body's wounds and blemishes. They make the remains look more natural for the grieving who want to have an open-boat funeral service. But they bond to human tissue and blend in so well that Cunningham can actually repair a gouged appendix and toss the body back into Tanria to get reanimated all over again. When the body comes back to him via the Tanrian Marshals, he cashes in on the Indigent Processing Grant."

"It's like patching a tire, McDouchebag, except the mechanic is the one leaving nails on the street and then profiting off the repair," Lil added.

"Which is why he wants to shut us down along with all the other grant recipients," Mercy finished before Nathan could object to Lilian's *McDouchebag* comment.

"I checked his records, Mercy. Every body is accounted for, including the indigents he processes and dumps in the burial pits."

"But what if he's sending home empty boats to the families of the people who bought funeral packages from him? Most folks request closed-boat services, and it's not like anyone is going to bust open the planks to make sure there's a body inside. Who knows what's in the urns he's sending home?"

"I'm humoring you for one night. If Curtis Cunningham turns out to be the heinous villain you say he is, I'm going to turn in my badge and take up professional macramé."

"Is that a promise?" Lil muttered.

"Are you sure you should be here?" Mercy asked her sister for the fifth time that evening. "Danny and Pop will both have my head when they find out I took you on a risky surveillance mission of a possible crime lord."

"Pish. I'm a grown woman. I do what I want."

Mercy heard the faint sound of the gate going up, and she trained her binoculars on Cunningham's dock. "There! Look!"

She saw Cunningham himself, clearly visible in the gaslight, before she handed the binoculars to Nathan. The team members of Operation Takedown sat in silence and watched as Cunningham and one of his men loaded six bodies into the hold of an unmarked duck.

"See?" Lilian hissed at Nathan.

"A funeral director is loading dead bodies into the hold of a duck. How shocking."

"At eleven o'clock at night on Allgodsday?"

"Fair point."

Both men got into the duck's cab, pulled away from the dock, and headed down the alley in the opposite direction.

Lil touched Mercy's arm. "Are we following them this time?"

"I'm on it," said Mercy. She started up the engine and followed Cunningham down Main Street, hoping he wouldn't notice the Birdsall autoduck in his rearview mirror.

Nathan gripped the window crank. "It's illegal to drive without your lights on, you know."

"Shut up!" Mercy and Lil told him in unison.

"Have you never tailed someone before?" Lil asked him.

"No. Have you?"

Lilian pursed her lips. "No comment."

The silence inside the Birdsall family autoduck grew thick with tension as they followed Cunningham at a distance.

"This is weird," Mercy said twenty minutes after they passed the exit for the West Station. When the duck in front of them pulled off the road and drove cross-country toward the Mist, she added, "And it just got weirder."

She turned the wheel, and now Mercy and her pregnant sister and her ex-boyfriend and her dog were jouncing in the cab as the duck rolled along the uneven ground.

"I hope this doesn't induce labor," Lilian said, and Nathan went green around the gills.

"Oh my gods, I am not delivering a baby tonight."

"No one asked you. Of course I'm going to make Mercy do it."

Mercy was too busy navigating Bushong's desert terrain to comment on her potential midwifery. She spotted two more vehicles in the distance, parked close to the Mist. Cunningham's duck pulled up beside them and parked. They all had their headlights on, so Mercy brought her duck to a halt, close enough to keep an eye on things, but far enough away to stay out of the beams of light.

Team Operation Takedown stayed in the cab and watched as the men unloaded body after body from the holds. Lil took her turn with the binoculars.

"They're putting a circular object onto the Mist. Do you know what one of those illegal portals looks like, Nathan?"

"It must be serious if you're calling me by my name instead of McDouchebag." He took the binoculars from her and peered through the lenses. "Oh, wow. Okay, you two might be onto something."

"I see a bright future in professional macramé for you."

"Ha ha. Stay here. I'm going in."

"What? Nathan, no," said Mercy. "There are six of them and one of you. Let's go back and report this to Sheriff Connolly."

"By the time we get to Eternity and notify the sheriff, these goons will be long gone."

"But we're eyewitnesses. Surely that's enough to arrest Cunningham first thing tomorrow morning."

Offended, Nathan placed a hand over his heart. "Mercy, I'm a professional. I've got this."

"I feel like he doesn't have this," Lil said as she and Mercy watched Nathan approach the men stuffing cadavers through a pirated portal into Tanria. "Maybe we should leave him here and get the sheriff?"

"We can't leave him. We're the reason he's here in the first place."

By now, Nathan had stepped into the beams of the headlights, waving his badge in the air, and while Mercy couldn't clearly hear what was being said, she could tell things were going downhill quickly. He dropped his badge and reached for his sidearm. There was shouting, followed by one of Cunningham's men drawing a pistol crossbow and firing at Nathan. He dove out of the way, losing his revolver as he hit the ground, and the arrow shot a hole through Mercy's windshield. Nathan rolled to his feet and tackled the shooter. Another man joined in the fray as Cunningham stumbled to the side.

"Stay here," Mercy told Lilian as she got out of the cab.

"That's what he said!"

"Are you seriously making a 'that's what he said' joke right now?"

"No, that's what Nathan literally said! And now they're shooting at us!"

Leonard squeezed past Lil and followed Mercy out of the duck.

"He's a weasel, but I can't throw him to the wolves." With that, Mercy ran toward the melee.

Leonard sprinted ahead of her, snarling and growling. Mercy's dog, who couldn't be bothered to lift his head most days, was now chasing two terrified employees of Cunningham's Funeral Services across the desert.

Cunningham climbed into his duck as Nathan traded blows with the three remaining thugs. On the other side of the portal, one of the cadavers shifted and rolled and got to its reanimated feet. Mercy watched in horror as it shambled through the portal and into the Bushong night. Everyone froze as the dead body of an elderly woman walked through the fray. One of the men fighting Nathan screamed and ran away into the night, while another staggered away in shock, tripped over his own boots, and hit his head on a rock, knocking himself unconscious. Nathan, who had a bloodied fist raised, ready to pummel the last of Cunningham's henchmen, gaped at the drudge, while the man in his grasp said, "Mom? You're putting my *mother's* remains in Tanria, Cunningham?"

The livid employee lunged out of Nathan's grasp and pulled Cunningham out of the autoduck. Mercy could see more cadavers reanimating on the other side of the Mist, so she raced to the portal and attempted to pull it loose. It wouldn't budge. She frantically pushed buttons and pulled levers as a bloodless arm reached for her from the Tanrian side of the border. She pounded her fist on the frame, and the portal slammed shut, cutting the arm off with it. Clawing her fingers around the edge, she finally yanked it out of the Mist and threw it to the ground.

The blast of a revolver shattered the air, and the man who had attacked Cunningham collapsed at the undertaker's feet. Another shot and the drudge went down, too. Disheveled and breathing hard, Cunningham leveled his revolver at Mercy. Fear flooded her bloodstream. The whole world narrowed to the barrel aimed at her face.

"Take one more step toward me, Deputy, and your girlfriend will get a bullet through the head."

Mercy sensed Nathan going still behind her. She wanted to tell Cunningham that Nathan was not her boyfriend and that her boyfriend was a Tanrian Marshal named Hart Ralston, and she did not want to die without seeing him again.

"Oh, Mercy, sweetheart, it didn't have to be like this," Cunningham said with appalling sincerity. "You could have made a tidy sum from my purchase of Birdsall & Son and sailed for better waters. Now I'll have to—oof!"

An unidentified object flew through the air and beaned Cunningham in the head. Nathan took the opportunity to launch himself at the seedy undertaker, disarming him, slamming him to the ground, and cuffing his hands behind his back.

Mercy's legs wouldn't hold her up, and she plopped onto the sandy earth as Nathan said, "Curtis Cunningham, you are under arrest."

Lil waddled into the light of the headlamps as quickly as her cankles would allow. "Mercy! Are you all right?"

"I think so? We took down the man," Mercy answered in stunned disbelief.

Lilian patted the top of her sister's head since she couldn't bend over to hug her. "Yes, we did. We took down that human hemorrhoid with a doughnut pillow."

Mercy looked over at the item that Lil had thrown at Curtis Cunningham's head and burst into a hysterical fit of giggles. Leonard trotted into the light and dropped a pair of torn plaid boxer shorts into her lap, his nubbin tail twirling.

Chapter Thirty-Six

With an afghan wrapped around his shoulders, Hart stepped out the screen door of Alma and Diane's house to let the west wind of Bushong tousle his hair, which was in need of a trim again. He watched the sun set over the pasture and thought of all the times he'd brought Gracie here, and for once, it gave him pleasure to remember his dog. The grief hadn't gone anywhere, but he could recall the happiness in equal measure now.

Maybe I should get another dog, he thought with sincerity for the first time as Alma stepped outside and stood next to him. They stayed like that as the sun sank lower over the horizon, obscuring their faces, covering them in dusk.

"How are you holding up?" she asked him.

Hart considered keeping his thoughts to himself, but what was the point of patching things up with Alma if he was going to go on bottling himself up all the time?

"I'm a wreck, but I'm hanging in there."

"Are you a wreck because Mercy dumped you?"

"That's one reason. I fucked up a good thing."

"Have you tried apologizing?"

"It was one of those fucked-up-too-much-for-apologies kind of fuckups."

"For what it's worth, I think whatever happened between you and Mercy did you more good than harm."

Hart nodded. It was easier to talk to his friend in the twilit world, where everything was dim and hard to see. It made him braver. He spoke again.

"The librarian in Herington helped me track down Bill's wife and daughter last month. His wife sailed the Salt Sea eleven years ago, but the daughter is living in southern Honek. She's a dentist, married, has a couple of kids. It sounds like she's doing well. She was kind when she wrote to me, but it's clear that she doesn't want to continue the correspondence. She doesn't want that connection to Bill in her life. I get that."

To his surprise, Alma slipped her arm around his waist and squeezed him gently. Not that there was a need to be gentle. His wounds were almost completely healed. Her affection made his eyes blur and his throat burn.

"You're a good man, Hart."

"And a messy demigod." He took a shaky breath. The night sky made him feel small, swallowing his voice when he spoke again. "How do you do it?"

"How do I do what?"

"Live like a normal person, when you're not sure if you're ever going to die."

"What else are you going to do?"

"It's not that easy."

"Sure it is." She took her arm from his waist and stood before him. The gaslight coming from the kitchen windows illuminated her face, and her aquamarine eyes gleamed in the twilight. "The odds aren't there. I mean, how many demigods do you know?"

"I can think of ten or eleven, all marshals."

"And how many of those demigods do you know for certain are immortal?"

"One."

"Rosie Fox?"

Hart nodded.

"Same. The New Gods aren't like the Old Gods. They're a generation removed from the Unknown, and to be honest, I don't think they're so different from us. The halfies of the Old Gods were far more likely to be immortal, and most of them found their way up there." Alma nodded toward the stars. Unbidden, one of Mercy's letters came to Hart's mind. He could see the way the words slanted and looped across the page: *I suppose it puts things into perspective—or it's more accurate to say that you put things in perspective for me—to gaze up at the night sky and feel a part of something bigger than myself.*

"I can see why you're worried, and to be honest, I'm worried for you," Alma continued. "I'd like to think that healing quickly is simply your gift. But if... All you can do is take things one day at a time, like anyone else."

Hart was tempted to tell her about his gifts and about what had happened to Bill, but he decided to save that for another time. Instead, he astonished both of them by dragging Alma into a hug. She sniffed hard against his chest.

"Sap," she called him, but she hugged him tighter.

He lay awake on the guest bed as the prospect of his immortality loomed over him, feeling more like a fact than a possibility. The bedsprings squeaked in protest as he turned onto his side, trying to get comfortable. The guest bed was better than his camping cot, but it paled in comparison to Mercy's giant, soft mattress. Then again, any bed without Mercy in it felt empty. He wondered if that emptiness would dissipate with time. Part of him hoped it would, and part of him hoped it wouldn't.

He thought of Mercy standing on the curb in her yellow skirt as a drudge reached out for her with a decayed arm. He thought of

Duckers at his back, fighting off a cluster of drudges well outside the bounds of Sector 28. He thought of Bill, bloodied and in pain, begging him to punch a hole in his appendix so that he wouldn't be reanimated. He thought of the smiling wives and doting husbands and all the families whose lives had been torn apart by the drudge problem inside Tanria, a problem that was slowly seeping outside the Mist as well, a problem that got worse every single day. And here he was, lying in bed when he was the one person in the world who might be able to solve the issue once and for all. He knew what needed to be done, and the more he thought about it, the more he knew he'd do it.

If he succeeded, Duckers and everyone else inside Tanria would be safer, and Mercy and everyone else in the border towns would be safer, too. If he failed, at least he'd find out if he was mortal or immortal. For thirty-six years, not knowing his fate had been slowly killing him. Tonight, at last, Hart intended to live.

He emptied out his pack, because everything he needed was at the station. He considered taking his grandfather's watch with him but decided to leave it behind. He wound it and set it on the bedside table and hoped it would still be ticking when and if he returned.

At dawn, he got up and tiptoed down the hall to press his palm against Alma and Diane's bedroom door, as if he could pass all the warmth and gratitude he felt for them through the wood grain. "Thank you," he whispered.

Then he sneaked out of the house, letting the front door snick shut behind him.

Hart stopped in Mayetta to treat himself to breakfast at the Little Wren Café. Sitting at the table where he and Mercy had quarreled, he spent a couple of hours finishing the copy of *Enemies*

and Lovers that he had checked out from the library during his last visit to Herington. He figured that if he could no longer love Mercy in person, he could at least love her through the pages of her favorite novel. He lost himself as he read, seeing his own loneliness and regret in the character of Samuel Dunn, and like Samuel, he fell a little in love with irreverent Eliza Canondale. When he finished, he noticed that his waiter was glaring at him for staying so long. He paid his tab, left an enormous tip, and listened to the jingling of the door chimes with fondness as he left.

He hopped into his duck and drove to Herington. The air was uncommonly cool as he stood outside the public library, waiting for it to open at ten o'clock.

"Good morning, Marshal Ralston," Mabel Scott, Hart's favorite librarian, greeted him at the door as she unlocked it. "What can I help you find this morning?"

"Nothing today. I'm returning books, but I'm not taking any out."

She pointed to a metal slot in the building's brickwork. "You know, there's a book drop outside. You needn't have waited for me to open up."

"I know, but I wanted to thank you for keeping me in books all these years," he told her as he handed her the stack he was returning.

"It's my pleasure. Oh, *Enemies and Lovers*. I love this book."

"So do I," he said, and then he walked to his duck and drove himself to the North Station. Not that anyone would question him at his home base, but it made more sense to enter Tanria through a point where no one knew he wasn't on duty. He skipped the commissary altogether and headed straight for the weapons lockers, where he checked out an extra machete with an accompanying sheath and backstrap, two extra pistol crossbows, two boxes of crossbow ammo, and an arm dagger. Normally,

Hart found arm daggers too showy for his taste. Today, it seemed practical. He passed by the flares for the same reason he passed by the commissary—there wasn't a point.

"Grandfather Bones, are you taking out an army or what?" commented the woman checking out his weapons, a lit cigarette fuming between her yellow teeth.

Hart said nothing in reply as he signed out. He packed up his supplies and headed for the stables. It had been less than two weeks since he and Duckers had faced the drudge cluster, but somehow, Saltlicker had wound up at the North Station, as if the Bride of Fortune had placed him there herself.

"Figures," Hart muttered, but then he remembered the way this beast had stuck around and rescued Duckers from the rising waters, the way he hadn't shied away from the drudges that night. He stroked the equimaris's soft nose, incongruously delicate beneath his calloused hand.

"You know what? You're exactly the asshole for the job."

He saddled up and rode into Tanria with a pack more full of weapons than food, because he wasn't planning to stay long. Halfway to his destination, he stopped to let Saltlicker rest and graze and curl his feet in a stream while Hart brewed a pot of tea and ate an apple. It wasn't much of a last meal, but he made a point of savoring the tea. As he drank, he sat quietly, his back against a tree trunk. One by one, he thought about the people who had mattered to him, pushing aside the remorse and regret that usually accompanied his memories. He wanted only love at his side now.

Mom.

Grandpa.

Aunt Patty (a tiny bit).

Bill.

Gracie.

Alma.

Diane.

Duckers.

Mercy.

He wished he could read Mercy's letters one last time, but he'd left them in her apartment that godsforsaken night she had sent him away.

When his cup was empty and there didn't seem to be any reason to linger, he tugged the equimaris from the stream. Saltlicker threw his head, protesting Hart's pulling him to dry land.

"You might be the last living creature I see on this earth, so quit being a dick," Hart told him.

The equimaris didn't care, but all of a sudden, Hart did. He'd tamped down his fear up till this point, but now that he was facing the last leg of the journey, it was creeping up his spine and spilling into his lungs. He closed his eyes and remembered Mercy's fingers in his hair, her thumbs wiping the tears from his cheeks.

Don't you ever go back there. Don't you ever try to open that door again.

Would she be angry with him if she knew what he was about to do? Or had she stopped caring about him the day she found out he'd lied to her? He couldn't stand the idea of causing her any more pain than he had already, but he'd be a liar if he said that he didn't want her to grieve his passing. Selfish bastard that he was, he still wanted to matter to her. And because he could not cling to Mercy, he threw his arms around the stallion's neck, pressing his face against the slimy mane. He hugged Saltlicker until he was ready to let go, and he climbed into the saddle, his resolve steady and true.

He arrived at Sector 28 at sunset, staring at the house in the field from the same vantage point he'd had all those years ago as he stood beside Bill. Given the failure of that mission, he probably should have started from a different point, but if Hart was going to finish what they'd begun, he'd go full circle. This was where he'd start.

"If it gets too rough, you get out of there. You hear me?" Hart told Saltlicker, who stamped and snorted. The stallion was already jittery, sensing the wrongness of this place. Hart had been hoping to steer with his knees to keep both hands free for pistol crossbows, but there was no way that was going to work now. He'd have to hold the reins in his left hand, leaving him with only a single six shooter in his right hand to protect himself.

So be it, he thought. For the tenth time in as many minutes, he made sure the pistol crossbows in his holsters were loaded. He slid the rapier in and out of the scabbard and touched the handle of each machete strapped to his back. The dagger on his arm was unfamiliar and uncomfortable, but he left it. Better to be overarmed than underarmed. He blew out a breath, as if he could cast his roiling thoughts into the wind along with it. Then he wrapped the reins around his left hand and kicked Saltlicker's sides.

The stallion launched from the trees into the open field, but he immediately began to fight the reins, trying to turn back as the first drudges stepped into their path. Hart pulled hard, keeping him on course. He took careful aim and pulled the trigger, taking down one of the drudges. The soul slipped out of the body as more drudges scrambled onto the field, putting themselves between him and the house. He fired another shot and missed, then another, taking out a second infected corpse. Another shot. Another. Another. He streaked across the meadow on the panicking stallion, barely keeping the creature in line as he tossed aside the empty pistol crossbow and pulled out the next. A few drudges dropped and released their souls, but more came, then more and more, a growing barrier between Hart and his destination. He grabbed the last crossbow from its holster, and when that was empty, too, he slid a machete from his back.

Equimaris and rider plunged into the bodies. Hart tried to hack a pathway through, but before he broke to the other side, Saltlicker shrieked, a sound that splintered the twilight. The stallion bucked hard, kicking out at drudges and casting his rider into the throng.

Hart smashed into bodies, fresh and rotted alike, losing his grip on the machete. A sea of drudges surrounded him, pulling him under. Teeth sank into the flesh of his shoulder, his stomach, his calf, an exquisite symphony of pain. A skeletal hand wrapped around his throat. He grabbed the only weapon within reach—the dagger on his arm—and sliced the hand off at the wrist. The drudge screeched as Hart kicked it in the chest, pushing it into the lethal horde.

Dagger clutched in his white-knuckled grasp, Hart slashed without thought or direction, clearing an opening above him. He crawled on top of the corpses, kicking free of a drudge clutching his ankle. He tumbled over the savage congregation until he got his feet beneath him. Bleeding and winded, he hurled himself off a drudge's back, landing and rolling onto the ground and staggering to his feet before he could get buried again.

The house was about thirty yards in front of him. He had enough time to think *It may as well be a thousand* before he was hacking away at another onslaught. He knew he couldn't outrun so many, but he sprinted ahead anyway as the bite in his calf screamed at him to stop.

Each time a hand reached for him, he hacked it away with his remaining machete. Each time teeth grazed his throat, he jabbed with the dagger. Each time they tried to stop him, he escaped. More and more disembodied souls gathered and swelled around him as he staggered and pitched and reeled his way to the house, blood dripping into one of his eyes and streaming out of his nose and trickling down his throat and soaking into his clothes. He swung his blades, hacking bodies into pieces. He coughed and spat blood, and still he went on, yard by yard, foot by foot.

He tumbled onto the steps of the front porch with a drudge over his back. He used the momentum of his fall to grab it and throw it onto the wood planks. Then he slammed the dagger into the thing's appendix. The soul billowed out as he pulled the blade free with a wet suck and got to his knees. Another drudge came for him as he reached for the doorknob, grabbing his arm and tearing the flesh of his forearm free of his body with bloodstained teeth. Blinded by pain, Hart howled in agony. The dagger fell from his useless hand and clattered on his front porch.

His front porch. He didn't care if this was the House of the Unknown God or his own death waiting for him in Tanria, disguised as the place where he grew up. As far as he was concerned, this was his home. He had been rocked to sleep in his grandfather's lap on that old swing. He had sat beside his mother on these steps, each of them holding a dripping ice-cream cone. He refused to fail here. This was *his* fucking house.

Gritting his teeth, Hart swung the machete and took off the drudge's head. He dragged himself the last two feet to the door on one hand and two knees. Throwing himself back on his heels with a shout of pain, he reached past the lights of all the souls gathering at the door and grasped the knob with his good hand.

The door was locked.

He tried again.

Locked.

He waved away the souls billowing around his face, and with one last grunt of effort, he slammed the blade of the machete into the wood, but the door remained shut against him.

"This door was never locked a day in my life!" he shouted, the words slurring one into the other over his broken teeth.

Then he remembered that there was a reason why people were given a key at birth, a reason why the ID tag around his neck was in the shape of a key. With a shaking hand, he pulled the chain from around his neck and fumbled for his Birdsall & Son tag, shoved it into the lock, and tried to turn it. The lock held firm. The tumblers didn't move.

"Fuck you!" he hurled at the Warden, the god who should have been waiting at the door, as two more drudges mounted the steps. He unsheathed his rapier, skewering first one, then the other. The souls flew free into the darkening sky.

More were coming. He was going to die here. He could feel his life leaking out of him. As his mind clung to thoughts of Duckers and Alma and Diane and Mercy and Mercy and Mercy, he was so relieved to know that he was mortal after all.

He dropped the rapier and grasped his mother's key in death-drunk fingers, pushing it into the lock and turning it clockwise. There was an answering *click* as the tumblers rolled into place. His chest flaring with hope, Hart pulled himself to his feet and twisted the knob. The door was heavy—so heavy—like lead rather than wood. He pushed hard, but it barely moved. A groan dribbled out of his mouth as he leaned his shoulder against the wood and put his body into it, nudging it open, inch by inch. He bled into the wood grain. His whole body burned with pain. There was something wrong with his lungs. All he could do was this one thing, this slow opening of a door that only he could see.

A strange silence thundered behind him. He watched the amber light of a single soul hover over his shoulder, then drift into the house. Another soul followed. Five more. Ten. Dozens.

Hart shoved harder, slid himself into the opening, propped his foot against the jamb, and held the door open with this body as the weight of it resisted, threatening to crush him.

The souls came rushing in, raising a violent wind that whipped around him and tore through him, tugging at his bones. One by one, the bodies of the drudges in the meadow and beyond dropped to the earth as the dead came home at last.

He cried out—a long, strangled vowel—but he would not let go, would not leave this spot until all the lost souls of Tanria had flown into the arms of the Unknown God. He would not fail Bill this time, and he wouldn't fail Duckers or Mercy either.

The souls kept coming, first in brightly lit waves, then sparsely, like embers popping from a fire, but the wind kept blowing into him. Hart's cry faded to breath, and his breath faded to nothing. His vision grayed and dimmed. The wind blew so strongly that his grip on the doorframe slipped, and he could no longer remember why he stood against it in the first place. He heard the soft liquid call of an equimaris, like the waves of the sea whispering over the sand when the tide goes out, and he turned his head to see Saltlicker on the edge of a field littered with bodies, bending his long neck to graze. Unable to hold on any longer, Hart let himself fly free. The wind carried him inside, and the last thing he saw was his own body dropping to the wooden floorboards of the porch as the door slammed shut behind him.

Chapter Thirty-Seven

The Birdsall family waited until the night following Mercy and Lil's triumph over Cunningham to celebrate. This was partially so that Mercy and Lilian could catch up on sleep, but mostly so that Zeddie could cook for them on his evening off. It coincided with Pen's last day of sick leave, so it was a farewell dinner as well.

Pop rose from his seat at the head of the table and raised his glass. "To my daughters! For the record, when you said that you wanted to take down Curtis Cunningham, putting yourselves in mortal danger was not what I had in mind."

Lil held up her glass of grape juice. "You say that like it's a bad thing."

Not for the first time in the past forty-eight hours, Danny erupted, like water bursting through a dam. "It is! Very bad! If you ever do something like that again, I'll—"

"Ooh!" Lil cut him off, her face screwing up in pain.

"Do not fake a contraction to get out of trouble with me."

"There. It's gone. I'm sure it was gas. You were saying?"

Danny's anger drained out of his face. "Was that a contraction?"

"No. I'm having these tiny pains here and there, mostly in my back, but I'm fine."

Mercy set down her wine goblet. "Lil? Are you in labor?"

"No, no. I'm sure the cramping is from indigestion."

"At regular intervals?"

"I guess?"

"Like contractions?"

Lilian went pale. "Maybe?"

"Okay then." Mercy turned to her brother. "Why don't you go see if Dr. Galdamez is at home?"

"I'd protest, but I don't want to be here when her water breaks. That sounds disgusting. Pen, are you coming with?"

"Yes, please." The way Pen launched himself from his chair made it clear that he was in agreement with his boyfriend.

Once they were out the door, Pop, Danny, and Mercy watched Lilian as they picked at their food. After several minutes of her family's gawking and poor attempts at light conversation, Lil glared at them. "I'm a pregnant woman, not a bomb that's about to go off. Ooh, except this one is starting to hurt."

Danny grasped his wife's hand. "Are you okay, honey?"

"MOTHER OF FUCKING SORROWS!"

Danny squeaked in pain, so Mercy reached over and gently peeled her sister's fingers off her brother-in-law's pulverized bones. "I hope Dr. Galdamez gets here soon."

"Did someone say, 'Dr. Galdamez'?" Zeddie said as he and Pen walked through the front door.

"She's here? Thank the gods," said Mercy.

"No, she's out on a house call, but I left a message with her husband."

Lil made a gurgle of rage that sounded like a feral equimaris ready to duke it out in a fight pool. Mercy and Danny shared a look of mutual despair. Pop was the sole Birdsall who didn't seem concerned, chuckling as he got up from the table and sat in his recliner. He unfolded his newspaper and brought his glasses from his eyebrows to the end of his nose. "Her contractions aren't even ten minutes apart yet. We've got hours to go."

"'We'?" Lil bristled.

"Hours?" Danny puled, gazing at his crushed fingers.

"I'm not sticking around for this," said Zeddie.

"Cosigned," said Pen.

Their duty discharged, they spirited themselves away upstairs, and soon the sounds of horseplay and giggling could be heard coming from Zeddie's room.

"Can Zeddie and Pen refrain from getting it on while I'm giving birth?" said Lilian as Danny guided her to sit down in one of the armchairs in the parlor.

"Seems like at least one person in this house should be able to have fun tonight," Danny murmured to Mercy. "Or two, I guess."

There was a knock at the front door. Mercy hoped it was Dr. Galdamez, but between Lilian's occasional bursts of profanity and Zeddie and Pen's antics upstairs, Mercy suspected she was more likely to find an irate neighbor on the doorstep. Instead, Marshals Twyla Banneker and Frank Ellis stood on the front porch, completely out of context on the threshold of the family home rather than at the Birdsall & Son dock. Frank doffed his hat, but it was Twyla who spoke.

"Hi, Mercy. Sorry to bother you, but we came to let you know that the Joint Chiefs of the Tanrian Marshals have petitioned the governor of Bushong to mandate the opening of all undertakers along the Tanrian border until further notice, and it's already been approved."

Pop levered himself out of his chair and stood behind Mercy. "What's going on?"

"I'm not sure, but from what I've heard, there are uninfected cadavers all over Tanria. You can expect a huge intake tonight."

Lilian gripped the arms of her chair, her fingers like talons. "Fuck the Salt fucking Sea!"

"We have a bit of a situation here," Mercy pointed out.

"I'm sorry, but you are required by law to open. Now. We need every berth we can get in every single town."

Frank nudged Twyla. "We've still got to get to Argentine and Mayetta." He nodded to Mercy and Roy and said "Apologies for the inconvenience" before putting on his hat and hopping into the waiting autoduck with his partner.

Zeddie and Pen were now standing at the bottom of the stairs. They must have caught the gist of the report, because Pen's lips thinned, and he headed upstairs toward the bedrooms.

"Where are you going?" Zeddie asked, following him.

"To get my pack."

Their heated discussion could be heard in the parlor, the words muffled and indistinct but the tones crystal clear.

"I don't like this," Zeddie persisted, dogging Pen's path down the stairs a minute later. "It sounds dangerous."

"It's a dangerous job, Z."

"You've barely recovered from the last time you were nearly killed on the job. If you were needed, I'm sure—" Zeddie paused, glanced at Mercy, and lowered his voice, although not enough to prevent her from hearing every word. "I'm sure you-know-who would've come to get you by now."

"I'm sure he's already there, probably in the thick of it." Pen slung his pack over his shoulder.

"Gods' tits and testicles, you don't even know what 'it' is!"

Pen took Zeddie by the cheeks and planted a deep kiss on his mouth. Then he pressed his forehead to Zeddie's. "I love you."

"I love you, too," Zeddie whispered in defeat.

They stood like that for long seconds before Pen said, "This is such a great exit, but I just realized, I need you to drive me to the station."

Mercy grabbed her purse and prodded Leonard until he rolled off the sofa. "Can you drop me off on the way?"

"I'm coming with you," said Pop.

"No. Nope."

"You're going to need help tonight. Your sister is going to be fine. Trust me."

"You're leaving me? All of you? Fucking fuck the Warden up the ass with Grandfather Bones's fucking tibia!"

"For someone ushering new life into the world, you sure know how to invoke the gods of death," Zeddie told Lilian before turning to Pen. "I'm super mad at you, but all things considered, driving you to the station is probably my best option at the moment."

Pen ruffled Zeddie's hair. "Childbirth is a beautiful thing."

"I hate you all," said Lilian as Danny hugged each of them in turn.

"I think I might be getting the better deal out of this," Mercy told him.

He shot her a wary look. "Pray for me."

With Zeddie behind the wheel and Pop installed in the passenger seat, Mercy hopped into the hold of the old autoduck with Pen, and off they went, bobbing as the duck trundled up the brick street. Pen gave her a tight smile, and Mercy realized that he was scared to go into Tanria. She thought of his words to Zeddie—*It's a dangerous job, Z*—and Hart's voice answered in her mind: *Comes with the territory.* A thick unease settled in her belly. In theory, she had relinquished the right to concern herself with Hart's well-being, but her heart refused to receive that memo. She squeezed Pen's arm. "Take care, all right?"

Buried in her words was *Take care of Hart, too.* She sensed that he understood what she meant without her having to say it.

"I will."

There were already two sets of marshals out front by the time they pulled up to Birdsall & Son. Mercy hugged Pen hard before he switched places with her father. She watched the autoduck climb Main Street before she and Pop walked up the steps to the boardwalk in front of the family business.

"Go ahead and pull around back. We'll meet you at the dock," Mercy told the marshals as she unlocked the front door.

"How many berths do we have open in the well?" Pop asked her as he followed her in.

"Most were cleared out for tomorrow's delivery, not that Danny's going to be able to take them if Lil's having a baby tonight. That also means we're pretty crowded on the dock. We've got two going to the burial pits and one going to the pyres later this week, so that leaves nine open berths in the well. Surely we won't get nine in one day."

By now, they had made it to the dock and heaved up the gate. Mercy had assumed the two sets of partners would have one corpse each, but in fact, they had five between them. Her breath hitched. "Five?"

"Yes, ma'am," one of the marshals confirmed as she wheeled the first one in. Mercy thought her name was Rosie, but she couldn't remember her surname. She usually worked out of the East Station, so they almost never saw her at Birdsall's.

"What in the Salt Sea is happening?" Roy asked. "Was there some kind of accident?"

"Not that we can tell. Drudges started dropping dead all over Tanria for no discernible reason. There are bodies everywhere."

They hadn't finished wheeling all five bodies into the boatworks lift before the next autoduck backed down the alley.

"We need a plan," Mercy told her father, stress making her pulse speed up. "Any thoughts?"

"I say that if they're in bad condition, we salt and wrap them immediately. If they're fairly fresh, we stow them in the well. If we run out of room, we leave the ones in the best condition downstairs against the walls outside the well. It's not as cold as inside the well, but it's cooler down there than it is up here."

Mercy blew out a steadying breath. "Okay. Right. Good thing one of us remembered to order more salt last week."

Roy gasped. "I completely forgot."

"I know. That's why I took care of it on Bonesday."

Mercy rubbed her weary eyes. She was already tired, and the night had barely begun. Roy wrapped his heavy arm around her shoulders like a much-needed blanket.

"It's going to be hard, but it won't last forever. We'll grit our teeth and get through it."

"Right. But don't overdo it."

"I'll be good. I promise."

It took them an hour or so to work out a rhythm. Pop assessed the condition of each corpse and sorted them while Mercy carted bodies down the lift and stowed them as best she could. Every time another cadaver (or two or three) arrived, Mercy met the marshals at the dock and pinned the paperwork to each body's sailcloth until she and Pop could fill it all out.

To Mercy's surprise, Zeddie arrived shortly after midnight with sandwiches and stale cream puffs in hand.

"What are you doing here?" she asked him as he set the food on the counter in the kitchenette.

"It was a zoo at the station when I dropped Pen off. I figured you could use some fortification tonight."

"Bless you. Any word on what's going on?"

"Apparently, most of the bodies seem to be coming from the central sectors, whatever that means."

The wisp of a memory surfaced, but Mercy couldn't recall why the central sectors should have any significance to her. She shrugged it off and took a bite of a ham sandwich. Leave it to Zeddie to throw together a ham sandwich that tasted like a four-star meal.

He shuffled his feet as he watched her chew. "I thought I might help you and Pop tonight, if I don't pass out first."

A warm glow lit up Mercy from within. "Think you can handle the paperwork, as long as the body is already salted and wrapped?"

His skin took on a pallid green hue, but he said, "I'll do my best."

She threw down her sandwich and hugged him, pinning his arms to his sides. "I love you!"

"Gross."

She let go and smacked him in the chest as Pop noticed them in the kitchenette. He looked at the sandwiches and cream puffs, then at his son. "Someone raised you right."

They got to work, Zeddie on the dock, clipboard in hand, and Mercy and Pop in the boatworks, salting and wrapping. The ribs of a half-finished vessel had to be shoved against the wall to make room for the human remains stacking up. None of the bodies appeared to be marshals, which went a long way toward alleviating Mercy's concern for Duckers. And anyone else who might be a Tanrian Marshal.

As the hours passed, the outside world disappeared. Mercy swam in a sea of death and salt and sailcloth. Her red transistor sat silent and watching as she worked side by side with Pop. She had no idea what time it was when Zeddie stepped into the doorway.

"Mercy?"

"Hmm?" She kept her focus on her work. There was so much work to do. Work behind her, before her, ahead of her. Pop nudged her to get her attention, because Zeddie wasn't alone. Pen stood behind him, and next to Pen was Alma Maguire. The grim set of the chief's jaw made that tiny pinprick of worry for Hart expand into a gaping pit inside Mercy.

"Have either of you seen Marshal Ralston come in this evening?"

"No," Pop answered.

Everyone looked to Mercy, and her mouth went dry. "I'm sure he's dropping off bodies like everyone else."

Alma stepped closer. "He was on sick leave, but we got word that he entered Tanria through the North Station this morning. They said he was armed to the teeth, like he knew something was going to happen, and now I've got hundreds of bodies on my hands—disinfected drudges, by the look of it—but no Ralston. Every other marshal assigned to the West Station is accounted for, except him. If you have any information, no matter how small or insignificant it might seem to you, I'd appreciate it if you could let us know."

The words dropped on Mercy like a load of bricks. Hart was missing, and hundreds of unexplained dead bodies had shown up all over Tanria. A lump of helplessness throbbed in her throat as she thought of Hart sitting on her settee, staring past her as he told her what had happened all those years ago when he and Bill had tried to send the lost souls into the afterlife, the weight of his voice a shadow of the burden he had carried around inside him for so long.

"There's a field in the middle of Tanria where his first partner died years ago. Have you searched there?"

Alma's brow furrowed. "That was in Sector 28."

"Why would he go there?" Pen asked, his alarm contagious.

Telling Alma and Pen where Hart might have gone was one thing. Telling them why he might be there—even if they were his friends—was a betrayal of his trust that Mercy couldn't bring herself to break. "You'll have to ask him that yourself. When you find him."

"And you have good reason to believe he went there?"

"More bodies coming in," Zeddie murmured from the open doorway.

Mercy gazed at Alma, feeling more helpless by the second. "Yes, I think that's where he went."

Alma patted Pen on the shoulder. "Let's go."

Mercy stood there, frozen, listening as Alma told the marshals on the dock to meet her at the station. Zeddie kissed Pen goodbye again, then leaned against the doorjamb of the boatworks, his chartreuse pants oddly lively, given his surroundings. Pop put an arm around Mercy. "I'm sure he's fine."

Mercy nodded but without much conviction.

Zeddie cleared his throat. "Is he... mortal? I mean, maybe he can't... you know."

Mercy wanted Hart to be alive more than anything in the world, but as she mulled over Zeddie's words, a horrible sadness filled her. "That's the last thing he'd want."

She took off her glasses and pressed the heels of her hands to her eyes, pushing against the tears. She couldn't help Hart now, but she could respect the final wishes of the unfortunates who had been delivered to Birdsall & Son tonight. She put her glasses on, blew her nose on the handkerchief that she kept in her pocket, and nodded at Pop.

"Let's get to work."

For the next several hours, they sorted, salted, wrapped, and stowed. Exhaustion tugged on Mercy's bones, but she treated each body with care and sang the incantations with as much fervor for the twentieth salting and wrapping as she had for the first. She gave all of them the dignity they deserved at the end, even as her worry for Hart pulled hard at her attention.

When she caught Pop leaning on the prep table, she sent him to the lobby to take a break. But there was no break for Mercy. The bodies kept coming, many of them from Sector 28. Mercy wouldn't and couldn't think about what that meant. The dead needed her more than the living.

By the time the Painter brushed the eastern horizon in shades of lavender and pink, there was no more room left on the dock, in the well, or on the floor around the well. The salt ran low, and there was only enough sailcloth left to wrap two, maybe three more bodies.

A lull finally hit around five in the morning. Mercy was teetering on her feet, so tired she hadn't noticed that Pop had come into the boatworks until his arm was around her. "Come on. Let's have a sit."

He guided her four steps toward the door before she protested, pulling away from him.

"I can't. I have to work."

"You need to rest."

"No."

"Muffin—"

"There are too many things to worry about right now—too many *people* to worry about—and if I stop working, I'm going to have to think about them."

"You're not doing them any good if you're dead on your feet."

He guided her toward the door again, and she let him. Both of them bone weary, they shuffled down the hall to the lobby.

"I know your sister is one of your worries. Mine, too. But it's going to be fine. Your mom yelled at me for twenty hours before the Three Mothers finally forked over your key."

Mercy let out a watery laugh and dropped into a chair. Pop sat down beside her, and Zeddie came out of the kitchenette with a mug of coffee for each of them.

"If you tell Pop he can't have a cup of coffee, I will beat you."

She laughed again, doing her best to keep her concerns at bay. "You're a terrible influence, Zeddie, but I'm glad you stayed to help tonight."

They heard footsteps pounding up the boardwalk seconds before Danny burst into the room, panting from his run over, a grin spread from rosy cheek to rosy cheek. “Emma Jane is here! Seven pounds, two ounces! Lil did great! Everyone’s fine!”

Mercy couldn’t hear the sound of her own cheers over her father’s and brother’s. She took turns with Pop and Zeddie to hug the breath out of Danny before fetching a plate of celebratory cream puffs from the kitchenette.

Danny’s cheeks glowed as he gushed. “You should have seen Lil! She was amazing! I don’t how know she—and Bride of Fortune, Emma Jane is perfect! Perfection! Wait until you see her toes!”

They toasted mother and child with cream puffs and hugged Danny a few more times before sending him home.

“I thought he was about to give us a play-by-play of the birth,” Zeddie said after ushering his brother-in-law out the door. “Thank gods he veered off that topic. I don’t think I could have handled the details.”

Zeddie was still holding open the door when Alma stepped into the lobby, her eyes bloodshot, her mouth drawn tight across her face.

The pit that had opened up inside Mercy earlier in the night stretched far and wide, dark as a moonless night, threatening to swallow her whole. “Did you . . . ?” she began, but the rest of the words refused to exit her mouth.

“We found him.” Alma’s bottom lip trembled. She took a shaky breath before she spoke again. “I’m sorry, Mercy. He’s sailed the Salt Sea.”

Chapter Thirty-Eight

When her mother died, Mercy had imagined herself diving into the deep end of a swimming pool and staying there, her senses muted and muffled, her body cold and weightless. The same sensation overtook her now, the blessed feeling of not feeling anything.

"Where's Pen?" Zeddie asked, his voice heavy with worry.

"Parked out back with the remains. He's taking it hard. We all are," Alma told him.

What did that mean, to take something hard? Mercy didn't want to take it at all, hard or soft or in between. Whatever "it" was, she was certain to bash against its sharp edges and break.

Alma glanced at her, but whatever she saw made her look to Roy instead.

"The body's too tall for a dolly, so we're going to have to bring him in on a stretcher, unless you'd prefer that we take him somewhere else. Given the circumstances—"

Alma's words yanked Mercy out of her icy numbness. "No! He stays here."

"Maybe it's better if he goes to Faber & Sons, muffin." Pop took her hands in his, but Mercy found no comfort in the gesture. She was so cold that she couldn't stop shivering.

"No," she repeated, her tone as hollow as she felt.

"Then let me take care of this one."

This one. The remains. The body. They were all talking about Hart as if he were no longer here. Because he wasn't. He was gone. He had *sailed the Salt Sea*, another unbearable euphemism. Why couldn't anyone say what he was? Dead. Hart was dead.

"I'll do it," Mercy insisted.

"Muffin—"

"He bought a package from us, and we're going to honor it. It's what we do here. You've already overextended yourself, Pop, so I'll take care of him."

"Mercy—"

"I need to take care of him!"

Alma studied her, her demigod eyes made more luminescent by unshed tears, and she nodded. Behind her, Mercy could see Zeddie take a sobbing Pen into his arms and walk him toward the kitchenette.

"Can you help me bring him in?" Alma asked Roy, but Mercy answered for him.

"He can't. Doctor's orders. I'll help you."

Mercy faced another probing look from the chief marshal before Alma acquiesced. "Do you want him in the lift?"

"That depends. What's the condition of the body?"

The body. Even Mercy was sidestepping the harsh reality of death.

Alma sniffed hard, and a single tear dropped down her left cheek. "He's in bad shape."

Bad shape meant he'd been in pain when he died. But he wasn't in pain now, so Mercy did her best to shove the thought to the side. She'd deal with it later. Right now, Hart needed her to do her job.

"We'll put him directly on the prep table," she said.

She followed Alma onto the dock and took the first breath of fresh air she'd had in hours before they climbed into the hold of the autoduck. A corpse wrapped in sailcloth lay on a stretcher, directly on the floor, too long to fit in any of the berths. There were several places where blood had stained the winding sheet.

Pain. He was in pain. The thought screamed through Mercy, but the anonymity of the sailcloth covering his face allowed her to ram it out of the way. Together, she and Alma lifted their burden. He was heavy, but both women were strong. They carried him the short distance to the boatworks and set the remains on the table. Alma helped Mercy maneuver the stretcher out from underneath the body.

"Are you sure about this?" Alma asked.

"I can handle it."

I can't handle this, said a voice deep inside herself.

"Well, I don't think I can, so I'll leave you to it." Alma reached across the table and brushed Mercy's arm before leaving her alone with the corpse of Hart Ralston.

Mercy had told him that she didn't want to see him again, and he had honored her wishes. Now, as she braced herself to see his remains, she'd give anything to hear the *ding* of the front bell and walk into the lobby to find him standing at the counter.

She could hear Alma and Pop speaking in low voices out front and Zeddie comforting Pen in the kitchenette with a combination of soft words and caresses and stale cream puffs, yet the silence of the boatworks reached down her throat, threatening to fill her with a grief that would level her. She reached for the precious transistor Hart had given her, wound the crank, and flipped the switch to *On*.

A trumpet blared into the boatworks, and she hurriedly spun down the volume dial until the music played softly. She didn't know the song, but it was an upbeat big-band number, the sort of thing she usually loved to listen to as she worked. It made what she was about to do seem normal, mundane. She willed her hands steady. Then she unwrapped him.

I can't handle this, she thought again, but her hands kept working, muscle memory taking over as her mind shrank from what she saw before her on the table.

His entire body was a catalog of agony.

Mercy swallowed a sob. *Get to work*, she told herself.

His clothing was unsalvageable, so she cut it away with scissors. She heard the rustle of paper in his vest pocket as she pulled the garment free of his stiffening arms, and she made a mental note to retrieve whatever it was once she had him cleaned and salted and wrapped. The shirt went, the dungarees, the underwear, and the one sock and boot he'd come in with, the other set left behind on a Tanrian field. She made a neat pile on the floor, remembering the careful way Hart had folded her overalls while she took a bath. She pushed the memory away as hard as she could.

All that remained was the chain around his neck with his mother's birth key and his shiny, new Birdsall & Son ID tag, but she couldn't bring herself to remove them yet.

She cried while she bathed him, not a deluge, but a slow steady leak as she rinsed the blood and dirt from his cool, pale skin. He appeared more at peace now that he was clean, but also less like his living self.

The wet keys glistened in the gaslight. Mercy touched the metal, fingering them the way she had when Hart was in her bed, her head resting in the crook of his shoulder, a concavity that seemed at once thin and cavernous in death. *My Nuzzle Nook*, she thought without meaning to.

Grief rammed into her so hard, she dropped the hose and cried out when the cold water doused her shoes and one of her pant legs. Still crying, she turned off the tap and gripped the table.

Pop appeared in the doorway. He looked haggard, but if he knew what a wreck she was, he'd barrel his way in and insist on taking care of Hart himself, when what he needed more than anything was a good night's sleep.

"Everything all right?" he asked.

Mercy swiped at the tears staining her cheeks. "Fine. I dropped the hose. That's all."

He walked across the room and stood opposite her, with Hart's corpse between them, but his focus was entirely on his daughter. "How are you doing?"

"I'm fine."

"Anything I can do?"

"You can go home and meet your granddaughter and rest."

"I will, but I want to go over a few things with you and Chief Maguire when she gets back."

"Where did she go?"

"To let her wife know. I guess they were close."

"Her name's Diane," Mercy told her father, remembering the warmth in Hart's voice when he had talked about her.

Leonard whined in the lobby.

"Probably needs to go out," Mercy said, the weight of exhaustion settling into her soul. It was bizarre to think of doing something as normal as letting her dog out to pee when Hart was dead and gone. He needed her to take care of him, but she had to take care of the living first, and it rankled her.

"I'll do it," said Pop, but Leonard's whines grew so sharp and pronounced that she followed him to the lobby anyway. The dog was pacing back and forth, skittish. Mercy tried to pet him, but he ducked away from her hand and barked, though there was nothing to bark at. She opened the door and tried to coax him outside, but he wouldn't go.

"He liked Marshal Ralston, didn't he?" Pop said quietly.

Mercy knew what he was getting at. A hard knot formed in her throat. She nodded. "Leonard, come," she called, moving toward the boatworks and the body of a man whose life had departed. Her dog followed her, sniffing the air as they got closer. She had Leonard sit beside the prep table, and she crouched down to be with him.

"He's gone," she told him, stroking his ears. "I'm sorry."

Leonard put his front paws on the table and sniffed the body, knocking Hart's hand loose so that it dangled off the table's surface. His nubbin tail wagged, then stopped. He whimpered piteously, a sound that echoed the keening ache inside Mercy. She wanted to bury her face in Leonard's brindle coat and feel his warmth against her cheek and hear his heart beating beneath his rib cage, but he yelped and bolted out of the room, leaving her alone with her sorrow.

Mercy took Hart's dangling hand, intending to put it on the table at his side. Instead, she intertwined her warm fingers with his cold, lifeless ones. She wished that she could sob, to get it out of the way so that she could do all the things that needed doing. But as she clutched Hart's frigid hand and made herself look at his battered face, the tears refused to come.

There was a knock at the front door, and Mercy bowed her head in frustration. "You've got to be kidding me. Pop, can you get that?"

In answer, her father's cigar smoke wafted in from the dock. He probably couldn't hear her or the knock.

"Zeddie?"

There was no answer. He was probably camped out in her apartment with Pen, or maybe they had gone home. And that left her to answer the door. She kissed Hart's palm—although she didn't have a right to do so, she thought with a guilt-laden pang—and set his hand down at his side.

The sounds of an argument on the other side of the door greeted her as she stepped into the lobby. "What fresh nightmare is this?" she asked Leonard, who gave her a sad wheeze from the chair that he wasn't supposed to be on, apparently recovered from whatever had bothered him earlier. She opened the door to find Horatio chewing out a nimkilim she had never seen before, a hard-bitten rabbit with a gold loop through one ear.

"You are infringing on my territory! The good people of Eternity do not need ruffians soiling their streets."

"Well, fuck you very much!"

Horatio flapped a dismissive wing at the rabbit and addressed Mercy. "My apologies, Miss Birdsall. I shall deal with this cur forthwith."

The other nimkilim marched past Mercy, lobbing his argument over his shoulder as he strode straight for the boatworks. "Federated Postal Code 27-C clearly states—"

"Excuse me!" cried Mercy, rushing after him alongside Horatio.

"—that in cases of decease, any undelivered mail is retrieved by the nimkilim of record, which is me." When Horatio hooted in outrage, the strange nimkilim stopped and added, "Suck. On. That," poking the owl in his puffed breast feathers.

"Remove your phalanges from my person at once before I am forced to do you harm."

"Please, I could wipe the floor with your tail feathers and still have time for a drink at the pub," the rabbit answered as he stepped into the boatworks.

Privately, Mercy agreed with that assessment, which was why she was not prepared when Horatio walloped the rabbit from behind and wrestled him to the floor. She scurried out of the way, pressing herself against the wall in shock and disgust as the nimkilim fought each other next to Hart's body. They rolled into the soiled clothing, wreaking havoc on Mercy's neat pile, both of them reaching for the vest and tearing it in half in the process with a violent *riiiiip*.

It was Horatio who came up victorious, waving a letter about in triumph as he declared, "Aha! To the victor go the spoils!" But his triumph evaporated when he read the address, and he gazed at Mercy with mournful eyes. "Oh, my dear. I am so sorry."

Bewildered, Mercy looked to the other nimkilim, but his attention was now on Hart.

"Aw, no. Not him." The rabbit stood on tiptoe to better see the body on the table. "No, no, no. You fucking asshole!" He tugged a red handkerchief from his pocket and sobbed into it.

"You can deliver it, if you like," Horatio told him, holding out the letter, his feathers ruffled, his cravat a mess.

The other nimkilim blew hard into his hankie and shook his head. "You do it."

"You knew Hart?" Mercy asked.

"Lemme see you." The rabbit approached her and studied her long and hard. "You know what? I bet you were probably worth it."

He took the letter from Horatio and delivered it to Mercy. "Mail for you, friend."

Mercy took the envelope from his paw. One corner was stained brown with Hart's blood, but the address was clearly legible.

To: Mercy Birdsall
C/O Birdsall & Son, Undertakers
26 Main Street
Eternity, Bushong

After all this time, her friend had finally written back to her.

"Well, I could do with a drink," said Horatio.

"That makes two of us. First one's on me?" offered the other nimkilim, and they let themselves out.

Mercy glanced at Hart's stiffening body before prying open the envelope with numb fingers and reading his last letter to her.

~~Dear Friend,~~

~~My dearest~~

Mercy,

My name is Hart Ralston.

I could tell you that I'm tall and have blond hair and gray eyes. I could tell you that my favorite color is yellow, because your favorite color is yellow. I could tell you that I'm a demigod and a Tanrian Marshal and, as I informed you in my first letter, a dickhead. I could even try to tell you that I'm "your friend," but how can I, in good conscience, claim that title? A friend doesn't lie or hide the truth the way I did.

This is my roundabout way of saying I'm sorry. Not "I'm sorry, but." I'm sorry. Full stop. I was afraid you wouldn't feel for me what I ~~have come to feel for y~~ have felt for you since the day I walked into Birdsall & Son and found a woman there who was color and light and joy in a world that had come to seem colorless and dismal and lousy to me. But that's not an excuse. There's no excuse for keeping the truth from you. I'm weak. That's all I can say for myself.

I am not a good man, as you well know, but at least I can tell you with absolute certainty that I am a <u>better</u> man for having known you. My letters to you have allowed me to be my best self the only way I know how, since I can't seem to make the right words come out of my mouth when I need them. And being with you—the real you—gods, what can I say? What words could do justice to the precious time you gave me? You've made me want to live my life, rather than spend my time worried about my mortality (or lack thereof). Maybe that's a mixed blessing, but it's more a blessing than a curse, so thank you, Mercy, for inspiring me to be better than I am. You have always been Merciful, whatever my stupid, foolish mouth has said to the contrary.

You once told me that I had a rapier for a heart and a depressing novel lodged in my appendix, but the truth is that, if anyone bothered to scratch my brittle, craggy surface, they would find that my heart and soul belong entirely and completely to Mercy Birdsall, the best human being whose surface I have ever had the privilege of scratching.

If I were brave, I'd send this letter to you. If I were braver, I'd destroy it. But I'm not brave and never was, not like you, so I'll keep it tucked beside my heart, unsent and unread, until the day I die. If I die. And who knows? Maybe then it will make its way to you somehow, my words too late as always and never worthy of you to begin with.

I hope one day you'll give your heart to someone good and decent and that you will cherish his heart in return. But it's a rare man who deserves you, so I'll leave you with this: I wish you a happy life, surrounded by the people you love and who love you in return.

~~Your friend,~~

~~Sincerely,~~

Love,

Hart

Mercy's eyes drifted from the page in her hand, past the body on the table, all the way to a point frozen in time, when she sat, miserable and alone, at a table in the Little Wren Café, believing her friend had stood her up. Except he hadn't stood her up. He had been there all along, right in front of her, and she had failed to see him for who he was. He had sat across the table from her, sipping his tea, his gray eyes cool and shuttered as he spoke, a challenge in his voice.

Maybe there are things about me that would surprise you, Merciless, if you bothered to scratch the surface.

One moment, she was standing against the boatworks wall; the next, she was bent over Hart's body, clutching the letter and clinging to an arm that could no longer hold her in return. She sobbed into the perfect curve where his shoulder met his neck, the spot that was supposed to belong to her for a long, long time.

I'm still waiting for you to do something stupid, he whispered in her mind.

"I was stupid all along," she wept, but he couldn't hear her now. Not where he was.

Chapter Thirty-Nine

Hart stole a cookie from the cooling rack on the counter when his mom wasn't watching. He had almost reached the back door when she asked, "Where are you going?"

His hand was on the knob. He didn't face her, because he didn't want her to see the cookie in his guilty hand, the still-warm chocolate chips melting all over his fingers.

"Down by the creek," he said.

"Okay. Put on your jacket."

"I'm fine. It's not cold."

"Jacket."

He rolled his eyes as he yanked his jacket off the coat hook, then sailed through the door and down the steps.

"Hartley James, put on your jacket!" Mom shouted at him from the kitchen window, but there was laughter in her voice.

"I will!"

"It doesn't do you any good if you're not wearing it."

"Okay! Bye, Mom! Love you!" he hollered over his shoulder, the jacket flapping in the wind as he ran, trailing from his hand like a kite.

"Love you, too!"

The sun shone bright in a cloudless sky, and the air was the perfect temperature, cool but not too cool. He ran past the chickens and the vegetable plot and waved at Grandpa, who was checking the rain gauge in the barley field. By the time Hart reached the creek, Gracie was at his heels, yipping. He found a stick and hurled it as far as he could and watched as she raced after it, lithe and swift as a deer. She brought it back to him and set it at his feet, her tongue lolling out of her mouth. The game of fetch went on for what felt like hours. Gracie was tireless, and Hart had nowhere he needed to be and nothing he needed to do. But as the sun arced high and began to drop toward the western horizon, he decided it was time to head home.

He walked past the cattle, which lowed in protest as Gracie tried to herd them, but the dog came running when Hart gave a sharp whistle through his teeth. She followed him in through the screen door and sniffed Diane's orange tabby, who arched his back and skittered away. Hart helped himself to a soda—they always seemed to have an unending supply in the icebox.

"Alma? Diane?" He stepped into the parlor, where dust motes floated in the shaft of afternoon sunlight pouring in through the open window. He took a sip of soda and liked the way the bubbles fizzed over his tongue. Bill had always insisted that soda would rot his teeth, but Hart couldn't help himself when he was at Alma and Diane's house.

Bill.

There was something about Bill that was supposed to make him sad, but he couldn't remember what it was.

He crossed the room and opened the front door and stepped into the lobby of Birdsall & Son, Undertakers, with a sensation akin to smacking into a wall.

I'm not supposed to be here, he thought with an accompanying dismay.

"Duckers, let's move it," he spoke into the empty air. But no, Duckers wasn't with him this time, was he?

"Gracie," he called, because he couldn't very well leave his dog behind. But then he remembered that Gracie wasn't supposed to be here either. This place belonged to a different dog. He wasn't sure of the name until it sneaked up on him and tripped off his tongue.

"Leonard?"

There was movement to his right. He turned his head and saw the boxer-and-other-things lift his head from the arm of a chair he should not have been occupying. The dog's nubbin wagged. He jumped off the chair and ambled toward his favorite marshal. Hart tried to pet him, but Leonard grew skittish, pacing the floor and whining in equal parts.

"Hey, what's the matter?" Hart asked him.

Leonard barked in distress and fled down the hallway.

The sound of a chair scooting away from a desk came from the office, followed by footfalls heading toward the door. A man came into the lobby, flipping through pages stuck to the clipboard in his hand. He startled when he noticed Hart. Then he studied the pages of his clipboard again.

"Well, shit. I guess that's today."

Hart stood frozen to the spot, stunned, unsure what he should be feeling. "Bill?"

"What? No." The man glanced down at his body. "Oh, right. That makes sense." He surveyed his surroundings. "Yeah, this all makes sense." He looked at Hart again and gave him a fond smile.

"Bill," Hart said again, except this time, it wasn't a question.

"No, sorry. You might not see Bill this go-around. He's holding on to a lot of guilt when it comes to you, worried that you're not going to forgive him, when obviously, you forgave him long ago, if you ever blamed him to begin with. Give him time. He'll come around."

Hart gaped at the man. He didn't know what to say, because this was definitely Bill, right down to the scar in his right eyebrow and the missing tips of the last two fingers of his left hand.

The man chucked the clipboard onto the counter. He came closer, stopping a few feet in front of Hart. "I'm your dad."

Hart continued to stare at the man before him, who, as far as he was concerned, was his mentor and the only real father he'd ever had. At last he spoke, his tone even when his feelings were not. "There's no way Bill could have fathered me. I don't have a dad."

"I look like Bill in your mind, but I'm not. I'm the Warden—you know, the guy who ushers souls into the House of the Unknown God. They need help sometimes, the lost and lonely ones. Hence, me."

Hart felt like the floorboards were tilting beneath his boots. "By 'guy,' you mean 'god'?"

"Yep."

"Right." It was the only response he could muster. His mind was a blank.

"Wow. Hartley James. I've waited thirty-six years for this day. Any chance I could get a hug?"

The man who was not Bill and who claimed to be one of the gods of death—who, to Hart's knowledge, had never fathered a child in all of recorded history—took a step toward him. He took an answering step back. He wanted nothing to do with the Warden, the father who was never there, the thing wearing Bill's skin as if he had any right to it.

The Warden stopped and held up his hands—Bill's hands. "Okay. No worries. I get it. I know you have some complicated feelings when it comes to me. Maybe it would be best if you called me Jeff."

Hart's jaw tightened. A familiar rage bled into his current state of confusion. "What is going on here, Jeff?" He said the name like a curse.

"You came home."

"I don't have a home."

"Sure you do. Several. Trust me. It's my job to know these things."

Hart exhaled in frustration as he glanced around the lobby. He knew this place, and he knew that he wasn't welcome here, although he was having trouble remembering why. It definitely was not his home.

The Warden leaned his elbow on the counter and clasped his fingers. The pleasant expression of his face turned commiserative. "We should talk."

"That ship sailed when you ditched my mom."

Warden dismissed Hart's resentment with a wave. "Well, I'm your dad, so too bad. We're talking."

Hart found himself sitting in a maple tree, on a limb that jutted out from the trunk in a nearly perpendicular line, matching the horizon. He knew this spot. It was his favorite climbing tree, the one that overlooked the west orchard. His feet dangled, and he kicked them through the air, first one, then the other, back and forth. The air smelled loamy, the scent of a plowed field before Grandpa seeded it. He didn't realize that the Warden was sitting next to him until the god spoke.

"I always thought that if I could have been a real dad—a normal dad—this is where we'd go when you had something you needed to say."

Hart regarded the Warden, who still looked every inch like Bill. Then he turned his attention to the hazy pink-and-orange sky. "This is where I went when I wished I had a dad to talk to."

"I know."

Bitterness filled Hart's mouth, spilling acidity off his tongue. "What are you doing here?"

"Existing. What are you doing here?"

Hart wanted to answer, but words alluded him. He took in the orchard and the familiar horizon beyond. He knew his house was behind him to his left, past the walnut grove. He was home. But it wasn't his home anymore, was it? Aunt Patty had sold this land years ago.

What are you doing here?

The question echoed in his head, and an answer slowly surfaced in his mind. There had been a field and a house. His house. And pain. So much pain. He had opened the door and had gone home. They'd all gone home, all the lost souls, his own included.

The god was closer now. Hart stiffened when the Warden's hand landed on his shoulder, but he didn't pull away. "I asked you a question, Hart. What are you doing here?"

"Dying, I guess," he answered, feeling empty and alone.

"Mortals usually do."

"So I *am* mortal?"

"Yep."

That was when he remembered Mercy, and the hurt that came with the memory made him wish he could forget her all over again. Except he didn't want to forget her. As soon as she returned to his mind, he latched on and refused to let go. *It'd be like reading a book that doesn't end*, she told him in his mind. *No matter how good the story is, you want it to be over at some point.* But she was wrong. Now that the grim, depressing novel that was his life had come to an end, he wanted to make the story keep going.

His mouth formed a hard line across his face before he spoke to the Warden again. "Nice of you to show up just in time for the end."

"The end?" The Warden shook his head. "I will never understand why mortals treat dying like it's the stroke of an axe rather than the slow steaming away of water in a pot."

"If you're going to talk like a fucking poem, you can keep your mouth shut. You know, like you've been doing for the past thirty-six years of my life."

"Thirty-six years is nothing."

"Sure feels that way."

"Are you saying your life was nothing? Because if that's the case, what a waste of thirty-six years."

"Sorry to disappoint you." Hart almost called him Father, but it seemed like the kind of tetchy work of irony a child would have wrought, and he was a grown man.

"Are you going to ask me why I left?"

"No."

"Too bad, because I'm going to tell you anyway."

"Fuck this." Hart intended to hop down off the branch, but suddenly, he froze, and not of his own volition. He could neither move nor speak. All he could do was sit and listen.

"As I was saying," the Warden continued, and when he looked on Hart this time, his eyes did not belong to Bill. They were lit with a cold gray light, great voids as vast as an overcast sky, immortal eyes—a god's eyes—infinite and immutable.

"I open the door for the souls who lose their keys or don't have keys to begin with. Always have, always will. Except once. Once, I wasn't there. And it caused a few problems, four hundred and seventy-two of them, to be exact, but I'm getting ahead of myself.

"Everyone crosses the threshold, right? So I've always found it bizarre that mortals are unpleasantly shocked when they find themselves either dead or on their way home. I mean, death is everywhere. Everywhere. Flowers die, and mortals have to replant them in the spring. Leaves fall from the trees year after year and rot. Birds drop dead out of the sky; their babies fall from the nest before they ever spread their wings. A beloved dog breathes one last breath and rips a hole in a man's heart, as if it were a surprise rather than an inevitability.

"How the fuck do humans manage to look away, and why do they want to look away to begin with? Especially when it comes to lost souls. Almost every time I open the door for one of them, they resist. They don't want to come in, when you'd think that out of all the souls of the world, these are the people who would be most grateful to come home. It made me wonder, what's so great about living that you wouldn't want to die?

"So I dressed myself up in flesh and blood and tried it out for a while, and the first thing I discovered was that living hurts. There are so many aches and pains. I stubbed my toe. Do you have any idea how much it hurts when you stub your toe?"

He looked at Hart, his eyes less eerie now, but Hart couldn't speak, couldn't move.

"I kept getting hungry. I caught the flu and lay shivering in a hotel bed for three days. But there was something else that hurt more than a stubbed toe or hunger or sickness. I couldn't put my finger on what it was, but it followed me wherever I went. And even that paled in comparison to the suffering I saw around me—people begging for food or money in the streets, people who were so ill they could barely move, people whose dreams had been crushed by time and fate and all the horrible things the Old Gods had unleashed into the world. I thought, if living is this miserable, why wouldn't people want to leave it behind?

"So I was about to give up and go home when I met your mom at Lennox's Comics and Games in Pettisville, Arvonia. Ever been there?"

Of course Hart had been there. His mother had taken him every time they went into town, and though they hadn't had much money, she'd bought him all the Gracie Goodfist comics he could carry in his small hands. Not that he could tell the Warden any of this; he was still frozen in place.

"She was arguing with the owner about the God of War and the God of Old Hell. Of course, back in the day, it was just Hell, but we New Gods got rid of it, so. Anyway, they were talking about the *Old Gods* comic series, and they were weighing the merits of each character, which one was superior, that kind of thing. It was a friendly argument. Obviously, I knew more about the subject than either of them, so I weighed in, saying that the Trickster is the most powerful villain, the one who caused more problems for humanity than any other god.

"I think she thought I was joking, because she laughed. I wasn't joking, but she had a gap between her front teeth, which some people think of as a fault, but to me, it made her lovely. Perfectly imperfect. Suddenly, all I wanted to do was make this woman laugh as often and as much as I could. It wasn't love at first sight, exactly—more like a knowing. I understood then and there that I was going to fall in love with her if I stuck around. So I stuck around. And that pain I felt, the one I couldn't figure out, went away. Poof. Just like that."

Hart could see his own hand writing the words on the page: *Maybe there's a strange comfort in knowing that at least one person feels something for me.* Of course, that hadn't been the end of the sentence. *Even if that feeling could best be described as hate,* his memory finished for him, and he remembered with a fresh stab of loneliness that Mercy hated him again.

"We had five months together," the Warden continued. "Five months. Five months is nothing, even by mortal standards."

It's longer than the time I got with Mercy, you fucking asshole. Hart frothed on the inside.

"You're wondering what happened, why I left if I was so happy?"

I don't care. The words were there on the tip of his useless tongue, but then he realized it was a lie. He did want to know. He had always wanted to know.

"Yes," he said, surprised to find that he could speak and move again.

The Warden's eyes seemed almost human now, black pupils rimmed in pale gray. Hart's own eyes, staring back at him.

"I left Grandfather Bones in charge of opening the door in my absence. Probably not the best choice, but it's not like there are a lot of gods of death to choose from, and the Unknown God is, well, unknown, and the Salt Sea deals with a lot of traffic, if you know what I mean. Anyway, bless his heart, Bones is deaf as a post, and he didn't hear the shuffling footsteps of the souls who needed help. By the time he figured it out, there were four hundred and seventy-two souls locked out of the House, and a lot of very pissed-off gods. Grandmother Wisdom hauled me to the door by my human ear. That hurts worse than a stubbed toe, by the way. I didn't even get to say goodbye to your mother. And I didn't get to meet you either, until now."

The god's single tear rolled down Bill's rugged face. He swiped at it and murmured, "I forgot about tears. Stupid Salt Sea."

"Did you *want* to meet me?" Hart asked, his voice high and light, a child's voice with all its unhidden fear and desolation.

"Fuck yes, I wanted to meet you."

The Warden no longer resembled Bill at all. He was tall and lean, his face angular, his eyes an innocuous shade of blue gray, and Hart knew this was what his mother had seen when she met a man named Jeff and fell in love with him. This was his father, and for the first time in his life, the notion didn't tear his heart in two.

"And you loved my mom?" Hart sounded even younger now.

The god's thin mouth curled up on one side. "Sure did. Sure do. She's home now. She came home to me."

"I saw her."

"I know."

"I really miss her."

"I know that, too."

Hart stared at his father, drinking him in, his heart breaking and stitching itself back together over and over. The sun disappeared over the horizon, and the stars blinked on, one by one. The Warden gazed on the world as if he could see all of it, well beyond what Hart could take in. When the god turned to his son again, his head moved in the opposite direction, so that it was his second face he showed Hart, with eyes as pale and colorlessly gray as the morning sky on a cloudy day.

"Anyway, all those souls wound up trapped in Tanria, which makes sense. They couldn't hang around in the mortal world, but thanks to me and Grandfather Bones, they couldn't enter the House of the Unknown God when they were supposed to, so they got stuck in the one place in the world that's in between life and death. Thing is, a soul without a body gets very confused in the mortal plane. After a while, that soul thinks it's supposed to be alive and searches for a body to inhabit so that it can keep on existing in its own terrible way. At the time, there weren't any humans in Tanria, so it wasn't a huge issue, but when people started coming in, things got ugly real fast. We tried to round up the lost souls, but by that point, it was like herding feral kittens, and there wasn't anything I could do about it but open the door to the souls who died too soon because I left my post thirty-six years ago and created the things I believe you call *drudges*."

"I don't understand. Why couldn't you open the door and let the lost souls in, too?"

"They wouldn't come."

"But they came when I opened the door."

"Technically, you opened *a* door: *your* door to *your* home. Tanria was always where you were going to die the first time. That's why it was there, and whew, the drudges didn't like that. You're like a bridge, you know? Half human, half god. When you opened the door from the outside, you fixed what your dad fucked up."

The Warden reached out, and when Hart didn't shrink from

him, he put his hand on his son's messy blond head, the reassuring heft of it like a benediction.

"I'm so confused," Hart admitted.

"Mortals usually are."

"So the drudges have all gone home? There are no more lost souls in Tanria?"

"That's right."

"And I'm mortal? I died?"

"Yep."

His skinny shoulders caved in, but he tried to be brave. "Okay."

The Warden jostled him affectionately. "See? You're sad to leave, like everyone else. So it wasn't a waste of thirty-six years after all."

Hart pulled away as a pressing question bubbled up from the depths of his muddled thoughts. "What did you mean about me dying 'the first time'?"

"You get two deaths to die, little demigod, one from me and one from your mother."

"Doesn't that mean I have two lives to live?"

"Same difference."

His father hopped off the limb and held out his arms. Hart jumped down and giggled when his father caught him and tickled him. They walked hand in hand to the house with the music of cicadas wheezing a late summer song around them. They were nearly home when his dad stopped, knelt beside him, and pointed to someone in the distance.

"See there? He came to say goodbye to you after all."

Standing in a moonlit field was a man holding a lamp in the darkness. It was hard to make out the features of his face from so far away, but he held up a hand with the tips of two fingers missing, a gesture that was both blessing and absolution. Hart held up his own hand in reply, and a heavy weight seemed to roll off him. He felt lighter than a cottonwood tuft floating lazily to the ground.

His father stood and nudged him toward the house. "Come on. Off to bed with you."

Grandpa sat on the back steps, smoking a pipe, the sweet aroma filling Hart's nose with the scent of home and comfort.

"Good night, Grandpa."

Grandpa tucked his pipe into his overalls pocket and patted Hart on the head. "Good night, peanut."

Peanut. Hart had forgotten that his grandfather called him that. He grinned at the old man as his father picked him up and carried him inside.

When they stepped through the door, Mom was in the kitchen, scrubbing a pot at the sink. She dried her hands on a dish towel when she saw him, and smiled, the gap in her front teeth on full display.

"Going to bed?"

Hart nodded, his cheek smooshing into his father's shoulder. She smoothed his hair and kissed the top of his head.

"Good night. Love you."

"Love you, too." He was so tired, he could barely form the words.

His father carried him up the stairs. His head lolled. His arms grew limp around his father's neck. His legs dangled and swayed with each step up. They turned into the first room on the left, and Hart's father laid him gently onto his bed. Hart was already in his favorite pajamas, the ones with dogs all over them—although he couldn't remember putting them on—and his mouth tasted of toothpaste. His eyes drifted shut as his father pulled up the blanket and tucked him in, but he fought sleep. There was something he meant to ask, something he needed to know.

"Dad?"

"Yep?"

"Why did the Old Gods go away?"

"Probably because infinity is a terrible thing. But you already knew that, didn't you?"

Hart did know that, but infinity didn't seem as scary when his father was beside him. He nodded, and his father leaned down to kiss his forehead.

"Good night, Hartley James. I'll wait for you."

Chapter Forty

It was time to sew up Hart's wounds. Some undertakers skipped this step, especially if the body was slated for cremation. Mercy had no idea what Hart's arrangements were yet, but only the Salt Sea could stop her from doing this for him at the end. Except, as she stood over him with needle and thread in hand, she couldn't bring herself to do it. If she sewed him up, she'd have to salt his body next, and if she salted his body, she'd have to say the incantations over him, and if she said the incantations, she'd have to wrap him in sailcloth, and if she wrapped him, she'd never see him again. If she did all those things, she would have to build his boat and send him over the Salt Sea to the House of the Unknown God.

He's already gone, her tired, sluggish brain begged her heart to understand, but her heart couldn't accept it yet.

"They're here."

Pop stood at the door. Mercy set down the needle and thread on the table, grateful for the interruption but reluctant to leave Hart, even if he wasn't going anywhere. "I'll be right there."

Her father left her alone with the body. Mercy kissed Hart's temple, then pulled a sailcloth over him as if she were tucking him into bed. She took off her sweaty headscarf, smoothed her hair, and made her way to the office, where she found her father, Alma Maguire, and a petite woman standing around the desk.

"I don't think you've met my wife, Diane," said Alma, more composed than she had been a few hours ago. "Diane, this is Mercy Birdsall. She's taking care of our Hart."

Our Hart. Why did he think he was alone, when clearly, these two women loved him as much as—

Mercy couldn't bring herself to finish that thought or to say "Nice to meet you," so she simply extended her hand. Diane bypassed the hand and dove straight into her, hugging her with birdlike arms that were stronger than they looked, arms that had probably hugged Hart in the same way.

Gird yourself: She's going to hug you. A lot, Hart had warned her.

Mercy had thought she didn't have any tears left to shed, but she was wrong. Hugging Diane felt like hugging her own mother, so she clung to the tiny woman far longer than she should have. And Diane, for her part, clung to Mercy as tightly, gasping with sobs as tiny as she was.

"Sorry," Mercy said when she could bring herself to pull away.

"You have nothing to apologize for." Diane took a handkerchief from her purse and dabbed Mercy's cheeks dry, though her own were damp. "It's clean. I promise."

A tearful laugh burst out of Mercy like the last, unexpected gurgle of a coffee percolator. She accepted the handkerchief and blew her nose. "I'll wash it and get it back to you."

"Please, don't worry about that. You have more important things on your plate."

Mercy knew that she was referring to the dozens of bodies that had piled up at Birdsall & Son overnight, and yet "more important things" made her think of Hart, and "on your plate" made her think of the prep table, and the fact that he was all alone in the boatworks. She knew he wasn't really there, and yet the guilt of abandoning him lay thick and heavy on her chest.

Pop picked up Hart's file from the desktop and glanced around at the three women crowded into the tiny office. "Everyone ready?"

They nodded, but Mercy was fairly certain that none of them were prepared for this. How could they be?

Pop shifted his reading glasses from the tops of his eyebrows to the tip of his nose and opened the file folder. Mercy caught a glimpse of Hart's signature at the bottom of the page, the strokes of each letter of his name created with his living hand. Diane's fingers slipped between hers and squeezed, an acknowledgment that this moment was next to unbearable. Mercy was certain that Alma's hand was held in an equally tight grip.

"He requested a boat in our Vinlandian series, made of teak, inside and out."

Mercy's heart dropped as her father looked at her over the top of his glasses.

"I . . . I've never made a Vinlandian."

"You'll do fine."

"And teak? He ordered *teak*?"

"Is teak bad?" Alma asked.

"No, it's the best material there is. It's incredibly expensive. Why would he order the most expensive boat we offer? That's so unlike him."

But in the question lay the answer. She hadn't closely examined the books lately, not since Lilian had begun the transition into the office manager job, but it would explain why Birdsall & Son was doing better than they ought to be. Clearly, that order alone had kept them afloat for the past two months. Mercy had refused to take Hart's money when he'd offered it, so he'd given it to her the one way he could. The lash of grief slapped her all over again. She pressed Diane's handkerchief to her eyes as if she could hide from the pain, and the fingers wrapped around hers squeezed more tightly.

"He requested that his remains be taken to the pyres and that the ashes be given to Alma Maguire and Diane Belinder."

Mercy let loose an incredulous huff. Leave it to Hart to order the most luxurious funereal boat money could buy, only to burn it as soon as he was inside.

"Did he say what he wanted us to do with the ashes?" Alma asked, her voice rough.

"He left that to your discretion."

Alma nodded, and Pop read through the next line of Hart's funeral arrangements.

"His mother's birth key is to be sent to his aunt, Patricia Lippett, whom he believed to be residing in Pettisville, Arvonia. Do you happen to know his aunt's whereabouts?"

Alma took up her wife's hand and pressed a kiss to it. "We can look into it."

"Good. As for his earthly belongings, including any and all assets and the contents of his bank account or accounts..." Pop tossed the file folder onto the desk, unfolded Hart's last will and testament, and scanned the document. He took off his glasses, rubbed his forehead, and looked his daughter square in the eye. "He left everything to you, Mercy."

It was almost nine in the morning, and Mercy had been awake for well over twenty-four hours, so the words coming out of her father's mouth made sense one by one, but she couldn't seem to string them together in any comprehensible way. "What?"

"He left you everything."

Mercy wasn't sure if she could handle any more shocks, and definitely not one of this magnitude. In the silence that followed, she pressed her hand to her cheek, trying to wrap her brain around what this meant.

Alma burst out laughing and clapped her hands together. "Good for him! Whew, Aunt Patty's not going to like that."

"Alma!" Diane chastised her, although a grin played at her own mouth.

"That hag was awful to him and you know it."

"Why?" Mercy asked. She meant *Why me?*, not *Why is Aunt Patty not going to like this?* But Alma answered the second question.

"It's got to be a small fortune."

"One million, two hundred thousand at the time he created his last will and testament, according to the document on file," Pop concurred with a numerical precision that stopped Mercy's heart.

"That kid never spent a penny on himself. Well, except to buy imported tea." Alma's voice broke at the end, a sound that echoed the fissure in Mercy's chest. Diane stroked her wife's back, sniffing hard.

"I can't take it," Mercy said.

"He wanted you to have it."

"You two should have it, not me."

Diane stood in front of her and took her by the arms, gazing at her with tired blue eyes lined with the kind of crow's feet that came from decades of sunlight and smiling. "This is what he wanted. Let him have this, here at the end."

Mercy was saved from answering by a knock at the office door. It was Danny, holding his hat over his heart.

"Sorry. Didn't mean to interrupt. Lil sent me to come bring you home, Pop."

"It's all right, Mr. Birdsall. Diane would like to say goodbye, and then we'll be on our way," Alma said, shaking Roy's hand.

Goodbye. The word was a blade in Mercy's chest.

Pop turned to her. "You need to go home, too."

"I am home."

"You know what I mean. Go to bed."

"I'm going to finish him up first."

Pop's eyes were bottomlessly sad. "He's not going anywhere."

"Go home, Pop," she begged him, this father of hers who had almost died a year ago. The sorrow of that near loss, mingled with her current misery, made Mercy cling to what she had left. She hurled herself at him, holding him tight. "I love you so much."

"I love you, too, muffin." He patted her back, comforting his first baby. "Zeddie's still here if you need anything."

Mercy snorted as she pulled away. "Is that supposed to make me feel better?"

He answered her laugh with a bittersweet one of his own. "You're incorrigible, the lot of you."

He left with Danny, and Mercy felt the crushing weight of the past few hours settle into her bones. She hadn't wanted to leave Hart's body in the boatworks; now she wasn't sure that she was up to the task ahead of her.

Diane placed a maternal hand on the side of Mercy's face, and Mercy couldn't help but nestle her cheek into its slender warmth. "I'm glad he had you, if only for a short while. And I'm glad he has you now."

"Thank you," Mercy told her, grateful for the woman's grace and kindness. She was certain she didn't deserve it, not when it came to Hart. She pocketed the handkerchief and led Diane to the boatworks, where they found Pen waiting beside the door. His eyes were puffy, and he seemed older than he had been a day ago.

"Can we make a deal that we're not going to hug each other, because we'll both lose it if we do?" he asked her.

"Thank you. Yes. Where's Zeddie?"

"He's asleep."

"In *my* bed?"

"Sorry. It was late, and we both crashed."

"I forgive you. Him? Not so much."

She was hoping to coax a small smile out of him, but he was as solemn as a shipyard.

"I want to say goodbye to him, but I also don't want to see him. I don't know what to do."

"I've got a sailcloth over him," Mercy told him. "You could come in and say goodbye and see him but not see him at the same time. Would you like that?"

Pen nodded. Mercy opened the door and stepped inside. Already, the room felt emptier, as if Hart were much farther away from her now. Diane followed her in, but Pen stood in the doorway for a long time before approaching the shrouded body on the table.

"Would you like for me to leave?" Mercy asked them both.

Diane squeezed her arm. "No, I'd like for you to stay."

"Me, too," said Pen.

Mercy stepped away to give them space as they stood over Hart's unmoving form.

Pen's hands fidgeted at his sides. "Hey, sir. I came to say goodbye. Sorry if I do it wrong.

"When my dad died a couple of years ago, it felt like Grandfather Bones dug a chunk out of me, and I've been carrying around a giant hole inside me ever since. Dad was always there for me. He really listened. He taught me... not the school stuff, but the *life* stuff I needed to know, like how to shave and how to deal with assholes and how to talk to a guy I liked. He was the man I wanted to be someday, and then all of a sudden he was gone, and I didn't have anyone to help me figure myself out. Until you. I thought I'd lost the only father I'd ever have, but now I'm losing you, too, and it feels like losing a dad all over again."

"Oh," Diane said and produced a fresh handkerchief for Pen. He took it, but he didn't use it. He coughed, fighting the urge to cry, then he cleared his throat and kept going.

"I think I'm part of the reason why you did whatever you did, which is what a good father does, I guess, but how could you leave me with that? I know I shouldn't yell at you when you're dead, but I'm pissed off at you, sir."

Mercy couldn't stand it. She put a hand on his shoulder. He reached up to brush her fingers with his.

"Can I see him?" he said.

"Are you sure about that?"

"I'm sure. I think I need to see his face to say goodbye."

"Okay."

Mercy let go of his shoulder, pulled down the shroud, and stepped away. She already felt like she was invading Pen's privacy as it was. Diane's, too.

"Wow, Mercy, this is amazing. How did you fix him?"

"What do you mean? I haven't done anything yet."

She looked down. Hart's eyes were closed, rather than open and staring. His lips were scarred but no longer cut. Then his chest moved, expanding in and out, the inhalation and exhalation audible.

"Oh," Diane breathed again, this time in wonder, and Pen stumbled backward.

Mercy's heart hammered so hard she could hear it galloping in her ears. She pulled down the shroud farther, revealing Hart's chest and stomach. His wounds were knitting themselves back together, and his color was beginning to return.

"What is happening?" Pen demanded.

"He's a demigod," Diane said softly.

"So, like... he's immortal?"

Mercy couldn't speak, but Pen didn't require an answer, not when he could see all the evidence he needed coming to life on the table in front of them.

"He's alive? He's alive!"

Mercy saw Pen dancing in her peripheral vision, but she couldn't tear her attention away from Hart. She placed a quaking hand on his chest. His skin was cool, but the flesh beneath was less rigid. She felt nothing. Until she did. One spasm of the heart followed by a long pause, then another beat, his life slowly but surely pumping through his veins.

"Is there a pulse?" Diane asked, a note of sadness tingeing her hope.

Mercy nodded.

"Oh," Diane said for the third time. The two women held each other's gaze over Hart, both of them understanding that this was not what he wanted. But because neither of them knew whether to laugh or cry, they wound up taking turns dancing with Pen, spinning a dizzying polka around the boatworks.

Breathless, Diane returned to the table, gave Hart a gentle nudge, and called his name. All three of them surrounded him, waiting for him to open his eyes, but he didn't move, save for the rise and fall of his chest.

"I don't want him waking up on the table," Mercy said. "Pen, do you think you can help me get him up the stairs and into bed?"

"Yes, ma'am! I'll get Zeddie to help us!" He smacked Mercy's cheek with a sloppy kiss and zipped up the stairs, his feet hammering on the treads as he shouted for Zeddie.

"I'll tell Alma," said Diane, exiting the room with less ebullience than Pen.

Mercy turned her shining face to Hart, but a bittersweet taste flavored her happiness. He should be dead, but he wasn't, and she knew that this was his worst nightmare coming true.

"Oh, Hart-ache, I'm sorry." She took up his hand, growing warm in hers, and pressed it against her heart. "And I'm sorry that I'm not sorry at all."

Chapter Forty-One

His eyes were closed, and he couldn't seem to open them. He was aware of sounds around him, but everything was muffled, as if he were underwater, although the *whoosh* of his breath and the thundering of his heart were deafening in his ears. His consciousness wove in and out, sometimes in blessed darkness, sometimes surfacing into the strange state of almost waking. When he did surface, his body was so heavy that he could not move it. There was no sense of time or place or memory, only drifting. A familiar softness enveloped him, above and below, smelling of comfort and contentment. *Her*, his mind whispered, unreeling the single syllable like the filament of a spider's web. He had the feeling that if he could latch onto it, it would pull him wherever he needed to go.

Something wet and smelly lashed his cheek with nauseating, slurping sounds. He lifted his leaden eyelids and found himself nose-to-nose with the ugliest, sweetest dog in Bushong.

Leonard, he remembered. He groaned, and with superhuman effort, he wiggled onto his side, away from the adoring onslaught. His gaze landed on a small woman sitting in a chair, her head lolling to the side in sleep. His breath was thin and his tongue thick as he pushed her name out of his mouth.

"Diane?"

She didn't stir. He watched her breathe, heard the sound of air weaving in and out of her body in time to the wagging of the dog's nubbin tail.

"Diane," he said again, louder, his mouth beginning to obey his will.

Her eyes eased open. Then she startled upright in her chair, as if she were a marionette, and the puppeteer had pulled on the strings.

"Hart!" She rushed to him and pressed her hand to his forehead, the way his mother had when he was sick. "How are you feeling?"

"Heavy," he said, but that seemed like a woefully inadequate response.

She cupped his face in her delicate hands and kissed his nose.

"Is Alma here?" he slurred. He felt drunk.

"I'll go get her. I'll go get everyone." She pressed her forehead to his, and Hart caught the scent of her bergamot soap before she relinquished him. She dragged Leonard off the bed and hurried out of the room, shouting "He's awake!" when Hart had never heard her raise her voice a day in his life.

His throat felt dry and crackly. He saw a glass of water on the table beside him, and it wasn't until he sat up that he realized he was in bed. Familiarity with his location mewled at the back of his mind like a cat that wanted to be let in, but all he could think of was how thirsty he was and how badly he wanted a drink. He reached for the glass and fumbled it, nearly knocking it over before he got a firm grip. He gulped down the water, cool in his burning throat, streams escaping on either side of his bottom lip and dripping onto his shirt. He put the glass on the table and frowned at the wet stains on the plain white cotton undershirt stretched taut over his chest. It was small on him. As a matter of fact, he didn't think it was his.

The metaphorical cat of his memory continued to scratch at

the back door of his brain with increasing insistence. Hart had hardly registered that he was not at Alma and Diane's house when Duckers burst into the room and tackled him onto the mattress with more enthusiasm than Leonard. Hart groaned as Alma's familiar voice barked, "Get off him, you dolt!"

"He's not gonna break. The man's unbreakable." Duckers smiled down at him before helping him sit up again.

Hart scanned the familiar faces hovering over him: Duckers, Alma, Diane, and... Zeddie Birdsall?

"This is Mercy's apartment," he said as the blood drained out of his cheeks.

"That's right." Alma smiled at him. Why on earth would she be smiling at a time like this?

"I'm not supposed to be here."

"Where's Mercy?" Diane asked Zeddie.

"In the boatworks."

Alma grabbed him by the arm and ushered him out the bedroom door—*Mercy's* bedroom door. "Well, go get her!"

"Oh, right."

Off Zeddie went to fetch the last person in the world Hart was supposed to see. He flung off the blankets and stood on unsteady feet. Suddenly, everyone had their hands on him, and he found himself in a sea of "No, no, no!" and "Lie down!" and "You've been out for three days!"

"I have to get out of here," he insisted at the same frenzied moment that he realized he was wearing nothing but the white undershirt and a pair of boxer shorts a size too small, covered in tiny hot dogs. Definitely not his. "Where are my clothes?"

No one would listen to him. They kept trying to convince him that he should stop or sit or lie down or listen as the cacophony of his own alarm spun in his head and came tumbling out of his mouth. "I have to go!"

"Hart, calm down."

"I'm not supposed to see her!"

"If you would—"

He yanked himself free of their hands, and his calves smacked painfully against the bed frame.

"I CAN'T SEE HER!"

"Hart?"

His name spoken from that mouth sliced through the noise. Everyone fell silent, Hart included.

Mercy stood in the doorway of her own bedroom with Zeddie shuffling nervously behind her. She wore the blouse with the yellow flowers printed on it, her dungarees riding high on her waist, her hair wrapped up in a yellow scarf. Her red glasses were a smidge crooked on her nose.

Hart froze as their eyes locked across the room. His heart had barely begun to mend, and seeing her now was like ripping open the wound all over again. He stood there, inexplicably wearing someone else's underwear, unable to mask how raw and broken he was, while too many people were there to witness how much it hurt him to see her.

Only then did it finally occur to him to wonder how he'd wound up half-naked in Mercy's bedroom in the first place, because he was 99 percent certain that it had nothing to do with sex. There was no earthly way he would forget making love to Mercy. Mercy, who looked at him with an emotion he couldn't identify. It wasn't anger, but it wasn't joy either.

"Do you remember what happened?" Alma asked him, touching his arm in a tender way that was very un-Alma-like.

He shook his head, although truth be told, he wasn't trying too hard to remember. He was pretty sure that recalling the events that had landed him at Mercy's apartment in a strange pair of underwear would be a bad idea.

"Let me talk to him," said Mercy, and to Hart's dismay, everyone obediently shuffled out of the room, leaving him alone with her.

He didn't know what to say, and apparently she didn't either. The silence screamed between them.

"I'm sorry," he said at last, directing his words to the hooked rug at his feet. "I know I shouldn't be here. I'll leave. Just need my...uh...clothes."

"We had to incinerate them."

"Oh."

He was more and more certain that he didn't want to remember what had happened, and the fact that it had led to the incineration of his clothing strengthened that resolve.

"I have extras in the hold of my duck," he offered, his desperation to escape tinting every word.

"You left your autoduck at the North Station. Zeddie and Pen are going to drive up to get it tomorrow."

The North Station? Why was his duck there?

His memory caught up to him in fractured bits and pieces. The resolve to open the door. Gearing up at the North Station. Saltlicker. The field. The fight. The pain. The lost souls of Tanria flying around him and through him. His body dropping as the door slammed shut.

"I died," he said. His face felt numb.

"Yes."

"I'm dead."

"No."

His attention snapped to her face. Her eyes were red rimmed behind her glasses, as if she'd been crying or was about to cry, a pitying look. He didn't think he could handle her pity. He wanted to run from the room—from her and that terrible compassion—but she stood between him and the door, so he stared at the rug again.

"I know this is the last thing you wanted," she said. "But I hope it's some comfort to know the truth now."

"What truth?" Hart repeated hollowly.

"That you're immortal."

He nodded absently, and then he remembered everything. Everything. His mother and Grandpa and Gracie and Bill and all the places he thought of as home. He remembered the Warden—his father—talking to him on the branch of a maple tree. He remembered the feel of his father's warm hands and gentle kiss as he tucked Hart into bed with the promise of two deaths to die and two lives to live.

He let his gaze drift to Mercy's face once more. He understood her pity now and was touched that she cared enough for him to feel sorrow on his behalf, especially when it was a worry he could dispel for a change.

"I'm not immortal."

"Hart, you were dead. And now you're not."

He almost told her everything, but what was the point? He had his life back, but he'd still have to live it without Mercy. In the end, he simply said, "I know. You have to trust me on this one. Not that I've given you much reason to trust me."

He watched her forehead furrow in confusion, an expression so sweet that he let himself enjoy it for a second before he said, "I'll get out of your hair. I'm sure Alma and Diane can give me a ride to their place."

"You can't leave."

"I think it's for the best."

She marched straight at him, and his heart jumped in his chest. His whole body went rigid with expectation, although he had no clue what exactly to expect. A slap across the face? A punch to the stomach? A kick to the nuts?

A kiss?

She yanked open the drawer beside the bed, pulled out a piece of paper, and held it up for him to see.

~~Dear friend,~~

~~My dearest~~

Mercy,

He wanted to howl at the Bride of Fortune, but it wouldn't change the fact that the letter was in Mercy's hand now, that she had read his words and seen his heart in a way that he could never take back or hide, and it made him feel like the skin had been peeled off his flesh.

"But my clothes were incinerated," he said helplessly, his eyes riveted to the brutal honesty of his own words.

The truth is that, if anyone bothered to scratch my brittle, craggy surface, they would find that my heart and soul belong entirely and completely to Mercy Birdsall.

"A nimkilim fished it out of your vest and delivered it before we burned your clothes. A rabbit."

Bassareus.

"Fuck," Hart uttered. He turned away from her and gripped the headboard of her bed. "I'm sorry."

"For what?"

"For everything."

"I need you to be more specific than that."

He could feel her eyes boring into his back. "I'm sorry I didn't tell you about the letters."

Another savage pause followed his apology.

"You are failing miserably at this, so I'm going to help you out. Let me tell you exactly why you should be sorry."

The fury in Mercy's voice was so acute that Hart braced himself.

"You should be sorry that you thought I wouldn't eventually forgive you for not telling me about the letters. You should be sorry that you couldn't push past what I said in anger and come talk to me. You should be sorry that you put yourself in danger when the people who love you would rather keep you here. You should be sorry that you went and saved the world and got yourself killed in the process and left me here without you!"

"I'm sorry," he sobbed.

"I don't want to hear 'I'm sorry, Mercy' or 'I don't deserve you, Mercy' or 'I hope you find someone else, Mercy'! I want to hear 'I love you, Mercy'!"

She slammed the letter onto the bedside table and gasped for air. Hart let go of the headboard and turned to stare at her, dumbfounded, before he found his words.

"Well, of course I love you, Mercy. Was that up for debate?"

She burst into tears. "For the love of the Mother of Sorrows, would you hold me please?"

Hart obeyed, his movements jerky and mechanical as he wrapped his arms around her. But holding Mercy was the same thing as coming home, and he drew her in closer and tighter, feeling her warmth against him, breathing in the pine scent of her hair.

"Please don't make me let you go," he whispered.

"If you ever let me go again, I will strangle you."

Mercy kissed him, and he thought he might fall to his knees. "I love you," she said against his lips.

"Gods, I love you, too. So much."

He kissed her and tried not to get snot or tears on her face. Then again, she was crying, too, and he didn't think he'd mind her snot or tears in the slightest.

"Aw, that's sweet," a familiar voice said behind him.

Hart turned to glare at Bassareus, who was, for reasons Hart could not begin to fathom, staring at him and Mercy through the open doorway, alongside Alma, Diane, Duckers, Zeddie, and an owl, all of them grinning.

"Isn't that the cutest fucking thing you've ever seen?" Bassareus asked the rest.

"It is," Zeddie agreed with an obnoxious smirk. "Nice boxers, Ralston."

"This is Zeddie's underwear, isn't it?" Hart asked Mercy under his breath.

"We were desperate."

The owl primly clapped his white wings. "Brava and bravo! What a marvelous finale. I do enjoy a happy ending."

"I want to remind you that I totally called this, sir," Duckers chimed in.

Bassareus blew his nose into his handkerchief. "Fucking beautiful," he wept.

Epilogue

Hey!"

Hart waited until he had the attention of the two adolescents, the charcoal in their fingers dusting their guilty hands. As they took in his six feet and nine inches, his gray demigod eyes, and his sheriff's badge winking sunlight at them, they looked like they might literally shit themselves.

Gods, this job was fun sometimes.

One of them—the girl—was smart enough to run. The boy remained pinioned in place by Hart's icy glare. Girls were always smarter than boys.

"What do you think you're doing there?" Hart asked him.

"Uh... uh..." The kid was so scared that the charcoal tumbled from his hand out of pure terror as Hart loomed over him and regarded the boy's handiwork on the exterior wall of the schoolhouse:

Ms. Sanderson is a bicth

"Ms. Sanderson may be a bicth"—he pronounced the word exactly as it was spelled: *bic-thuh*—"but the poor woman's got her work cut out for her if she has to teach you lot how to spell *bitch* right."

Hart picked up the charcoal, crossed out *bicth*, and demonstrated the proper spelling in his neat, blocky print. Then he chucked the charcoal and leveled the boy with his steeliest glare. The kid whimpered.

"Let's go say hi to your dad, Thomas, and see if he'll let us borrow a bucket of soapy water and some rags so that you can clean this up."

Hart oversaw the whole endeavor, from Thomas's father's excoriation of his son to the boy's cleaning of the besmirched clapboard. Toward the end, Hart relented and let his dog Trudie go over to the kid for a pet.

When Thomas was finished, it was time for Hart to head home. En route, he stopped to watch the workmen take down the sign at Cunningham's Funeral Services with smug satisfaction. Mercy's coordination with the other undertakers along the border, combined with her investigation into the undertaker's shady practices, had put Cunningham out of business and into jail. Hart was so proud of Mercy, he could hardly see straight. And privately, he was thrilled that Nathan McDevitt's involvement in arresting Cunningham had led to Mercy's ex pursuing a career with the FICBI—the Federated Islands of Cadmus's Bureau of Investigation—far away from Eternity.

A sharp bark pulled his attention away from the defunct undertaking business. Trudie wiggled her butt, knowing she was supposed to sit as instructed but losing patience quickly. The second Hart met her slightly bugged eyes, her thick tail thumped the ground.

"Ready to go, Trudie True?" he asked his comic-book-superhero sidekick, named for Gracie Goodfist's best friend. The metronome of her tail increased its tempo dramatically. She was short but stocky, with the kind of barreled rib cage Hart liked to pat with a satisfying *thump*. "Come on, then."

She walked at his side like his shadow, her tail always moving, her mouth a constant smile as they headed to Mercy's

Undertakings, passing by the family home on the way. Roy was sitting in a rocker on the front porch, whittling a boat. When he wasn't whittling boats, he could frequently be found taking naps with Emma Jane. It was the cutest thing Hart had ever seen. Trudie ran ahead of him to receive the affection that was due to her from her human grandfather.

"Hi, Sheriff," Roy called as he set down his knife and ran his big hand over Trudie's adoring head.

"Hey, Pop. Remember, there's a barbecue tonight at Alma and Diane's."

"Between all you kids, I've already been reminded seven times. Zeddie's made roughly twenty side dishes. And cookies."

Hart lit up. "Snickerdoodles?"

"I think so, but he won't let me eat any."

"Brutal," Hart commiserated before stepping inside to steal one. He ducked into the kitchen, where the plate of snickerdoodles sat on the counter. Zeddie and Duckers were too busy making out against the icebox to notice that Hart was standing there, eating one.

"Shouldn't you be working?" he asked his former apprentice.

Duckers continued to keep his lips locked with Zeddie's as Zeddie flipped Hart the bird behind his back.

"Barbecue tonight at Alma and Diane's," Hart reminded them as he took another bite. "Bring these."

Duckers finally pulled away from Zeddie's mouth. "No offense, sir, but please go away."

"You know you can call me Hart now, right, Duckers?"

"You know you can call me Pen now, right, Hart?"

Hart considered this as the taste of cinnamon lingered on his tongue. "Nope. Can't do it."

"You're as bad as Mercy," Zeddie groused as he grabbed Duckers's hand and led him toward the staircase.

"Thank you."

"Hey, sir, I spotted a dragon flying over Sector W-13. No joke," Duckers called over his shoulder as Zeddie dragged him up the stairs.

Hart had to raise his voice to be heard as the two young men went into Zeddie's bedroom and closed the door. "Salt fucking Sea, how many times do I have to tell you there are no dragons in Tanria?"

Duckers snickered loudly behind the door. Hart shook his head, but he was laughing, too.

On his way out, Hart patted Roy on the shoulder and handed him a pilfered cookie before heading home. A half block from Mercy's Undertakings, he caught up to Danny, who was pushing Emma Jane in a stroller up the boardwalk.

"Ready for ribs?"

"I am ready for any meal I don't have to cook or clean up," Danny said.

Trudie stuck her nose in Emma Jane's face. The baby laughed, revealing all two of her bottom teeth. Hart reached into the stroller and picked her up. She loved it when Uncle Hart swept her into his arms, because he made her taller than everyone else. He kissed her neck—her tickle spot—and made her screech with laughter.

"Would you like me to collect your wife?" Hart asked Danny when they arrived at Mercy's Undertakings.

"By all means."

"Come on, Emma Jane Little Bottom."

He carried the baby inside with him, bouncing her and her dark curls as they walked through the lobby, the music from Mercy's transistor filtering in from behind the closed boatworks door. Leonard lifted his head from his favorite chair and wagged his nubbin.

"Leonard, get down," Hart ordered him, but when Trudie hopped into the other chair, he gave it up as a lost cause. He popped into the office, where Lilian was tidying up her desk.

"Look what I found," he said.

"There's my baby girl!" Lil held out her hands, but Hart hugged his niece to his chest and tickled her fat belly, making her giggle. That giggle was the best sound in the world.

"I'm sorry, ma'am, but possession is nine-tenths of the law," Hart said in his best Sheriff's Voice.

The baby screwed up her face as a horrid squirting sound came from her diaper. An equally horrid stench followed it. Hart handed Emma Jane to her mother forthwith. "Here you go. She's all yours."

He barely darted out of the way as Lilian swiped at him with one hand while clutching Emma Jane with the other.

"Your mother is a terrifying woman, E. J.," he informed his niece.

"At least I don't look like a charcoal pit."

Hart glanced down at his shirt and frowned at the black streaks. "Good point."

He left Lilian to deal with the baby and the diaper and headed upstairs. When he stepped into the apartment, he dipped his hand in the blue flowered bowl of salt water next to the door and touched his mother's key on the altar. He changed his shirt and combed his hair before heading downstairs in time to see Horatio and Bassareus stepping onto the dock.

"Helloooo!" Horatio hooted, hoisting his driving goggles up on his forehead.

"Hiya, asshole," said Bassareus.

"I thought you weren't due back until tomorrow."

"Darling, we are so much better at escorting the dearly departed to their final catafalques than our human counterparts," Horatio drawled as he headed straight for the new icebox on the dock and retrieved a bottle of Veuf Didier sparkling wine. "And the pay is far superior to that of the Federated Postal Service. It keeps one motivated, does it not, Bassie?"

Bassareus grabbed the whiskey bottle sitting on top of the icebox and pulled out the cork with his teeth. "If he calls me Bassie one more time, I'm going to shove this bottle up his ass."

Hart took his watch from his pocket and saw that it was nearly time to leave. "There's a barbecue at Alma and Diane's tonight, if you want to go."

The nimkilim burst into hysterical laughter.

"He thinks we want to go to a *mortal* party," Horatio chortled.

"Loser!"

"You're fired," Hart told them both, which made them laugh harder. He shook his head, but he was smiling as he headed for the boatworks. The volume of the music rose sharply when he opened the door and found Mercy counting urns in the supply closet. She wore her yellow dress, the one she had been wearing when Hart stepped into the lobby of Birdsall & Son years ago and nearly blew it with the love of his life—or the love of his *lives*, as it were. He took her by surprise, sweeping her into his arms and dancing her around the boatworks.

"You scared me to death!" she half laughed, half protested as he moved her through an anchor step, spun her out, then brought her into him again, dancing in time to the music. She smacked him on the chest in exasperation. "Most people start with *hello*."

He bent down to kiss her. "Hello, Merciful."

She smiled at him, dimples and all. "Hello, Sweet-Hart."

Acknowledgments

I'll start by heaping gratitude upon my agent, Holly Root, whose sage advice ("Go nuts. Get weird.") and boundless enthusiasm were critical to the hatching of this book. Cheers to you, Holly, and to Alyssa Moore and the whole amazing gang at Root Literary.

Thank you to my editor, Angeline Rodriguez, for believing in my work. I'm also grateful to have UK editor Nadia Saward in my corner along with everyone at Orbit, including Paola Crespo, Casey Davoren, Rachel Hairston, Madeleine Hall, Stephanie A. Hess, Tim Holman, Nazia Khatun, Aimee Kitson, Joanna Kramer, Bryn A. McDonald, Amanda Melfi, Lisa Marie Pompilio, Ellen Wright, and many others. With their combined powers, they ushered this novel from a typo-filled manuscript to a beautiful object to be read. And I am forever obliged to Janice Lee for copyediting the book, thereby saving me from public humiliation.

Thank you to Tanaz Bhathena, Kathee Goldsich, Sarah Henning, Jenny Mendez, and Sierra Simone for your feedback and for spitballing ideas with me. Katie Korte, bless you for reading bits and pieces along the way. Additionally, I must raise a cup to Adib Khorram, my personal tea consultant. And while I know that I functioned for more than forty years on this earth without Miranda Asebedo and Amanda Sellet, I'm not sure how. Thank you, Miranda and Amanda, for your constant brilliance and your ride-or-die friendship (and for rhyming so conveniently).

Finally, thank you to my friends and family for the love and support, especially my sons, Hank and Gus, and my husband, Mike, who made sure that I had the time and space I needed to write this undead-infested love story in relative peace while we were stuck at home together during the Quarantimes. This one's for you, Dr. Mike. You're the best love interest a girl could ask for.

extras

meet the author

Megan Bannen is a former public librarian whose YA debut *The Bird and the Blade* was an Indies Introduce Summer/Fall 2018 pick, a Summer 2018 Kids' Indie Next List pick, and a Kirkus Best YA Historical Fiction of 2018 pick. While most of her professional career has been spent in public libraries, she has also sold luggage, written grants, and taught English at home and abroad. She lives in the Kansas City area with her husband and their two sons. She can be found online at meganbannen.com.

Find out more about Megan Bannen and other Orbit authors by registering for the free monthly newsletter at orbitbooks.net.

if you enjoyed
THE UNDERTAKING OF HART AND MERCY
look out for
THE BALLAD OF PERILOUS GRAVES
by
Alex Jennings

In a fantastical version of New Orleans where music is magic, a battle for the city's soul brews between two young mages, a vengeful wraith, and one powerful song in this vibrant and imaginative debut.

Nola is a city full of wonders. A place of sky trolleys and dead cabs, where haints dance the night away and Wise Women keep the order, and where songs walk, talk, and keep the spirit of the city alive. To those from far away, Nola might seem strange. To failed magician Perilous "Perry" Graves, it's simply home. Then the rhythm stutters.

Nine songs of power have escaped from the magical piano that maintains the city's beat, and without them, Nola will fail. Unexpectedly, Perry and his sister, Brendy, are tasked with saving the city. But a storm is brewing, and the Haint of All Haints is awake. Even if they capture the songs, Nola's time might be coming to an end.

1

HERE I'M IS!

Perry Graves tried not to think about summer's arrival—the heat devils hovering, breathless, over the blacktop as if waiting for something to happen—or even about the city streets. Tomorrow was the last day of school, and he'd be free to roam the neighborhood soon enough...But it *wouldn't* be soon enough. Perry and his little sister, Brendy, sat cross-legged on the living room floor watching Morgus the Magnificent on the TV. The unkempt, hollow-eyed scientist was trying to convince a gray-haired opera singer to stick his head into a machine that would allow Morgus to amputate the singer's voice with a flip of the switch. From here, Perry could hear his parents and their friends gabbing on the front porch as they sipped sweet tea and played dominoes.

"Why you ain't laughing?" Brendy said.

"Don't talk like that," Perry said. "Daddy hears you, he'll

get you good." Then, "I don't always have to laugh just because something's funny."

"Oh, I know, Perry-berry-derry-larry." Brendy stuck her tongue out at him. "You in a *mood* 'cause you ain't seen Peaches in a week. You don't want me talkin' like her because it remind you of the paaaaaain in yo heaaaaaaaaart!"

Perry scowled. "Shut up."

"I'm sorry," Brendy said. "I'm sorry you luuuuuuvs Peaches like she yo wiiiiiiiife!"

"Little bit, you be sorry you don't shut your mouth," Perry threatened. He had no idea what he could do to silence her without getting into trouble.

"Nyeeeeowm! Zzzzzrack!" For a moment, Brendy absently imitated the sound effects from Morgus. "You just want her to say 'Oh! Perilous! I luuuuuvs yew tew! Keeeeeeess me, Perry! Like zey do een—' " Perry was ready to grab his baby sister, clap his hand over her mouth at least, but before he could, a clamor rose up outside. "Looka there!" some grown-up shouted from the porch, his voice marbling through a hubbub of startled adult exclamations.

Whatever was going on out there had nothing to do with Perry, so he ignored it. He was sure that someone had just walked through some graffiti, or that a parade of paintbodies was making its way down Jackson Avenue. He grabbed Brendy's wrist, all set to give her a good tickle, but when the first piano chord sounded on the night air, Perry's body took notice.

Perry let go of his sister, and his legs unfolded him to standing. By the time the second bar began, his knees had begun to flex. He danced in place for a moment before he realized what was happening, then turned and made for the front door. Brendy bounced along right beside him, her single Afro pouf bobbing atop her little round head.

Ooooooh—ooh-wee!
Ooooooh—ooh-wee!
Ooo-ooh baby, oooooh—ooh-wee!

Outside, Perry's parents and their friends had already descended to the street. Perry's grandfather, Daddy Deke, stood at the base of the porch steps, pumping his knees and elbows in time with the music. "Something ain't right!" he shouted. "He don't never show up this far uptown—not even at Mardi Gras!"

Perry bounced on his toes in the blast of the electric fan sitting at the far end of the porch. The night beyond the stream of air was hot and close—like dog breath, but without the smell. As soon as Perry left the breeze, dancing to the edge of the porch steps, little beads of sweat sprang out on his forehead and started running down.

From here, as he wobbled his legs and rolled his shoulders, Perry saw a shadow forming under the streetlight. It was the silhouette of a man sitting at a piano, and the music came from him. The spirit's piano resolved into view. It was a glittery-gold baby grand festooned with stickers and beads, its keys moving on their own. Shortly thereafter, Doctor Professor himself appeared, hunched over, playing hard as he threw his head back in song. He wore a fuzzy purple fur hat, great big sunglasses with star-shaped lenses, and a purple-sequined tuxedo jacket and bow tie. Big clunky rings stood out on his knuckles as his hands blurred across the keyboard, striking notes and chords. Perry smelled licorice, but couldn't tell whether the smell came from Doctor Professor or from somewhere else. The scent was so powerful, it was almost unpleasant.

All Perry's senses seemed sharper now, and he tried to drink in every impression. He danced in place to the piano and the bass, but as he did, guitars and horns played right along, their sound pouring right out of Fess's mouth.

Ooh-wee, baby, ooooooh—wee
What did you done to meeeee...!

By now, everyone for blocks around had come out of their houses and onto the blacktop. A line of cars waited patiently at Carondelet Street, their doors open, their drivers dancing on the hoods and on the roofs. It was just what you did when Doctor Professor appeared, whatever time of day or night. They danced along to the music, and those who knew the lyrics even sang along.

You told me I'm yo man
You won't have nobody else
Now I'm sittin' home at night
With nobody but myself—!

Perry gave himself up to the sound and the rhythm of the music. The saxophone solo had begun, and it spun Perry around, carried him down the steps and across the yard. His feet swiveled on the sidewalk, turning in and out as he threw his arms up above his head.

Just as quickly as he'd come, Doctor Professor began to fade from sight. First, the man disappeared except for his hands, then his stool disappeared, and then the piano itself. He had become another disturbance in the air—a weird blot of not-really-anything smudged inside the cone cast by the streetlight, and just before he had gone entirely away, Perry heard another song starting up. The music released him, and the crowd stopped moving.

"Oh, have mercy!" Perry's mother crowed. "That's what I needed, baby!"

"That Doctor Professor sure can play."

"Baby, you know it. Take your bounce, take your zydeco—this a jazz city through and through!"

Wilting in the heat, Perry turned to head back inside and saw Daddy Deke still standing by the porch. The old man wore a black-and-crimson zoot suit, and now that he'd finished his dance, he took off his broad-brimmed hat and held it in his left hand. He looked down his beaky nose at Perry, staring like a bird. "Things like that don't happen for no reason," he said. "Something up."

"Something bad?" Perry asked.

"Couldn't tell ya, baby," he said. "Daddy Deke don't know much about magic or spirits. But I gotta wonder...why *that* streetlight in particular? That one right there in front of Peaches's house?"

Now Perry turned to look back at the space where Doctor Professor had appeared. Daddy Deke was right. It stood exactly in front of Peaches's big white birthday cake of a house.

"I didn't see her dancing," Perry said. "Did you?"

"If she'da been there, we'da known it," Daddy Deke said. "Can't miss that Peaches, now, can you?"

Perry and Brendy's parents resumed their seats on the porch, but Daddy Deke headed past them into the house. Perry and his sister followed. In the foyer, Daddy Deke paused to breathe in the cool of the AC and mop his brow with a handkerchief. "Ain't danced like that in a minute," he said.

The living room TV was still gabbling away. Brendy twirled and glided over to shut it off—and Perry wasn't surprised. After seeing Doctor Professor, the idea of staring at the TV screen seemed terminally boring—but so did porch-sitting.

"What you doing tonight anyhows, Daddy Deke?" Brendy asked.

"Caught a couple bass in the park this morning," the old man said. "Might as well fry some up and eat it."

"You went fishing without us?"

"Y'all had school," Daddy Deke said. "If you comin', come on."

Daddy Deke's house sat around the corner on Brainard Street, a stubby little avenue that ran from St. Andrew to Philip, parallel with St. Charles. The low, ranch-style bungalow with the terracotta roof and stucco walls looked a little out-of-place for the Central City—it was the kind of place Perry would expect to see in Broadmoor, crouching back from the street like ThunderCats Lair.

As Perry and Brendy crossed the lawn, Daddy Deke broke away to head for his car, an old Ford Comet that seemed like a good match for the house in that it was also catlike. But instead of ThunderCats Lair, it reminded Perry of Panthor, Skeletor's evil-but-harmless familiar. Daddy Deke turned to look at his grandchildren over his narrow shoulder. "Gwan, y'all. I just gotta stash something real quick, me."

As always, the door to Daddy Deke's house was unlocked. Perry let himself and Brendy inside and took a deep breath. Daddy Deke's place had a smell he couldn't quite identify, but it was unmistakable. A mix of incense, frying oil, and Daddy Deke's own particular aroma—the one he wore beneath his cologne and his mouthwash, the scent that was only his.

At one time, the house had been a doubled shotgun. Daddy Deke had had the central dividing wall and a couple others knocked down, but the second front door remained. Perry and Brendy took off their shoes and stored them in the cubby underneath the coat rack. By then, Daddy Deke had followed them inside.

"Do the fish need scaling?" Perry asked. Daddy Deke had shown him how to descale, gut, and fillet a fish, but Perry was still refining his grasp on the process. There was something about it he enjoyed; figuring out how to get rid of all those fins, bones, and scales felt a little like alchemy—transmuting an animal into food. It made Perry think of the Bible story where Jesus fed thousands on a couple fish and two loaves.

"Naw," Daddy Deke said. "Did it my own self this time—wanted to get them heads in the freezer. Gonna make a stew later on."

Perry's mouth watered. Daddy Deke's fish-head stew was legendary—no matter what form it took. He could make it French-style, Cajun, or even Thai. On those nights when Daddy Deke made a pot for the family and carried it around the corner, the family would eat in near silence, punctuated with satisfied grunts and hums of approval.

"Why I can't never fix the fishes?" Brendy asked. "I wanna help make dinner!"

"You didn't want to learn," Perry said. "You said it was gross."

A flash of anger lit Brendy's face, but it blinked away as quickly as it had come.

"You promise to be careful with the knife," Daddy Deke said, "and we put you on salad duty, heard?"

"Yesss!" Brendy hissed. "Knife knife knife knife *knife*!"

"Lord," Perry said with a roll of his eyes.

In the kitchen, Daddy Deke turned on the countertop radio and stride piano poured forth to fill the room like water. "You know who that is?" Daddy Deke said.

Perry listened closely. He recognized the song—"Summertime"—but not the expert hands that played it. Hearing it made him feel a sharp pang of loss. He hadn't touched a keyboard in more than a year. He pushed that thought away—thinking about playing was a dark road that led nowhere good. "No," Perry said. "Who is it?"

"That's Willie 'The Lion' Smith," Daddy Deke said, "outta New Jersey. Used to work in a slaughterhouse with his daddy when he was a boy. He said it was horrible, hearing them animals done in, but there was something musical about it, too. That's the thing about music, about a symphony: destruction, war, peace, and beauty all mixed up, ya heard?"

Perry frowned and shut his eyes, listening more closely. He could hear it. At first the tone of the music reminded him of water, and it was still liquid, but now he imagined a bit of darkness and blood mixed in. He saw flowers unfurling to catch rain in a storm. Some of them were destroyed, pulverized by the water or swept away in the high wind.

"That's the thing about music," Daddy Deke said. "It can destroy as much as it creates. It's wild and powerful, dig?"

Perry opened his eyes. "Yes," he said, trying to keep the sadness from his voice. "I understand—a little bit, I think."

"Hey, now," Daddy Deke said.

Perry shook his head. His attention had been off in the ozone somewhere as he, Daddy Deke, and Brendy played rummy. Perry liked rummy okay—he liked the shape of the rules, the feel of the game itself—the cards against his palms, raising and lowering them to the table, keeping track of points—but tonight, he'd been going through the motions. "I'm sorry," he said. "What's going on?"

"What's going on is you won and you don't even care!" Brendy huffed.

"Y'all, I'm sorry," Perry said. "I just—I still feel the music on me. I'm thinking about what it means and what Doctor Professor wants with Peaches."

Brendy rolled her eyes. " 'And where she at? What she doing? She thinking bout me?' Blah blah blippity."

Daddy Deke laid down his cards and shook his head. "Don't tease ya brother for caring—and besides, Perry ain't the only one miss Peaches when she gone. Is he?"

Brendy pulled a face where she flexed her neck muscles and drew her mouth into a flat, toadish line. Then she let the expression go and sucked in a huge mouthful of air to pooch out her checks. She let that go, too. "Okay, no he ain't," she said. "We all be missing Peaches. I get left alone, too, but I don't make a big deal. Just like when—"

Perry knew his expression must have darkened because Brendy cast aside whatever she'd meant to say next. "En EE ways, Peaches *always* go away for a lil bit after a fight."

This was true. Thirteen days ago, Peaches had fought Maddy Bombz on the roof of One Shell Square after Perry and Peaches figured out how to predict the location of her next display. Each of her fusillades was part of a grander display—similar to the ones above the Missus Hipp on Juneteenth or on New Year's—and since she didn't care about the safety of her "audience," of course she intended to launch her grand finale atop the tallest building in Nola. Perry and Brendy watched from a Poydras Street sidewalk as one of the explosions tossed Peaches down to the street.

She hit hard and lay still for a moment, then sat up, shaking her head angrily. A glance into the parking lot to his right told Perry what she'd do next. Peaches pushed up imaginary sleeves and bounded over to a big green dumpster. She lifted the bulky metal thing over her head easy-as-you-please and jumped. *Hard.* Watching her reminded Perry of the moon landing videos. It was as if gravity simply worked differently for her when she wanted it to.

When she leaped back to the street, the dumpster she carried had been crimped closed like a pie crust. She set it down right there on the pavement.

"Five-oh on the way," she said. "I seen 'em from up above. Let's get to steppin'." And they had. Perry and Brendy had spent the night at Peaches's house, watching TV and eating huckabucks and Sixlets late into the night because there was no school the next day.

Perry and his sister awakened the next morning to find Peaches's pocket of pillows and blankets empty—and nobody had seen her since.

"I know she coming back," Perry said.

"I know you know," Daddy Deke said. "But I'll tell you sumn for free—there ain't nothing wrong with the feelings you having, but them feelings are yours. Ain't nobody else responsible for 'em, dig? You can't carry nothing for nobody else, and cain't nobody carry what's yours for you."

Perry frowned. In the past, Daddy Deke had never failed to offer him comfort when he was feeling low, but this advice seemed important. He turned Daddy Deke's words over in his mind for the rest of the night. *Cain't nobody carry what's yours for you.* What burdens did he carry, and why? Well, there was the dream he'd had...but some dark, quiet presence in the back of Perry's mind told him that it hadn't been a dream, it had been a warning, and he'd be a fool not to heed it.

Music might be the most powerful magic in Nola, but it couldn't help Perry—not really.

Dryades Academy was an old square-built art deco building that looked more like a courthouse than a place of learning. Its façade was a riot of ivy, full of ladybugs the size of baseballs, which marched up and down the outer walls, keeping them clean. Chickens roosted in the trees out front, and one of the substitute teachers, Mr. Ghiazi, had told Brendy that every evening, after hours, when the last students and teachers had gone home, the chickens would come inside and hold their own lessons, learning about corn and how to find the best worms and bugs. Something about the way he said it made Brendy think Mr. Ghiazi was probably joking—or at least that he thought he was.

Inside, the building boasted green marble floors, old-fashioned mosaics, and vintage furniture maintained by an invisible custodial staff. What Brendy loved most about the place, what she couldn't imagine ever parting with, was its smell. Crayons, glitter, oil soap, and cooking. It smelled best on cold winter days, but even on the last day of school, Dryades Academy smelled like home. How her brother could leave it made no sense to her.

This year, Perry and Brendy had attended separate schools. Last summer, Perry abruptly asked to transfer out of Dryades Academy and wound up at a new school over on Esplanade Avenue. Brendy didn't understand the choice, and she knew she should have asked Perry about it, but every time she tried to bring it up, Perry's face took on a lost, hunted look, and she backed down. Still, it made her sad and angry to be without him, and sometimes those feelings formed a little knot of tension in her throat—like she'd tried to swallow a pill and failed.

All year she had avoided thinking about it, but now, as she sat at her desk by the window in Mr. Evans's class, ignoring the movie playing on the classroom livescreen in favor of a Popeye the Sailor Man coloring book, she wondered whether Perry had decided to leave because he wasn't good at music.

Brendy bore down with her Fuzzy Wuzzy brown, filling in the outline of Popeye's left arm as he slung a string of chained-together oil barrels over his head. She'd taught herself a trick earlier this year: She liked to color in her figures hard, in layer after layer—careful, of course, to stay inside the lines—then go back with a plastic lunch knife and scrape away the wax. The process resulted in smoother, richer colors that had won her an award from the Chamber of Commerce in its Carnival Coloring Competition. The grand prize had been a beautiful purple-and-white bicycle that Daddy Deke taught her to ride without training wheels.

Brendy frowned, listening hard, as she finished coloring Popeye's exposed skin and tried to decide what color Olive Oyl should be this time. The chickens in the tree outside had gone quiet. Brendy had earned the right to sit by the broad classroom window because Mr. Evans thought she did such a good job fighting the temptation to stare outside at the trees and the play yard, and the neighborhood beyond. This was only partly true. Brendy found it easy to keep from staring out the window because she tended to listen out it instead. Most of the time she spent at her desk found her listening to the swish of cars on the street, the noise of other classes bouncing balls and running riot on the play yard blacktop, the squabbles of the chickens and the neighborhood cats—who seemed, lately, to have resolved their differences by banding together against the raccoons and possums.

Hey, girl!

Was that Peaches? Brendy raised an eyebrow.

Hey, girl. Hey!

Brendy frowned and selected another crayon. “Peaches?” she whispered.

Yeah, girl. Come on. We gots to go!

Brendy considered briefly, then raised her hand.

It took a while, but Mr. Evans noticed. “Brendy?”

“Can I go use it?”

Mr. Evans nodded curtly. “Two minutes.” But he’d never remember.

orbit